Grumpy Pucking Orc

Orcs On Ice
Book 1

Debra Dunbar

Chapter 1

Ozar

I glared at the bright white of the ice at the end of the tunnel, a low growl escaping my lips. I'd always hated the waiting right before a battle, that period of inaction until the call to charge was given.

Only we weren't heading into battle, we were about to play a human game called hockey. Shirtless. With strangely curved sticks instead of swords.

"This is stupid," Eng muttered in Orcish. "We came here to find wives and take them home, not waste time dancing around on knife-blades for human entertainment."

Bwat shrugged. "Perhaps this is how we win a human female. Many species require the male to perform dance-like displays to show their suitability as a life-partner."

Ugwyll snorted. "What we need to do is grab the first sturdy female of childbearing years and drag her back home. That's how we show our suitability as a husband. Not dancing and not wearing these stupid fucking shoes."

We all hated these stupid fucking shoes, but none with the white-hot passion of Ugwyll. The orc faced the same struggle as the rest of us, trying to balance on the knife-blades that ran the vertical length of our shoes, but it angered Ugwyll far more than it bothered the others. Ugwyll was agile and gifted in sports and battle, as well as being a scout of great renown beyond his clan. Repeatedly falling while wearing these things called skates was absolutely humiliating to him.

It was humiliating to *all* of us. Except for Eng, that is, who had spent our one practice before this game leaning against the wall with a bored expression on his face.

"This isn't a dance, it's a fight," I reminded the group of orcs.

"I thought it was a contest," Ugwyll said. "Hitting the flat minotaur turd with a curved stick past the enemy team and into their nest."

"Net," Bwat corrected. "They call it a net. And the turd is a cuck."

"Cuck." Ugwyll laughed. "Isn't that what the humans call their hand-axes?"

"That's 'cock.'" Bwat had been diligently studying the human language of English. We all had, but Bwat knew far more than any of us. "They also call their cock a Johnson, a dick, a penis, a—"

"I don't care what humans call their hand-axe." Eng reached down to cup his, a gesture hindered by the large gloves he wore on his hands and the hard plastic device we'd all needed to affix over the area between our legs.

"Shut your mouths and focus," I growled. "We're about to go into battle and we need to win."

A muscle twitched in Ugwyll's jaw. He glared out into the arena as if that were the foe we were facing and not the humans twirling around on the ice like they were indeed dancing. Eng, on the other hand, just snorted.

"Right. We're *not* going to win. First, none of us know

the rules of this game beyond putting the minotaur turd into the other team's net. Second, none of us can remain upright on these knife blades for more than a few seconds. There will be no winning. This isn't a fight or a contest or anything we should lower ourselves to participate in. You idiots can slide around out there for the next hour or so but I'm not going to make a fool of myself."

"It's our job," Bwat insisted. "We were told we needed to have jobs if we wanted to stay here, and this was the only job we were offered."

"Don't care," Eng announced. "I'm not doing this, and I'd like to see the human brave enough to try and make me."

It wasn't the humans we needed to worry about, it was the demon who owned this team, and the angels who set the rules in this world. The days of raids, of plunder, of snatching human women and hauling them home over our shoulders were over. And that change couldn't have come at a worse time.

The noise from the crowd in the stadium increased in volume, and I adjusted my stance, trying to balance on the knife blades without having to hold onto the wall. Eng was right—this *was* ridiculous. But I'd dance around in these shoes if it meant I could return home with a wife.

A wife meant children, and there was nothing in the world I wanted more than children. Pudgy, green-skinned babies to bounce on my knees. I'd teach them to fight, watch their tusks come in, celebrate their victories and comfort their tears. I'd had no siblings, but I wanted as many orclets as my wife would be willing and able to provide.

Years ago, before the plague took the lives of so many, I would have been wed and have sired several orclets by this age. But with the deaths, my hopes had also died.

Humans had been compatible breeding partners

centuries ago when orcs regularly raided the human lands, bringing their females home along with gold, jewels, and livestock. Many of the orcs in our tribes had some human blood running through their veins.

So here we were again. Leaving our clans and crossing the portals once more, but this time to only bring home human brides to have children with.

Although if some pillage occurred along the way, that would have been icing on the cake.

I'd expected to face battle. I'd expected screaming unwilling females. I hadn't expected a group of winged beings to incapacitate the lot of us orcs as if we were newborns.

It was the first of what would be many humiliations.

We'd needed to agree to certain rules before we were released from the custody of the angels. No kidnapping unwilling human females to be our brides. No plundering. And jobs. The maintaining of gainful employment.

So here we were, in our gainful employment, about to participate in a contest known among the humans as hockey while walking on these knife blades.

An amplified voice shouted something unintelligible from the arena, and the crowd roared again.

"Go, go, go," urged one of the human assistants from behind us.

Once more, I growled—this time louder.

I was Ozar, son of Meig and Oala, a skilled warrior and a Guardian of Clan Heregut, a Commander of my Squadron. I wore the marks awarded to those who'd excelled in battle. I had much to offer a wife. And if this ridiculous contest was what it took to get one, then I would perform to the best of my ability.

And I'd do my damndest to win. Because above all, I *hated* losing.

Letting go of the wall, I stomped forward down the tunnel into the bright light. My bare shoulders brushed the sides of the hallway. Humans reached down from nearby seats, touching me. Again I growled, jutting my lower jaw forward so my tusks were even more visible as I stepped onto the ice.

The stupid knife-blade shoes slid forward and I nearly fell on my ass, as I'd done the first and only time I'd attempted this. Thankfully I managed to shift my balance and somehow remain upright. The other orcs on my team exited the tunnel behind me, pushing me forward and sliding me across the ice. Ignoring the din of the crowd and the shouting of the amplified human announcer, I tried to focus on slowing my speed so I wouldn't careen clear across the rink and into a wall.

Most of the others didn't have as graceful of an entrance. Eng groped his way along the wall. Bwat shot forward and flailed about, eventually face-planting on the ice. Ugwyll managed to remain on his feet until one shoe went wide and he fell backward. The line behind him went down like those dominos I'd seen the humans set up, until the last eight orcs ended up in a pile just outside the hallway.

The roar went from cheers to laughter, and I felt a sharp surge of anger.

No. I could not kill the humans. Not unless I wanted the angels to send me back home in shame. Without a wife. Doomed to be forever childless.

"This way. This way." One of the humans that worked for our team was ushering us over toward a seating area.

Several other human support staff glided out to us, assisting the fallen onto their feet and helping them over to the box.

I waved off a human who was trying to take my arm and stomped my knife-blades into the ice as I made my way to our seating area, breaking off chunks and leaving scars on the smooth white surface.

This was going to be a long and humiliating evening. And it would only be one of many. I sat in my chair, glaring at the human team and hoping that I found a willing human female to be my wife soon. Because it probably wouldn't be long until I killed a human, or more likely killed a few dozen humans. And then my dreams of a wife and children would be over.

Chapter 2

Jordan

"It was wonderful of your parents to get us all tickets," Abby said, handing me one of the beers she'd carried over from the concession area.

"Yeah, and the seats are awe-some," Willa added as she took her own beer from Abby.

The *seats* were awesome. The tickets to see the new Baltimore Tusks? Well, the jury was still out on that one.

At first I'd been excited by my parents' gift. I'd grown up in Buffalo, New York, practically skating before I could walk. While I'd never played on a children's league or school hockey team, I'd participated in plenty of pickup games with the local kids, goofing off on an ice-covered pond near our house. And I'd loved the occasional professional games my parents had taken my brother and me to.

An NHL team for Baltimore seemed like a dream come true for hockey fans, but when it was announced that this team would be made up of orcs, my excitement had wavered. It wasn't that I had anything against orcs; I'd never even heard of them being real until last month. Supernaturals seemed to be all over the place in the last few years. The angels practically ran things. There were demons, shifters, vampires, elves...

And now orcs.

This would no doubt be the first of many supernatural sports teams. It felt strange, but teams like the Tusks were a logical step toward reflecting the changes all around us. One of my friends from the gym was a werewolf. Demons owned several Baltimore area businesses. There was an elf barista at my favorite Starbucks. The trio of enthusiastic black dudes in line for beer beside us were vampires.

But *orcs?*

Advertisements had shown these giant, muscle-bound, green, half-naked guys with tusks jutting from their lower jaws and a steely look in their eyes. I'll admit, they looked impressive. But my first thought was that it wouldn't be fair to pit orcs against humans. Who in the world had approved this? It had to be against some NHL regulation, or occupational health and safety code. The humans would be slaughtered—and some of these human players made millions of dollars a year. Why would any NHL team agree to risk their players against a team of orcs? And who in their right mind would be willing to watch such carnage? Not *me.*

But my parents had bought me tickets, excited for me to attend this inaugural game of our new hockey team in Baltimore. So here I was.

"Let's hurry up and get to our seats." Abby bounced in excitement, nearly spilling her beer.

"Orcs on ice," Willa drawled as she followed me through the rows to our spot. "Sounds like a Disney movie... or a reality show. I wonder who will get voted off the island?"

"Or who will get the rose?" Abby laughed. "It'll be fun. I love hockey."

We all did, but I wasn't sure if what we were about to see would be hockey or a gladiatorial contest. Hopefully the Red Wings wouldn't end the game carried out on stretchers.

We settled in with our beers, commenting on the hotness level of the visiting team as they warmed up on the ice. No matter how the game turned out, it was good to get together with Abby and Willa. The past few weeks we'd all been swamped at work, and our schedules hadn't seemed to align. Sitting here drinking cheap draft beer and ogling guys made me feel like I was back in college and not an over-worked professional trying to grow my practice in a competitive market.

"Here come the orcs," Willa announced.

I turned my attention to the huge green dude skating out of the tunnel. He didn't seem to be very steady on his skates, but he remained upright. The ones who followed him were worse. Within seconds, there was a pile of green bodies at the edge of the ice.

"Why are they shirtless? Not that I'm complaining or anything," Abby said.

"I wonder if their dicks are proportionate to the rest of their bodies," Willa said. "If so, they're gonna have a hard time getting laid. I mean, I like to think there's a hole for every rod, but anatomy has its limits, and nobody wants to explain that kind of injury to an ER doc."

"None of them can skate," I said, because although the naked chests and questions about penis-proportion were important, the orcs' lack of basic skills on the ice took priority in my weird mind.

Yes, I was more fixated on the orcs slipping and sliding than their sculpted chests or their potentially painful cock size.

Although now that I thought about it, the one guy who

had remained standing and wasn't hugging the wall *did* have an amazing set of pecs. And arms. And abs. And the thighs filling out those tight pants weren't exactly shabby, either.

"That first dude has to be nearly seven feet tall," Willa commented. "I'm not a particularly short woman, but I wouldn't even come to his shoulder. He'd need to pick me up to kiss me. I could give him a blow job from a squat."

Abby sighed. "It would need to be a fast blow job because I just can't hold a squat for long."

"We can work on that," Willa told her. "Give me six months and you'll be able to crack walnuts with your ass cheeks."

She wasn't kidding. Willa was a personal trainer at our gym and had a dedicated group of clients on the side for private sessions. I was pretty sure army sergeants could learn a thing or two from her. And I'd bet good money she actually *could* crack walnuts with her ass.

"Oh, jeez, this is gonna be a shit show," Abby said as others skated onto the field to help the orcs stand and make their way to the bench. "They really *can't* skate. How the heck does Baltimore have a hockey team that can't even skate?"

I had no idea. It wasn't cheap to buy an NHL franchise, and I knew there were a lot of hoops to jump through. Why the owner had gone to all that trouble only to populate his team with a bunch of supernaturals that couldn't skate was beyond me.

Although the owner *was* a demon, which might explain everything.

At least this wasn't going to be the human bloodbath I'd feared. The orcs would likely spend most of the game sprawled out on the ice while the Red Wings evaded the bodies and scored goals left and right.

I wasn't sure how I felt about that. Initially, I'd been worried about the human team and the unbalanced matchup. Now, I was worried about an opposite unbalanced matchup.

Orcs. I was worried about a bunch of seven-foot-tall, muscle-bound, green-skinned, fierce dudes who looked like they could take on a team of dragons and come out on top. I know it was weird, but I felt sorry for these guys.

"Maybe we should drink every time an orc falls down?" Abby suggested, interrupting my angsty thoughts.

"I don't know about you two, but *I* don't want to spend tomorrow puking from a massive hangover," I said.

"From the way those guys skate, we'll all end up dead of alcohol poisoning before the first intermission," Willa added.

I sighed, looking as the orc who'd been first out of the tunnel returned to the ice, skidding his way to the center of the rink. "I guess this means we won't be taking bets on the winner or the score."

Abby laughed. "Score? I'll wager twenty bucks that the Red Wings win by more than ten goals."

"More like twenty goals," Willa scoffed.

It felt kind of wrong to be making fun of the orc team like this. It *was* funny, but I got the impression that the orcs weren't in on the joke. I wondered if they'd been shoved into this with no training, no preparation, and no knowledge at all of the game. It was one thing to be a clown or a stand-up comic by choice, another to be laughed at when you had no idea you were there to play the fool.

As the game began, I felt less and less like laughing. The Red Wings were racking up goals at a speed that made it likely Willa's prediction would come true. The orcs truly did not know how to skate and had taken to stomping around the ice instead, hacking at the puck as though they were trying to split firewood. Their sticks were breaking at an alarming rate, and the one time they got the puck, they sent it flying toward the ceiling, where it took out one of the lights. One orc did nothing but lean against the wall and scowl at everyone, while the forward seemed to think his main goal was to tackle members of the opposing team. That could have resulted in serious injury had the guy ever been able to get within a foot of any of the humans.

At the first intermission, our cups of beer were empty, and the Tusks had scored no goals.

The Red Wings had scored five.

I felt strangely heartsick as I went out into the concession area to get more beers. Then I overheard the commentary while in line. Hockey fans were leaving, disappointed that the game was so one-sided. The people that were remaining seemed to view the whole thing as if it were a circus event.

I got three beers and returned just as the players were taking to the ice again. The Tusks didn't seem to have improved their skating skills during intermission, but I could instantly see a difference in the orcs' attitudes. They were pissed—a least *some* of them were pissed. The one guy continued to lean against the wall, sneering at the whole thing.

The forward, who'd been the only one managing to stay on his skates the first third of the game, took possession of the puck and used his size to slam into any human who came near. Unfortunately, the humans managed to get their sticks in front of him, and he tripped over one, falling face-first to the ground.

The rest seemed to happen in slow motion. One of the Red Wings went for the puck and drove it straight into the orc's face. Green blood flew, and the orc shouted a guttural word in a strange language, throwing out his arm to clothesline the human in the shins.

I jumped to my feet and gasped, expecting the orc to have a broken arm and probably a dislocated shoulder in addition to the damage the puck must have done to his face, but clearly orc arms were made of sturdier stuff than what we humans had. The human hockey player went flying, slamming onto the ice and sliding forward with a streak of pink from blood of his own.

The crowd roared. The Red Wings roared. The Tusks roared. Suddenly, everyone had their gloves off and punches were being thrown as the human officials tried in vain to get the players separated. What the orcs lacked in skating ability, they clearly made up for in brawling skills. When order was finally restored, the ice was painted with red and green blood—but mostly red. The Red Wings were battered, and while the Tusks had their share of scratches and cuts, for the first time tonight they seemed proud and confident.

That confidence was gone in minutes. When the game resumed, the Red Wings kept their distance, taunting and showboating their superior skating skills by zooming around the clumsy orcs. They passed the puck like they were playing Monkey in the Middle. They twirled like they were figure skating. They skated backward toward the goal, spinning at the last minute to easily scoot the puck into the net. Meanwhile, the orcs stumbled when they weren't sprawled helpless on the ice. The third period went pretty much the same.

It was a massacre. The Red Wings won with a twelve-point lead, but the Tusks did score a point. In the third period, their gutsy forward managed to keep the puck long enough to slam it into the goal as the Red Wings' goalie tried in vain to block it.

Ozar. That was the name on the back of the guy's jersey. I'd looked him up on my phone to see if that was his last or first name to find that Ozar was evidently his only name.

My breath weirdly stuttered when I watched him, a strange electricity zinging from my chest to between my legs. What the hell was that about? Yeah, there was that superstar thing about professional male athletes that made most straight girls hot and bothered, but I usually didn't get this way over sport-dudes. Or musicians. Or actors.

Actually, I *did* get turned on; I just knew better than to act on it. Wham, bam, thank you ma'am wasn't my thing. Some of my friends were thrilled to participate in a good one-night stand, but I'd always wanted more. And I'd learned over the years that athletes, musicians, and actors were seldom interested in more.

"What do you think?" Willa asked as we left the arena. "Are we Tusks fans? Should we get season tickets? T-shirts? Their logo tattooed on our asses?"

Abby wrinkled her nose. "I want to support the local team, but this didn't feel like hockey."

"The game was really unfair," I agreed. "Maybe if the orcs knew how to skate and how to play the game, it would be worth going, but I don't want to see them get the shit kicked out of them on the regular."

Willa bumped my hip with hers. "But we *do* want to see half naked, muscular green guys, right, Jordan? I mean, *tusks*? Come on, you know you're dying to get a close-up look at those bad boys."

She wasn't wrong. A tooth fetish wasn't what made me curious about the orcs' tusks, it was a passion for my profession. I was a dentist—a reconstructive dentist, to be exact.

"I wonder if they continue to grow and need filing down, or if they're more like human teeth?" I mused.

Abby laughed. "Twenty bucks says there'll be an orc mouth X-ray on her Instagram within the next month."

I had to laugh at that too, more than a little excited at the idea. My Instagram had lost me dozens of dates. It was the first thing that showed up if someone Googled me, and the photos on my account weren't the typical fitness or food pics. No, my images were close-ups of toothless mouths, bone-graft procedures, and implant anchors. Disappointingly, guys I'd gone out with over the last few years didn't seem to have the same fascination for dental reconstruction as I did.

"Let's grab a drink at Puck's," Willa suggested, pointing down the street at the pub. "I'll buy."

"Then I'm totally up for another beer," Abby teased. "If you're buying, I'm drinking."

I hesitated, because I'd already had two beers and I wasn't much of a drinker. But those beers were watery drafts, and I hadn't exactly slammed them. I had the bandwidth for another alcoholic beverage or two. And it had been weeks since Willa, Abby, and I had gotten together.

What the hell. Might as well.

"Okay." I pulled at the opening of my jacket. "Let me drop this back off at the car so I don't die of heat stroke in there. I'll meet you guys inside."

Willa and Abby continued on as I headed down the side street toward the parking lot behind the stadium. It was chilly enough to warrant a jacket outside, but I'd survive a quick three-block dash to Puck's without it, and I'd be a whole lot more comfortable without the extra layer. Demons had taken over ownership of many of the area bars, and the one who owned Puck's seemed to think the establishment was back in hell from the temperature inside.

Gripping my keys between my fingers, I turned the corner into the parking lot. It was well-lit, but Baltimore was still a large city, especially to a Buffalo, New York, gal, and I was always a little nervous while walking alone. When I saw a large figure leaning against the back of my car, I abruptly stopped, wondering if I should dig the pepper spray out of my purse or turn around and get the hell out of here.

Then I realized the figure had green skin, a pair of skates slung over a bulky shoulder, and a shirt with the Tusks team logo on it. Taking a few tentative steps forward, I saw a drop of green liquid fall to the asphalt.

An orc—and a member of the hockey team, judging from his attire. It made me hesitate, undecided what I should do. Not that I was afraid a professional athlete would harm me, but he was muttering under his breath and probably wanted some alone time since he was out here solo in the parking lot.

Okay, he was seven feet of muscle, and I didn't know anything about orcs, so I *was* a little afraid.

After a few seconds of contemplation, I didn't get the pepper spray out, but I still kept my hold on the keys as I continued walking. The orc glanced up, and I saw the blood on his one tusk, his chin, and on the front of his jersey.

My heart lurched. This huge, powerful green dude was hurt. And teeth...I couldn't help but be sympathetic over anyone with a mouth injury. It was then that I pocketed the keys, the medical-me—specifically the dentist-me—trying to dispel my fear.

His skin was the color of fresh spring leaves, with a darker green section on the left side of his jaw. The orc's muscles were barely contained under the hockey jersey that neither he nor any of his teammates had worn during the game. His long onyx hair was tied back at the nape of his neck and reached down mid-back, with some of it in thin braids. His eyebrows and absurdly long lashes were the same black, as was the short beard that lined his jaw and chin. It was his eyes that held me, though. I'd expected them to also be black or dark brown, but they were a warm, lighter shade, like whiskey in the firelight.

Oh, I did love me some whiskey. *And* a fire on a cold winter night.

"Um." I stood ten feet from the orc like a total idiot, not sure what to say or remembering why I'd come into the parking lot to begin with.

"Sorry. This is your car?"

The growl of his low, accented voice sent heat spiraling down through my body. The orc pushed away from my car trunk and took a step forward then stopped, clearly sensing my unease.

"Yeah, but..."

Another drop of green slid down the bloodied tusk, hovering at the end.

I'd gotten used to other supernatural creatures. Well, maybe not demons, but *other* supernatural creatures. But orcs were new here. Were they like demons? Like the shifters? Like the elves?

"I'll just...go to the stadium." The drop of blood splattered onto the pavement. "Or another place. No bleeding is allowed in the locker room."

Dentist-me warred with woman-me and with woman-alone-in-a-city-me. He was huge, and he had a rather large knife strapped to one thigh over his sweatpants. It was understandable that even someone as large and intimidating as this guy wouldn't want to walk around Baltimore unarmed, but that knife looked kinda big to be legal and it made me nervous. But his mouth was bleeding, so knife or not, dentist-me was winning the fight.

No surprise there.

I realized he was waiting for me to move, so he wouldn't come closer as he edged past me to walk back to the stadium or another part of the parking lot. I also realized that this was the team forward I'd been ogling during the game, the only one who'd scored a goal, the only one who'd managed to stay on his feet, as inexpertly as he skated. He was also the one who'd sent a member of the opposing team flying and initiated that huge fight.

A fight that had no doubt resulted in his injury. I thought of that puck slamming into the side of his face and winced.

I was torn between moving away and letting the orc walk off elsewhere or being polite—being a dentist.

Polite dentist finally won.

"Are you okay?" I asked, stepping closer to the orc.

Chapter 3

Ozar

We'd lost the battle...or contest. Whatever. It was no surprise, but I was still furious and felt a wave of humiliation every time I thought of the score. The only thing saving me from a murderous rage was that we'd gotten into a fight with the humans on the opposing team, and they'd limped off the ice, injured far worse off than we had been.

Although, as I felt the empty sockets where two teeth had been and wiggled my loose tusk, I might reconsider whether we'd truly won that fight or not.

The rest of the team had headed for showers and out to a bar, but I'd quickly changed and left the arena, needing some privacy. I hadn't initially gotten it, finding a crowd of humans waiting outside. Most of them were just there to gawk, but my eyes had been drawn to a small boy clutching a program and hopping around with excitement.

"Mr. Ozar?" His voice had reached me over the din of traffic and the loud conversation from the adults. "Mr. Ozar? Can you sign this?"

The adults parted as I stepped forward, everyone giving

me a wide berth. Except the child who sucked in a breath and grinned at me, lifting the program and a pen upward.

I knelt because I towered over this little one, taking the paper and the writing implement. There had been several stereotypes about orcs that I'd encountered since coming here, and our assumed lack of literacy was one of them. We had libraries. We had a written language. And I could indeed sign my name.

Which I did, handing the paper and pen back to the boy. "Do you like hockey?"

He nodded. "Yes, but I want to be an orc when I grow up."

A man nearby, perhaps his father, chuckled and sent me a look that was both apologetic and wary.

"Why wait to grow up?" I told the boy, gently placing a hand on his slim shoulder. "What is your name?"

His eyes shined as he looked up into mine. "Mike. Mike Miller."

I nodded solemnly. "I, Ozar, warrior and guardian of Clan Heregut, announce that Mike Miller, human of Baltimore, is a friend and now a member of our clan. I vouch for his strength and courage. He will honor the clan with his deeds and forever be known as an orc brother."

Tears sparkled in the boy's eyes, and his mouth wobbled. I patted his shoulder, taking care not to knock the tiny child over, and stood. "I hope to see you soon, brother Mike Miller."

He clutched the program and pen to his chest, his smile telling me all the things his voice couldn't. As I went to walk away, I glanced at the male standing next to the child. "Thank you," he said as he gathered the boy close to him. "Thank you."

There was nothing to thank me for. Children were a precious gift, no matter if they were orc, or human, or even fae. I'd meant what I'd said to the boy. If he ever found himself in our lands, all he'd need to do is say that Ozar of Clan Heregut had given him clan rites, and he would be welcomed.

He'd be welcomed regardless. Our clan had no children. Few clans had more than two or three at the most. There wasn't an orc in the realm that wouldn't embrace Mike Miller and call him brother. Or son.

My heart ached after the encounter with the human child, but my mouth ached even more, so I kept walking until I'd reached the parking area. It was still half-full of vehicles, but there wasn't a human to be seen. Leaning against a blue sedan, I felt the bruise on my cheek, then explored the holes where this morning two teeth had resided.

The bruise would be gone in a day—two at most. We orcs healed fast. The teeth? I wasn't the only orc to have lost a tooth or two, although the injury upset me. After a hundred and twenty-two years I still had all my teeth, and it was something I was proud of.

Had. Past tense.

At least it hadn't been one of my tusks that had been knocked out. An orc's tusks were their pride and joy. And while there was honor in a battlefield injury that resulted in a disfigurement, orcs with only one—or no tusks—were still regarded with pity.

I might have claimed we were going into battle tonight, but we weren't. Losing a tusk in some silly game against humans would have been mortifying. Maybe Eng was right. Maybe we should refuse to play this stupid game. Maybe I should stand against the wall and scowl, biding my time until I could convince an eligible human female to return home with me as my bride.

The idea flitted away with only a second of consideration. I'd made a commitment when I'd accepted this job, and I took my responsibilities seriously. Eng might refuse to play, but I couldn't do that. I'd give this team and this sport my sincere efforts until I could return home with my bride.

Jerking my head up at a noise, I saw a human standing close to me. The female eyed me with big eyes and a set of keys gripped tightly in one hand. She was scared, just like most of the humans I'd encountered since I'd come here. Legends said that humans, females in particular, were always afraid of us, but that after we kidnapped them and brought them home, they changed their minds and became wonderful spouses and mothers. None of that gave me comfort. I didn't want to start out my marriage with fear. Even if the angels hadn't forbidden us from snatching unwilling human females, I wouldn't have done so. I wanted a wife. I wanted children. But there were lines I was unwilling to cross.

"Sorry. This is your car?" I pushed away from the vehicle, unwilling to move much farther in case the female thought I had ill intent toward her.

Then she stepped forward and asked me if I was okay.

How was I supposed to respond to that? Our team had suffered a humiliating defeat, and I was trying hard not to care since no one else on the team, including our owner, did. I'd lost two teeth. I hadn't yet found a human female willing to be my bride. I hated this place with all its loud noise, lack of trees and wildlife, and tall buildings. I was homesick. Lonely. And seeing that little boy outside of the stadium brought an arrow to my heart, reminding me of all we had lost.

But I doubted this female cared about any of that. I wished she did. I wished someone did, outside of my clan back home.

Wiggling my loose tusk, I shrugged. "I am not dead. That makes me okay."

I wasn't sure how much longer I could continue to do this. So far, none of the human females I'd met were at all interested in becoming my wife. Bwat had suggested I might have better luck if I didn't broach the topic of marriage within the first five minutes of meeting them, that I should try wooing the female for a few days before telling her I intended to marry her and fill her womb with as many children as possible.

I'd been wallowing in pain, simmering anger, and self-pity when this small, slim woman had suddenly appeared. And under the glare of the buzzing parking lot lights, she seemed to have a glow about her.

Something clicked deep inside me—something I'd given up hoping to ever experience.

"Don't do that," she told me.

I frowned, wondering what I wasn't supposed to do. Die? I'd always done my best to avoid that.

The human female took a few steps closer to me. She had silky brown hair, was wearing what humans here considered casual attire, and had a satchel slung over her shoulder.

Purse. Bwat had said it was called a purse.

"Stop doing that," she insisted, striding purposefully right up to me and gripping my wrist in her small hand.

Her touch sent an electric current through me. Rooted in place, I sucked in a deep breath and smelled a citrus and floral scent that complimented the warm, complex aroma of *her*.

It was as if everything that lay deeply dormant inside me came alive. I vibrated from her touch, stepping in to her and breathing in her scent. Her eyes widened, their stormy-gray irises flecked with gold. I felt invisible chains twist around my heart, tying me to her with deceptively delicate bonds.

With a gasp, she jerked her hand away and took a step back.

"I am sorry," I said. But I wasn't sorry. There was nothing to be sorry for and everything to celebrate.

A mate bond. I'd just experienced a mate bond. With a human female.

Impossible. Yet it was exactly as my father and other males with my clan had described.

I'd come here ready to wed and bring home any female who was of an appropriate age to breed. It was a cynical view of marriage, but I'd had no choice. It was that or watch as my clan died out.

But now...

As a child I'd seen the bond between my father and mother. I'd grown up hearing stories from orcs who'd had the bond, who'd experienced that connection with their spouse.

Then the plague had happened.

Many orcs lost their mates. Some of them died soon after as well. Others struggled to continue on, living so that there would be enough of our elders to tell the stories of our ancestors and share their wisdom.

Even with the stories, none of us young males ever expected to be able to have a mate bond.

Yet here I was, bleeding in a parking lot, the threads of awareness braiding and twisting, tying me to this human female in front of me. It shouldn't have been possible, but there could be no other explanation for that instant sense of connection, for the song awakening in my heart, for the emotions soaring through me.

I had an almost overwhelming urge to pick her up, carry her back home to my den, and worship her, body and soul.

I resisted that urge. First, forcibly taking unwilling females was not allowed, and the screaming and flailing from this female might bring enough humans to take her away from me. I didn't want anyone to take her away. A rush of fierce protectiveness surged through me at the thought.

Second, I was already injured with my tusk loose, and two teeth gone and back on the ice somewhere in a streak of green blood. I didn't live in a den; it was something called an apartment. These apartments weren't built for securing unwilling females, so even if I managed to get her there without the humans incapacitating me, I'd have no way of ensuring she didn't escape.

How embarrassing that my first meeting with the female who was my true mate had taken place while I was injured and in pain. It wasn't a good start to our courtship, and I reached up to my tusk, mortified that I was making such a poor first impression on the female I'd already bonded with.

"Stop wiggling your tooth...tusk." The female stepped close again and smacked my hand. Hers was a slim, delicate hand tipped with equally delicate claws painted an attractive pink. It wasn't anywhere near large or strong enough to move my own massive green one.

Not registering what she was saying, I wiggled my tusk again, grunting as pain spiked through my mouth.

"*Stop.*" The female reached out again but hesitated

before she touched me this time. "You're going to pull it out if you keep that up."

That got me to stop. The thought of losing one of my tusks was terrifying. Losing my tusk while playing with stick-wielding humans? I'd never live it down.

And I'd never get her to be my wife with only one tusk. This female's concern clearly told me that she would only consider a mate who had *two* tusks.

The female opened up the bag she had on her shoulder and pulled out a small packet of white sheets. "Open up. Let me see."

For some reason, I instantly obeyed this bossy female and opened my mouth. An orc female would never have demanded I show her the inside of my mouth. They were bossy, yes, but my loose and missing teeth were not something another orc would have bothered over. In fact—"Ah!"

The female jumped a little at my shout but kept poking the white sheets in my mouth. They were coming away stained with my green blood, but none of that seemed to worry her. Finally, she stood back and balled the bloody sheets up into a wad, folding her arms across her chest and glaring at me.

I shut my mouth, oddly subdued and strangely concerned that she was going to scold me.

"You have lost two of your teeth!"

My fears were realized. Yes, she was scolding me. Along with my unfamiliar nervousness, I also felt respect and a surge of lust. This slight human was feisty. The mate bond flared, roaring into a flame. I straightened to my full height, wincing as my engorged hand-axe fought the confines of that stupid plastic cup they'd made all of us wear during the game.

"Do *not* wiggle that tusk."

I dropped my hand at the fierce tone of her voice. Me. A Clan Guardian. A warrior. A hero, who'd defended our territory and had made a name for myself for my strength and bravery, was cowed by a tiny human female.

I'd do anything for her, anything she demanded. Anything. She was my life, my very breath. I would breed with no other female, marry no other. If she rejected me, then I would spend my life alone and mourning the loss of the very reason for my existence.

"Where are those teeth you lost?" the female demanded, jabbing a finger at me. "You're still bleeding, so they had to have come out during the game."

I nodded. "I lost the teeth during the game. But they may be in the dumpster if the human with Zamboni-beast has already cleaned the ice."

My teeth had been knocked out when a hockey male had hit me in the face with the minotaur turd. Or maybe I'd lost those teeth when I'd accidentally gotten hit with a teammate's hockey stick. Yeah, it might have been that.

At least I'd scored a goal. Losing a couple of teeth was worth that, in my opinion.

The female swore, making me even harder. I shifted, widening my stance and wondering if I could reach into my pants and rip the plastic cup off. I'd feel a lot better without it cutting off circulation, and maybe a display of my arousal would impress this female. But before I could decide on a course of action, the female had yanked my head lower and pried my mouth open, once more poking at the empty sockets in my mouth and continuing to swear.

Humans had quite the vivid vocabulary. It was really very impressive.

My brain short circuited as she gently touched my loose tusk. Did she know what that meant? Probably not.

Humans didn't have tusks, so this female probably had no idea how intimate it was to fondle another's tusk.

The female stepped back again, wiping her hands on more of the little white cloths and digging into her purse. "I'm going to need to see that Monday morning. I'll squeeze you in first thing at eight, so be there on time."

I took the card that she held out and read it. I'd been working hard on learning the humans' scribbly language and recognized an address and phone number along with two lines that must be her name. Names? Why were there two lines? The humans I'd met so far didn't have this many names. Maybe she was a special human? Maybe this included her titles and rank? Was she also a military officer?

Her voice broke me from my thoughts. "And if you can find those two teeth, wrap them in wet cloths and bring them in with you. I doubt I can put them back in, but I can use them to mold new teeth for you. I'll also need to do X-rays and see if there are any broken sections left that I need to remove and determine if you need a bone graft to support the implants."

I nodded, glancing once more at the card. I hadn't understood most of what she said, but it was clear she wanted me to meet her Monday morning at this address. "I will be there. My gratitude, Schooner Dental Reconstruction. You are kind and beautiful."

I was proud of my careful pronunciation, and equally proud to remember not to add "spinster" to her name. I'd learned that last night when trying to buy a human female a beverage at the bar near the stadium.

She made a snort-noise that I thankfully realized was the human version of expressing mirth.

"It's Doctor Schooner, but you can call me Jordan." The female extended her hand.

"Ozar." I gently took her hand in mine, trying not to crush it or break any of the pretty, painted, delicate claws. "Please call me Ozar."

"Ozar. A powerful name. It suits you." She smiled, and I released her hand. "I'll see you Monday morning, Ozar."

Staring as she walked away, I noticed that she hadn't wiped her hand off after touching me as so many human women did.

She'd expressed concern over my damaged tusk—even touching it. She hadn't appeared repulsed by me; in fact, she'd invited me to visit her at a very indecent hour Monday morning. Even if the mate bond hadn't wrapped its delicate threads about my heart, I would have been transfixed by her.

My hand-axe more than liked her, but that was typical. I hadn't been with another in quite a while. Abstinence plus the euphoria of a mate bond had me hard as a metal rod.

No other female would do. I wanted my hand-axe to rise for no one but her, spill seed for no one but her. I knew that future self-pleasure releases would only occur when thinking of her.

Jordan. My mate, Jordan.

Reaching into my pants, I ripped the plastic cup off and tossed it across the parking lot. My member sprung free inside the pants, and I reached down to adjust it.

A mate.

Hopefully she felt the same way. I might have lost two teeth, and my team may have lost the game, but I'd won in every way that mattered. I'd found my true mate.

Chapter 4

Jordan

This is ridiculous, I thought as I made my way to the pub where my friends and I were going to grab drinks. Why had I gone into dentist mode the moment I'd seen that orc wiggle his tusk? Why had I offered to provide him with dental care and given him what amounted to a VIP appointment when my practice was booked for three months out?

It wasn't like I was doing this pro bono, though. The guy probably had great insurance. And doing reconstructive work for a hockey player would boost the status of my practice, even if that hockey player was an orc.

But none of that was why I'd offered to help him. Good insurance and a pro-athlete patient wasn't an adequate excuse for examining a total stranger's mouth in the middle of a parking lot—a stranger who hadn't filled out a ton of paperwork and hadn't been seated in a chair in my office by one of my staff. Why had I *done* that? Was it the challenge of fixing an orc's teeth? Was it an academic interest in his unusual jaw and dental structures?

Was it the sparks that danced along my nerve endings

when I'd touched him? The very non-professional concern I'd felt as I'd examined his tusk? Or the heat that had pooled between my thighs when he'd so gently taken my offered hand and shook it? His hand had been huge, easily able to break the bones in mine with a hard squeeze, but he'd been so careful. And his golden-brown whisky eyes had shown with kindness, reverence...attraction.

He wasn't my type. The orc thing...it was horrible to think this, but I'd never imagined dating anyone but a human male. Even without the green skin and the tusks, he was just...big. The guy was seven feet tall and a wall of hard muscles—muscles so defined I could clearly see them from the stands at the game.

I'd never gone for the jocks. I made it a hard rule not to date sports figures, musicians, or actors.

And he was an *orc*.

But orc or not, something about him stirred me like no one had in over a year—like no one *ever* had.

Shaking my head to clear it of such thoughts, I opened the door to the pub and headed straight for the ladies' room to wash my hands. Good grief. I'd examined someone's teeth without even wearing gloves, with nothing but cheap pocket-sized tissues to sponge up his blood. Again, *what* had I been thinking?

After I'd washed my hands twice and applied sanitizer from my purse, I headed back into the dining area and saw Willa waving at me from a back table.

"What took you so long?" Abby asked. "We were ready to send out the cavalry to search for you."

"And you still have your jacket." Willa pulled on one of the sleeves. "Wasn't the whole trip to your car so you could ditch this?"

Now I'd have to tell them what happened. How embarrassing. I grimaced and slid into a seat, relaying the story of finding Ozar leaning against the back of my car, and his dental issues.

Abby rolled her eyes. "Let me guess, you pulled a portable X-ray machine from your purse and took images right in the parking lot."

"You are *such* a dentist." Willa laughed. "Although I've got to say, hockey players probably all need reconstructive work multiple times in their careers."

I shuddered at the thought of all those broken and dislodged teeth. "They wear mouth guards."

But *did* the orcs wear mouth guards? The humans had pads, while the orcs had been skating around bare-chested. Maybe they weren't provided with mouth guards, either.

The thought infuriated me. Did OSHA know about this? The National Hockey League? There had to be safety standards in place and those should apply to orcs as well as humans playing the sport.

Willa elbowed me. "Well, now you have a new client who probably has great insurance and deep pockets if they're paying the orcs what they pay the human players. Maybe you'll end up the official dentist to the team."

"Maybe." The thought didn't really appeal to me. I preferred my current clientele and didn't really want to turn into a sports specialist. But if my friends thought this was some sort of strategic career move, then they wouldn't suspect the weird attraction I'd felt toward Ozar.

I'd never hear the end of it if Willa and Abby thought I was getting all hot and bothered over an orc.

Abby eyed me over her beer. "So, which one was he? The goalie? That forward? He was totally hot."

I blinked in surprise. "You think the forward was *hot*?"

My friend grinned. "I mean, they're *all* hot. Tall, muscles out the wazoo."

"Tusks?" Willa laughed. "I'll admit they are totally jacked, and the green skin doesn't bother me one bit, but how would kissing one work with those tusks jutting out of their lower jaw?"

They both turned to me, and I felt my face heat up at the scrutiny. "What? I've never kissed an orc. How am I supposed to know?"

Abby snorted. "We're looking at you for a dental-expert perspective. And you *did* get up close and personal to those tusks tonight. Do you think an orc is kissable? Or more importantly, is oral out of the question?"

And now there were images running through my mind of Ozar going down on me. The tusks were long enough that, with care, the points wouldn't jab anything...important. And skillful pressure with one of them in the right place could be absolutely amazing.

I sucked in a breath, realizing that Abby and Willa were still staring at me, silent and waiting for my verdict.

"I think kissing could be...logistically different, and...oral could be interesting and enjoyable."

Abby did a fist-pump. "I *knew* it. Should we become Baltimore Tusks groupies, girls? Go to the parties and experiment with some orc loving?"

Willa shrugged, lifting her wine glass. "Hell, I'm up for anything. Count me in."

"Uh, count me out." I grimaced. I was too busy with my career to squeeze in all the partying and casual sex.

Although I couldn't help but wonder...

I took a deep pull on the cold draft beer, wondering why it was extra hot in here. Puck's was always hot, but I felt like I was ready to melt.

"I'm buying tickets for the next home game," Abby announced, picking up her phone.

"I'll research what bars they hang out at, and if anyone is hosting an after party," Willa said. "Twitter and Insta, here I come."

"Isn't it called 'X' now?" I said.

Willa shrugged. "Fuck that. It's always gonna be Twitter. And National Airport will never be called Reagan National. And McDaniel College is forever Western Maryland College."

For a woman who was known for being adaptable, Willa was surprisingly inflexible about some things. I hid a smile behind my beer and took another sip. I'd arrived in Baltimore five years ago to start my practice, feeling out of place and lonely in the city. Willa had been a personal trainer at the health club I'd joined, and we'd quickly become friends. Abby had gone to college with Willa, and after a few happy hours, the marketing consultant ended up my friend as well. They were both smart, funny, and they kept me from becoming a slave to my job.

"There." Abby set her phone down. "We've got tickets to watch the Tusks play Toronto at the next home game. My treat."

Willa turned her phone to face us. "Judging from some pics on Insta, it looks like the Tusks like to grab a post-game beer at McHenry's Bar and Grill. It's just four blocks the other side of the stadium. You ladies should down those brews so we can go ogle some buff green dudes."

"Yes!"

"No!" I spoke the same time as Abby, then sighed as the two other women turned to face me, eyebrows raised.

"That felt like an oddly emphatic no," Willa commented.

Abby rested her elbows on the table and propped up her chin. "Is there a reason you don't want to go to McHenry's?"

"I have to get home to my cat?" It was a lame excuse, but it was the only one I could think of that wouldn't expose this strange insta-crush thing I'd developed on one of the orc players.

"Bullshit." Willa laughed. "Your cat is going to be pissed at you whether you go home now or in three hours. I'm thinking there's another reason you don't want to go. You're blushing like crazy."

"There's probably a whole team worth of teeth and tusks to examine at McHenry's," Abby teased. "And if you want to examine other body parts of a certain hot forward, I'm guessing he'd be eager and willing."

Damn. My face was on fire, and all I could think about was the idea of my leg pressed against Ozar's as I sat next to him at the bar. He'd offer to walk me to my car, then pull me into a walkway between two buildings, pushing me up against the wall and kissing me. His lips would be soft, his tongue insistent, his tusks firm against my face. He'd grab my ass with his big hands, hauling me up so I could wrap my legs around him and press myself against the hardness of his—

"McHenry's it is." Abby downed the rest of her beer, then pushed mine toward me. "Drink up, girl. We've got hockey-orcs to ogle."

Chapter 5

Ozar

I watched Jordan leave, then I went back into the stadium, strategizing my plan of attack.

Could she really be my true mate?

Did humans feel the mate bond like orcs did? If not, I'd need to plan my wooing very carefully to make sure I didn't lose her to another. I'd been told stories of how orcs had won their mates, but those had been *orc* females, and those females had felt the mating bond connection just as strongly as their partners. It would be a challenge for me to win Jordan over—especially since I knew so little about human females and human mating customs.

And I could be wrong. I'd never experienced a mate bond, and while this had felt like what those in my clan had described, it might just be simple lust. Either way, I wanted to explore these sudden emotions, wanted to see if what I'd felt when Jordan stepped close to me and touched my tusk lasted beyond tonight. Even if this wasn't a mate bond, I was still attracted to her. From what I could tell in those brief minutes, I liked her. And that was enough for me to commit to wooing her. I needed a wife, and I had no doubt that

Jordan would make me happy as we went through our lives together.

But how to woo her?

The two months I'd been here had been spent getting used to things like banking, public transit, and what humans considered crimes. We'd all been focused on learning English, knowing that not only would we need it to navigate this world while we remained here, but we'd also need to be able to speak to our potential brides. I hadn't had time to delve into common human habits or their wooing customs, so I'd need to learn quickly to make sure I didn't screw this up.

And then there was sex.

Did human females like the same things as orcs? I knew the nuts and bolts of the process were the same, but the rest of it was a mystery. I'd heard enough conversations to have determined that human females, just like orc females, had sex prior to marriage—most likely as part of their selection criteria. The thought made me break out in a sweat. What if I didn't please Jordan? Releasing my seed in her would cement the mating bond for me—if there even *was* a mate bond. But if I failed to impress her with my prowess and she left my bed for another, more skilled male, I would be crushed.

And there was the question of whether I could even coax her to lay with me. I'd need to impress her long before I invited her to my furs. And I hadn't the foggiest idea how to do that.

Thoughts of my failure filled my mind. Sweat broke out on my forehead, and rage filled my heart at the thought of losing Jordan to another. I prided myself on my control and dismissed the idea that I might harm Jordan or her chosen partner if I failed. Although the thought of her with another did bring up violent thoughts. I'd just have to make sure I did everything correctly in wooing her, and that she found the sex beyond reproach. *Everything* needed to be beyond reproach.

Thankfully, the Zamboni machine hadn't swept the ice yet, and I quickly found my two missing teeth. Then I headed into the locker room, looking for my teammates. As embarrassing as this situation was, I needed advice.

I especially needed Bwat to recommend materials to study on courting and sexually pleasing human females. Bwat had been the one who'd learned the spoken and written English the fastest, and he'd been devouring written materials and video programs in his spare time. Among the orcs on the team, Bwat was considered the expert on humans and life here in their realm.

The locker room was empty except for Sizzle. The slight demon was our equipment manager, and he was currently sorting through hockey sticks, muttering about the damage they'd suffered as a result of tonight's game. I put my skates in front of my locker and eyed the demon.

Sizzle wasn't a human, but demons had been living here far longer than I had, and the equipment manager might have good insights into how I should woo my mate.

I sat down next to the demon, who ignored me. "I have found a human female that I want to marry. I wish to make her mine," I announced.

"Congratulations. Good for you."

Sizzle's monotone drawl sent the very clear message that he wanted me to go away, but I knew the value of perseverance. Wearing down an opponent with strength and stamina worked in battle, and there was no reason to think it wouldn't work in conversation as well.

"I need advice on courting human females," I continued. "When wooing female orcs, we slay beasts and present them as gifts or build homes to entice them to accept our marriage offer."

The demon put down the stick he was looking over and turned to me, a glimmer of interest in his dark eyes. "Same with demons. Well, except the house thing. Bring them food and the head of their enemy on a pike. Sometimes the head serves as food, which is a win-win situation. Less effort, double the impact."

I frowned. "I do not know who her enemies are, and I fear murdering a random human for a trophy gift would offend. What if I accidentally kill one of her clansmen? Or a family member?"

Sizzle grunted. "Yeah. Most demons wouldn't care about that, but humans *are* stupidly sentimental about their families."

I'd be upset if someone killed a clansman as well, so we and the humans agreed on this point.

"There are not many beasts in Baltimore to kill," I complained. "Gifting a squirrel or one of the birds that eats crumbs from the sidewalk does not seem like it would impress a female."

"You're right," Sizzle agreed. "Lots of humans hunt, but all the larger animals are outside the city. Except for the zoo, that is, and humans get really pissed off when you kill one of *those* animals. Trust me, I know. You're probably better off buying her a steak from the grocery store. Or a gift card from Starbucks. Human women love their coffee."

I nodded slowly, thinking that I'd need to look up the definition of "gift card" later. I'd seen the Starbucks businesses and also enjoyed the human coffee beverage, so that might be a good option. Buying a steak at the grocery store for her seemed like it would get me labeled as a poor hunter, and I didn't want that.

Thanking the demon for his help, I showered, changed, and went in search of my teammates. I found some of them down the street at a local food establishment that had proven to be hospitable to orcs.

Eng, Bwat, and Ugwyll were all at the bar, each holding a large mug of beer. They were the only ones seated there, with the human customers huddled at tables as far away from the bar as they could get.

The wait staff didn't seem to mind us orcs. A bearded male human bartender gave me a wave and began pouring me a mug of the dark beer I enjoyed. A human waitress with short, spiked pink hair and a pierced nose smiled at me as she walked by with a plate full of food. Careful not to get too close to the nervous human customers, I made my way to the bar and sat down beside Bwat.

"What took you so long?" Ugwyll asked. "We put in an order for snack-tizers because we're starving and didn't want to wait."

"I went outside and spoke with a human child. Then I met the female I intend to marry."

Eng saluted me with his beer. "Does she have any sisters or friends you could introduce me to?"

Not if he were the last orc male alive. Eng was an entitled, pompous jerk. If Jordan had any friends or sisters, I'd make sure Eng never met them.

"So, when are you leaving with your new bride?" Bwat asked.

I squirmed. "I have to court her first. You are the one who warned me that I shouldn't propose right away, so I intend to woo her for at least a week before discussing marriage."

"Pfft." Eng scowled. "Courting? Human females? Just grab her and haul her back home. Slap some of that goose-tape on her mouth first so the other humans don't hear her screaming and shoot you or alert the angels."

"It's called duct tape," Bwat told him.

"You can try to kidnap *your* bride, but from what I've seen of human females, I don't want to have an angry, unwilling bride in my bed. We've got to rest sometime, and I have no doubt she would stab me in my sleep," I said.

"Not if you tie her up before you slumber," Ugwyll told me.

I was *not* going to tie Jordan up. Unless she liked that sort of thing. Then I'd absolutely tie her up.

We drank our beers in silence. The snack-tizers came. Once all the wings and tots and poppers had been consumed, I broached the topic that had been occupying my mind since I'd first seen Jordan in that parking lot.

"Do you think it's possible to have a mate bond with a human female?" I asked.

Bwat regarded me with sympathy, patting my shoulder. "None of us will ever experience a mate bond. We can only hope to have a satisfying marriage with a human female and know that our children may be able to find a true mate of their own."

"The orcs who have human blood in their veins were able to have a mate bond. We can breed with humans. We can have loving partnerships with humans. Perhaps a mate bond isn't out of the question," I argued.

Ugwyll frowned. "Orcs in the past have brought home human wives when they came here to plunder and raid. If it were possible, wouldn't some of *them* have experienced a mate bond with their human spouses?"

No one had an answer to that. We had historical texts,

but they didn't detail the marital life of orcs. And no one living during my lifetime had ever had a human wife, although several of my friends back home had known a human grandmother.

We all stared into our pint glasses with broody gazes. Even Eng seemed saddened by our mate-less fate. Their gloom and despair made me want to give them some hope to hold on to, even though revealing such personal feelings was uncharacteristic for me.

"When I met this human female tonight, I felt more than physical attraction," I confessed. "I believe I may have felt the stirrings of a mate bond."

They all jerked their heads to look at me.

"There is a human with orc blood in Baltimore?" Ugwyll's voice rang with excitement. "Are there more? Females who live here and have orc blood would not have died from the plague. If so, we could all possibly find true mates. But could we bring them home? I don't want to experience the joy of a mate bond, only to possibly lose my wife to the plague when we returned."

"We'd need to stay here," Eng gloomily announced. "I can't stay here. I'm a very important orc, a son of the clan chieftain. A prince in my kingdom. I'm needed at home. I'm better off just grabbing a fertile human female than having to suffer through the loss of a part-orc mate."

"I'd stay," Bwat said. "As much as I dislike life here, I would stay if it meant I was able to bond for life with a female who had orc blood."

"Is her skin green?" Ugwyll asked. "Green-tinged? Tiny tusks? Those back home with human blood in their veins are only slightly smaller than full-blooded orcs, so she must be larger than most human females."

I finally managed to break into the conversation. "She

does not appear to have *any* orc blood; she's a human female."

Silence fell once more.

"You think you felt a mate bond for a *human* female?" Bwat asked.

"How hard did you hit your head on the ice?" Eng scoffed.

"Not *that* hard," I grumbled. "I'm sure—"

"Maybe you confused lust for a mate bond." Ugwyll reached down and adjusted his hand-axe through his pants. "Human females can be very enticing. Their lithe bodies, their tantalizing smell... I wonder about their tuskless mouths, and how that might feel—"

"It was more than lust," I snapped. "I'm sure—"

"Bonded mates are orc-orc." Bwat frowned. "This human female *must* be orc. An orc with a glamor to make her appear human? Although with our resistance to magic, I can't see that ever working."

"She is a human, and I am sure she is one hundred percent human. And I believe she may be my true mate." I slugged down my beer and waved at the bartender for another. "Even if she is not, I want her to be my wife. We will return home together, live out our long lives together, and have many orclets."

I couldn't hide my smile at the thought. I'd built a den back home before leaving, intending to present it to my wife. It was the traditional wedding gift from a male to his bride, and I'd carefully crafted every bit of the home, thinking the whole time about a contented wife and the rowdy, adorable children we'd raise together. But Jordan... I'd expand the sitting room, add a second porch onto the back, build a detached kitchen for when the days grew too hot to cook in the house. I'd save my earnings and buy the very best furs, purchase anything that caught her eye, make myself available to satisfy her every whim.

Eng's laughter broke through my happy thoughts.

"Does *she* know about this? Assuming this truly is a mate bond you feel, then who is to say a human female is even able to experience the same? You may forever be pining for a female who is not interested in being your wife, or one who never accepts the bond."

"True." Ugwyll nodded. "If she's your mate, then you should grab her and race home as fast as you can."

"Don't give her a choice," Eng added. "Once you're home with her, she'll have to accept you as her husband. She'll have no other option."

I glared at him. Eng was such an asshole. The other orc claimed to be a king's son from a different mountain range's clan and acted as if he were better than the rest of us. One day Eng would realize he was working the same job, living in the same sort of accommodations, and under the same restrictions as we were. Here, no one gave a river rat's ass whether Eng was a king's son or a dung-pile turner.

"It would be dishonorable to break my vow, even though that promise was made to an angel and not another orc," I told him. "And I cannot abduct her. She is the female I want to make my bride. I could never do anything to cause her distress or harm her in any way. Besides, the human female in question has indicated she is open to my advances. She gave me a piece of paper with her name, title, and the location of her domicile. And she told me to meet her there Monday morning at the hour of eight."

Bwat sucked in a breath. "In the *morning*? At the hour of *eight*? Whoa."

I puffed my chest out. It *was* a promising situation.

"Good job." Ugwyll punched me in the shoulder. "Figures you'd find a willing female first. Is she comely?"

I snarled at the other orc, ready to come to blows at the questioning of my true mate's attractiveness.

Bwat put a hand on my arm. "Easy. We just want you to tell us of her beauty."

Oh. Well, that was okay, then.

"My mate's name is Jordan Schooner, and she holds a title of 'Doctor' among her people. She is slight in build, but bold of character, with skin the color of foam on a dark beer, and eyes like storm-waters. Her hair is the shade of oak-bark and sunshine, and her voice as soothing as Maxten song at night."

Bwat nodded approvingly. "Very poetic. Your mate sounds truly gorgeous."

Eng snorted. "Not to me. 'Bold of character'? She's a shrew who will make your life a nightmare of arguments. I want a quiet, submissive woman who will do as I say."

Ugwyll took a swig of his beer. "I don't care either way as long as she can bear my children. I plan to have at least twelve and intend to have her checked before we wed to ensure her fitness for duty."

Bwat glared at them both. "Ozar has the right idea. My mate must inspire me to song and poetry. She should be skilled in all forms of art and be able to garden. Our plants and flowers back home will be the envy of the clan, and we will entertain everyone with our duets on the famous orc battles of old."

I kept quiet. Yesterday I would have agreed that a healthy, compatible bride was enough, but now I hoped for the love that only a mate bond could bring. I wanted conceiving offspring to be more than a duty, more than just a physical pleasure. I wanted my wife to yearn for my touch as much as I would yearn for hers. I wanted my hand-axe to harden just thinking about her. I wanted sex to strengthen our bond, not just to put a child in my female's womb.

"You are meeting this female on Monday morning at her invitation? What are you going to bring her as your first gift?" Bwat asked.

"I'm not sure," I confessed. "I spoke to Sizzle in the locker room tonight, and he suggested I give her a steak from the grocery store or a Starbucks gift card."

"What in the name of every mountain god is a 'Starbucks gift card'?" Ugwyll asked.

"Gift cards are a type of currency only exchangeable in certain stores. Humans find them an appropriate reciprocation for a kindness done to them, but I don't believe it would be substantial enough to impress a human female that one is courting, let alone one who might possibly be a true mate," Bwat said, reaffirming my decision that he was the correct one to ask about how to woo human females.

"A steak? From a grocery store?" Eng's eyebrows shot up. "Maybe a slab of meat if you actually killed the beast yourself. Even then, presenting the entire animal would be a better choice. Always go overboard on gifts to show that you are not only serious about making her your bride, but that you have the skill and riches to provide for her."

"I agree." I shrugged. "But there are no large beasts nearby for me to slay, and my meeting with her is Monday morning. That gives me tomorrow to procure something, and I doubt I could locate a large beast within the city of Baltimore to kill in that timeframe. What would make a suitable first gift for a human female that I can acquire by tomorrow night?"

"Jewelry. Or clothing," Eng suggested.

"I could research what sorts of jewelry or clothing

human females find appealing," Bwat said. "But it's a risk. She might have particular tastes, and the gift might not gain her favor."

"I think it might be too early in my courting for such a gift anyway," I said. Although it might be a good idea to have Bwat do this research for a future gift.

"How about food prepared by you and fed to your intended by hand," Ugwyll suggested. "That is how my father wooed my mother. Good food that is hand-fed shouldn't fail to please even the most selective of females."

I frowned. "What if I choose a food she does not like?"

Eng shrugged. "Then feed it to her anyway. Forcibly if need be. Hold her down. Human females must be provided suitable nourishment, whether they want it or not."

"Maybe I should give her a knife? Or a mace?" I suggested, thinking that Jordan might appreciate a well-crafted weapon, although I doubted I'd be able to make one by Monday morning.

Bwat tapped his lower lip. "What does she enjoy? I know you have only just met her, but what are your first impressions?"

I thought for a moment. I didn't know much about her yet. She was beautiful. My hand-axe wanted to bury itself in her warmth. She had a small transportation vehicle that was blue. She was kind, concerned about my missing teeth and the injury to my tusk—

"She is very interested in teeth," I said.

The other orcs put down their beers and stared at me.

"Teeth?" Ugwyll finally asked.

"She collects them as trophies and wears them as a necklace?" Eng nodded approvingly. "She is truly a warrior and a good match for you. Perhaps a longer chain or a second one to display her growing collection?"

I hadn't seen a necklace of trophies around Jordan's neck, and surely if that was something of importance to her, she would proudly display them every time she left her home.

"I believe she has great concern that humans and orcs retain their teeth," I finally said. "She was upset that I had lost two teeth in tonight's game and asked me to find them if I could. I believe she intends on creating new teeth for me in place of the ones I lost."

I didn't say anything about my tusk, because some things were not meant to be shared with others, even if these males *were* the only other orcs in the city.

"That is quite the magic," Ugwyll said in an awed tone of voice. "Creating new teeth? You truly have found a valuable mate, Ozar."

"She wanted you to find your lost teeth?" Eng asked. "Perhaps that is her way of hinting to you about a suitable gift. She wants to keep them. And I cannot think of any reason a female would want an orc's teeth unless she had romantic feelings toward him."

I patted my pocket where I'd stuck the teeth. Should I string them on a chain for Jordan to wear?

"Human gifts are given in festively wrapped boxes tied with bright ribbons," Bwat informed us all before turning toward me. "There are some boxes, paper, and supplies in the closet in the coach's office."

"We have a coach?" Ugwyll asked.

No, we did not have a coach, but we did indeed have a coach's office with a thin layer of dust on the desk.

"If she finds the teeth a suitable gift, and indicates she is interested in me as a potential husband, should I follow up with an offer for dinner? Or perhaps I should give her an enemy's head on a pike?" I asked.

"I vote for the head-on-a-pike," Eng said.

"I'm voting for the Starbucks gift card," Ugwyll chimed in.

"I think you should wait until after you meet her Monday to decide on your next gift," Bwat said. "You will have learned more about her likes and dislikes, and perhaps she will subtly hint at an appropriate next gift, like she did with the teeth."

I considered the options, finally deciding to go with Bwat's suggestion. Although I might just stop by a Starbucks and pick up a gift card, just in case.

Chapter 6

Jordan

We walked into McHenry's and came to an immediate halt. The orcs were clearly visible at the bar, giant and green, and huddled together as they discussed something. The human clientele had given them a wide berth. The only open tables were the ones immediately around the orcs. Willa headed for the bar seats next to the hockey players, but I grabbed her arm and steered her toward a table instead, not wanting to look like a desperate puck bunny following Ozar here from the parking lot where I'd met him.

"Spoil sport," Willa muttered, taking her seat.

She and Abby both sat beside me, angling their chairs so we were facing the orcs. The guys hadn't seen us yet, and I was already dreading the moment one of them turned around and noticed the three of us gawking at them. Or smirking, as Willa was doing.

"That one on the end is typing on a cell phone," Abby leaned over and whispered. "I had no idea they'd be tech savvy."

"Maybe they have similar devices at home," I suggested.

For some reason, I'd assumed orcs lived a medieval-era existence with fire pits for cooking and beasts for transportation, but they could have the magical or technological equivalent of cell phones. Maybe they could teleport like the angels or whisk across the skies on magic carpets. Stereotypes were harmful, and if anything, the past few years had taught all of us that we were not the superior race we'd assumed ourselves to be.

"Do you think they're discussing the game and strategizing for their next one?" Abby asked.

Willa laughed. "I think they're rating the women in the bar and betting on who can get laid tonight."

They both turned to me.

"I've got no idea what they're discussing," I confessed, wishing I'd left and gone home to my cat.

Abby elbowed me. "Go find out. You've met one of them. Get your butt up to the bar and do the whole 'fancy meeting you here' thing."

No. Fucking. Way. I slouched lower in my seat, regretting that I'd ever been talked into this.

"How are they not breaking those barstools?" Willa asked. "They're all like seven feet tall and probably weigh over three hundred pounds with those muscles. And they're carrying knives. I'm not talking Boy Scout Swiss Army Knives, either. Those things have *got* to be illegal."

"Why is everyone scared of them?" Abby looked around the bar. "I mean, yeah, they're big and muscled, and have tusks, but they're hockey players. I'd expect people would be wanting to take selfies with them."

"Screw it." Willa got up from her chair, tossing her long braids over one shoulder and tugging the neckline of her shirt low enough to show off her cleavage. I tried to pull her back down into her seat and failed.

"Hey, boys! Great fight tonight. You might not have won the game, but you beat the snot out of those Red Wings."

The orcs all turned around. I hunched lower in my chair, but it didn't matter. Ozar's eyes found mine, and I knew I was red as a damned tomato. He jumped from his seat, took two steps toward me, then stopped. I could see he was just as confused about how to handle this situation as I was, so I took a deep breath, smiled, and waved him over.

"Did you and your friends want to join us?" I asked him once he'd walked the rest of the way to our table.

Ozar glanced behind him where Willa was chatting with one of the orc hockey players. Then he looked at Abby.

"Please join us," Abby told him. "That is, if you want to. We saw the game tonight and would love to buy you all a beer."

Where Willa was bold and brash, Abby was all friendly flattery. No man could resist either of my friends, for very different reasons.

And it seemed that orcs were just as susceptible to their charms as humans were. In seconds, we were all crowded around the table, bumping knees and rubbing elbows, literally, with the local hockey team. I'd expected loud bragging and pickup lines, but the orcs seemed to be nervous with us right next to them. It was kind of endearing. We all introduced ourselves. Abby ordered a round of beverages. Then there was an awkward silence.

The one named Bwat was staring at his phone in a way that reminded me a lot of the guys I'd recently gone out with from a dating site. He was a bit shorter and leaner than the others but still was well over six feet tall with muscles that a bodybuilder would envy. The one name Ugwyll looked like he was sizing us up—for what, I had no idea.

Eng I recognized as the guy who'd propped up a wall the entire game. He had an arrogant, brooding expression, like he considered this whole night a giant waste of time. For some reason, that was the orc Willa had locked her sights on. I shouldn't have been surprised. That woman always loved a challenge. And an argument.

Ozar shifted in his chair, scowling at his teammates, then his lips turned upward as he glanced my way. "I didn't expect to see you until Monday morning."

Ugh. Did he think I was stalking him? There definitely was an intriguing attraction going on here between us, but I needed time to think that out. I wasn't one to rush...well, rush *anything*. And being here probably gave him the impression I was.

"I'm glad to see you again," he confessed. "Do you like hockey games? Do you often attend?"

"I like hockey, but the last professional game I remember going to was when I was a teenager," I told him. "Baltimore hasn't had an NHL team before the Tusks. There are some minor league teams around here, but I've never gone to any of their games. Did you play hockey back home...where you're from? Or something like hockey?"

It was a stupid question given how badly they'd played —and skated—but I felt it was polite to ask.

He shook his head. "We had no ice-games. Our sports involve feats of strength, running, and hand-to-hand combat."

"I'm sure you won many of those." It wasn't false flattery. He was huge and strong, and after watching him fight tonight, I couldn't imagine him losing to anyone—even other orcs back in his homeland.

Ozar looked a little embarrassed. "I won some, but not what I would call many. At home I am a warrior, a Clan

Guardian. I fight, but I also lead my...team? I think that is your word."

I guessed it was, not knowing much about even human military terms. Which brought me to something I'd been dying to ask him since I'd talked to him in the parking lot.

"Your English is very good. Did you learn to speak it when you were young? Back home?" I was guilty of assuming the orcs lived a primitive existence, like green cavemen. For all I knew, they could have cities, schools, and libraries, as well as the equivalent of cell phones.

"Other than a few basic words and phrases, we all learned your language when we came here two months ago." He grinned at my surprised expression, flashing a line of white teeth and those tusks. "There are many languages in my world. It's good to know as many as possible, so we learn fast."

"Are there humans living in your orc cities? Is that how you learned those basic words and phrases?" I asked, really curious about his life before coming here and playing hockey.

He shook his head. "Not for many of your centuries has there been a human living with an orc clan. But there are orcs who have human blood in their veins from an ancestor, and while the human language has mostly been lost, their descendants know some of the language that was passed down in their family. My friend Gax had a human grandmother and taught me what he knew of her language."

"Humans have a lot of languages. Did you all only learn English or others? Did Gax's grandmother speak English?" That initial awkward silence was broken, and now I was excited to know everything I could about orcs—and about this orc in particular.

"Gax's grandmother spoke English, and that is what we

learned when we arrived since our passageway to this world led us here."

He had made a gesture with his arm as he spoke, and I couldn't help but tease him. "You arrived from your world via a portal to The McHenry Tavern? Is the passageway in the basement? The walk-in fridge?"

Ozar frowned, consulting his phone. After a few long seconds of typing and reading, he chuckled, the sound low and warm. "We arrived in this country, but not in this particular business."

"I still think your being able to speak English in two months is remarkable," I told him. "I doubt I'd be able to do more than ask where the restroom was and maybe comment on the color of your clothing in *your* language after two months."

He leaned over, his arm brushing my shoulder. "I think you would learn quickly. Gax's grandmother did."

I had so many questions.

"How did Gax's grandfather meet his human grand-mother?" I wondered. The elves and fae had a long history of kidnapping humans, but that wasn't exactly a situation that led to romance. Unless Gax's grandfather had rescued her from her kidnappers, that is.

Ozar squirmed. "I don't know the exact circumstances of their meeting."

"He kidnapped her?" My voice was flat. I didn't care if I offended him or not.

The orc sighed, then nodded. "He did. I believe there were some difficult early times between them, but they ended up in love."

Right. "Maybe you should Google 'Stockholm Syndrome' on your phone," I snapped.

He stilled, his expression worried as he looked at me.

"We no longer raid and plunder your world like we used to."

I noticed he didn't say anything about kidnapping women.

"And I vow to you on my honor and my clan that I will *never* take a female against her will."

My eyes met his, and I was surprised by the intensity in those golden-brown irises. I believed him. I didn't know what the other orcs intended, but I believed Ozar.

"Okay. Just so we're clear, I carry pepper spray in my purse," I informed him, thinking that might not be that much of a deterrent to an orc. Maybe I needed to find a reputable magic shop and invest in a protective amulet. Or just buy a gun.

Ozar solemnly nodded. "Understood. I will give you no reason to use seasoning to defend yourself."

I snort laughed at that, because the cultural barrier helped to make him seem less threatening, and more of an earnest, seven-foot-tall, musclebound, Boy Scout.

"So, what sort of English words and phrases did your friend Gax teach you?" I asked.

He grinned again, and a little zing went through me. "I will tell you those another time, because they are not words a male should say in the company of an *oranwgiel*."

Yeah, a total Boy Scout. It was so incongruous compared to his appearance that my attraction to him flared hotter. I scooted my chair closer, taking the beer that Abby had bought for us and clinking it against Ozar's pint of dark brew.

He frowned.

"It's a ritual," I explained. "Touching our glasses together signifies friendship and trust."

Ozar grunted, picked up his pint, then rapped it against

mine with a bit more force than I had done. "I trust you, Jordan."

I smiled. "And now we drink."

The orc took that to mean he should down his entire pint, then wave at the waitress for another round. I'd intended to just sip mine but didn't want to insult the guy so I quickly gulped the pint down, knowing I'd regret all these beers in the morning.

"What made you decide to play hockey if you didn't have the sport back home?" I asked as the waitress distributed another round of brim-full pints to each of us at the table.

"Angels," Ozar informed me. "We were not allowed to remain here unless we had what they call 'gainful employment.'"

My mouth dropped open. "So, all the bouncer jobs were taken? Overnight convenience store clerk positions? Wrestling coach openings? Why hockey?"

He consulted his phone again. "We were offered none of those jobs. The only employment opportunity was to play hockey for this team, and we accepted."

Sweet Jesus. My anger flared, totally pissed at the demon owner of the Tusks. He'd taken advantage of these orcs who'd thought they were getting a regular job instead of becoming the equivalent of freaks in a circus sideshow. There wasn't much payback I could do to a demon, but if that guy ever found himself in my chair, he was getting an unnecessary root canal without Novocain, professional ethics be damned.

Ozar took a long pull at his beer, then stared at the dark brew with a moody expression. "We were arrogant. Comparing our size and strength to the humans, we assumed we would easily win at any game. But we did not win, and we were laughed at. I think *that* is why we were asked to do this job, so we could play the fools and humans could pay their coin to watch the big powerful orcs be beaten by humans."

I put a hand on his shoulder, feeling the muscles under his T-shirt jump at my touch. "*I* wasn't laughing. You scored a point—that's no small thing in hockey, especially since you all aren't experienced in skating or in the game. You also kicked some serious ass in the fight."

He looked a few things up on his phone, then smiled sheepishly. "It was a lucky shot. And of course we kicked asses in the fight. We're orcs."

Now *there* was the arrogance I'd expected. Surprisingly, it didn't turn me off like it did with other guys.

"Lucky shot or not, you nailed it right into the net. I'll bet with some practice and good coaching, you all will be more than a laughingstock by the end of this season."

"We all hope to be gone by the end of the season," he confessed.

My heart sank at that. "What do you mean?"

He looked embarrassed, as if he'd spoken without thinking. "None of us are good at hockey. It's best for us to get other jobs. I hope to stay in Baltimore, though."

There was a meaningful glance that accompanied his last words, as if he was planning to stay in Baltimore because of me. I'd been fed a lot of lines in my life, but I got the feeling this orc Boy Scout wasn't delivering empty promises to help him get laid.

"I'd like it if you stayed in Baltimore," I confessed, feeling a little uneasy at expressing my interest so clearly.

"Then I will." That intensity was back in his eyes. "And I will continue to play hockey if you wish."

I winced. "You need to do what you want in terms of

employment. I'm just saying that I think you all could be contenders. You're physically...well, damned buff. All you need is coaching on the game and loads of practice on the ice. I get the impression none of you are averse to a challenge."

He typed again on his phone, then nodded. "I accept the challenge."

Sucking in a breath, I held up my hands. "No! I don't want you to do this for me or for anyone else. If you're going to continue with the Tusks, it has to be for *you*."

"Or for the team?" He looked at the other orcs, and I got the impression they were about to be whipped into shape, whether they liked it or not.

"Ozar, you need to do what *you* want." I put my hand back on his arm.

"There are things I want. And if being a fool on a hockey team gets me those, then I will play this game."

I shivered a little at his tone, that non-practical, romantic piece of my heart thrilling at the intimation that he wanted *me*—that he'd do anything to win *me*.

"How about you not be a fool on a hockey team," I said, a daring tone in my voice. "How about you be a winner on a hockey team? How about you score goals and play in a way that the other team is scared to death of you?"

Ozar grinned at that, his gaze focusing on some distant point, visualizing his success. "I like that idea, Doctor Jordan Schooner of Schooner Dental Reconstruction. I like that."

"Jordan," I reminded him. "Please just call me Jordan."

"Jordan." He took another drink from his beer. "I have told you many things about me, and now I want to hear everything about you."

By last call, I hadn't told him *everything* about me. As

usual, I'd gone on at length about my more challenging reconstructive dentistry cases. I'd even pulled out my phone and showed him pictures. I wanted to blame the number of beers I'd had this evening, but honestly, I was always like this—a total tooth nerd who lived for her profession.

Ozar was either incredibly polite, or he was determined to suffer though anything for a chance to take me to bed. Except at the end of the night when the staff was shooing our drunk butts out the door, Ozar didn't insist on taking me back to his place. Instead, he expressed concern about my ability to drive my vehicle and offered to walk me home.

I laughed at the idea of stumbling several miles through the city to my house. I was wearing comfortable shoes, but I was also extremely tipsy and knew I'd end up having to pee in a couple of people's landscaping on the way if I walked home. It was a better plan to order an Uber and pick up my car sometime tomorrow. Abby had left before us, as had Willa. The other orcs had also left, leaving Ozar and I drinking another round and talking until closing.

Ozar was intrigued by the Uber app, saying he wanted to download that for himself as he didn't have a vehicle or know how to drive one. I finished, then asked him how orcs and others in his world got around.

"We walk. We can also run at a fast pace for very long distances. And if we need to haul lumber or something else, we hitch *pzacki* to a cart. They are like..." He jutted out his lower lip in thought. "Horse and moose. And shark, although they do not need to live in the water."

What the hell kind of monster was that? "Do you ride them? Or do they just pull carts?"

"Both, although they tend to bond to one orc and will only allow them to ride or approach. They are dangerous creatures and can be vicious to those they do not like."

My Uber pulled up to the curb.

"Thank you for an enjoyable evening," I told him, really meaning it. I'd had a great conversation with him, and the initial attraction had strengthened, winding its silky strands tightly around me as we'd gotten to know each other. Without thinking, I reached up and pulled his head down to mine, kissing him firmly.

He was taken by surprise, but quickly got with the program, gathering my body against his. His arms scooped me up off my feet, nestling my hips to the firm hardness between his legs. He was so tall he still needed to arch his back to continue kissing me, but the awkward position didn't seem to bother him, and it certainly didn't bother me. Neither did his tusks, which pressed firmly but not painfully against the sides of my mouth.

All the while, my Uber driver waited patiently. I doubted this was the first time he'd seen two people at closing time locking lips, waiting for their drunk-drive home.

When we finally pulled apart, Ozar opened the back door for me, ushering me into the seat and gently closing the door. The driver pulled from the curb, smirking at me in the rearview. I twisted to look back at the giant orc who watched until we rounded a corner.

It had been so easy to offer Ozar my business card in that parking lot under the guise of having him come in as a patient. That excuse for seeing him meant my heart would be safe. If he showed up Monday morning, fine. If not, then it wouldn't be a personal rejection *or* a slight on my abilities as a dentist. But we'd gone to McHenry's, and I'd gotten to know him better, and now there was so much more at stake. What would happen Monday morning when he walked into my practice? *If* he walked into my practice?

And what would happen if he didn't? My heart ached at the thought. Was this just a drunken flirtation that the orc would regret in the morning? He was a sports figure, losing team or not. And there was a reason I didn't date athletes.

But if he *did* show up at my office, and he acted totally professional, then I'd have to do the same. If he flirted, then maybe I'd work up the nerve to ask him out.

Maybe.

How the hell was I supposed to ask out a patient? Or even *flirt* with a patient? Ugh. Maybe I shouldn't have told him to come to my office after all. Playing it safe meant that I was now going to face an ethical dilemma.

And there *would* be a dilemma, because I wanted more from Ozar than just a chance to take care of his teeth. But it was too late for that now. If he arrived Monday morning for his appointment, I'd just need to be brave, throw professionalism out the window… and possibly ask him out to dinner.

Chapter 7

Ozar

I tossed and turned through the night, having dreams about Jordan and the orclets we would have together interspersed with nightmares of her rejecting me. Giving up on sleep, I rose. The sky was gray with the coming sun as I sat on my apartment's porch with a glass of milk and the last two cinnamon rolls from the dozen I'd picked up from a street vendor a few days ago.

The milk reminded me of home. It was a special kind that Bwat had found on the internet. A truck delivered the bottles to me three times a week from a farm west of the city. I'd discovered that with the addition of a vanilla bean, it tasted just like our *woanja* back home. It was so thick it coated my upper lip. Creamy and sweet and icy cold on my tongue and throat.

It was an orclet's drink, but my youth had been cut short with tragedy and this milk conjured up the joy of childhood and family.

Back home I would have been embarrassed to be caught enjoying a large cold mug of *woanja*, but none of my teammates lived in this building. They'd never been to my apartment to come across the bottles in my fridge. What I drank in private was my own business. And the humans didn't seem to view this as a beverage they needed to put aside when they became adults. The delivery man didn't seem surprised by my standing order and the lack of orclets behind me when I opened the door. And just yesterday the human male next door had been sitting on his porch, dunking sweet, baked disks into his own glass of milk.

Cookies. From what I could tell, most human adults enjoyed milk, and they all relished sweets. I hadn't quite worked up the nerve to put a packet of cookies in my basket at the market. Maybe someday I'd pretend I was buying them for a child, go home, and dunk them in my milk as the neighbor had done.

My orclets would have the time to drink *woanja*, eat sweets, and learn to enjoy their youth without the specter of loss cutting their childhood short. Jordan and I would blanket them with love, teach them important survival skills, all while making sure they learned the importance of kindness and clan bonds.

She was perfect. My mate. My female. The future mother of our orclets. She was smart, warm, and although I didn't understand human females at all, I got the impression she was as attracted to me as I was to her.

But that didn't mean I'd win her. A female like Jordan? There were probably dozens of males competing for her favor. I'd bring her my lost teeth that I'd managed to find on the ice, but I needed to do more. I'd need to impress her, to show her that I was the male best suited to be her partner in life.

To be her mate.

Downing the last of my milk, I went inside to shower and put on what the humans called "workout clothes."

There was a room full of equipment at the arena that we were supposed to use to maintain our strength and speed, but no one knew how to use any of the machines. Bwat had nearly toppled one over on himself last week, and our demon boss had screamed at Ugwyll for throwing the heavy disks through the wall. So we'd given up on the gym, and since we all hated sliding around on the ice while wearing knives on our shoes, I maintained my strength and speed as I would at home.

Trotting down the five flights of stairs, I exited the building and began to run.

It had taken me a while to learn to ignore the stares and the way humans quickly edged out of my way, sometimes crossing to the other side of the street when they saw me coming.

Some things had improved since last night, though. The human police didn't stop to interrogate me about what I was doing in the city and why I was running down the sidewalk. A human male shouted "Go Tusks" from a passing car, even though the fist he was shaking at me wouldn't have been an encouragement back home. A group of human females made whistling noises, commanding me to remove my shirt as I ran by.

After looping around Druid Hill, I headed slightly north and east to the waterfront, up to Canton, then circled back and slowed down as I entered Patterson Park.

Normally the park was close to empty with only a few human joggers and a handful of human females pushing babies in elaborate, shaded carts. Today, it felt like half the human population of Baltimore was here, having meals in large groups, kicking balls, or throwing colorful disks back and forth. Groups of children played team sports while adults watched and cheered. The metal structures arrayed on a sandy base were full of younger children, all of them climbing, swinging, spinning, and shrieking with joy.

Sitting on a bench, I watched the children. Orclets were larger and heavier than human young, but I'd seen the occasional adult male on the playground equipment. If the structures could support their weight, then they would hopefully hold up under a rambunctious orclet.

I'd been a little envious of that human male, swinging high and laughing as his child did the same by his side. If I tried that and broke the children's play equipment, I'd feel terrible. Maybe I could find a metalsmith in the city willing to let me use his forge and make a climbing structure and swinging apparatus built for an adult orc's weight. Certainly, larger humans would appreciate that too.

But Jordan and I would be living at home with my clan. There would be no need to construct playground equipment for orcs here. Besides, adult orcs would not be caught dead frolicking with orclet toys or on their play structures. There were adult structures for conditioning and athletic contests, and there were toys.

A black and white ball bigger than my fist rolled against my foot, interrupting my thoughts. I looked down at the ball, then up at the two male human children who stood four feet away, eyeing me expectantly. Reaching down, I picked up the ball and bounced it off my head toward the children, careful not to hit it too far.

They cheered, letting the ball hit the ground before rushing it. One child managed to maneuver it away, using his feet in complicated shuffling movements to keep the ball from the others. I watched them, thinking that human young were surprisingly agile with excellent balance. We might be stronger and faster, but humans had physical skills of their own. We'd always discounted them as weak, but last night's hockey game had been a humiliating lesson. As a Guardian, I'd learned not to let hubris put my clan at risk. These were not life-or-death contests, but I still should not be blind to my opponents' abilities on the ice.

I felt a tug on my shirt and looked down to see a female human child, her multitude of thick, dark braids capped with large colorful beads.

"Push me," she demanded.

My eyes widened, because there was no way I was going to shove this tiny, fragile creature.

She stomped a pink sneaker-clad foot. "Swing. Push me."

I looked in the direction she was pointing and understood. Before I could stand, a human female whose multiple braids were considerably longer than the child's rushed forward.

"I'm so sorry, sir. Melly, hon, I'll push you on the swing."

The child held her ground in spite of her mother's tugs, so I stood. "I will assist," I told the female. "Children are precious, and their needs are always a priority."

The female gawked at me as I stood to tower over her. "Wait. You're one of those hockey players, aren't you? An ogre?"

I winced but knew the insult was unintentional. "My name is Ozar, and I am an orc. A member of the Tusks hockey team."

"Ozar." She dug her phone from her pocket, following us as little Melly reached up to take my hand and drag me to the swing set.

After assisting the tiny human onto the woven seat, I gently pushed her, careful not to let her go too fast or too high. The activity wasn't as easy as I'd thought. My hands needed to connect at the right spot on her body at the right time, or I risked pushing her off the woven seat. It was a great responsibility that took all of my focus, and by the time she'd commanded me to stop so she could play on other equipment, I was sweating with anxiety.

With Melly off to ride on a structure shaped to mimic a fanciful pink animal, I'd thought my job was done, but the moment I turned from the swing, there were other human children clamoring for my attention. I climbed on top of a structure that protested my weight with a squawk and lifted the smallest to the next level of handholds. I spotted young humans who scaled a wall with only tiny plastic pieces to support their upward movements. I huddled underneath a swinging set of planks connected by loose rope, reaching between the gaps to mock-threaten children who squealed in delight.

I was hungry and thirsty, but I remained at the park until the humans had gathered their young together and left. Walking back to my apartment, I scared several humans with the toothy grin I could not keep from my face. Other than meeting Jordan, this had been the best moment of my time here among the humans.

And I fully intended on returning.

Chapter 8

Jordan

Even with a couple of Tylenol and a giant glass of water before bed, I still awoke with a hangover. My internal clock, my bladder, and my cat, Judy, all had me up at six in the morning. Knowing that I couldn't ignore two of those three things, I stumbled out of bed, took care of my need to relieve myself, fed Judy, downed another giant glass of water, and went back to bed.

At ten, I was feeling better—at least until I heard the distinctive sounds of Judy throwing up.

I adored my cat, but Judy revenge puked. Six hundred dollars in veterinary testing had only told me that she was exceedingly healthy without any physical concerns. Desperate, I'd experimented with anti-hairball food, sensitive stomach food, and a variety of grain-free, chicken-free, and limited ingredient kibble. At one point I'd actually started preparing her food from scratch, which involved weekly trips to the butcher shop and hours of prep. A year later, I'd collected enough data in the food diary I'd kept for my cat that I realized Judy vomited when events upset her need for a consistent schedule. A late work night, not enough attention, or business trips to a conference all resulted in unexpected surprises planted like land mines around my house.

It was unusual for her to puke within my hearing. Usually she was stealthier, but this morning she was clearly upset at my sleeping in and wanted me to know it.

"I'm up. I'm up," I shouted as I staggered once more from bed. Judy still tossed her breakfast, but she shifted slightly so the mess landed on the hardwood floor and not the rug where she'd previously been aiming.

It was the little things that I appreciated. All my rugs were washable, but that didn't mean I enjoyed cleaning them in the laundry sink and running them through the washing machine every few days. In appreciation for Judy's redirection, I scooped the tuxedo cat into my arms. She snuggled against me, purring and butting the top of her head against my jaw as I walked into the kitchen.

Coffee now. Vomit cleanup later.

"I'm guessing you want more breakfast since you just emptied your stomach," I said to Judy.

She purred louder, then meowed and twisted out of my arms, landing with grace on the kitchen floor. I knew my place in the hierarchy of the house, so I gave her a cup of kibble before I started brewing my coffee.

I couldn't blame Judy since I was a girl who liked my routine as well. The timing shifted a little on the weekend, but everything else was the same. Coffee, a light breakfast, and the newspaper on my phone. Gym. Shower and change. Then either work or whatever I had planned for the day if it was Saturday or Sunday. Today was supposed to involve all the household chores I had no time for during the week, then an evening movie and work on my latest article on bone reconstruction options for patients with jaw deformities who needed dental implants.

Last night's alcohol had pretty much blown that schedule to hell—aside for the coffee and newspaper, that is.

I was too old for this shit. A couple of beers were acceptable. Three or four was a party. The six or seven or eight or whatever I'd happily swilled down last night was not good. I wanted to blame my friends, but it was my own darned fault. I'd been all tingly-happy over meeting Ozar and had regressed into college coed me who used to be able to drink a six-pack and a couple of shots without repercussions. That college coed me would also have had no problem semi-stalking a hot orc hockey player, but in the cold light of day, I was embarrassed about my actions.

I groaned, putting my forehead down on the cool oak of my kitchen table. Ozar hadn't seemed to think my groupie behavior was weird. And he'd clearly had an interest in me beyond my professional ability to repair his teeth. So that meant the only real harm from last night was my headache and queasy stomach.

"Maybe I should puke on the floor too," I told Judy.

She chirped a reply and walked over to wind herself around my legs. The food bowl was empty, and I hoped this time the kibble stayed in her stomach.

Coffee. A slice of lightly buttered toast to settle my stomach. *The Baltimore Sun* on my phone.

I was feeling a bit better after all that, so I changed into my workout clothes, kissed Judy on her furry forehead, and headed to the gym.

I knew it wouldn't be a good day for a spin class, or running intervals on the treadmill, so instead I opted for deep-water swim-running with a floatation belt, then an easy session on the rower followed by some hot yoga.

Feeling a bit guilty over my neglected cleaning chores, I headed home and got in my vacuuming, bathroom cleaning, and a few loads of laundry before grabbing a shower and relaxing in a pair of comfy pajama pants and a tank top—no bra, because no one needs to wear that kind of torture device in the sanctity of their own home.

The day hadn't started out all that great, but it certainly was ending well. The exercise, the water, and the light breakfast had chased my hangover away, and I was ready to relax.

Judy was ready to relax as well, although I was pretty sure she'd spent most of the day snoozing. I whipped up a quick salad with leftover grilled chicken for dinner, adding half the leftover grilled chicken to Judy's bowl along with her kibble. Then my girl and I curled up on the couch. I put on some classical music in the background, grabbed my laptop, and got to work.

Was it really work if I enjoyed it this much?

It wasn't like I'd grown up obsessed with teeth. As a kid I'd wanted to be a baker, then a firefighter, then a spy. In high school, I'd loved biology but hadn't felt particularly inspired by the botany focus of high-school classes, and dissecting an earthworm hadn't lit my fire, either. It wasn't until college that I'd gone down the anatomy rabbit hole, to find myself intrigued with teeth.

At eighteen I'd been with my maternal grandmother as she'd talked to the hospice nurse who would be assisting with her palliative care. Cancer had taken a brutal toll on her, but she'd proudly told the nurse that she had all her own teeth and no need for denture care. It had hit me then that so many of my elderly relatives had chosen to have all their teeth removed and gone the route of dentures. Implants were still a radical and terribly expensive procedure, and for many people, gum disease and poor preventative care had left them with no option but dentures. I remembered that this very grandmother had spent a large amount of her savings a few decades prior to her cancer diagnosis to treat a periodontal issue, and that investment had paid off. Even facing the end of her life, she was proud that she'd be buried with her teeth still intact.

Maybe it wasn't such a surprise that dentistry became my passion. Preventative care was key, but it was the periodontal and restorative work that really fired me up. I loved seeing patients like my late grandmother who wanted to make sure they met their end with as many of their own teeth as possible. I'd gone the extra mile to reduce my patients' gum recession, restore lost enamel, go below the surface of the tooth to take care of even the slightest infection that might threaten someone's smile. It was the children and young adults that really tugged at my heart. Some of them had been born with deformities or had been in accidents where years of plastic surgery and skin grafts had put them in my chair to do what I could on what remained of their teeth, gums, and jaw. And my favorite patient...he was a ten-year-old boy who'd struggled with weak enamel and gum issues. I'd made progress in saving his teeth and loved seeing his smile as he sat in my chair.

My career didn't devour my *entire* life, though. I loved my family and my friends. I enjoyed morning workouts at the gym and spending time with Judy. I wanted a husband, but I wanted one who also loved his job, who would come home and curl up with Judy and me to talk about our day, to discuss what excited us in our different careers. There would be respect, admiration, and attraction. We'd want the same future, and we'd be excited to walk side by side throughout our lives together as partners. We'd support each other, cheer each other on, be there as a shoulder to cry on when things were hard. Maybe we'd raise a child together, loving and supporting every moment of their lives just as my parents had done for my brother and me.

I couldn't help but envision Ozar in that role as my husband. It was stupid. I'd just met him, and everything seemed roses and sunshine when you first met someone. It might not work out between us. We could be looking for very different things in a date or partner, or whatever. And he was a hockey player. He'd be gone weeks at a time, a slave to a brutal training schedule that only slightly eased up in the off season. And for all I knew, he might not even want a marriage.

It wasn't healthy to put all these expectations on him. He was a great guy, and all I needed to do was enjoy our time together. Anything else would happen, or it wouldn't. I needed to live for the moment, for the day, and stop obsessing over my failed past relationships or what might or might not happen in the future. Now. Focus on now.

Which was the paper I was writing. I would fall into the world of bone-grafts, with a purring warm cat by my side. Then bed. And tomorrow will be another day.

Chapter 9

Ozar

Early Monday morning I ran by the arena and found a suitable small box in the coach's office closet. The box had been pre-wrapped with a soft, slightly fuzzy dark blue covering—which was a relief since I doubted I had the skill to neatly fold paper around the awkward shape. None of the bows with the sticky backing would remain on the blue surface, so after putting my teeth inside, I tied a silky white ribbon around the box in a bow that was slightly lopsided.

Anxiety burned in my stomach. Jordan was the first female I'd ever wooed, and due to the scarcity of female orcs, I hadn't been able to witness many courtship processes myself. All I had to go on was stories from my father and other orcs in my clan, and what Bwat had told me about human dating customs.

My walk to the address on the card Jordan had given me took less time than I'd expected, so I meandered around the block a few times. It was important to be on time, but arriving too early would be rude. My timing did give me a chance to stop in a nearby Starbucks, though.

The guy at the register did a double-take when he saw me, then grinned. "Hey, you're one of the Tusks, aren't you? Ozar, right?"

It was one of the few times someone outside of the stadium had recognized me as being on the hockey team, and it sent a strange feeling through my chest, like when I'd returned home to my clan after successfully defending the western boundary. But what did I have to be proud of? The Tusks were nothing but comic relief, laughingstocks on ice. I was just doing this job so I could remain here until I found a wife. Then I would go home. Something deep down inside of me wanted to take this job seriously. I'd wanted to win this past weekend against the enemy...other team, but we didn't have the skills or any sort of team cohesion. None of my teammates cared about the game, and it seemed like the audience hadn't, either. They were just there to see a bunch of orcs get the crap beat out of them.

"Yeah. I'm Ozar," I replied gruffly to the cashier. The brief feeling of pride had been replaced by shame. I wasn't recognized because of valor; this human male knew me because I was earning a reputation as a buffoon.

The employee's smile was sympathetic. "Rough first game, but you'll get them next time. We're rooting for ya."

Was he serious? I grunted, then placed my order, grabbed a gift card, and paid for it all, waiting awkwardly at the pick-up end of the counter while keeping my eye on the time.

"Go Tusks!" A female who had her dark curls streaked with purple slid the coffee drink toward me with a smile.

Maybe they did mean it. Maybe they wanted us to keep trying and hopefully win a game—eventually. Their comments felt genuine, and my cup not only had my name on it, but a cute drawing of an orc with a hockey stick.

I left feeling conflicted. After last night's game, I'd decided not to put any additional effort into this hockey thing. But if there were people in this town that actually wanted the Tusks to win, I didn't want to let them down. I'd marched out of my clan's homeland on hopeless missions dozens of times in my life, determined to do my best because I owed it to my clan. They had put their faith in me. And I would die before I let them down.

Weirdly enough, I was beginning to get the same feeling of responsibility and duty toward the people of Baltimore, who wanted the Tusks to win. Which was ridiculous. These were humans, and this was a silly game. It wasn't at all like my duties as a Clan Guardian back home. I owed nothing to these humans and nothing to the other orcs who'd been forced onto this team of ours.

Jordan's residence was six floors up in a large, concrete building with glass doors, thickly carpeted floors, and an elevator. I took the stairs since I didn't really trust a metal box suspended on ropes to safely haul me up six stories. Once I was on the correct floor, I quickly identified her dwelling by the gold writing on the glass door.

Unsure what human protocol was, I tapped on the glass door and peered through it. Two females sat behind a desk, and there were two males and a female sitting in chairs across from them. Jordan was nowhere to be seen, and for a second, I was worried that I'd gone to the wrong place, despite the fact that her name was painted on the door.

One of the females behind the desk waved me in, so I entered and approached her.

"Good morning. Doctor Jordan Schooner told me to arrive here at this time," I said, proud that I'd memorized several different greetings in case I'd need to gain entrance from a doorman or security person.

"You must be Ozar." The female smiled at me. "Here's a form we ask all of our new patients to fill out. Take a seat over there with the others, and we'll call you when we're ready."

What was going on? Was Jordan such a high-ranking female that she had staff answering her door and screening her visitors? And who were these other people? I took a seat, glaring at the other two males, hoping to intimidate them into leaving. Could Jordan have others vying for her favor? Was I in competition with these other two males? And what about the female? Why was *she* here?

Had I misread the whole situation? I knew nothing about human customs, and I was beginning to doubt that Bwat did either, in spite of all his supposed research.

I sat and looked at the form, struggling to understand most of the questions. We didn't have all this paperwork back home, but in the human world it seemed like everything required I fill out ten of these pages, all of them requesting the same information. It was annoying. I found myself muttering in Orcish under my breath and jabbing the writing implement into the paper with a force that left holes in it.

Fed up with the whole thing, I took it all back to the female at the desk, slapping it down on the counter and returning to my chair.

I thought about leaving, but I hadn't imagined the chemistry between us Saturday night. It wasn't just our chance meeting in the parking lot, either. She and her friends had appeared at the bar where my teammates and I were congregating, and I got the impression that they'd arrived knowing we'd be there. And that kiss Jordan had given me as she left...

Quickly evaluating the possible prowess and attraction of the other two males made me feel slightly better. Neither looked like they were anywhere near the optimal age for breeding, and I seriously doubted their ability to bring Jordan pleasure or provide for her. Perhaps there was another reason for their presence here. Although I knew absolutely zero about human female preferences when it came to males.

I was still second guessing myself when another female walked from a back room and called my name. I stood, following her into a small room with a reclining chair, two stools, and all sorts of metallic equipment. The female indicated that I should sit, but instead I stiffened, looking around at all the small metal tools and the large arm-like protuberances jutting from the sides of the chair. I didn't like the look of this room. Or the feel of it. Or the smell of it either. And where was Jordan?

I growled, thinking I should have brought an additional weapon. Although I could easily overpower these humans and escape, I'd feel more confident with a sword, or at least something more than my one knife.

"Um, it's your first time at the dentist?" the female squeaked, clutching her clipboard against her chest. "Maybe I should get Doctor Schooner."

The female dashed out of the room, leaving me to take up a defensive position facing the only exit. When Jordan came in, I felt the tension leave my shoulders. She was giving me a kind smile and looked especially nice with her nut-brown hair pulled back and a long white jacket over her gray shirt and pants.

"Everything okay?" She walked up to me until she was so close that I could see the gold flecks in her gray eyes.

"You scared the heck out of Makena, but she needs to get used to nonhuman patients. I'll talk to her, but for today, I'll handle your imaging and exam."

"I might have growled at her," I admitted sheepishly.

Jordan laughed, putting a hand on my arm. "Humans have done worse than growl at their dental appointments. Here. Sit in the chair, and I'll go over the intake form with you."

I did as she asked, finding the chair surprisingly comfortable, even though I still didn't like the look of the metal arms and trays full of what looked to be torture devices.

"So, I'm guessing you might have some concerns about the questions on our form?" She held up the piece of paper I'd returned to the female out front. Black ink slashed across the neat lines, and light shown through the holes.

I thought she'd be angry at my disrespect, but Jordan looked like she was struggling not to laugh.

"Name. Address. Employer. I'll have Shanelle call for your insurance information, so don't worry about that. I'm guessing from these slashes that you either don't want to share your medical history, or that you don't have any medical history?"

She glanced at me with her eyebrows raised and that faint smile on her face.

"Sorry." I grunted. "We have healers at home who take care of wounds and injuries. If broken, our tusks will grow back. Our other teeth don't grow, so if they are damaged, our healers help the pain, and they stay in our mouth."

She tapped her pen against her lips, and I watched, fascinated. Her lips had felt so soft and full against mine. I wanted to touch them, taste them again, suck them into my mouth and nibble gently down on them.

"Your tusks regrow?"

Jordan interrupted my thoughts with her question, which was okay because she seemed genuinely interested to know about my second favorite part of my anatomy.

"For our whole lives, our tusks always grow. We need to shape and trim them often, or they can curl around to sometimes hurt our face."

She stepped forward, reaching out a hand before looking up to me for permission.

I grunted. "You may touch."

She had my permission to touch all sorts of things. Once more, my mind wandered to fantasy, only to be jerked back to reality when she ran her fingers over the loose tusk she'd examined last night. It wasn't that our tusks were sensitive; in fact, I could barely feel her touch on the tooth. It was such an intimacy for someone to run gentle hands over my tusk and the edge of my lips, though. We orcs were physically demonstrative, but that mostly meant slaps on the back, hugs, shoulder clasps, and head-butts, not...this.

Fuck. My hand-axe was absolutely rising to the occasion.

She glanced down, then stepped back, her face going pink. "So...uh...how long have you ever grown your tusks?"

I shook my head, a little embarrassed. "When I was a foolish youngling, I refused to trim and shape them. They grew to here." I held my fingers mid-cheek. "Then they curled out like this. My father said 'enough,' and I trimmed them back like they are now. It was not a good look, having my tusks curled on my face. In our clan, only very old orcs, hermits, and those who lose their minds let their tusks grow so long without a trim."

My father had always been strict about keeping my tusks neat and a reasonable length, but after losing his mate, my mother, in the plague, he stopped caring about his own. When I'd left, his one tusk had curled around in a circle while the other one had grown in a long arc just past the outer corner of his eye. He had wanted to stop living after losing his life mate, but he—as well as many of our other clansmen suffering such a loss—would not allow himself that relief until he was assured our clan would continue.

"I can imagine it would be difficult to eat and drink and…do other things with such long, curled tusks," Jordan commented.

She'd blushed at the "other things," and I smiled, knowing where her mind had gone.

"I am capable of eating, drinking, and doing many pleasurable things to satisfy my partner no matter the length of my tusks," I confidently assured her.

Her inhalation was sharp, and she wouldn't meet my gaze. After a few seconds, she cleared her throat and finally looked at me once more.

"Well, your injured tusk seems firmly in place this morning with no signs of lasting damage," she continued. "I want to have images of all your teeth, but especially that tusk to make sure there isn't something going on under your gumline. And…and if you like, I can clean, shape, and polish them as well as the rest of your teeth."

My smile grew. "I would very much like that."

She was clearly flustered, and it made me want to laugh. I was feeling lighter and happier than I had…actually than I had since the last time I'd seen her.

"Um, okay, then. Let me take a look at the rest of your teeth. Oh! Were you able to find the ones that were knocked out?"

My eyes widened as I remembered my gift. Digging the box out of my pocket, I presented it to her with both hands.

She stared at it a moment, paling slightly. I felt my stomach twist. Was this wrong? Should I have gone with the grocery store steak instead?

Then she opened the box and made a snort-noise.

"The teeth! For a second, I thought..." Pink once more stole up her neck into her cheeks. "Never mind. I'm glad you were able to find them. Please let me take a look in your mouth to see if there are any broken pieces that I'll need to extract."

I relaxed completely as she looked at my teeth, poking around with a metal stick and checking each tooth, including the gaps where I'd lost those two. The whole time she chatted, asking me questions about my home, my family, and the team.

It was impossible for me to talk properly with my mouth wide open, so I just grunted and garbled monosyllabic replies.

"I still can't believe that your English is this good," she said, finally taking her hands away to make notes on what looked like yet another form. "I know I told you that before, but I'm just amazed at how proficient you are. If I'd arrived in some foreign land a few months ago, knowing only a few words and phrases, I doubt I would have progressed so quickly."

"Orcs need to learn other languages," I reminded her. "I know ten orc dialects and six other languages from my home. Plus, we had help when we arrived here."

Jordan tilted her head, and once more, I thought of how beautiful and alluring she was.

"Help?" she asked.

"When the demon offered us jobs on the hockey team, we all needed to learn English quickly, so the angels gave us these." I showed her the communication device we'd all received.

She blinked at it. "A cell phone. The angels gave you all cell phones and what? A Duolingo app? Do they even have language learning apps for orcs?"

I didn't know this Duolingo thing, but I pushed the button on the communications device that we'd spent two months using.

"I eat my breakfast in the hallway," the device said.

Jordan burst out laughing, taking it from my hand. "Seriously? That's terrible. Why don't these things ever teach you usable phrases? When are you ever going to need to tell someone where you eat breakfast? And who the hell eats in their hallway?"

"I also know the word 'pillowcase,'" I informed her.

She laughed again. "You're joking."

"And 'the brown cat eats pie during winter.'"

"Oh, stop." She was laughing so hard that tears fell from her eyes.

"May I borrow your bathtub?"

"No! Seriously? That's not even possible!"

I let her get control of herself after that one, although I wanted to go on. Making Jordan laugh was addictive.

She wiped her eyes. "I should have known the angels would screw up a simple language learning app. Although some of the apps we humans have developed aren't any better." She handed me back my device. "Really, how *did* you learn English beyond what your friend taught you?"

I stuck the phone back in my pocket. "Radio, television, being close to humans. Although the device did help, silly as some lessons are."

She tilted her head. "Say something in your language.

Not the bathtub or the cat thing, but something you'd actually say to another person."

I didn't have to even pause to think.

"*Grumem-esch-ach metanekan schlonakanap-tsknt.*"

She smiled. "What does it mean?"

"You need to learn Orcish, and then you will know what it means."

Chapter 10

Ozar

After asking again for permission, Jordan once more inspected my mouth, poking and prodding at the various teeth and muttering under her breath.

"You have wonderful teeth and gums for someone who claims to have had minimal dental care," she said with a voice that held more than a tinge of envy. "I had to clear only the slightest bit of plaque, and there are no cavities. Your gumline is perfect, and your gums are so pink and healthy. Everything looks great outside of those few teeth you lost, but I'd still feel better taking some X-rays."

I nodded, agreeing with anything she wanted. I trusted this female. With my teeth. With all of my body. With my heart.

"Please talk to your teammates about regular dental care while they're living here," she continued. "The plaque I scraped off looked fairly recent, which makes me believe that the food here isn't as healthy for your teeth as the food back home. I strongly recommend you orcs all visit a dentist every six months for a cleaning and a checkup, otherwise I fear your beautiful teeth won't be so lovely the longer you remain here, eating human food."

My eyes widened at that, and I made a mental note to warn my teammates.

"I'll send you home with a toothbrush as well as some samples of toothpaste and dental floss. It'll be very important to use those while you're living here to maintain your teeth. If you have any questions on how to use any of the products, please contact us."

Her whole spiel felt like...well, a spiel. Once again, my stomach contracted with worry and doubt. Was she hovering on the edge of a decision? Was she going to write me off as just a patient or accept me as a candidate for her heart?

"I need to see a couple of other patients. Is it okay if Makena or Mike comes in for your imaging?"

At my perplexed expression, she went on to explain the procedure. As much as I wanted her to stay, I realized that she'd already taken valuable time from her job to personally provide for my care. To insist she ignore her other clients and remain with me would be wrong.

It was clear this was her job. Her place of business. She had not invited me to her home to woo her, and while other orcs might be discouraged by the professional setting, I wasn't. I knew what it was like to kiss this female. Her interest in me was beyond the professional care of my teeth. So I'd agree to whatever she wanted and then convince her to see me again in a more romantic setting.

"Are you fine with one of my staff helping?" she asked again. "I promise they are professional and follow the procedures I've established."

"Your employees can do my imaging," I told her, even

though I wasn't sure what the word "imaging" meant. "I will try not to growl at them."

She chuckled. "Maybe I'll send Mike then, just in case you growl a little."

I grabbed her hand as she turned to leave. "But you'll be back? I'll see you again before I go?"

Her eyes met mine, and I saw the indecision in them.

"Tusks are important to orcs. I trust you with mine, and I do not trust others." I was absolutely playing dirty here, but it was kind of true. I did trust her. I didn't trust many—humans *or* orcs. And I wasn't above a little manipulation to ensure I had a chance to woo her some more before I left.

"Yes. Absolutely." She turned her hand to grip mine and smiled. "I'll be back. Don't worry."

I trusted her, so I didn't worry. Instead, I settled back in the comfy chair, eyeing the metal sticks. This Mike human could take images of my mouth and teeth, but if he so much as picked up one of those things, I was getting out my knife.

Ten minutes went by. I was so bored that I got up to retrieve one of the magazines on a nearby table and sat back down. I'd just gotten to the article about a female named Taylor Swift and her secret vacation getaway when a human male entered the room. Even if I couldn't have smelled his sweaty fearful aroma, I would have known how terrified he was. His eyes wouldn't look anywhere near my face. His hands shook. His voice was pitched high and wavered. And he swallowed every few seconds, his Adam's apple bobbing each time.

I might be a grumpy orc, but I felt sorry for this guy, so I kept my grunts and grumbles to myself and tried to be friendly. Unfortunately, my toothy grin seemed to make the male even more nervous. That meant it took him forever to place the pieces of cardboard in my mouth in the correct way to get the needed images.

I'd seen Bwat take pictures with the phone device we'd used to learn English, but he'd never had to drape a heavy bib over someone's body or exit the room before he did so. I was beginning to think that this imaging process involved a possible long-term health risk and was annoyed at the number of re-takes Mike had to do because his hands shook too much to do his damned job.

It made me growl.

Which evidently made Mike realize that all the images he'd taken were sufficient.

I went back to my magazine.

"Ryan Reynolds had a wardrobe malfunction at Petunia's Hot Dog Shoppe last week," I read out loud as Jordan came back into the room.

She jerked to a halt, then grabbed the magazine to look at the article and pictures. "Wow. Just...wow."

"Human pants are not very durable," I commented.

"Holy..." She turned the magazine sideways. "They didn't even black that out. I'm impressed. Super impressed."

Mine is bigger. I clamped my mouth shut before the words left it.

"As interesting as this is, let's look at these images of your teeth." Her smile creased her cheeks as she put the magazine aside and started typing on a keyboard positioned on the narrow table along the wall beside me. In seconds, images sprang to life on the huge monitor—images of teeth.

I looked at the pictures with interest. We had nothing like this at home. Not only were my teeth shown in stark white against the black background, but I could also see the roots buried under my gumline and the solid structure of my jaw. My tusks looked huge, and in these pictures seemed to be fused deep into the bone of my lower jaw.

"I can't believe there aren't any broken pieces of tooth left behind," Jordan marveled, pointing at one of the images Mike had taken of my mouth. "There's no need for bone grafting or any work on your jaw. The only thing I'm concerned about is placing the implant. I need to make sure our equipment is sufficient to drill into orc bone, and that we have the correct anesthesia and numbing medicines."

She went on about abutments and how she wanted to ensure the replacement teeth were of equal strength to my originals. I didn't understand half of what she was saying, but her voice wove its golden chains around my heart, and I loved that she was so passionate about something—even if it was something as strangely mundane as teeth.

Jordan stepped out again to see another patient, but she came back, and she continued to do everything herself, including polishing my teeth and tusks with a substance that tasted both gritty and minty.

I'd never had my tusks polished before and was breathless from the intimacy of the act as well as Jordan's body so close to mine. She smelled like flowers and coconut, and I found myself fantasizing about her pushing the tray aside, straddling my body, shedding that white jacket, then slowly unbuttoning her shirt.

But that wasn't going to happen. I was here as a patient, and any opportunity to get her undressed and bring her pleasure would need to occur elsewhere, at a later time and day.

I'd been relieved to realize that the other males in the front room weren't suitors, but that meant *I* wasn't here as a suitor, either. And an invitation to meet her at such an early hour clearly didn't mean the same thing to humans as it did to orcs. For a second, I'd been worried that I'd misread her intentions. Then I'd remembered last night in the street, and our kiss. I'd felt a spark between us that had been a second from turning into a bonfire.

All too quickly she was done, putting away the metal sticks and moving the tray so I could stand.

"Leave your number with Ava up front, and I'll call you when I have everything I need for the implant procedure," she told me. "It'll probably be three or four weeks since I'll have to get them from a different manufacturer than I usually use. I'll let you know if it'll be more than a month, though."

No! I couldn't let her slip away like this. I couldn't let this just be about my teeth and nothing else. I couldn't wait three weeks or more before I saw her again.

"This is for you." Desperate, I pulled the Starbucks gift card out of my pocket and handed it to her, thankful that I'd grabbed one when buying my coffee. "And...and...I would like to cook dinner for you. Tomorrow night. At my house."

It was probably way too soon for me to offer her a meal, but I didn't have time to figure out the glacial pace and weird rituals of human wooing, so I was going with what I would have done had she been an orc female.

Jordan seemed perplexed as she took the gift card, but her gaze shot up to meet mine at the dinner offer. "Tomorrow night?"

"Yes. Or the next night—whenever you are free." Suddenly, it was very hard to breathe. If she said no... I pushed the panicked thought away. If she said no, I'd just have to go buy her a steak or kill a few squirrels in the park and leave them at her house as a gift. I didn't know where she lived, but if I followed her this evening, I could easily find out. If I could track a Mennt across the plains, I could easily follow a human female home without being noticed.

"You want to cook me a traditional orc meal? At your house?" she asked.

I nodded, hoping I could find reasonable substitutions for the scant orc meals I knew how to make. "We can order pizza delivery if you don't like it."

She laughed, and my heart felt lighter at the sound. "Then it's a date. Tomorrow night at your house. What can I bring? Wine? Bread from the bakery? A dessert?"

"Just you," I told her.

She dimpled again. "That's not fair. You're cooking a whole meal for me. The least I can do is bring wine. Red or white?"

I stared at her, concerned that I would answer wrong. Was there a difference? I'd never drunk wine before, being a beer kind of orc myself.

"How about one of each?" she suggested. "That way you can keep what you're cooking a surprise."

"Okay." And now I could breathe again. She'd accepted my offer to cook for her, at my home. Tomorrow night. And she'd said it was a "date," which, according to Bwat, was what humans called their wooing activities.

I wasn't just another mouth of teeth in her job. I was a date. And I was cooking her dinner.

Chapter 11

Jordan

I honestly had no idea what the heck was going on with my new patient.

Was he *really* a patient?

Of course he was, since I'd cleaned and polished his teeth and was going to take care of his implants, but I didn't ever have dinner at my patients' houses. And I certainly didn't have any patients that I'd drunkenly kissed outside of McHenry's Tavern at two in the morning after closing time.

And then there was the velvet engagement ring box that I'd nearly had a heart attack over. Had it been a joke? Because I could barely stifle my laugh when I'd opened the box and saw what was inside. Orc customs were clearly different than human ones, so maybe he'd not known that he was carrying his teeth in a ring box? Or did he actually mean to propose to me? With teeth?

Then there was the Starbucks gift card he'd given to me right before he'd left. Never had a patient given me a gift card—even during the Christmas holidays. But it was clear that he considered me more than his reconstructive dentist.

I doubted he invited his medical providers over for dinner. Unless that was an orc thing?

No. There'd been some sort of zing between us there in the parking lot, and that kiss... Plus, the zing had still been there today while I'd been trying my best to be professional.

Trying and failing.

Professional wasn't "accidentally" rubbing my boobs against his arm while I examined his teeth. Professional wasn't eyeing his near-constant erection.

Professional definitely wasn't eagerly accepting his offer to cook me dinner tomorrow at his place. I was already imagining this dinner would lead to me staying over and getting sweaty in the sheets with a muscled orc.

The guy wasn't boring, I'd give him that. Actually, he was far from boring. His tales of his homeland and clan had been fascinating, and he'd truly seemed interested when I'd gone on and on about dental matters.

He'd told me how orc tusks continuously grew and needed to be trimmed and sharpened annually. He'd told me that they used something similar to pine needles to floss with and an herbal paste for daily dental care. I'd been fascinated to learn that tusk length was a matter of personal preference, and that he'd always worn his between two and three inches long. I was fascinated by the fact that if they were left untrimmed, the tusks would curl around, possibly growing into the orc's cheek. Some orcs' tusks curled more than others, requiring those with "curly" tusks to maintain shorter lengths, while those whose tusks grew straight might sport seven- or eight-inch tusks rising up past their cheekbones.

Ozar told me he wasn't a fan of the long, curled tusk styles, saying they looked barbaric and that outside of some rebellious teen years, he'd sported a shorter style. I'd listened with rapt attention and was thrilled when he'd agreed to let me smooth the surface of his tusks and polish them to a bright white.

It wasn't just his teeth. I *really* liked this orc. I liked the way his golden-brown eyes focused intently on me, the way his muscles strained against his T-shirt and the smooth, warm green of his skin. I liked his obvious admiration of me, his polite and engaging conversation. He was clearly physically attracted to me if the bulge in his pants was any indication, but instead of delivering a bunch of lame propositions, he'd asked me about my work, my hobbies, and my favorite foods, as well as a very strange question about any enemies that I might have.

And then he'd asked me to dinner—even better, he'd offered to cook for me.

Was it wise for me to go over to his house for dinner? I didn't really know him, and he was an orc, physically capable of overpowering me with both hands tied behind his back. I'd give his address to my friends, set up a time to check in with them and let them know all was well. It couldn't be *that* dangerous to go to his home for dinner. He was on the Baltimore Tusks hockey team. It wasn't like he'd jeopardize his job and risk imprisonment just to get some action.

And honestly, the thought of getting it on with Ozar was appealing. *Very* appealing. I'd taken far longer than I'd needed to polish his tusks, enjoying the effect my closeness had on him. I wished I'd unbuttoned my shirt a bit before I'd gone into the room, just to flash a little cleavage as I bent over him, so I could see the desire burning in his dark eyes.

"Are you seriously going to take on an orc as a client?" Mike's words cut through my thoughts, and I sucked in a quick breath as I turned to face the dental hygienist.

"Of course I am. I've been thinking for a while now about marketing my practice to nonhumans." It wasn't completely a lie. I'd briefly considered reconstructive work for werewolves but had been concerned about how the implants would fare when they shifted. At least that wasn't a concern with Ozar—at least, I didn't think so.

"He *growled* at me," Mike complained.

"You took nearly forty images of his teeth," I shot back. "Even with the lead shielding, that's an unacceptable amount of radiation. I can't charge his insurance for forty images. It makes us look like we're sloppy when we can't manage to get decent pics with the usual ten or fifteen."

"It's not easy trying to position the film in an orc mouth," he argued. "Especially when you're worried that orc is going to snap your neck with one hand."

I blew out a frustrated breath. "There was no reason for him to snap your neck, Mike. He was here to replace lost teeth, just like the majority of our human patients." *He was here to see me. He didn't care about the teeth.* I blocked out that thought and got back to arguing with my hygienist. "And humans all have different shaped and sized mouths. An orc's teeth might be a bit unusual, but placement of the films in his mouth shouldn't be any more difficult than placing them in those of our other patients like Mr. Cooper or Mrs. VanNestor."

"Orcs are violent. Mr. Cooper and Mrs. VanNestor aren't. Besides, that orc scared Makena," Mike said. "She said he growled at her, too. Do you really think it's a good idea to have him here? What if he gets angry and trashes the place?"

I rolled my eyes. "He's an orc, Mike, not the Hulk. And he's a member of the local hockey team. He's not going to trash the place. *Or* hurt anyone."

"What's next? Werewolves? Vampires? Demons?" Mike muttered as he walked away.

I couldn't really blame him. It had taken me a while to get used to all the supernaturals, but now I was ashamed about my initial wariness around them. It had helped that I'd made friends with one of the werewolves at the gym, met a vampire at book club, and chatted with the demon who was my Uber driver one night. I was still a *little* wary about demons, but it wasn't like all humans were perfect. I was more likely to be robbed by a human than a demon, or any other supernatural being.

Up until now, I'd limited my practice to humans, not because I didn't want supernatural clients here, but because I'd worried I couldn't provide the specialized care they might need. But now I realized that was just laziness on my part. I'd never found out if they even *needed* different medical devices or care; I'd just assumed so.

Which made me no different than Mike.

Later tonight I would do some research—a whole lot of research. And tomorrow I was going to announce to my staff that I had every intention of expanding my practice. But tonight...I was going to see if Willa and Abby were available for dinner, because I needed their input on what to wear and bring for a home-cooked meal at an orc's house.

I had a dozen other clients scheduled today. But first I was going to run to Starbucks for an iced chai latte, courtesy of Ozar.

"He's *making* you dinner? Not ordering carry out?" Willa asked before popping a couple of sweet potato fries into her mouth.

"Yes. He's cooking me dinner. At his house. Tomorrow night," I repeated.

"What's he making?" Abby asked. "What do orcs eat?"

"He wouldn't say. I'm bringing a bottle of red and one of white, so we'll be covered either way," I told her.

"He's probably going to serve a haunch of beef that he roasted over a fire pit," Willa said. "No sides, no vegetables. I'm guessing that orcs are strict carnivores."

"He was drinking a Starbucks coffee when he came into the office this morning," I countered. "And we saw them drinking beer and eating appetizers last night."

"They were wings though," Abby reminded me. "Chicken wings. That's meat."

"But the artichoke dip and jalapeño poppers weren't meat," I argued.

"The one time my ex cooked me dinner it was canned chili with hot dogs chopped up in it," Willa said, wrinkling her nose.

"*My* ex once made his grandmother's lasagna recipe, so let's not stereotype men as being bad cooks," Abby said.

"Was it any good though?" Willa asked. "I'll bet grandma was turning over in her grave because he forgot the bay leaves or added too much oregano."

"It was better than canned chili with hot dogs." Abby laughed.

"Seriously, I *really* think you better eat a full meal before you go over, just in case it's terrible," Willa advised. "You can always claim you're on a diet and that's why you're not eating whatever hideous food he's serving you."

"Or say that you had a big lunch," Abby added.

"Or tell him that you might have gotten food poisoning from a lunchtime shrimp salad," Willa said. "That way you'll also have an excuse for leaving early if the date is truly horrible."

"We should set up a rescue plan." Abby leaned forward across the table. "I'll call at eight o'clock, and you can pretend I'm a dental emergency."

"Guys, no!" I threw up my hands. "I don't need to set up a rescue plan, or some elaborate lies to get out of eating whatever he's cooking. He said if I didn't like it, we'd order pizza."

"He *said* that, but did he really *mean* it?" Willa gave me a sideways look. "Fragile egos, you know."

"I'm pretty sure he meant it. But it won't matter. Whatever he cooks, it can't be worse than the stuff I had to choke down at the college cafeteria," I told them. "I like him. I've met him three times now, and I really like him."

"She's inspected his teeth, and she still likes him," Abby told Willa.

"Well, he bought her a Starbucks gift card and presented his teeth in a velvet engagement ring box. What's not to like?" Willa replied to her.

I sighed. "Okay, ladies. If you're done teasing me, then help me decide what to wear. Dressy or casual?"

"Casual," both said in unison.

"But not *too* casual," Abby cautioned. "Jeans, but a tight tank top under a nice jacket."

"Wear those dark wash jeans that make your butt look amazing," Willa added. "And a push-up bra so the girls are front and center. I'll bet he's a boob man...or boob orc."

"What if he actually *is* grilling on the patio?" I fretted. "Because nothing says sexy like a parka and mittens."

"It's a high of fifty-two tomorrow," Abby said, looking at

her phone. "It won't be colder than mid-forties by the time you're there. There's no need for a parka."

"Plus, you can act all cold on the patio, and he'll need to warm you up." Willa winked. "Grill tongs in one hand, squeezing some Jordan ass with the other hand."

Now *that* was a plan.

"He *is* very warm," I commented. "I think orcs' body temperature might be higher than ours."

"I predict some snuggling in your future," Abby said.

"I predict a hell of a lot more than snuggling in her future." Willa laughed.

After some lurid guesses on how my date might end, we finally shifted the topic of conversation to Abby and Willa. An hour later, I was driving back to my home in Federal Hill, anticipating tomorrow's date with a mixture of excitement and nervous apprehension.

With a stroke of luck, I managed to find a parking spot a block away from my home. When the real estate agent had shown me the three-story row house in Federal Hill, I'd fallen in love with the industrial interior vibe, the huge windows overlooking the tidy back garden, the spacious master bath with both a walk-in tiled shower and a giant soaking tub with clawed feet. Love blinded me to the fact that this dream house didn't have a garage or any off-street parking. The freezing or sweaty-humid walk to my door from whatever parking spot I'd managed to find was no picnic, and scraping ice and snow off my car on winter mornings was a downright pain in the butt.

Tonight though, the walk was short—a blessing since it was pouring down rain this evening. Judy bounded toward me the second I opened the door, meowing her displeasure over my absence. Tossing my wet coat on the hallway rack and setting my tote on a table, I scooped her up and cuddled her close.

"I'm happy to see you too, Your Honor."

Judy was actually named Judge Judy, partly due to the lacy-looking collar of white around the black of her neck, and partly because she greeted any guests with a narrow, suspicious gaze. The cat liked her rules and routines, and her opinion of people was something I took seriously. Both Willa and Abby had eventually won her over. I was hoping that Ozar would as well.

I had an automatic feeder in the kitchen and a watering fountain on each floor, so I knew she wasn't hungry or thirsty, but we had a ritual. Each night when I came home, she got a few pieces of chicken, and some fresh catnip sprinkled on her scratching pad. She struggled out of my arms when we were a few feet into the kitchen, running to the fridge and staring at the stainless steel door.

After chicken and catnip, I left Judy in the kitchen and went on my daily scavenger hunt for anything I didn't want to accidentally step in later. There was only one hairball coughed up tonight, and it was thankfully on the hardwood floor of the dining room.

Like Judy, I was a woman who loved my routine. I changed into pajamas, scrubbed the makeup from my face, and twisted my hair onto the top of my head, securing it with a bright red scrunchie. Then I grabbed my laptop and plopped on my couch with Judy curled up beside me as I researched paranormal dentistry.

Sadly, there wasn't much to research. I scoured published research papers and was disappointed to only find one about vampire fangs and two about dental care among the shifter population.

The vampire paper was at least interesting with images and illustrations showing two canals in the dissected fang, one of which attached to a series of glands and the other which led to a channel across the roof of the vampire's mouth that forked and opened near the back set of molars. I guessed this allowed the vampire to somewhat taste the blood they were imbibing before swallowing, although I also imagined that some of the blood was not pulled into the fang cavities and was instead sucked into their mouths and over their tongue in a more typical fashion. The section on the glands attached to a vampire's fangs was sparse and mainly filled with conjecture as the author had been working with a long-deceased vampire skull and not a live subject. I wondered what those glands held, and what their importance was in vampire's feeding. Regardless, I came away from the paper thinking that vampire dental reconstruction wouldn't differ significantly from human dentistry, aside from the tricky nature of their fangs.

It made me think of Ozar's tusks, and how the X-rays had shown them to be thick and solid aside from a long nerve that ran along their length, terminating only half an inch from the point.

Moving on, I opened the two papers on shifter dentistry. One detailed the failure in clinical trials of implants when it came to surviving the shift from human to animal form. There was hope that a joint venture between a medical device company and an entrepreneurial wizard in Florida might yield an implant suitable for shifters, though. The other paper was a lengthy study of dental hygiene and the reduced rate of both plaque and cavities among shifters. It seemed that periodontal disease was unheard of among their populations.

Digging around more, I realized there was nothing on

dentistry for demons as the vast majority could just recreate damaged or lost teeth within a fraction of a second.

I sighed and set my laptop aside so I could pet Judy. "It doesn't seem like there would be opportunity to target the shifter market. The technology might not be there for reconstruction, and shifters probably wouldn't need much in the way of routine dental care—not that I do much routine care beyond my reconstructive patients anyway. Should I offer night hours for vampires? I know some can walk around in the daylight, but the ones who might need my services the most probably are restricted to moonlight only."

Judy purred and rolled over so I could scratch the side of her neck and chest.

"I could offer a discount and see if I can become the official dentist of the Baltimore Tusks, but I don't want it to seem like I'm using Ozar just to get a contract with the team. And what if this date doesn't go well? Or goes *really* well? It might be awkward campaigning for their business if Ozar and I become an item."

My cat didn't deliver an opinion, so I continued to pet her and muse over my options.

"How about I call this medical equipment company and ask if I can assist with any clinical trials of their potential shifter implants? And advertise for vampires needing skilled dental care? And wait to see how things go with Ozar's implants before I approach the team about a contract?"

Judy meowed. I took that as a sign of her approval.

The rest of the evening was spent ransacking my closet in search of an outfit that was casual, but not too casual, one that would show off my assets but not make me look like I was at Ozar's just for a booty call.

We might end up in bed tomorrow night.

I *wanted* us to end up in bed tomorrow night.

I wanted him, but I didn't have the best track record when it came to sex on the first or second date. If I let hormones take the wheel, I might miss red flags. I might lose my heart only to find out we weren't a good fit. I might lose my heart only to find out he just wanted a fling with a human woman, and nothing more.

Did *I* want something more? Or was I overthinking this whole thing like I always did?

I needed to calm down. Wear something casual and comfortable and nice tomorrow night. Get to know Ozar. If things went well, do a little first-base action to see if the attraction I felt was real.

And *not* sleep with him. At least, not sleep with him on the first date.

Or...maybe sleep with him on the first date if I wanted to. I was a grown woman, after all, and there was nothing wrong with letting my heart, and my hormones, take the wheel.

Chapter 12

Ozar

Leaving Jordan's place of business, I headed straight to the stadium. I was expecting to be grilled by my teammates about my meeting with Jordan. I was not expecting to have a wad of paper shoved in my face the moment I walked into our locker room.

"Clan Guardian?" Eng mocked. "You should have been an *Rkwanala*."

Snatching the paper from his hands, I saw there was a large picture on the front—me with the human children at the playground. It looked like it had been taken yesterday, which made sense since I'd spent several hours playing with the human young at Patterson Park. Curiosity about the picture meant it took a few seconds for Eng's words to sink in.

Rkwanalas were orclet caretakers, mainly for the royalty of Eng's kingdom since most orcs prided themselves on having a hands-on approach to the care of our young. Eng had meant the word as an insult, a slur on my maleness, but the slight missed the mark. Even though it wasn't typical for adult orcs to indulge in play with young, let alone young that weren't their own, I refused to be shamed about my actions this weekend.

"There's still time," Eng continued. "No female will accept courtship from a *Rkwanala*, but you can live a happy life taking care of other orcs' offspring."

That stung. But before I could hit Eng so hard his nose flattened, Ugwyll spoke up.

"*Rkwanala* to who?" the other orc snapped. "There are no orclets to care for in most of our clans. None. No wives. No orclets."

Instantly the mood in the locker room shifted. The lack of orc offspring was a somber fact that no one wanted to think about.

"That's what *I* want when I go home," Bwat said as he looked over my shoulder at the paper. "Dozens of happy, healthy, well-fed orclets playing in the center of our village. They won't have to watch their mothers and sisters die. They won't have to see their fathers waste away with grief. They won't have to grow up and be adults before their tusks are more than nubs."

And now the mood was downright funereal. Our heads lowered. Ugwyll slumped down onto a bench. Eng turned away, leaning his forearm against a locker.

"I understand why Ozar was playing with the human young," Bwat confessed. "Every one of us would give a year of earnings for the chance to join a group of orclets on a play structure, even if those orclets weren't our own. Each moment witnessing the play of youth is precious. We shouldn't let the old rules govern us—not when we've lost so much."

"Everything we now do is for our clans' future. For our hoped-for children." Ugwyll's voice was soft and husky.

"And for our hoped-for wives," Bwat added.

"For the continuance of the royal line and the stability of my kingdom," Eng said.

I bit back a growl. Eng still deserved a good nose-flattening. All that orc cared about was his title and his inheritance. I'm sure he'd barely even look at his wife other than to bed her, and he'd probably confine her to a remote estate once she was beyond breeding age. His offspring would be raised by others and would most likely end up just like him. Selfish. Uncaring.

Instead of taking a swing at Eng, I stood and stretched. "Should we practice on the ice this afternoon? Or find heavy objects to toss back and forth?"

Bwat snorted. "Neither. I'm just here because the demon said we needed to be for a few hours of each day. As soon as the timekeeping device says I can leave, I'm going."

Eng nodded. "Same. I might go to this place where Ozar found all the human children and see if any females would qualify to be my wife. They have proven their ability to breed, and I can promise them honor and wealth if they become my spouse."

I growled, still thinking about punching Eng in the nose. "I plan on throwing some weights, then going for a run. Perhaps I might find a few suitable trees to climb as well."

We all turned to Ugwyll.

"There are some booklets in the coach's office with pictures of naked human females in suggestive poses," he said. "I'll look at those, then probably go to the McHenry for a beer."

"Naked human females?" Eng grinned. "Can I see those booklets when you're done? Just put them in my locker and I'll grab them tomorrow."

I scowled. "Those human females are wives or sisters or daughters. Leering at their naked bodies is disrespectful."

Ugwyll shrugged. "Perhaps their culture is different, and they are happy to be leered at."

"I'm the prince of the kingdom. They should be honored I'm leering at their pictures," Eng announced.

Bwat was furiously typing on his phone. "It seems that it is the profession of some human females to be seen naked and leered at. There are even sites where males pay money to look at videos and something called live-streams of human females who are naked and who occasionally perform sexual acts."

I was torn, appalled at the disrespect males showed these human females, but intrigued at the possibility of learning what human females found sexually appealing.

"How do I access this site?" I asked, feeling as if I were betraying all my female ancestors.

"I'll text it to you," Bwat said.

"Text it to all of us," Eng said. "That and these booklets Ugwyll found might help pass the time until I find a wife."

There was a loud *thunk* noise from outside the locker room. Escellates Johnson, the demon who owned the Tusks, burst through the door, waving a thick wad of papers in his hand. My heart sank, knowing he'd probably seen the image of me playing with human children on the front page. I was done taking shit for that. It was probably not a good idea to punch the boss, but I was in the mood to knock this demon right through the wall if he so much as said a word to me about it.

"Did you see this?"

He slapped me on the shoulder, then on the arm. I would have hit him back, but I was thrown off by the fact that he was smiling. That demon never smiled. Never.

"'A Baltimore Tusks' forward, Ozar, was seen this

weekend at Patterson Park entertaining local children,'" he read.

I growled, ready to punch him. Hard.

"Marylynn Boyd of Druid Hill said this of Ozar: 'He's a great guy. Friendly and happy to talk to the fans. And he clearly loves kids as much as they love him.' There's a whole list of quotes in this article." Escellates started waving the paper around again.

I lowered my fist slightly. "Yeah? Do you have a problem with that?"

The demon barked out a laugh. "Hell no! Ticket sales doubled in the last three hours. Merch is flying out the door. This is better than you clowns getting your asses whipped this weekend."

Bwat's fingers were flying once more over his phone screen, no doubt translating "asses whipped." Growling silently, I vowed not to have our "asses whipped" ever again.

"From now on, you're going to be the 'kid' orc." The demon poked my chest with his index finger. "Playgrounds. Schools. Charity fundraisers. Make-A-Wish stuff. Anything to do with kids."

I nodded, having no idea what he was talking about, but willing to spend time with human children—as long as it didn't cut into my courtship of Jordan.

"You!" Escellates hopped over and slapped Eng on the back. "You're in charge of old people."

"W-what?"

I bit back a laugh at Eng's shocked expression.

"Old. People," the demon shouted as if Eng were deaf. "Nursing homes. I want you there every weekend we're playing at home. Maybe even in the evenings during the week. There better be articles in the paper about you playing bingo with them and all that shit. Got it?"

Eng's eyes were wide as he looked at each of us. I shrugged.

"And you are going to be focusing on animal shelters." The demon turned away from Eng to point at Bwat.

"Animals? Shelters?" The orc's forehead creased, and he glanced down at his phone. "Am I building homes for these creatures? How big are they?"

"You don't need to build homes for them. Take them for walks. Help the staff at the shelter. Make sure there are lots of pictures of you with the animals."

Bwat stared at the demon. "What sort of animals are these?"

Escellates threw up his hands. "Hell if I know. Dogs and cats mostly, but I'm guessing they have other animals too. If it's at the shelter, I want you looking like you love it."

"I...I will do that," Bwat stuttered.

Ugwyll snorted, as if he didn't realize he was next. "You!"

Ugwyll jumped as Escellates ran toward him.

"You are going to spend time with the homeless."

"Building homes for homeless animals?" Ugwyll asked hopefully.

"Humans. And in addition to building homes, you're going to work at the soup kitchen and at the shelter."

Ugwyll looked over at Bwat, then at the demon. "The homeless humans are at the same shelter as the animals Bwat is taking care of?"

The demon chuckled. "No, although that would be an incredible savings. The homeless humans helping the homeless animals? For free? A huge reduction in labor costs. But sadly, that hasn't happened, so you're going to be at the *human* homeless shelter. And the soup kitchen. And the home building."

None of us really heard whatever the demon said next. We were all too shocked. Even after he left, still waving the papers around, we just stared silently at each other.

"What does this homeless animal care mean?" Bwat finally asked.

"Am I supposed to take the homeless humans for a walk as well?" Ugwyll asked.

"*Old humans?*" Eng curled his lip. "I am *not* going to spend any time with a bunch of smelly old humans."

"This might be a good chance to meet and woo our brides," Bwat said, cheerful as usual.

"So, you intend to marry a dog or a cat?" Eng scowled. "Ugwyll might find a suitable homeless female, especially since his standards are so low, but I doubt an elderly human female will be of breeding age. This is a waste of my time."

"Why can't *I* be in charge of children?" Ugwyll complained. "Not that I am opposed to marrying a homeless female, but a human who has proven her ability to have offspring would be a better choice."

Bwat snorted. "Those females are already married, you shit-brain. That's why they have children."

"Maybe her husband has died," Ugwyll argued. "And if not, I can just kill him myself. The female will be thrilled to be free of that human male loser and marry a strong virile orc instead. I will even adopt his children as my own and ensure the males have careers and the females good orc husbands."

Eng nodded. "It isn't fair that Ozar is in charge of children since he already has a female he plans to marry. Let him take the old humans or the animals."

"I'm keeping the animals," Bwat snapped. "No one else can have them."

"With your tiny hand-axe, you are more suitable to satisfy a small mammal bride than a human female."

Eng laughed at his own statement, but Bwat growled, his hands tightening into fists. "I do not lay with *animals*."

I stepped between the two before this escalated into a brawl. "Enough. We do what the demon says or risk losing our jobs and being sent home without brides. Save your fights for our next match on the ice. Even better, spend your anger by running, climbing, or throwing weights."

Nobody took my advice, but at least Eng and Bwat walked away, Eng heading for the showers and Bwat leaving the locker room. Ugwyll loitered but looked like he was preparing for a nap rather than any sort of exercise, so I left.

Throwing the weights across the room wasn't as enjoyable without someone to catch them and throw them back. After an hour, I left the gym and the arena to go for my run. This time I didn't stop by the park to play with the children, going straight home instead to shower and change.

Worried that Jordan might leave her work before I got there, I headed straight back and wandered from store to store, staying where I could see the building exit and Jordan's little blue car in the parking lot, while hopefully remaining out of view.

Clouds had covered the descending sun by the time she emerged, her head tilted as she cradled her phone between her shoulder and ear, a large leather bag over her opposite shoulder. I scooted behind a large black vehicle, but she didn't even look in my direction. Clearly preoccupied, she climbed into her blue car and drove out of the lot.

There were many vehicles in the streets. That and the hanging lights that organized the traffic flow meant I didn't need to do more than an occasional jog to keep Jordan's car in sight. My behavior was absolutely suspicious as I hid in doorways, behind parked vehicles, even crouching behind the sign outside a store. The passing humans didn't seem bothered. Several called out my name, wishing me and the Tusks luck at this weekend's game. I waved and smiled, trying to look as non-threatening as a seven-foot green orc could in a world of humans. Ages ago, humans screamed and ran at the sight of us, a few brave warriors daring to challenge us to a fight. But things had changed. Instead of challenges, I was met with excited requests to write my name on various pieces of paper and even body parts.

I complied, having to pick up the pace to keep Jordan's blue car in sight. It wasn't long before she pulled into a parking spot at the side of a street and got out, heading into a restaurant.

Anxiety gripped me, catching my breath. Was she here on a date? Meeting a human male? I waited a few minutes, then tried to casually look through the windows. It was a Monday night, and the place was far from packed, but it still took me a while to find Jordan at a back table. She was with the two women she'd been with last night. I relaxed and retreated a step, backing right into a large human male's torso.

"What are you—wait...you're the hockey player. Ozar, right?"

The male's voice had started with a menacing tone but quickly shifted to friendly excitement. Any second now, I would need to write my name on something for him.

"Yes, I am Ozar. I am with the Tusks hockey team."

The human took a step back and swept one arm toward the door. "Can I get you a table? Are you heading for the bar? First drink is on me."

I knew that if Jordan or her friends spotted me, it would not go well. I was following her, and any lie I told to explain my presence in the exact same dining establishment would be regarded with suspicion if not outright disbelief.

"No...I am looking for a place to take a female for a date this week."

Clearly, it was easier to lie to human males than their females. While I stepped away from the window, the male ran inside and returned with a paper menu. He pointed out their number to call for reservations and said they would be thrilled if I chose their restaurant for my date.

Tucking the menu under my arm, I walked around the block to wait, occasionally peering around the corner to make sure Jordan's car was still parked at the curb.

It started to rain. The menu was quickly soaked. Feeling slightly guilty, I balled it up and stuck it in a nearby trash bin. I didn't mind that I too was wet. There had been campaigns where we'd marched through downpours for days, bedding in soggy furs and limited to eating dried fruit and fat-coated nuts because starting a fire was impossible. This cold rain didn't bother me, especially when I knew a warm, dry home awaited me only a few miles from here. The stove would quickly cook a hot meal, and I'd just received a delivery this afternoon of cold, creamy milk.

And I'd endure the most brutal weather for Jordan. I didn't just want to know where she lived, I wanted to make sure she returned home safe.

Okay, I did want to know where she lived, mainly so I could leave her courting gifts. Plus, it would be easier to sleep at night knowing exactly how far from my home she was, sleeping in her own furs and hopefully dreaming of me.

I waited for nearly two hours before I saw her blue car head down the street. Breaking into a run, I followed my previous strategy of keeping track of her without obviously stalking. Finally, she turned down a street lined on either side with tall brick homes and parked. I hid behind a large black vehicle and wiped the rain from my face as I watched her run down the street, her leather bag on top of her head.

Jordan dashed up a set of stairs, huddling close to the door as she struggled to open it. I stealthily moved closer and saw a small black-and-white bundle of fur inside before she quickly shut the door. I was sure this was her home, but just in case, I lingered outside for another hour, walking around the block and pretending to check my phone. She didn't come out, and once the lights came on downstairs in her house, they stayed on. Taking a huge risk, I walked by her house. The curtains twitched aside, and I froze, but instead of Jordan, it was the black-and-white furry animal that stared accusingly at me from the window.

I'd cook her dinner tomorrow night. I'd brought her the requested teeth, and I'd given her a Starbucks gift card. But that might not be enough. It was important that she knew my intentions and interest, and with my lack of knowledge of human wooing rituals, I wasn't taking any chances.

So I left Jordan's neighborhood and headed to the nearest grocery store.

Chapter 13

Jordan

The next morning, there was a steak on my doorstep—a New York strip steak from Safeway, the price tag still on it. Glancing up and down my street, I wondered how someone could have been walking by on their way from the grocery store at five in the morning and dropped their twenty-dollar steak on my doorstep—the doorstep that was a good ten feet from the sidewalk.

Kneeling down, I picked it up. It was cold—colder than I would have expected a steak to be in Baltimore in October. We weren't the tropics, but we still had a few nights where the temps didn't get below forty-five.

"Hey," I called out—not super loud because it was really early and some of my neighbors weren't up yet. "Did anyone drop their steak?"

I felt like an idiot half-shouting that into the pre-dawn, my breath fogging in front of me. There were no cars coming or going down my street. The sidewalks were empty. No one was awake but me. If someone had accidentally dropped their steak, they were long gone.

Ducking back inside, I put the steak in the fridge. All

sorts of weird thoughts ran through my head—warnings from my childhood about poisoned Halloween candy fueling my imagination. But why would someone poison a twenty-dollar steak and leave it on my doorstep? It's not like I had enemies. If a customer was dissatisfied, they'd leave a horrible internet review for me, not figure out where I lived and deliver a poisoned steak to my door.

I intended on eating it eventually because I absolutely was not going to let a good steak go to waste. It wasn't destined for dinner tonight, because I had a date. Maybe tomorrow night. Or I could just freeze it for later. And if a random person showed up on my doorstep asking if I'd happened to find a New York strip steak, I'd give it back.

After my usual morning search for cat puke, I threw on my workout clothes and grabbed my bag and purse before heading out to the gym. I wasn't the only one there for an early workout. Parking, I joined ten other people, each of us nodding to each other and filing inside the moment the doors were unlocked.

Treadmill. Weights. Yoga.

It was my routine, and I loved a good routine. Spreading my mat out for the yoga class, I saw Stephanie and waved the werewolf over. We exchanged the usual pleasantries then dove into our vinyasa sequence, led by a very bendy man named Mario. When we finished, I smiled over at Stephanie.

"Do you need to rush right out to work? This might sound weird, but there is something I wanted to talk to you about. If you're free, I'd love to buy you breakfast and pick your brain a bit."

I felt a little awkward imposing on Stephanie like this. We were friendly enough to chat at the gym, but it wasn't like we hung out together after a workout. Sadly, she was the only werewolf I knew well enough to even broach the topic of supernatural dental procedures with.

It was embarrassing. Why did I only know one shifter, and barely knew her at that? Plus, it wasn't her responsibility to educate me on the medical industry and werewolves.

Stephanie smiled back. "I'd love breakfast. Two spin classes and arm day has me ready to eat a herd of deer."

We drove separately and met inside Miss Shirley's by the Inner Harbor. The place was packed, as usual, but we lucked out and got a small table for two by the window. I eyed the neighboring customers who were indulging in the famous Bloody Marys with an Old Bay Seasoning Rim and a garnish that included green tomato, pickled okra, and a jalapeño slice.

"Thinking of day drinking?" Stephanie asked with a grin.

"Thinking, but not doing," I told her with regret. "I've got four implant procedures today."

She made a face. "I hope you'll be drinking after work, then. I don't know how you do that, working in people's mouths all day."

I shrugged. "I'll admit it's not the most glamorous job in the world, but I love it. And I feel like I'm really making a difference in people's lives."

"Think I'll stick with home renovations."

"Did you finish work on that house in Reisterstown?" I asked.

"Finally." Stephanie rolled her eyes. "I thought the plumbing in that master bath would be the death of me, and the wiring didn't look like it had been touched since nineteen-twenty."

I winced in sympathy, remembering how much I'd

needed to spend to get my row house in Federal Hill up to code.

"I've got exciting news, though." The werewolf looked at the other customers and leaned closer. "I'm afraid to jinx it, but I've *got* to tell someone. I'm a finalist in the running to have my own season on *Home Sweet Home*."

My mouth dropped open. Then I squealed, clapping a hand over my mouth to hold further excitement back as I looked around to see if anyone noticed. *Home Sweet Home* was a nationally syndicated show that each season highlighted a historic remodel of a celebrity's home. It was immensely popular, and contractors who were featured found their careers skyrocketing as a result of the viewership.

"Oh my God! Oh my *God*!" I bounced in my seat, the only way I could manage to keep my voice reasonably quiet.

"I *know*!" Stephanie bounced in her seat as well. "Don't tell anyone. I'm so afraid if it gets out, the whole deal will vanish in the wind."

I made a zipped-lips motion. "Who is the celebrity?"

"They'd only tell me that it's a sports figure. I'm guessing it's Jorge Sanchez with the Orioles. Rumor is he's got an offer in on a huge eighteenth-century farmhouse this side of the Liberty Reservoir."

"Wow. That's amazing." I wasn't as sports-focused as Stephanie and had no idea who Jorge Sanchez was, but a season featuring my gym buddy helping restore/modernize an old farmhouse was a must-watch.

We both fell silent and glanced down at the menu as our waitress approached.

I ordered the crabmeat hash and Fried Green Tomato Eggs Benedict with a cup of black coffee. Stephanie ordered the fried chicken, biscuit, and gravy omelet with a side of chicken andouille sausage and a large latte.

"Man, I love this place," I told her once the waitress had left. "If I ate here every day, I'd be huge, so it's once-a-month only."

"You need to have a werewolf metabolism. I'll probably need second breakfast in a few hours even after all this food," Stephanie said.

"How much of that is werewolf metabolism, and how much is you swinging a sledgehammer and framing out new walls?" I asked.

"A little of both, honestly." She settled back in her chair, smiling at me. "So? Enough about my job. What did you need to talk to me about?"

"It's about being a werewolf. I wanted to know what happens to any man-made material in your body when you shift forms?" I asked, diving right into the matter.

"Well, we have to take out piercings beforehand, or they just fall out." She laughed. "Except there was one hunt where Jazmine's gold hoop stayed in her left ear. We teased the heck out of her. Matt still calls her 'Pirate Jaz.' Tattoos vanish in our wolf form but reappear when we turn human again. I've got no idea how that works, but I'm glad because I don't want to have to get new ink every time I go for a hunt."

"How about things like fillings, or dental implants, or knee replacements?" I asked, wanting to confirm what I'd read in that medical paper.

Stephanie steepled her fingers and rested her chin on them. "That depends a lot on the individual shifter. Since we're all descended from angels—Nephilim, actually—we each have varying degrees of what you'd call magic. Some of us can't tolerate silver at all—we're talking Epi-pen level reactions—others just get itchy, others have no problem at all with the metal. Things like hip and knee replacements? It's a toss-up whether the device will tear through us during a shift, or if it stays and remains there when we shift back."

I sucked in a breath, horrified at the thought of a titanium knee replacement breaking through skin, muscle, and bone as a werewolf changed form.

"It's bad," she said in response to the expression on my face. "There's a demon-owned company that's been working with a sorcerer and an angel to produce medical equipment that adjusts to a shifter's change in form. I've heard their products are in clinical trials and aren't available outside of a few select practices. And they'd be expensive. Either way, not many doctors would probably be willing to perform the surgery since there are certain methods that need to be followed with shifters, and we're not always good under anesthesia."

"Is the equipment manufacturer DarRafi Inc.?" I'd done some internet research and hadn't been sure if the company was a fake or not. A demon, an archangel, and a human sorcerer working together? It sounded like the prelude to a joke about them walking into a bar.

She nodded. "That's them. They're based out of Chicago. Are you thinking of offering services to supernaturals? Because sign me up as your first client." Stephanie pulled the corner of her mouth aside and showed me a gap where her number fifteen tooth should be. "Cracked a molar on a deer bone five years ago and could never get the crown to stay on through a shift, so I just had the dentist pull it. I saved up for one of those fancy implants, but the closest reconstruction dentist that is approved for the clinical trials and works with shifters is in Boston."

Excitement coursed through me. I'd emailed DarRafi

Inc. and requested to be added to their clinical trials, high-lighting my extensive experience with human dentistry and mentioning that I also had an orc as a client. I might be jumping the gun here, but I was eager to expand my prac-tice...and to help Stephanie replace that missing molar.

"After five years without that tooth you might need some realignment and possibly a bone graft. Call my office and I'll have them squeeze you in for imaging and an evalu-ation," I told her. "Even if I don't get the approval to use these new implants, I can send the information and images to the dentist up in Boston and hopefully save you an evalu-ation appointment."

"That would be *awesome!*" She grinned. "Werewolves have good regenerative abilities, but obviously it's not all encompassing since some of us have bum knees and my broken tooth never magically fixed itself. I'd like to hope I wouldn't need a bone graft, but reality is that I probably do."

"I'm sure DarRafi has all the equipment I need, and I'd be grafting your own bone, so that would shift when you do."

At least, I hoped so. I'd need to further dig into medical journals and articles to see. And I'd need to contact DarRafi again for their training videos and materials on the procedure.

"If you get approved for this, you're going to be swamped with new clients," Stephanie said. "There are more shifters in the city than you realize, and lots of them need fillings, crowns, partials, and implants. Get ready for a whole lot of clients."

I wasn't ready, but I'd get there. I'd hire another dentist willing to specialize in supernatural work if needed. Orcs, humans, and shifters. There were so many beings I could help, so much I could learn.

And all of this was because I'd met a sexy orc hockey player leaning against my car in a parking lot.

Our food and drinks arrived, and we settled into additional conversation about our jobs. Stephanie told me about a house in Hampden she was just beginning work on and the gorgeous chestnut floors that had been buried under layers of carpet for nearly eighty years.

"I'm doing this job solo," she added. "Remember Dillon? We broke up and there's no way I'm still employing *or* sleeping with his cheating ass. Gave him two weeks' pay and handed him a garbage bag full of his clothes and his half-empty box of Fruit Loops. Good riddance."

I made a sympathetic noise.

"How about you?" she asked. "Dating anyone?"

"I've got a first date tonight with a guy who plays for the Tusks," I told her, feeling a flush of excitement at the thought of seeing Ozar again.

Stephanie nearly choked on her omelet. "An orc? The hockey team Tusks? Damn. You go, girl. Where's he taking you?"

"His house." I wiggled my eyebrows. "He's cooking me a traditional orc meal, but I'm hoping the proximity of his bedroom inspires some after-dinner activity."

"Now you're talking! Those guys look like they have muscles on muscles. I never pegged you for a puck bunny, though," she teased.

"I'm not normally, but there's something about him." I smiled. "He's kind of grumpy and growly, but not with me. He's kind, thoughtful, and a good listener. And I really like hearing about his home and culture."

"Does he have a brother?" Stephanie grinned. "One who might be interesting in going out with a werewolf who can also swing a hammer?"

"I really have no idea," I confessed. "He didn't mention siblings, so maybe he's an only child. There's a whole team of orcs in town, though. If things work out with Ozar and me, then maybe I can introduce you to one of them."

The werewolf held up her hands. "Actually, thanks, but no thanks. I make it a rule not to date actors, musicians, or sports players. Or werewolves named Dillon."

I nodded. "Got it. I'll absolutely ask Ozar if he has non-actor/musician/sports player friends who are single and aren't named Dillon and have at least basic carpentry skills."

Stephanie gave me a thumbs-up. "Thanks. It's a nightmare out there when it comes to dating."

It was. I'd given up on the apps and had pretty much given up on dating all together, deciding to take a break and just focus on my career and my friends. I'd never thought that I'd meet a guy in a parking lot and end up with him offering to cook me dinner.

Chapter 14

Ozar

I got to the stadium at six in the morning, tired and jittery from a combination of the pot of coffee I'd downed and nervous anticipation over my date tonight. There had been many, many sleepless nights when I'd been out on patrol, but I'd felt particularly drained after my restless night, hence the pot of coffee.

Tonight, I'd see Jordan. I'd feed her, spend time talking about her life and about my home. Then later, if she was amenable, I'd show her that I could satisfy her as only a true mate could.

But step one was dinner. I had a few ideas, but I wanted to run them by the other orcs for feedback before I went to the grocery store. And since I had a ton of nervous energy to burn off, I intended to strap those stupid knife blade shoes on my feet and see if I could improve my skills on the ice.

On my way to the equipment room, I peeked out at the rink and was astonished to find Ugwyll out there, sliding and falling, and cursing in a loud, frustrated voice. I could sympathize with the orc. No one on the team seemed to care at all about the game we were to play here or whether we won or lost. I wasn't sure Ugwyll did either, but I knew he had pride in his athletic abilities and that it must be a horrible blow to his ego that he couldn't manage to stay on these stupid skates.

My own competitive spirit sparked as I looked at the rink, the boxes, the empty stands, the blank scoreboard. I didn't *want* to care about this game, but I did. Even if I was only here a few more weeks, I still wanted to excel at this activity. I wanted to beat our opposing team. I wanted to win.

If I won Jordan's heart, we'd return to my home as soon as possible, but even if I never needed to glide across the ice on these knife-blades again, I still wanted to win at least one game before I left. I didn't want to be a laughingstock, a fool. I might have managed to score one goal the last game, but it wasn't enough.

It couldn't let it be the last goal I scored. If I had to punch every human on the opposing team, I wasn't going to let them win easily. Even though they would probably end up with the top score, I'd still feel good watching them limp out of the arena, bruised and bleeding.

I left Ugwyll falling and cursing on the ice and went to get my skates. He was still there when I stomped out of the tunnel onto the ice, sprawled out by one of the nets.

"Here." I slid a stick over to him and dropped a puck on the ground.

"Eat shit," he snarled as the stick slid to a stop against his knee. "I hate this game. I hate these knife-shoes. I hate ice."

"I hate the smug opposing team," I continued his rant. "I hate being laughed at by the humans in the stands. I hate our demon team owner who gives zero fucks whether we look like fools or not as long as he rakes in the ticket and sponsorship money."

Ugwyll struggled to his feet, using the stick for support and holding on to the goal with his other hand. "I should just go home, but there's no way I'm going back without a bride, a total failure and a loser."

"So, stop being a loser." I slid him a second stick.

"What did you call me?" Ugwyll snarled as he reached down to grab the second stick.

I waited until the other orc was fully upright and using the two sticks for balance. "A loser. At least I scored a point. You couldn't even get from one side of the rink to the other without falling."

Ugwyll roared, propelling himself forward. His feet slid all over, but he managed to stay standing and somehow moved forward. When he got close to me, he swung one of the hockey sticks and missed, almost toppling over in the process. I waited until he was balanced and stabilized, then slowly skated away.

I wasn't as good as the humans we'd played against, but I'd slowly been figuring out how to walk on these things without stomping huge dents in the ice.

I led Ugwyll for two laps around the ice, noticing that the other orc hadn't fallen once and was now starting to rely less on the sticks for balance. And he was picking up speed. I also noticed my own walking was becoming less choppy and quicker as well. As I tried to turn around and skate backward, I immediately fell on my ass. Ugwyll skated up and smacked me with one of his sticks. I grabbed it out of his hand and the other orc spun around, gliding backward into the wall—all without falling.

I couldn't help but feel smug as I got to my feet. Ugwyll was the most athletically talented of the whole team, and he was livid over his inability to master this sport within seconds of stepping onto the ice. I'd wondered if his fury over not being instantly good at something was keeping him from making progress, so I'd given the other orc something else to be angry at—me.

"You're a *wyndall's* ass," Ugwyll said, the words tempered by his slightly embarrassed smile.

"And you're better at this than you thought," I pointed out. "Maybe next game you'll manage to stay on your feet, even if you never do score a goal."

Ugwyll's growl made me laugh. I reached out with my stick and brought the puck I'd dropped when I first came on the ice closer.

"All right, loser, try to keep me from scoring a goal."

I stood and walked forward, slower than before since I had to concentrate to keep control of the puck. Ugwyll easily caught up, cutting in front of me and slapping the puck away. We both ran for it, Ugwyll taking possession. I managed to stay even with him, the loud crack of our sticks echoing off the empty stadium seats as we fought for the puck.

Again and again, Ugwyll stole the puck from me, making progress toward the goal net until he eventually knocked the puck in. He lost his balance and fell in the process, and there wasn't anyone to try to stop the puck, but he'd still scored a goal.

After a few more rounds, I was done. I headed back to the locker room, leaving Ugwyll still on the ice practicing. Eng and Bwat were there, along with six of the other orcs on the team. Four of the orcs were playing a game of *Misk* with plastic chips they'd found in one of the closets. Bwat was looking through a stack of magazines. Eng was in his usual pose, leaning back against a locker and scowling at everyone.

"You weren't actually practicing, were you?" Eng asked me.

I nodded. "Ugwyll and I were, yes."

"Why?" Eng screwed his eyebrows together. "I understand Ugwyll, with his obsession to be the best at every sporting event, but why are *you* bothering? The owner doesn't care. The humans watching the games don't care."

I thought about the two employees at Starbucks yesterday. "Some of the humans watching care. More of them might if we actually practiced and made an effort instead of standing against the wall the whole game."

Eng shrugged. "I didn't come here to play stupid games for human entertainment, I came to find a suitable bride. None of this"—he waved his hand around—"is going to help me get a bride."

"It helped Ozar," Bwat chimed in. "Maybe if you get a couple of teeth knocked out, you'll find your true mate as well, Eng."

"I'm not interested in finding a human true mate. I just want to find a suitable female so I can go home and leave all this nonsense behind." Eng pushed away from the lockers and snatched the magazine from Bwat. "Here. This female will do."

Bwat and I stood next to Eng to see the picture he was pointing at.

"I don't think Pussy Galore would be interested in being your bride," Bwat commented, reading the caption under the picture.

Eng glared at him. "She should be honored to marry me. I'm Eng, son of the Chieftain Mrong of Clan Waragur. I am a prince, the heir to the largest of the orc clans. Waragur is a kingdom, and I will be the king one day."

Bwat rolled his eyes. "Maybe Ozar's mate has a sister or a friend who would be willing to be your bride, although I doubt it."

"I could never do such a disservice to Jordan's sister or friend," I said, horrified at the thought of having to spend any more time with Eng than absolutely necessary.

Thankfully, Eng ignored the idea, continuing to look through the magazine for other matrimonial candidates.

"Speaking of your mate, how did your date go with Jordan yesterday?" Bwat asked me. "Did she like your gift of teeth? When is the wedding?"

"I misunderstood and yesterday morning wasn't a date after all. It seems that her job involves repairing teeth, and she wanted me to meet her at her place of business to begin the process of replacing my two teeth that were knocked out." It was embarrassing to admit this, but we were all learning about human customs, and it would help Bwat to know about my error.

"Oh." Bwat winced. "I'm so sorry. Is the mate bond not reciprocated by her?"

"I think it might be." I told him about her polishing my teeth. And I told him about our planned date for this evening.

Bwat punched my shoulder. "That's amazing. Food seems to be just as critical in human courtship as it is in ours. From what I've read, I think Sizzle might be right about the steak idea."

"Actually, I did go to her house last night to leave a gift of steak," I told him, glad that I seemed to be doing this correctly. "It wasn't easy, though. Since I didn't know where she lived, I had to follow her around all evening until she returned home. Then I got to the food store right before they closed and went back to her house early this morning to leave the gift."

Bwat's mouth fell open. "You followed her around? All night? To her home? That's not a good thing, Ozar. Humans don't like that. Human females especially don't like that. Stalking is not a good thing."

"But she knows where *I* live," I protested. "She made me write it on a piece of paper before she took care of my teeth. It's only fair that I know where her home is too, especially since I couldn't otherwise gift her with the steak. Back home, I would know because everyone knows where everyone else lives. Or I could just ask a member of her clan to direct me to her house. There are too many humans in this city for that, and no one even seems to know who their neighbors are."

"It's still not good," Bwat grumbled.

"Well, she didn't see me, so she'll never know I was following her," I reassured him.

"Wait." Eng looked up from his magazine. "If she didn't know you were following her, how is she supposed to know the steak is from you? Did you leave a note on it?"

"I hadn't thought of that." I frowned. "She has to know it's from me. I'm courting her. I gave her my teeth, gave her a Starbuck's gift card, and am going to cook her dinner. Who else would be leaving meat on her doorstep?"

Eng shrugged. "A human male? Why do you think you're the only one courting her? For all you know, there are a dozen males leaving meat on her doorstep. She probably has more meat than she knows what to do with."

I was torn between a sense of panic and an urge to rip Eng's head off and punt it out of the locker room. Thankfully before I acted on that last urge, Bwat spoke up.

"What are you going to cook for her?" he asked. "This is a very important moment in your courtship. Everything needs to be perfect."

The panic grew, but I no longer felt like decapitating Eng.

"I'm not sure. She's expecting a traditional orc meal, but I don't know what the equivalent spices or meats would be here."

Plus, there was the fact that I wasn't exactly a culinary genius. We had orcs in our clan that were skilled at preparing meals, but most of us just went with the basics. I doubted Jordan would be impressed with the basics, and I really did want to impress her.

"*Fikmak* pie?" Bwat suggested. "I'm sure you could find an appropriate meat substitute, and I believe human root vegetables would work."

It was definitely a tasty and very traditional orc meal, but there was one problem.

"I can never get my crust to be flakey," I told him.

"How about *Milowen*?" he asked.

I frowned. "That's not really a traditional *meal*." The dried meat was an orc staple, but it was mainly used when hunters or scouts needed something portable and non-perishable to take with them. "I could cook *Swakega* stew," I volunteered. It wasn't the most sophisticated meal, but it was hearty and filling, and I'd prepared it enough back home that I was pretty sure the end result would be edible. "Although I'm not sure I can get *Swakega* here."

"They're kind of like horses, but smaller," Bwat said. "If they don't have *Swakega*, then maybe horse meat will do."

I'd been to the food store many times since I'd arrived in Baltimore, and I'd yet to see anything beyond pork, beef, chicken, lamb, and an assortment of fish and sea creatures, but I could always ask the humans who I'd seen working in that area.

After making a quick list with substitution suggestions by Bwat, I headed out to the store. It still amazed me that humans purchased all their food at these places. Although Bwat insisted that many humans did hunt, I'd yet to see any of them bringing a kill back home to the apartment building I shared with at least a hundred humans.

The stores themselves were beyond anything we had back home. They were huge, with ten different brands of the exact same thing. There was an entire aisle of breads, another one of cheeses. Were these toilet paper types really that different? Did humans need multiple kinds of sheets just to wipe their butts? It was overwhelming every time I went. I ended up just throwing random items in my cart and hoping I wasn't buying the wrong dish soap or food that was meant for animals.

Although those dog biscuits had actually been pretty tasty.

I grabbed a cart and went straight to the meat section, ignoring the stares of the customers I passed. Once there, I carefully scrutinized the different packages, using my phone app to translate all the unfamiliar words. None of the products were the same as back home, but the app thankfully showed pictures of the animals the meat came from and gave a description. I'd spent about ten minutes trying to figure out the difference between a rump roast and a chuck roast when a human female wearing the store's uniform came up to me. Her hair was hidden under a scarf, and her name tag said "Amina."

"You're one of the hockey players, aren't you? Ozar?"

"I am." I waited, wondering if she'd express support like

the two employees at Starbucks or ask me to write my name on something.

"Can I help you find anything?" Her smile widened. "It must be really hard figuring out our food."

"It is." I held up the two roasts. "I'm cooking *Swakega* stew tonight for a human female that I'm wooing. Which of these is best?"

Amina clapped her hands. "A date! How exciting! I've obviously never had *Swakega* stew. Describe it and I'll do my best to help."

I told her about the dish, how it was meat-heavy with a rich and spicy sauce and that it was served over a slightly firm, steamed vegetable called *moa*.

She frowned. "Is the meat chopped? It doesn't sound like the human version of stew."

"No, but it falls off the bone when cooked, so we remove the bone and serve the meat in large chunks with the sauce," I explained.

"It sounds a lot like a dish my grandmother makes." She tilted her head and looked up at me. "Do you trust me?"

"Yes." I was so relieved to have an actual human helping me. If the stew turned out good and Jordan was pleased, I was going to give Amina tickets to our next game. And a Starbucks gift card, just in case she didn't enjoy sporting events.

She grabbed the two roasts out of my hands and put them back. "Lamb. A leg of lamb, but you need to rub the spices on it and start slow cooking it as soon as you get home in order for it to be spicy and tender like you're describing."

I nodded, taking notes on my phone as she led me down the shelves of meat, looking through the different packages until she held one up and put it in my cart.

"Leg of lamb. Now let's head for the veggie section."

I followed her, jotting down that I should thinly slice the onions, and that the garlic should be peeled, separated, and wedged into the slits I needed to cut in the meat. There were three types of unpronounceable spices I was supposed to rub on the lamb, then tomatoes, olives, and little salted fish that came in a tin were to go on the bottom of the heavy Dutch oven she'd placed in my cart. By the time she was done, I had a cart full of groceries and instructions to make something that hopefully would be similar to *Swakega* stew.

It was far more than I could carry in the flimsy plastic bags they usually put my purchases in, so after I paid, I got a large box from the back of the store, transferred everything into it, and walked home with it up on my shoulder.

With my notes and all of my groceries spread out, I began chopping and slicing, preheating the oven as Amina had told me. Back home our stoves were heated with wood, but this human one was powered by a cord attached to the wall and that certainly was convenient. It heated quickly without all the smoke, although I missed the smell of the burning wood.

I was nervous about leaving the stove unattended, so I cleaned my small apartment. Back home, I would have shown my mate my spacious dwelling with my handcrafted furniture and beautiful, warm furs, but here I would have to make do with what I'd been able to afford with my job as a hockey player.

After a few hours I realized that my cooking wasn't going to burn the building down. Reassured, I left to go buy some additional items to make the apartment seem less sparse. Bwat had composed a list of must-have items when inviting a female to my home, so I found myself running all over the city to buy decorative pillows, flowers, candles, fur blankets, and a fancy little towel for the bathroom.

The flowers went on the table, along with the dishes that had come with the furnished apartment. I put jars of candles on every flat surface, deciding I should wait to light them until a few minutes before Jordan was to come over. I scattered the decorative pillows on the couch, propping some of the larger ones up against a wall. Half of the furs went on the couch, and the other half went on my bed. I'd really gone overboard on them, but back home, furs didn't just provide comfort and warmth, they were a symbol of virility. I had no idea whether that was true with humans, but I figured it wouldn't hurt to have an overabundance of them just in case.

With nothing else to do, I showered, put on clean clothes, checked on dinner, then waited.

Chapter 15

Jordan

I staggered up the steps to Ozar's fifth floor apartment, wishing I hadn't worn the boots with the high heels since his apartment didn't have a working elevator. It wasn't a particularly disreputable neighborhood or a bad apartment building; it was just very average and not what I expected someone playing for an NHL team to have rented. But what did I know? Maybe he was sending money home to his family, or saving up to buy a swanky house, or maybe the demon who owned the Tusks paid them crap wages. Whatever the reason, I was carrying two bottles of wine and a box of cannoli from Vaccaros as well as a Brazo de Gitano from Tio Pepe's. Those packages plus my heels meant I was forced to take several breaks as I climbed the stairs.

Arriving slightly out of breath and hoping I hadn't accidentally crushed the pine nut roll, I knocked at Ozar's door. He opened it as if he'd been hovering right by the entrance. We stared at each other, sparks flying.

"*Mawrk!*" he said, reaching out to take the bags. "Greetings! Come in. I didn't mean to make you stand at my door holding all this."

Some of my nervousness fled seeing that he was just as anxious. The orc spun around, looking for a spot to put the bags before just setting them down on the floor and reaching to take my coat.

"I'll put this…" He spun around again.

I bit back a smile. "In the closet?" I pointed to the door that led, I assumed, to a hallway closet.

Ozar opened the door, then cursed—at least, I thought it was a curse. "There are no pegs. Why would someone build a coat room and not put in pegs to hang your coats?"

"Probably because we use hangers." I laughed at his perplexed expression. "I'll buy you some. Just put my coat over a chair or on your bed or something."

"I will do that."

He vanished into a back room with my coat while I looked around. Ozar's apartment was sparsely furnished, but he'd clearly tried to brighten the place up a bit with some personal touches. There was only one couch in front of a wall-mounted television, but he had some big cushions against the wall that I guess he used for additional seating. The sofa's upholstery was hidden beneath a pile of furry blankets and red geometric-printed pillows. Furry pillows sat against the back of the dining chairs, and a furry rug lay between the laminate coffee table and the wall with the television.

I was sensing a fur theme here. And a candle theme.

The fur probably was Ozar's aesthetic, but the fact that there were fresh flowers on the table made me wonder if the candles were also for my benefit. They were all lit, and that definitely shouted, "romantic dinner."

Ozar came back and picked up the two bags with the pastries. I grabbed the other one.

"I bought a few things for dessert—some local sweets

that everyone who lives in Baltimore should try," I told him. "Why don't you put them in the fridge, and I'll open up the wine for us?"

He looked down into the bag and sniffed, making an appreciative noise before ushering me into the kitchen. I wondered how good his sense of smell was. Better than a human's? Better than a dog's? I hoped my deodorant held up through the marathon climb to his apartment, or this was going to be an awkward first date.

I had noticed an incredible aroma wafting from the kitchen the moment I walked into the apartment. Entering the kitchen made my mouth water. Whatever Ozar was cooking, it smelled amazing—rich and meaty and spicy.

It wasn't canned chili with hotdogs, and I'll admit I fell a little more in love knowing he'd gone to the trouble to cook what smelled like a gourmet meal for me.

Ozar opened the fridge and slid the boxes inside. I'm nosy, so I looked over his shoulder and was surprised to see a variety of fresh vegetables, a couple of nice steaks, a six-pack of dark beer, and a tub of unsweetened Greek yogurt, and what looked to be farmhouse milk in an actual glass container. Not at all what I expected from a bachelor orc.

I easily found a corkscrew and opened the red while Ozar pulled two glasses from the cabinet. They weren't wine glasses, but I wasn't about to get snobby about drinking from highballs when that incredible smell was coming from his oven.

"I'm dying to know what you're cooking," I said as I poured and handed him a glass of wine.

"It's supposed to be *Swakega* stew." He put on a surprisingly frilly apron and a matching pair of floral-patterned oven mitts then opened the oven, sliding out the rack and lifting the lid off the Dutch oven.

I thought dinner had smelled good before, but this... I'd left my house determined to delay having sex with Ozar, but this was totally changing my mind.

"Here." He took a spoon off the stove, ladled some of the sauce, blew on it, then held it out. I gingerly sipped it while the orc watched, an anxious expression on his face.

The sauce was spicy and hearty and reminded me a lot of a Moroccan dish I'd once had. I made an appreciative noise, then took the spoon in my mouth for the rest of the sauce, my eyes on Ozar the whole time. The tension in his shoulders vanished, and a flare of lust lit up his eyes as I slowly slid the spoon out of my mouth. It was one of the most overtly suggestive things I'd ever done, but any self-consciousness fled at his expression.

He wanted me as much as I wanted him. And just like me, he was imagining his cock between my lips instead of that spoon. But that would need to wait because I was starving, and I wanted to get to know this orc a little better before we got naked in the sheets.

Ozar stared at my lips, then put the spoon on top of the stove before returning the lid to the Dutch oven and closing up the stove. Taking off his oven mitts, he made a grumbling noise and scratched his head. "I don't know if any of the ingredients I found in the grocery store are the same as what we have back home. A female employee at the grocery store named Amina assisted me. It's similar to *Swakega* stew, but not exactly the same. I'm sorry. I really wanted you to have a traditional orc meal."

There was no need for him to apologize. I'm sure it was difficult trying to find similar ingredients, and I truly appreciated all the effort he'd put into this dinner, even if I felt a flare of jealousy over his mention of this Amina woman.

"Someday I'd like you to have the real thing, served to you in my clan's homeland," he said with a shy smile.

"I'd love that." It had been years since I'd taken a day off from my dental practice, and I didn't have the staff to cover for an actual vacation, but I really did want to see his homeland and try the authentic version of his foods. It would require a lot of advanced planning, but I did need to start taking time off now and then. I'd covered Aaron Steinman's practice when he and his wife celebrated their thirty-year anniversary in Italy last year. He'd offered several times to return the favor.

"Shall we sit down and wait for the dinner to finish?" He gestured to the living room, that worried frown back.

I grabbed our wines and followed him into the room, watched him adjust the pillows and furs, then placed our drinks on the coffee table and sat down smack in the middle of the sofa, making sure that he was going to end up against me no matter which side of the sofa he took.

Without the slightest hesitation, he sat to my right, draping his arm across the back of the sofa where it brushed against my shoulders. His thigh pressed against mine, and the warmth of his body was like a heater. I wondered what the body temperature of an orc was? Sitting here beside him, I thought it had to be close to a hundred degrees.

"Tell me about *Swakega* stew back where you grew up," I said, continuing to think some rather uncharitable thoughts about Amina, even though the employee was most likely in her sixties and had probably only been helping Ozar navigate human foodstuff as part of her job.

"*Swakega* is a game meat, similar to your horses, although I used lamb," he hurriedly added, no doubt in response to the look of horror on my face. "It has lots of spices and root vegetables. We cook it in a pot all day, then serve it over another root vegetable. It is a common winter food at home. All orcs growing up have eaten it. We have lots of memories and heart-feelings about *Swakega* stew."

I nodded. "Comfort food. We humans have those same feelings and memories, although the foods are different for each of us depending on our upbringing and cultural heritage."

"What are *your* comfort foods?" he asked, brushing his hand against my hair.

I leaned back, feeling the heat of his skin against my neck. "Macaroni and cheese—the kind in the box with the squeeze packet of cheese. Pizza. Brownies. Oh—and chocolate chip mint ice cream."

He scooted over so that I was nestled in the crook of his arm. "I've had pizza, and I like it. We have fried bread and cheese at home, but I actually like the human version better. I've never had these other foods, though."

"I'm not about to cook you boxed macaroni and cheese after the meal you're making for me, but I'll buy you some to try yourself. Ice cream, though—that's an experience that's better shared."

"So, it's cold milk?" he asked, a strange note of hopefulness in his voice.

I turned to him, surprised that he didn't know what ice cream was. He was so close, his face only a few inches from mine. His brown eyes met mine, and I sucked in a breath.

"Cold milk and cream, sugar, and other ingredients. It's frozen while being churned," I whispered.

"Sweet milky slush." Ozar leaned closer, his dark eyes warm. "I should try it."

"You should." I closed the distance and kissed him.

His tusks were smooth and hard against the corners of my mouth. His lips brushed against mine, gentle and sweet until I nipped at his lower lip. With a sharp inhalation, he gathered me close, his tongue tangling with mine. I felt his fingers tighten on my shoulder while his other hand worked its way up my waist to cup my breast.

My stomach growled loud enough that we both could hear it. The rumble probably shook the floor. Laughing, I broke the kiss and pulled back. His eyes were soft and warm, with a hint of concern. Reaching out, he lightly traced my jaw with a calloused finger.

"I need to feed you now." His smile was sheepish. "I meant to feed you before kissing."

"Well, that was my fault." I grinned. "I couldn't resist."

The rough edge of his thumb brushed against my lower lip. "I don't want to stop but tonight is supposed to be about dinner. And the food should be ready now."

He stood, and I watched as he walked to the kitchen. Ozar moved with a stealthy grace for such a large guy. And every ounce of him was muscle. I'd done a bit of a reacharound when we'd kissed and there wasn't even a hint of a spare tire going on under his shirt—not that I hadn't seen him naked from the waist up as all the Tusks were during the game.

His hockey uniform had told me in no uncertain terms that his legs and ass were totally solid, but I'd known plenty of buff guys who were sporting a little softness around their midsection. I'd never minded that at all; in fact, it was a weird turn-on for me, but Ozar's rock-like physique lit an unexpected fire between my legs.

A few seconds later, the orc appeared again with that ridiculous apron tied around his waist and a steaming bowl of stew in his hands. As amused as I was by the rose-printed apron bordered with several rows of ruffles, it was the food that got my attention. I jumped up, prepared to help, but

Ozar growled at me to sit while he served. I did as he demanded, my stomach growling again as he brought in hot bread and a container of what looked to be farm-fresh butter. Finally, he sat, pulling off the apron at the last minute and tossing it over the back of the couch.

Then he served me. Dishing everything into a bowl, he picked up a spoon and hesitated. I tilted my head, wondering if he was going to sample my food or spoon it into my mouth. Either scenario would be uncomfortably weird, but I'd go along with whatever, not wanting to offend his dining customs.

Thankfully, he flipped the spoon, handing it to me. I waited for him to serve himself, but he just stared at me expectantly. As respectful as I wanted to be of his customs, I wasn't about to chow down with him hovering and watching me, so I motioned toward the serving bowl.

"Humans who are dining together eat at the same time," I finally said.

He let out a breath, nodded sharply, then filled his own bowl before sitting down. Still, he waited.

"Um, *bon appetit?*" I scooped a hearty spoonful into my mouth and my taste buds exploded with the flavor. "Oh, God. This is amazing." It was so amazing that I was talking with my mouth full.

His shoulders relaxed and he grunted something unin-telligible and began to eat.

We sat side by side, our knees touching as we ate in silence. As conscious as I was of his muscled thigh so close to mine, the food took center stage. The meat was flavorful and tender, the sauce spicy and rich. Instead of resting on a bed of rice, Ozar had served it all on top of steamed sweet potatoes, which were the perfect complement to the stew. I'd imagined orcs as some sort of fantasy barbarian, dining solely on unseasoned roasted meat and hard, crusty bread. I was thrilled to realize that once again, my stereotypical assumptions were all wrong. Their lives and homes were clearly different, but from what Ozar had told me, theirs were no less nuanced and full than our own lives. A difference in culture didn't mean the orcs were savages, it just meant they'd discovered different ways of enjoying the same things we did.

Ozar insisted I relax with another glass of wine while he cleared the plates and cleaned up. I smelled coffee brewing, and he brought me a mug, then went back into the kitchen to return with the two boxes from the fridge.

"Milk and sugar?" he asked with a smile.

"Just milk, please," I replied.

He brought me the giant bottle of milk I'd seen in the fridge as well as two plates, two forks, and a knife. We each had half a cannoli and a slice of the pine-nut cake. As we ate, I told him about my favorite bakery in Little Italy and the amazing Spanish food at Tio Pepe's, promising to take him to both places soon.

All through dinner and afterward, I still felt the fire, the sexual flame that being so close to him sparked, but unlike before, the intense physical attraction was blended with an incredibly cozy feeling of companionship. I *liked* Ozar. Talking to him was so easy. And even the silences that sometimes fell, the lulls between our conversation...these were comfortable. There was no doubt in my mind that we'd see each other again, that I'd buy him dinner at Tio Pepe's, that we'd explore the Inner Harbor then walk to Little Italy for an espresso and a cannoli, that we'd eat crabs on the deck at Nick's Fishhouse, listening to reggae music while watching the boats come in to dock.

I couldn't imagine a future without Ozar by my side. I didn't *want* to imagine a future without him.

At thirty, I'd dated a lot. I'd had a few relationships. I'd been in love. But none of those prior experiences had ever been like this. What I felt for this orc was so much more than sexual attraction. Being with him felt right. It was like we were meant to walk through our lives side by side, in partnership forever.

"These are both very good." He pointed his fork at each of the boxes, scraping the last of the cannoli filling off his plate.

"Keep the leftovers," I told him. "You can take them in to your team tomorrow for them to eat."

He growled, reaching out and pulling the boxes closer. "These are mine and I will not share. I plan to have them for breakfast."

I laughed, because in spite of his fierce glare, his lips twitched upward. "Okay, then. Breakfast of champions. You all probably burn off a million calories in practice and work-outs anyway."

"We don't." He sighed, his expression suddenly serious. "Practice and workout, I mean. We have no coach, no one to teach us to skate or show us what exercises will help us perform our best. We don't even know the rules of the game beyond getting the turd...I mean the puck into the opponent's net and preventing them from doing the same. Our owner only wants us to play the bumbling fools. I thought the humans in the stadium wanted the same, but I think some humans do want us to win."

I reached out to put my hand on his arm. "There are lots of fans that want you to win, including me. I'm sorry you've got so little support from your owner and staff."

He grunted. "There are times in life when you must

accomplish things without the help of others. I have been running and exercising each morning on my own, and today I skated with Ugwyll. I am trying to get my teammates to care about the game but in this I am failing as well."

Ozar was a strategist, a leader. I'd seen that from the first time I'd laid eyes on him. I knew he had a plan, and I was willing to help any way I could—although I doubted a reconstructive dentist could do much to assist a struggling orc hockey team.

Sliding my hand down his arm, I curled my hand in his. "What's the most important thing the team needs to learn?"

I was thinking I could pull together some YouTube videos of games, a bullet list of hockey rules, and maybe even ask Willa for a basic workout plan they could follow, but his reply surprised me.

"To skate. We will always be the fools unless we can stay on our feet and at least manage a tiny bit of defense. We may never win, but I hate that our opponents win by so many points."

The muscles in his arm had bunched at his words, and his hand squeezed mine.

"What time do you get to the stadium in the morning?" I might not be as skilled as an NHL player, but I'd grown up with skates in a part of the country where we'd had a long winter season to play on the ice.

"Six," he replied.

Well, I was up earlier than that most mornings for a gym workout anyway. But before I offered to help the team, I wanted to have some one-on-one with Ozar.

"How about tomorrow night I give you a skating lesson, and afterward, we'll go out for ice cream?"

His eyebrows shot up. "You skate?"

I grinned. "Pretty much since I could walk."

A whole host of complex emotions chased across his face, and I worried that maybe I'd said the wrong thing. Was it emasculating in his culture to have a woman be better than a man at something? For her to teach him? That was one stereotype I hadn't assumed about orcs.

Ozar cleared his throat. "I would very much enjoy you teaching me to skate and taking me for ice cream."

His voice was husky, with something approaching awe. I felt my breath catch, my heart swell.

"Then I'll meet you at the stadium at seven tomorrow night?" I asked, my voice suddenly just as husky.

"I'll make sure the security human knows to let you in." He released my hand, stood, and smiled warmly. "But if you are to teach me something, then I need to return the favor. Wait here."

Chapter 16

Jordan

Ozar went into the bedroom, then reappeared with his arms full of weapons.

Okay. That was unexpected.

"You're going to teach me to *fight?*" Not that I was opposed to the idea, but I had serious concerns about accidentally cutting him with a knife or slicing his pillows and furs with a sword.

"Yes." He tossed a knife onto the table. It bounced twice before coming to a stop by my dessert plate.

"Rubber weapons?" I was astonished. Why would he have a bunch of rubber weapons in his apartment? Or anywhere, for that matter?

He grinned sheepishly. "I thought to bring them home for future children in my clan to use. They would learn much quicker if there was no fear of injury."

It made sense. I picked up the rubber knife and stood, testing it with a few inexpert thrusts.

"Are there a lot of children in your clan?" I was envisioning Ozar teaching little orcs, tiny green toddlers with budding tusks tugging at his pants' legs, and chubby babies squealing as he swung them in his arms.

His smile fell. "No. We have no children in our clan. But I hope that soon we will."

No children? What had happened? I should have asked, but I didn't want us to discuss what was clearly such a heavy subject on our first date. Instead, I wondered what *our* children would look like. Could we even *have* children together? Would they be a lighter green? With smaller tusks? Shorter and less muscular?

"You should stand more like this."

He'd come over as I'd been daydreaming and began positioning me, turning me so my right side was forward, the knife low. As he went to move my legs, I turned and stabbed him in the ass with my rubber knife.

It was a gorgeous ass, begging to be stabbed...or grabbed with both hands.

"Attacking an unarmed opponent." He shook a finger at me, his eyes dancing with laughter. "Very dishonorable."

"You're almost twice my size. I've got to fight dirty, or I'll never win," I told him.

"You're supposed to learn, not win."

I raised my eyebrows and tilted my head at Ozar, thinking that he probably never learned anything without the desire to win lurking not so quietly in the background. He left my side, unbuckled the scabbard with the giant knife from his hip, and set it on the table.

"Do you always carry that?" I asked, wondering again if the blade was legal. It was a truly big knife, but then again, things had changed a lot with werewolves, demons, and other supernatural beings walking around the city streets.

"Of course. As well as my hand-axe." He smirked.

I tilted my head, my eyes roaming all over his body.

"Where are you keeping this axe? And why do you have it? Do you need to chop firewood in the middle of Baltimore? Are there random trees that need felling?"

"This is my hand-axe." He reached between his legs. "It is not just a weapon for close-range fighting, or a tool to cut trees. A hand-axe is sometimes a male body part meant for pleasure and breeding."

Oh. Naughty innuendo. And how typical that a guy would refer to his cock as a weapon.

"So I'm bringing a knife to an axe-fight?" I waved the words away as soon as I saw his confused look. "Never mind."

"I hope to use my hand-axe later," he teased. Then he took off his shirt, tossing it on the table on top of his scabbard.

My brain completely derailed. The guy was fucking huge. I'd known this from standing next to him and from leaning over him at my office, but seeing his naked arms, shoulders, and chest so close brought it all home to me. Humans would need to dedicate a substantial percentage of their waking hours to attain this orc's level of muscle mass. Actually, humans would probably need pharmaceutical help to be this buff. And they'd need to be severely dehydrated to look as cut and defined as the muscles Ozar was sporting. The guy was just a giant wall of sculpted granite, and I couldn't stop looking. My eyes traced the expanse of green skin, the scar that cut a diagonal across his ribs, the sprinkling of ebony hair that veed into a line that vanished at the pants slung low on his hips.

"Should I take off *my* shirt?" I finally managed to ask.

"If you do, then we will be doing something other than a knife-fighting lesson."

There was a hopeful note in his voice that made me grin. "Later," I told him. "When you get your hand-axe out."

He smirked, and I couldn't help but eye the bulge that strained the fly of his pants. It grew under my scrutiny, and I knew if I didn't steer this in a different direction, we were going to end up naked and in bed within the next ten minutes. Or less.

Did I want that? I did, but I barely knew this guy, and any time I'd rushed physical intimacy it seemed to drastically accelerate the end of a budding relationship. Not that my relationships where sex had been delayed fared any better.

"So, what do we do? Just start stabbing until someone begs for mercy?" I tried to twirl the knife around my fingers and ended up holding the blade. Good thing it was rubber.

I was kidding but Ozar seemed to seriously consider my suggestion.

"If you were trapped and had no other options, that approach might be good," he commented. "An attack from a small human female might surprise enough to disable or kill if you planned your strike well."

"Then—" Wait. What had he said? What had he called me? "Did...did you just call me a *female?*"

He froze. His eyes widened. "Yes." He drew the word out cautiously. "You *are* a female. A human female."

I bristled. I might have snarled a little. "I am a *woman*. Not a female. Woman."

He took a step back. "It is the same thing. A female bears young. I may not know much of human culture but there are males and females. There was a time when it was not uncommon for an orc to take a female human for a bride."

"Stop saying that word." It all came out through gritted

teeth. I was ready to stab him, except the rubber knife I held wouldn't do anything. Was this really how he saw women? Just females to breed and bear offspring?

Ozar held up his hands, dropping the rubber knife. His eyes grew even wider. "I am sorry, Jordan. I am very sorry. What am I saying wrong? Please tell me why you are so angry."

Sanity edged out my fury. He didn't know. He truly didn't know. This wasn't a red flag, it was at best a pale yellow one.

I sucked in a big breath and slowly blew it out. "The term 'female' is scientifically correct, but carries negative social connotations. It should be used for animals, not human women. When you call us, call *me* a female, it makes you sound like one of those incels."

He frowned. "Incels?"

Ugh. How did I explain this? "Men who are involuntarily celibate. They think they are entitled to have any attractive young woman they want and are angry and bitter that they cannot have any woman they choose. They think that women owe them sex and fidelity because they are men. They are arrogant, controlling assholes who offer nothing to any relationship because they feel that men are superior to women and that they don't need to do more than maybe provide minimal food, clothing, and shelter. They feel that women should act as servants and sex slaves to them. They call women females, because it degrades us, makes us on the level of an animal."

"I am not this incel male. I am an orc. The word we use in our language translates to 'female' in our English app. I did not know it would cause insult."

Of course he didn't. I was overreacting, jumping to the worst conclusion because in the past, I'd made excuses for a man's bad behavior and ended up hurt. It wasn't fair for me to think the worst of Ozar based on my past horrible dating choices.

"So...all human...women are to be called women. But others are females?" He asked, tilting his head in curiosity. "Demons, shifters, vampires, and elves are females?"

"No." I wrinkled my nose in thought. "Any sentient beings should be referred to as men and women. Unless they are non-binary. That's probably a lot to go into right now. Just remember that 'male' and 'female' are words only used for animals."

He nodded. "I will remember."

Damn it. I had totally ruined our sexy knife-fight vibe, but it was better to have this conversation now than later. Our first fight. Or misunderstanding. Either way, I knew his insult was unintentional and desperately wanted to get back to where we were, so I stepped in to him, jabbed his chest with my rubber knife, then kissed the spot where I'd fake-wounded him.

"I am forgiven?" His voice rumbled low. Uncertain. Hopeful. Turned on.

It was as if I felt his emotions floating through me. This connection between us...I didn't quite trust it yet, but it was like a heady drug taking over my body, my emotions, my very soul. There was danger ahead. This was a man who could break me. I'd be risking so much giving my heart to him.

But like a moth to a flame, I couldn't help myself.

"You are forgiven." I tilted my face up, closing my eyes and pursing my lips.

He didn't hesitate, lowering his head to kiss me. Once more, he began with a soft brush of his lips, those tusks smooth as cool ivory on my skin, then he pulled me to him, devouring my mouth, his tongue tangling with mine. I felt heat rise through me as I ran my hands over his chest, skating them around his sides to the hard muscles of his back. Then I stabbed him right where his kidneys should be.

"Dead!" I shouted, jumping back from him and raising my arms in triumph.

He laughed, the sound resonating from deep in his massive chest. "Clever fe...woman! Take every advantage in a fight. Although I would not be happy to know you used this tactic with someone other than me, I *would* be happy that you defeated your enemy and returned to me alive with his head as a trophy."

This orc was *not* an incel. Not at all.

Ozar lunged at me, taking me by surprise. The rubber knife swiped diagonally from my right shoulder to my left boob before I could jump back.

"Keep fighting," he commanded as he lunged again.

I swung my knife like a crazed woman, frantically retreating until I felt the wall at my back. He went to jab his knife into my stomach, and I dropped, hitting the floor hard and scrambling between the tree trunks of his legs. On the way out, I reached up and stabbed his ass.

"Good," he roared, swinging around and bending low to slash again.

The movement put him off balance, so I kicked his knee, rolling away before realizing what I'd done.

"Oh God! I'm sorry." I stood, holding my hands up. "Time out, time out! Did I hurt your knee?"

This wasn't the sexy knife-play I'd envisioned. Something about Ozar's size and skill had spiked my adrenaline and made me act as if I were really under attack.

He reached out, grabbed my wrist, and spun me around

until my back was against his front, held there within the bands of his muscled arms.

"No, you did not hurt my knee, but you would have disabled an attacker." He kissed my temple, then bent his head low to nibble gently on my neck. "I love that you are fierce and clever. You would not hesitate to protect yourself and your family. You would fight side by side with your mate, protecting your offspring."

I leaned against him, tilting my head to encourage him to continue with the kisses and bites. Compared to him, I was fragile and weak. I hadn't expected him to compliment me like this, and I had no doubt that he truly did believe me fierce and clever, a warrior worthy of fighting by an orc's side. Regular gym attendance and an athletic youth meant I wasn't built like the stereotypical nerdy dentist, but I didn't consider myself particularly buff. *Stephanie* was, but some of that came from her being a shifter. Willa was more likely than any of us to fit into a human-warrior role since she made her living as a personal trainer, but *me?*

"It's more than muscles," he murmured as he uncrossed his arms and slid his hands down my waist to my hips. "Fighting is about being smart, thinking quickly, and using your advantages."

I laughed, standing on my tip toes to rub the top of my butt against his very obvious erection. "This is the only advantage I have."

He chuckled. "You have more advantages than this."

Spinning me around again, he put his hands on my shoulders, holding me arms'-length from him. I pouted at the distance.

"Try to reach my shoulders," he commanded.

Right.

I put both arms forward like I was in a campy '60s zombie movie. The best I could do was grab his biceps.

"You will always have a shorter reach than your opponent," he told me. "So, you must reduce the distance. Your fighting needs to be close. Run forward quickly, before he has a chance to swing."

"Like this?" I rushed him, stabbing at his torso.

"Yes," he praised even as he blocked my swing with a rubber knife he'd quickly pulled from his waistband. "Get inside my reach and force me to be always acting in defense with no time for attack."

I tried to do as he said.

"That's good," he encouraged, as my swing arced through the space where he'd stood half a second ago.

"I didn't stab you, so it's *not* good." I tried again, still failing to hit him.

Sweat had made his muscles look like he'd oiled himself up for some weight-lifting contest. I was equally sweaty, but not as glamorous. My hair had partially come loose from the scrunchie I bundled it up in when we started to fight, making what was supposed to be a messy bun just plain messy. My clothes felt like they were glued to my chest and back. I probably *should* have taken my shirt off. In fact, taking my shirt off sounded like a damn good idea right now.

Time to put an end to this knife fight and get out the hand-axe.

I changed tactics, diving into his chest. It was like throwing myself against a boulder. He didn't budge but did wrap an arm around my waist to steady me. I took advantage of my position and stabbed him repeatedly in the back.

"There. You're dead. I killed you."

He tightened his grip, lowering his arm so I could feel

the hard length of him against my stomach. "It would take more than a few knife wounds to kill me."

No doubt, as evidenced by that scar across his ribs.

I stabbed him a few more times. "Have you bled out yet?"

"Still alive." Dropping his rubber knife, he reached up with his other hand, wrapped his fingers around the nape of my neck, and leaned down to kiss me.

Chapter 17

Ozar

Orc romances were an explosion of emotions and physical attraction. I'd expected my courtship of a human female to be slower in pace and more cerebral, even though I'd immediately felt that Jordan was as physically attracted to me as I was to her. From the moment she'd walked through my door, I'd sensed that Jordan was on the edge of sharing my furs. Indecision? Yes, but that glow in her eyes, the way she took every opportunity to touch me, how she'd leaned in to initiate our kiss on the couch—all of that gave me hope.

Everything was so much better than I'd hoped for. She'd honestly loved the food I'd prepared. I'd been so ready to feed her by hand as our customs dictated, but her uneasiness had me switch course, and it had been the right choice. The wine and the sweets she'd brought were incredible, and it seemed that she shared my unusual love of dairy products from her pledge to treat me to ice cream. When she'd offered to teach me to skate, I'd realized that my courtship had been scoring me points.

So I'd taken a chance and offered to teach her knife-play

with the rubber weapons I'd impulsively purchased for our clan. It had been a risky decision but had paid off. Her eyes sparkled. Her creamy skin gleamed with sweat. Her hair had escaped its ties and was damp and wild, teasing me with what she would look like after I'd brought her to ecstasy.

Jordan was a natural. Physically fit and with that agility and incredible instinct I'd observed in the human hockey team that had opposed us, she darted around, surpassing me with unexpected feints and attacks. My admiration for her grew by the second, and my hand-axe was solid with approval.

A female...*woman* that used every wile and advantage to win against an opponent? I didn't think I could love her any more, but tonight Jordan had won my heart and soul.

Once more, she dove forward into my arms. She'd employed this tactic so many times before and succeeded as she always had. I wrapped my arms around her, reveling in the softness of her against me, the sinewy muscles, the fragile bones in my embrace.

So delicate. So fierce. I didn't know if it was the mate bond or not, but I could not imagine ever spending my life with another.

I felt the jab of the rubber knife into my back and couldn't help but smile at her cleverness. She'd declared me dead, and even though I'd protested that it would take more than a few stabs to kill me, she was right. I was dead. I was hers for the taking, my very life in her soft hands.

I pulled back, a shudder coursing through me. "I would be honored if you would share my furs."

Jordan tilted her head, eyeing me quizzically.

"I want to take you to my bed and lay you upon my furs," I explained. "But I cannot do this without your permission and consent. If you allow, I will show you my dedication to giving you pleasure. I want you to be my fem —woman. And I hope that my skills on my furs will convince you that you will be the first in my every thought, that I will put your wants and needs above the mountains, the heavens, and the land."

Her eyes widened, her pupils darkening to the point that her eyes appeared nearly black.

"Yes. Consent. Full consent. I am enthusiastic and eagerly willing to share your furs," she said in a breathless whisper.

With a growl, I scooped her into my arms and lifted her into my embrace. Then I tossed her over my shoulder.

She burst out laughing. "I was thinking this was a bride-carry, but it's turned into me being carted off like a warrior's prize."

I hesitated, shifting my grip on her. "Is that unacceptable for an orc to do to a woman?"

She raked her nails across the skin of my back, hard enough for me to feel it, but light enough that she would not draw blood. "No. Take me to your furs, Ozar. And let's show each other the pleasure we can give and receive."

I hauled her into my bedroom, restraining myself enough to lay her gently on my fur-covered bed. Straddling her body, I gently removed her shirt and frowned at the seamless, lacy device wrapped around her breasts.

Jordan let out a breathy laugh and reached behind her back. "It clasps in the back. Then slides off my shoulders."

She did just that, releasing a pair of treasures that made my breath catch in my throat. Orc females...women, were known for large breasts that overflowed an orc's palms. Jordan's were small and firm. They curved upward with dark rose-colored nipples and a faint network of blue veins showing through the pale skin.

With a cool fingertip, she traced a line across my collarbone and down my sternum to tug at my waistband. "Take these off."

I obeyed, scooting off the bed to drop my pants and free my hand-axe before climbing back on the mattress to straddle her. "Your turn."

I wasn't about to let her up, so I took charge. Unbuttoning and unzipping her pants, I slid them off her hips only to realize I hadn't yet removed her footwear.

Jordan giggled. "Let me—"

"No." I fumbled around the tall boots, finally finding the zipper and removing them one at a time. Then I proceeded to take off her pants and her socks. Then the gorgeous blue lace garments that were the only fabric remaining between me and her soft skin.

"You're gorgeous," she murmured, running a hand down my chest once I'd made my way back onto the bed.

She was gorgeous, all creamy skin and lean muscle. I traced a finger across her collarbone, then leaned forward to kiss her. Not the slightest bit shy, Jordan gripped my waist with her hands, then wrapped her legs around my hips. My kiss deepened as I invaded her mouth with my tongue. But there was so much more of Jordan that I wanted to taste, that I wanted to touch. Breaking off my kiss, I brushed my tusks along her cheeks, nuzzling her as I inhaled her warm scent. Then I kissed down the soft skin of her neck, my tongue gently tasting her.

Her legs tightened around me and she lifted her hips off the bed, wiggling in an attempt to align herself with my hand-axe.

"No. Not yet." I'd meant that to be teasingly stern, but instead my breathy voice came out as pleading instead.

She laughed, but lowered her hips, her hands exploring my waist and abdomen as I made my way down her body, taking in her taste, her scent, and the texture of her skin.

With my hand on the small of her back, I pulled her close and knelt between her legs. She gasped as my tongue traced her slit, arching herself against me. Slowly, I explored her, noting every reaction and memorizing her most sensitive spots as well as whether those areas preferred a firm or feather-light touch. The taste of her was intoxicating, but it was her gasps and whimpers that drove all other thoughts from my mind but to bring her joy, to make her come against my tongue and fingers.

"Ozar!" She squirmed against me, arching her back. "I'm so close. Please. Please."

There was no denying her. Without hesitation, I moved my mouth to her nub, and swirled it with my tongue, licking and tasting. Then with my tongue on her clit, I plunged into her depths with my fingers, curling them slightly as I moved them in and out. She moaned, her legs shaking, tightening against the sides of my head. Then her muscles tightened around my fingers and with a strong pull of my mouth against her nub, the orgasm rolled through her. She shattered beneath me with a cry.

I paused, not wanting to overwhelm all the sensitive areas but anxious to make her come again. And again. I could do this all night. I could do this for the rest of my life and be perfectly happy. She was so warm and wet, and even though my balls ached with need, I was satisfied.

"*Grumem-esch-ach metanekan schlonakanap-tsknt*," I told her, meaning every word.

She blinked down at me, then reached her fingers to my

shoulders, urging me up along her body. I complied, feeling myself throb as she kissed me, her hands skating along my hips before moving between us.

"I want you inside me," she whispered, stretching her arms to slide her fingers along the shaft of my hand-axe.

"I want you to come many more times before." The protest wavered, my vision going white as her nimble fingers circled the head of my hand-axe.

"I want you inside me, and you're too much of a gentleman orc to deny a woman what she wants."

That saucy little smile on her face, her fingers on me, the smell of her sex surrounding me... She was right. I could never deny her what she wanted. Never.

So, I eased slowly into her, pulling out a little to tease her. At her protest, I slid all the way in until my pelvis touched hers. She clenched around me, her tightness, her heat embracing me.

I felt the strands of the mating bond strengthen, becoming ropes of steel that could never be broken. We were one. She was my mate. Mine.

My hands gripped her hips as I moved, slowly, then faster as she urged me on. Her hands gripped my waist, firmly at first, then with a frantic pressure that drove her nails into my skin.

Her moans, whimpers, breathy incoherent words intensified my already wild desire for her. With a final, erratic thrust, we both slid over the edge. The world around me disappeared, and all I knew was her—my love, my mate, the one who would forever hold me, body, heart, and soul.

Chapter 18

Jordan

I lay there, spent and drowsy, floating in a haze of affection and sexual bliss, curled up in Ozar's arms. I snuggled against his chest, breathing in his scent, then traced the big scar across his ribs. The muscles jumped under my light touch, and I smiled to know he was ticklish there.

"How did you get this?" I asked, my voice low and husky as though we were trying to be unnoticed, hiding away from the world.

"In a battle against a minotaur clan that was attempting to take the western section of our territory." His hand gently caressed my back. "I had defeated five of them and was fighting two more. When I turned to block a sword strike, the other minotaur tried to stab me with his horns. He would have gutted me, but I moved, and his horn tore me here along my ribs."

I sucked in a breath, my mind going down a rabbit hole of what would have happened had he died that day. I never would have met him. I never would have experienced...this.

"It must have been horrible," I said, my fingers still moving over the raised, bumpy flesh.

He grunted in agreement. "Three ribs broken and the muscle torn. Blood filled that lung and needed to be drained. It was five days before the healers could take the tube out and let the muscle fully heal. We orcs heal fast, but I needed to walk and move, or my lungs and muscles would have been forever damaged. I bled for ten more days, but the wound eventually healed."

"That's a very dangerous injury, even here with our medical technology," I told him. "The risk of pneumonia and infection are high."

He nodded. "Orcs rarely have infections and our healers are good, but I was lucky to have survived."

I leaned forward and kissed the scar, my lips trailing its length. "Do you have any others? Scars, that is?"

I felt him shrug. "Many small ones that are no longer visible. I do have one from when I was an orclet that is very embarrassing. Few know about it."

"Tell me." I looked up at him, intrigued.

He laughed. "My friends and I climbed Skilmagh Mountain. They turned back because it was almost dinner time and orc parents are very strict about family dinner. I was...conterous? Contras?"

"Contrary," I helpfully supplied.

"Contrary. I was a contrary orclet. If there was a rule, I was ready to break it."

"Seriously?" I couldn't imagine Ozar as a rebel. He seemed to be an orc of honor, whose word was his bond. I would have thought him the last orc to break the rules, even as a youngster.

Ozar laughed. "I broke *many* rules. And that day, I kept climbing to the summit long after my friends had gone home. The view was amazing. I could see clear to the sea. But the climb down was more difficult and slower, partly because it was close to sunset. I slipped and fell and went over a cliff. When I awoke, I was soaked in blood, my head ached, and everything was blurry."

The thought of a child Ozar with a serious head injury halfway up a mountain made tears spring up in my eyes. If he had been my child, I would have covered him in bubble wrap and locked him in his room for the rest of his life.

"I very slowly made my way down the mountain. It was not easy since my vision was affected, and it was so dark. I cried," he admitted. "My parents had organized a search party, and thankfully my father found me. He carried me home, swore the healer to secrecy, and told the others in the search party that I'd made it home on my own and was going to be confined to the house for weeks as a punishment."

"Was it so shameful to have a serious head injury from a fall? You were a child. I can't imagine why your father would need to keep your injury a secret," I said.

His smile held a hint of nostalgia. "It was considered a private matter, for my family to deal with. If the others had known how injured I was, it would have painted me as more than a rebel. It would have shown me to be a fool, who makes poor choices and can't be trusted to lead others. I can see that you don't understand, but what my father did allowed me to correct my mistake and eventually become a Clan Guardian."

I didn't understand, but I kept an open mind, knowing that his father had done the right thing according to their culture. And he'd saved Ozar, finding him and carrying him home where he could get immediate medical attention, then covering up his recuperation as though he'd been "grounded."

"Your mother must have been so worried." I couldn't help but think of how I'd feel in this woman's place, on the edge of a panic attack as others searched for her missing son.

"She was. My mother feared I'd never make it to adulthood after that. It's one reason I have no siblings." He sighed and the sound was full of grief. "She and my father delayed having more orclets, planning to wait until I was older. But then she died."

I reached up to cup his face. "Oh God! Ozar, I'm so sorry."

He swallowed hard. "An illness swept among the orc clans and while all it touched became sick, more females died then males. It is why we have no children in our clan. The females who survived were young and have only been recently wed, so we hope to have children soon. We were lucky, though. Some clans only have two or three females that survived the plague; others have none at all that survived."

"I'm so sorry," I repeated, unable to process how horrible this must have been for him and the others. "There was nothing your healers could do?"

He shook his head. "They tried but could not stop the spread or the deaths."

I stroked his cheeks, leaning forward to plant a soft kiss on his jaw. "Tell me about her."

His smile was wistful. "Her parents were metal workers from a clan in one of the western mountain ranges. She was strong and gifted in her family's art. I still have some of the knives she made me as well as the war hammer she'd made and gifted to my father on their wedding day. She was truly an equal to my father, his forever mate. The moment he set his eyes on her, he knew no other would hold his heart."

"That's so romantic," I whispered.

He nodded. "Her hair was as dark as mine, but hers had curls. She was tall, and very muscular from working with metal. Three times she won the stone toss contest at our fall festival and was legendary across the region in *Xalba*, which is similar to your wrestling sport. As a mother, she always encouraged me, inspired me, and pushed me to expand my talents. While my father was a major influence in my becoming a Guardian, a commander of our clan, my mother encouraged me to explore what other orcs would consider silly hobbies."

"Like what?" I asked.

Ozar smiled fondly. "I never had her skill at making blades, but she showed me how to use metal to create small creatures for amusement and decoration. On her name-day one year, I gifted her a tiny bird I'd forged. Her name was Gruexal, which is what the little bird is called in our language."

Gruexal. I wondered if they were like the chickadees that visited my backyard feeder. It seemed odd for a tall and muscular woman to be named after a tiny bird, but I imagined as a baby it had seemed fitting.

"That's such a wonderful gift for your mother." It wasn't a surprise that Ozar was so thoughtful when it came to gifts. He'd gone to such lengths to make tonight special. He'd given me a Starbuck's gift card, and he barely knew me. I did love my coffee, so his guess had been correct. I bit back a smile, thinking of how he had presented me his teeth in an engagement ring box. For such a large, intimidating guy, he was sweet, sensitive, and funny. Even his grumpy side was endearing.

Reaching up, Ozar took my hands in his. His eyes were serious as they met mine.

"I came here hoping to find a bride, Jordan. We are compatible with humans and can have orclets with them. I hoped to somehow find a human woman, wed her, and have the family I never could have back home."

My heart ached for Ozar. I grieved for his mother and the others who'd died of this horrible illness. And I absolutely understood why he had chosen to come here. Companionship. Partnership. Love. Creating a life together, a family.

He wanted commitment. He wanted to settle down. And while I'd thought those things would never happen for me, I found myself wanting the same. With Ozar.

"Does that bother you, Jordan?" He let go of my hand to take a lock of my hair in his fingers, weaving it between them. "That I want a bride? A family?"

I snuggled against his chest as he played with my hair. "It's not so different than what we humans want."

"But what do *you* want?" he pressed.

"I...I don't know." I hesitated, biting back the words my heart wanted to shout to the heavens. It hadn't even been a week since I'd met this orc. And while everything so far had been hearts and flowers—and a Starbuck's gift card—there could be a minefield ahead that I never suspected.

"So how many of these children are you thinking?" I lifted my head to smile up at him.

"As many as the mountain gods gift me. As many as my wife agrees to bear for me."

"That's not an answer." I poked him just below his ribs. "How many do *you* want?"

He smiled sheepishly. "Six. It's a good number, and the players needed for a *Ghug* team."

I rolled my eyes. "And you'll expect your wife to do all the childrearing in addition to cooking and cleaning and sitting by your feet every night?"

I tried to keep my tone light, but Ozar scowled. "Males...*men* are equal parents. We provide for our families and pamper our wives. We teach our orclets. We provide for their basic care, which involves cleaning and feeding and arguing over bedtimes."

"Good. My dad was a very involved parent, so I've got high expectations."

"Tell me about him." Ozar's voice held a soft nostalgic note that nearly brought tears to my eyes. "Tell me about your family, about growing up as a human child."

I did. I told him stories of my teacher father, and my mom who'd been a sort of administrative do-all at a local scrapyard. We'd had an ancient car held together mostly by duct tape, and a split-level rancher for our home. Both parents spent most weekends fixing what had broken in either the car or the house, and neither my brother nor I had owned the latest version of any electronic game. But we always had food, and we always were warm. Summer vacations were an excursion to tent camp for a week in a national park, or a week at Aunt Jan and Uncle Mark's house only a few miles from the Jersey shore, and winter breaks were spent skiing at whatever east coast spot my parents got the best deal at. We weren't poor, just solidly middle class. And my parents had spent our youth being carefully frugal, which meant that both my brother and I had been able to go to college with only a minimal amount of student loans.

My loans were bigger thanks to the dental doctorate my parents hadn't budgeted for, but I still was absolutely grateful for their shrewd financial planning.

I told him how Dad had given me my love of the theater, and my inability to go for a hike without coming home with my pockets full of interesting rocks, how my mom collected old cookbooks and would spring strange side dishes of aspic and mysterious casseroles on us every week or so for dinner. About how she'd gotten me my first car from the salvage yard and secretly worked on it with Dad for months before presenting it to me for my eighteenth birthday.

I must have rambled on for an hour, but Ozar never interrupted. He continued to play with my hair, his breathing rhythmic and his chest rising and falling under my cheek.

Lifting my head, I met his eyes. "Sorry. It's probably not a great first-date move to give you a not-so-abridged version of my childhood."

"Courtship is learning about each other," he said. "Physically and emotionally. These things either bring us closer, or pull us apart, but it's important to show all of us to each other. Seeing the beauty is easy, but love is about knowing the scars, too."

I traced the groove in his chest again. "I love your scars, even though how you got this one still scares me."

He slid me up along his body and kissed me, softly, slowly, with tenderness.

"Now it is your turn. Show me *your* scars." His smile was teasing.

"They aren't from any battles," I warned him.

"Are any of them from falling off a cliff as a child?"

I chuckled. "No. Well, there's this one on my knee from when I came off a skateboard as a teen."

"I will slay the skateboard beast for daring to harm you."

He was teasing again, and I absolutely loved it.

"Then there's this one on my thumb. I was trying to slice a stale bagel, and the knife slipped. Oh, and the one on my forehead from when I was little and decided to slide down the stairs on an outdoor lounge-chair mattress, like it was a toboggan."

He examined each scar, tutting over every one as if they'd been life-threatening injuries. Most of them were tiny, barely visible after all this time. It's not like I'd had a minotaur try to impale me or had fallen off a cliff.

"Stay the night with me," he murmured, pulling me against his chest once more. "We can eat cannoli and the rest of the cake for breakfast."

I sighed, wanting nothing more than to spend the night in his arms. Tomorrow too. Maybe the whole week. But when you owned your own practice and were the only dentist, you were in the office rain or shine, sexy new boyfriend or not.

"I've got some early patients tomorrow. I want to stay with you, really I do, but I need to be up early, showered, and in the office for work, and that won't happen if I'm here having sex with you all night and eating sugar for breakfast."

I expected an argument or pouting, but instead he kissed my forehead, then lightly patted my ass. "Next time?"

"Next time," I promised, thinking that I should bring a change of clothes. Maybe leave some toiletries in his bathroom and take over a drawer in his dresser with some basic clothing. Yes, we were moving at the speed of light in this relationship, but I honestly had no worries at all. Ozar was incredible. No red flags. No friction. No doubts.

I'd never thought that an orc would be my soulmate, but that's what this felt like.

With incredible regret, I eased out of his arms and out

of his bed. It took me a while to find my clothing—especially since I was distracted by Ozar watching me with a satisfied smile on his face. I pulled on my bra, a wrinkled shirt, and pants, stuffing my underwear in one pocket. When I was slipping shoes on, Ozar finally rolled out of his bed. He stood and stretched, and my eyes were riveted by the perfection of his body.

"I will walk you to your car," he informed me in a tone that brooked no argument.

"Like that?" I waved a hand to indicate his undressed state. "First, it's close to freezing out there. Second, nudity in public is a crime, and I don't want to watch the police cart you off."

He smiled, then reached down and pulled on his pants. The fact that he had a half-mast going on meant he required some adjustments when zipping up.

"Better." I figured he probably didn't feel cold the way we humans did. The orc's normal body temperature felt about one hundred degrees, and he had grown up in an area with high mountains, so our mild fall weather in Baltimore was probably nothing out of the ordinary for him.

I gathered up my purse, deciding I'd leave the bottle of white wine here along with the desserts. I hadn't seen anything but the beer in his fridge, and it would be nice to have a decent Pino Grigio here when I came back. Ozar walked with me down the stairs, his hand gently on my lower back. I'd decided to carry my heels, so it was far easier going down than climbing up. Once we were on the ground floor, I balanced with a hand against Ozar as I put my heels on. Then he walked with me to where I'd parked my car, his eyes scanning our surroundings and his hand still protectively on my back. He waited as I climbed in and started the car, remaining vigilant even as I pulled away from the curb and down the street.

It was a little weird. I'd always been self-sufficient, bristling at any hint that I might not be able to take care of myself even in a large city that had far more crime than where I'd grown up. But Ozar's attention and watchfulness didn't feel like a slight on my strength or ability to take care of myself. It felt no different than a friend, a loved one who looked out for me just as I'd look out for him, a partnership where two people knew each other's strengths and weaknesses and gratefully allowed the other to help where they could.

I was falling fast. I was falling in love with this orc. And that scared me. Would this be a love that flamed out as quickly as it caught fire? That worry hovered around the edges of my bliss, but I knew that nothing except time would prove my fears right or wrong.

Chapter 19

Ozar

I slept fitfully without Jordan in bed beside me. Her scent was all over my sheets, all over me. Every time I'd doze off, I'd reach for her, only to wake up in a panic when I found the bed empty beside me.

She was my mate, my soul-bond, the only woman I'd ever love. When she'd consented to our joining, I'd hesitated, knowing she had no idea what that action would mean for me. But in the end, I'd done it, willing to risk a lifetime of painful solitude for even a moment of that joyous connection.

I knew she'd felt it too. I could see it in her eyes. Sex between us had been more than just an orgasm for her. But she was human, and I wasn't sure if the mate bond meant the same thing for them as it did for orcs.

I'd take what I could get, though. Whatever love she was capable of giving. And if her love was fleeting, not for forever, then I'd watch her leave. And I'd thank the mountain gods for every moment she was mine.

After tossing and turning, I finally got out of bed, finished off the pine-nut cake, and made a pot of coffee. My bed furs smelled of Jordan. My skin smelled of Jordan. Faint traces of her scent lingered all over my apartment. I debated taking a shower but decided to leave her scent on my skin for a little while longer. At six, I dressed, grabbed the box of leftover cannoli, and headed over to the stadium.

Just like yesterday, Ugwyll was on the ice. This time he wasn't on his back, cursing with his legs and arms splayed out. I watched as he made his way around the rink, pushing a puck side to side in front of him with the stick. After two laps, he slowed and turned around, then began to skate backward, still maneuvering the puck as he went. These laps were punctuated with several stops and starts, but the orc managed it without falling or running into anything. I kept watching, letting Ugwyll have his solo time on the ice, then I went to the locker room to get my gear on.

By the time I joined him, Ugwyll was circling the far goal, shooting from a line of pucks as he came around. As I skated over, he halted and turned to face me. Lifting his head, he sniffed the air then put out his hand for a fist-bump.

I completed the human-style acknowledgement.

"When's the wedding?" he asked, a broad grin on his face.

I shifted on my skates. "We're not at the wedding stage yet. Humans take these things slower. I've got more wooing to do, but things are looking promising."

Ugwyll gave me a worried look, then shot another puck into the net. "You locked your mate bond with her. Why would you do that when you weren't sure she was ready for that kind of commitment?"

Because I am a love-sick idiot. "There will be no other for me. I'd rather complete the mate bond and experience a moment of that bliss, than risk having a partial bond for the rest of my life."

Ugwyll sighed and hit another puck. "If she doesn't return the mate bond—if she doesn't even *feel* the mate bond, then you risk a painful, short life. Personally, I'd rather live with a partial bond."

"I will accept whatever she can give," I said with far more confidence than I felt. "I will continue to woo her, and if she commits to be my bride, that will be enough."

I wanted her to feel the mate bond and accept it, but I would take whatever the human equivalent of that might be. If the worst happened and she decided she wanted another... I clenched my teeth, not wanting to think about that. Last night, I'd thought I could accept that horrible alternative, but now I wasn't so sure. Not that I'd have any choice. I would never force her to be my bride.

"She's moving into your den, though?" Ugwyll asked.

I winced. "Not yet."

The other orc turned to face me. "Please at least tell me she remained in your furs until sunup."

"She had commitments to her patients this morning," I protested. "And she didn't have appropriate clothing with her for her employment."

Ugwyll's eyebrows shot up, and he tilted his head.

"She is taking me to eat ice cream tonight. She also wants to skate with me." I left out the teaching me part because I was feeling rather pitiful as it was. "She also said she wanted to take me to other places in the city."

The other orc stared at me in surprise. "*She's* wooing *you?* A female is wooing a male?"

I nodded. "I think this is the way humans do things. But it must mean that she has similar feelings. She is attracted to me. She's been receptive and even eager. I satisfied her several times last night and she was reluctant to leave."

Ugwyll shrugged and turned back to the pucks. "You're a *wyndall*'s ass, and I shouldn't care whether you get hurt or not, but I do. You're absolutely committed to this female without knowing if her feelings for you will last a week or a month or forever."

He was right, but I couldn't be any other way. I'd been bold and strategic in warfare, and while I'd never put my team in unnecessary danger, I'd always been willing to take great personal risk. I could do no different with Jordan.

Pushing my doubts and fears to the back of my mind, I did laps around the ice as Ugwyll had done, attempting to skate backward and failing miserably. I did better at getting the puck in the net, even managing to speed up and aim my shots to specific sections of the goal. Two hours later, Ugwyll and I were both sweaty and tired—and the only two who'd been on the ice this morning.

"Where is the rest of the team?" I asked during one of our water breaks.

"In bed? Playing games in the locker room? Tugging their hand-axes?" Ugwyll speculated.

"We have a game in two days," I fretted. "I don't know about you, but I don't want to continue to be the fool."

Ugwyll snorted. "These humans have been playing this game for much of their lives. We're not going to win against them."

"I don't need to win; I just need to make them respect us." I waved a hand at the empty stadium seats. "I want those who watch to respect us as well."

"Me too," Ugwyll confessed. "But that's going to take more than just the two of us."

I tossed my empty water bottle into the plastic bin. "Then let's go try to recruit some hockey players."

Ugwyll followed me off the ice and into the locker room where I found six of our teammates lounging around. Whacking my stick against one of the lockers got their attention.

"You're interrupting my nap, you *wyndall's* ass," Eng said as he leaned his head back against the wall and closed his eyes.

"Team meeting," I yelled. "Now. On the ice. Put your skates on and get out there."

Bwat ignored me and kept looking at his phone. Eng yawned and folded his arms across his chest. Two of the guys eyed me nervously and grabbed their skates. The other two edged toward the door.

Ugwyll slapped his stick across the doorway and glared at the two potential deserters. "Get. Your. Skates. On."

They hustled back to the benches and did as he said, which left me to deal with Bwat and Eng.

"Bwat," I barked out. "Meeting. On the ice. Skates on."

He looked up from his phone. "Do you know that hockey players are known for their foul language, taunts to members of the opposing team, and fights in the middle of the games?"

My eyebrows shot up, impressed that Bwat had been researching something related to hockey and not just generic human culture and language.

"That's...helpful," I reluctantly admitted.

"The main curse word used is 'fuck,'" he continued. "If we want to be taken seriously at this hockey game thing, then we need to say 'fuck' a lot."

I nodded. "Everyone say 'fuck' as often as you can in your communications. Bwat, you're in charge of coming up with appropriate taunts for us to use against the opposing team. Now, skates on and hit the ice. That means you too, Eng."

Eng rolled his eyes. "Why should I bother? No fuck-one cares if we win or lose, if we try or not. If there's no payoff, why exert any effort?"

"No *fucking* one," Bwat corrected. "When it's describing—"

"There *is* a payoff." I grabbed my box of leftover cannoli from my locker. "Now everyone get on the ice."

Eng muttered something about how my finding a mate and getting laid had pushed me over the edge of insanity, but he did as I said and strapped on his skates.

We all went onto the ice, Ugwyll and I moving with a whole lot more ease than the other orcs who hadn't been practicing. Just to torture them, I skated to the center and waited for them to slip and slide their way to me. Eng, as usual, refused to cross the ice and instead stomped his way around the wall until he was as close to us as he could get while still clinging to the barrier.

"Our owner might not care if we win or lose," I began. "Some fans might not care if we win or lose—although many do. But no matter what others' expectations are, *we* need to care. We need to stop being the fools they come to laugh at, and be the players they respect, the ones they cheer for."

"We're not going to win," Ugwyll reminded me. "I can barely fuck-skate, and you're not much better."

"*Fucking* skate," Bwat interrupted.

I scowled. "We might lose, but we'll make the other team pay for every point in fuck-blood."

"*Fucking* blood," Bwat corrected. "Because—"

"We try to win. We try to score every point we can. But

our primary goal is to make the other team respect us. And we do that by hitting them hard and often."

For the first time, probably in his life, Eng looked mildly interested. "You want us to beat the shit out of the human team?"

"Yes but make it look like a series of unfortunate accidents," I explained. "We're clumsy and don't know how to skate, so we slam into them, trip them, accidentally sucker punch them while flailing around for balance, rack them in their hand-axes with our sticks."

Ugwyll grinned. "I can do that."

"They'll put us in the box if we fight," Bwat said.

I shrugged. "So, we go in the box. I don't care as long as we rattle them."

"How hard can we hit them?" Eng asked.

"Don't kill them or cause any serious injuries," I said. "Bruises, blood, concussion, a few knocked-out teeth are all okay."

"Can we shoot the puck into their faces?" one of the other orcs asked.

"I don't think the rules allow that," Bwat replied.

I didn't give a fuck about the rules right now. "No, if we have control of the puck, we need to try to score. Don't waste that opportunity caving a human's skull in."

"You said we could hit them with sticks?" another orc asked. "You mentioned nailing them in the hand-axe with our stick, but what if we take out their knees or break a few ribs with one?"

"You might break a stick doing that. And Sizzle gets mad when we break the sticks," Bwat warned.

"Fuck Sizzle." I must have said that right because Bwat didn't correct me. "Now we're all going to skate and practice. If you stick around until I say so, then I'll give you some of my cannoli."

"What's a cannoli?" Eng asked.

"This." I pulled one out of the box and took a big bite.

Everyone sniffed, then edged closer.

"That looks good," Bwat said, wiping some drool from the edge of his mouth.

"It *is* good," I told him. "Jordan brought me some last night."

"Smells like cannoli wasn't the only thing you were eating last night." Eng smirked.

The others all laughed, the ones closest to me thumping my shoulders and offering congratulations. A few asked about wedding dates and when I planned to go back home. I managed to avoid answering any of those questions, not wanting to go through the same judgement I'd gotten from Ugwyll.

"So, we get a cannoli if we stay on the ice until you say so?" Eng asked, getting back to business.

"Yes, but you need to skate and try to hit pucks into the nets," I told him. "Standing on the wall doesn't count."

"Do the pucks have to actually go into the net?" Bwat asked.

"No, but you have to try." Finishing the cannoli, I closed up the box and gestured to everyone. "Three laps. Go. Now."

They all groaned, but surprisingly did as I said— even Eng.

"I already worked my fuck off this morning," Ugwyll complained. "Why do I have to do twice the workout?"

"Do you want the crowd chanting your name as our best player? Or do you want them chanting, 'loser, loser'?"

A muscle in the orc's jaw twitched.

"Do you want women lined up outside the locker room, ready to ride your hand-axe? Or do you want to spend your life sleeping alone, with only your right hand for comfort?"

"Fine," Ugwyll snarled as he skated out to the edge of the rink. He immediately passed three of his teammates, and I saw everyone's fighting spirit kick in as they tried to catch him.

After their three laps, I separated them into groups of two so Ugwyll and I could hit pucks to each of them, practicing our passing and receiving skills. I had no idea what I was doing, but I'd watched the human team during our game and had figured out what abilities we absolutely had to develop in order to be competitive—or at least not look like total idiots on the ice.

The guys were staying on their feet and starting to get reasonably good at slowly passing the puck, even though they often missed ones hit their way. Bwat was just skating out to retrieve his puck when our owner walked onto the ice.

I'd only seen Escellates Johnson a handful of times since he'd shown up to offer us a job on his new hockey team, and now I'd seen him twice in two days—and I felt deep down in my bones that his increased interest in our daily activities wasn't a good thing.

"What the fuck are you doing?" the demon shouted.

It seemed that human hockey players weren't the only ones who employed liberal use of the word "fuck."

"Practice," Ugwyll shouted back.

The demon made a "pfft" noise. "You don't need to fucking practice. I don't care if you can skate or hit the puck. Go back to the locker room and play checkers or something."

He left, and the moment he was off the ice, all the orcs turned to stare at me.

"Keep practicing. We're *not* going to go play checkers until we're done here," I told them, whacking the puck to Bwat. "We're going to practice, no matter what that demon says. We might work for him, but he hired us to play hockey, and we're going to play fucking hockey."

"Yeah!" Ugwyll roared, raising his stick in the air. The others did the same, except for Eng, who just rolled his eyes.

"We're going to make the other team respect us," I yelled over their shouts. "We're going to have fans cheering us on. And by the end of the season, we're going to fucking win a game."

Everyone except for Eng raised their sticks at that, slamming them down on the ice as they shouted in agreement.

"We're not fools, no matter what the demon says," I added once they'd calmed down.

"They'll respect us. And that demon is going to respect us too," Ugwyll said.

"Yes! That fuckwad of a demon is going to respect us," Bwat agreed.

"Fuckwad." Eng nodded from where he'd been standing against the wall for most of the practice.

"Yeah. All of the fuckwads are going to respect us." I turned and hit a puck into the net. "Thirty more minutes of practice, then we'll all eat cannoli."

And *then* we'd play checkers.

Chapter 20

Jordan

Leaving Ozar last night had been so difficult. I'd been attracted to him the moment I'd seen him on the ice during their game, and that attraction had grown each time I'd seen him since. It wasn't just lust. I *liked* him. He was interesting. He made me laugh. He made me feel admired, wanted, cherished...loved.

There had been some pretty good sex in my past, but nothing had rocked my world like last night with Ozar. It wasn't just magnetism and orgasms though. Something had happened when we'd had sex, and I just couldn't explain it. Everything had clicked together in a split second—physical ecstasy, emotional connection, admiration, respect, affection. Love.

And an odd linking that felt as if my very soul was now connected to his.

All I'd wanted to do was spend the night in his arms, cancel my appointments for the next day, and remain in his bed until the sun went down again. But I was a professional who had her own practice, and there were patients who'd planned their days around their appointments. As much as my heart wanted otherwise, my responsibilities and commitments weren't something I took lightly.

I knew that Ozar respected that—even admired that in me.

He'd watched me drive off, and I'd looked at him in my rearview mirror until I could no longer see him. Distance seemed to be no hinderance to the strange connection we'd forged last night, though. I'd felt those silken tethers as I'd slept, as I'd driven to the gym, even as I'd showered and dressed, and driven to work.

This was crazy. I couldn't be so in love after just one date, after having known him for only a few days. Was this some orc magic? The elves were said to have the ability to enthrall a human's mind. Did orcs have the same sort of skill? Or was this truly a case of fated, insta-love, soulmates that the romance novels I read on vacation extolled?

As flustered as I was over last night, I still kept to my schedule. Thankfully Judy had managed to keep her stomach contents inside her this morning. I spent forty minutes at the gym running on the treadmill before showering and getting into the office early. I was just pouring a cup of coffee before my first appointment when Shanelle came into the back to tell me that Abby was up front.

Concerned that my friend's unplanned visit meant she had a dental emergency, I left my coffee and rushed up front.

"Crown?" I asked her. "Pain? Broken tooth?"

"Nope. I'm here about this." She slapped a copy of the *Baltimore Sun* on the front counter.

Part of my morning routine involved reading the paper, but it was the online version and since I had a limited amount of time, I tended to hit certain sections and call it done. Clearly, I'd missed an important article, because on the Sunday edition sitting on the counter was a picture of Ozar in a playground full of children.

I grabbed the paper and read the article, looking up at Abby with wide eyes once I was done.

"Are your ovaries exploding?" she asked me. "Because mine sure as hell are."

"I might be having triplets just reading this," I replied.

"No birth control can hold up against this kind of thing," she added.

"Which might be a problem given what we were up to after dinner last night," I told her.

Abby's mouth fell open, then she screamed, throwing both hands in the air before hugging me. It was weird. I mean, good sex *was* a cause for celebration, but it wasn't like I'd won the Nobel Prize or cured cancer or anything.

"I've got a good feeling about this orc," she told me. "Especially after seeing this article in the *Sun*. Kids, Jordan. The guy loves kids. And they love him."

My face heated up. It's not that I had a ticking biological clock, but at thirty, I had frequently thought about what my future might hold. The career was a given, but my daydreams had often included a husband and had sometimes included a couple of children. It wasn't top of my priority list, but the knowledge that Ozar was so easy and friendly with little humans warmed my heart. The guy had a whole lot of checks in the positive column, and this was a giant addition to those traits I admired in a guy.

"Sooo." Abby glanced over at Shanelle, who was obviously listening as she pretended to go through patient charts. "How *was* last night?"

"Good." I eyed Shanelle, trying to keep this suitable for work. "We had a lovely dinner. He's a good cook and an excellent host. We played with some rubber knives, then… relaxed."

Abby snorted at "relaxed." "Wait…rubber *knives*? Is that a euphemism for something naughty?"

"No, he had rubber weapons, and he and I sparred. He was teaching me self-defense."

Shanelle had given up all pretense of doing work at this point.

"That's a good excuse for the two of you to get handsy with each other. Not that you need an excuse," Abby said.

"It absolutely led to romance." I'd lowered my voice, but Shanelle edged closer. Which was fine. My going on a date with Ozar wasn't something I wanted to hide, but with her listening, I wasn't about to tell Abby anything about the spicy part of the evening.

"Meet me and Willa after work for drinks and tell us all the details," Abby insisted. "The guy cooks. He loves kids. I'm hoping the mattress aerobics add yet one more plus in the tally."

There were a whole lot of pluses in the tally so far. A whole lot.

"I'm going to the hockey stadium after work to skate with Ozar, then I wanted to take him for ice cream. He's never had it. Can you imagine?"

"A world without ice cream? No, I can't imagine that at all. What sort of hell is his homeland?" Abby teased. "And are you sure you want to skate with him? We saw him at the hockey game. He's liable to fall and crush you within the first five seconds."

"He was better than anyone else on the team," I reminded her. "I'm going to teach him a few things because he wants to try to make something of this team. And yes, I trust him not to fall on me."

She quirked an eyebrow. "He *wants to make something of the team?* Make *what* of the team? Because the Tusks are not going to be walking home with the cup anytime in the next decade. They're a group of orcs who don't know how to play hockey and have never skated before up against teams that have been on the ice before they could walk and who have lived and breathed hockey from grade school on."

"If they score a point occasionally, it's a start," I argued. "Don't underestimate them. They're clearly gifted when it comes to physical activities, and they learn quickly. They might suck this year, but they'll suck less each game they play, and I'm sure that within a few years, they might actually win a game. Maybe two."

"Hopeless optimist," Abby teased. "But I'm not going to argue with you about your boyfriend's hockey team—especially because I'm longing for some comped tickets."

The door opened, and my first patient for the day came in so I waved my hands at Abby. "I've gotta get back to work. Tomorrow night I'll meet you girls for happy hour and spill the goods."

My friend pushed the paper toward me. "Keep that. I'm not sure Willa or I can wait for tomorrow night to hear the juicy details, but we'll try."

The rest of the day was a crazed blur. I had my implant procedures, an emergency root canal, and a tricky set of enamels that caused me to work late. Just as I was getting ready to finish for the evening, the rep with DarRafi Inc. returned my call about their supplying me with medical equipment for the nonhuman population. It made me extra late leaving the office, but by the end of the day, we had an approved account with DarRafi and they had emailed me a link with access to a library of training videos on their products.

If my plans had been anything besides spending time with Ozar, I would have canceled and spent the evening watching those videos and going through the catalogue of products. Instead, I rushed home and changed—four times. It wasn't easy finding an outfit that would work for skating, but was still sexy—but not *too* sexy. I got the feeling that Ozar's affections mirrored mine, but just in case, I didn't want to make our relationship all about the physical.

Even though I fully intended on inviting him home to my house tonight.

Finally, I decided on black yoga tights paired with the Baltimore Tusks jersey I'd ordered after last weekend's game layered over a long-sleeve silk T-shirt. It was warm enough that I skipped the coat and threw on a down-filled vest instead. Sticking my phone and my wallet into a small cross-body bag, I blew the dust off my skates and left for the stadium.

The parking lot was vacant aside from a couple of cars, and the main entrance was locked up tight with those folding metal security gates. I walked left to a gray, window-less door and pressed the intercom button.

There was a pause while the guard checked my name, then I heard a *click*. I wrestled the heavy door open and walked across a small room to the guard booth. I slid my ID through the slot in the probably bulletproof glass. The man checked it, radioed for Ozar, then slid my ID back to me.

I'd barely stuffed it back into my purse before another door opened, a huge green, muscle-bound orc blocking the entrance.

"Jordan."

Chapter 21

Jordan

I felt a flush of heat at his deep voice. Memories filled my mind from last night—his hands on my body, his mouth on my body, that noise of satisfaction that he'd made deep in his throat when I came. But I wanted more than sex from this orc, so I pushed those tantalizing thoughts to the back of my mind and held up my skates.

"Ready to have some fun?" What was meant to come out light and flirty, instead was husky and full of innuendo.

"By fun, do you mean am I ready to have you ride my hand-axe?" His gaze roamed over my body. "Yes, I am. Should our fun happen before or after we skate?"

Both? I sucked in a breath at the idea. "You pick."

He considered his options for a few, long seconds. "After. If we do the sex now, that's all we'll be doing for the rest of the night. When you are naked on my furs, I know I will lack the resolve to do anything but pleasure you until the sun rises."

That sounded amazing to me, but getting to know him outside the bedroom was important, too.

"Then I agree. We should skate first, eat some ice cream, and see where the night takes us."

The night was going to take us straight back to either his house or mine.

I followed him through the door, just now realizing that the guard was an amused audience to our conversation. The stadium was empty and mostly dark except for the hallway leading down to the team areas. Everything was industrial in design with concrete floors, block walls, and ductwork overhead. Ozar gave me a brief tour, showing me the luxurious—and empty—gym, as well as the meeting room and offices. Then he ushered me into the team's locker room. I hesitated a brief second, not sure if I'd find a bunch of naked orcs inside or not.

The locker room was just as empty as every other room and hallway we'd been through. It was pretty standard. Walls of metal lockers with wooden benches lined up parallel to them in the center of the room. Toward the back, an open doorway led to tiled showers, the individual spots separated by half-walls. To the right, another open doorway led to toilet stalls with urinals and sinks. Glancing around, I noticed there were not the expected motivational posters on the walls, no action pictures, not even graffiti. This could have been an upscale high school locker room instead of one for an NHL team.

I was more disappointed that it was immaculately clean, with the faint scent of lemony cleaning product, than anything else. Not that I wanted to be hit with the aroma of damp, dirty socks, but there should be that warm odor of muscular athletes. And orc sweat had a fresh, earthy smell that from last night's knife fight I'd discovered really turned me on.

Ozar opened a locker and pulled out a pair of skates. As

we sat side by side to lace up our footwear, I broke our companionable silence.

"None of you wear pads or helmets when you play?"

He grunted. "Except for the goalie, no. Only the humans wear those."

I hesitated, not sure if that was because they weren't as susceptible to injury, or because their pride kept them from wearing safety gear.

"We only have pants, skates, and our sticks," he continued. "And a plastic device to protect our hand-axe from impact. We didn't used to have those, but after Morag took a puck between the legs, the team owner provided them."

I sucked in a horrified breath, and Ozar grimaced.

"Morag's walnuts were the size of oranges for days, and his hand-axe still curves to the right."

"Oh God!" I couldn't imagine how painful that had been. "What did the team doctor say? Did Morag need to see a specialist? Is he still on medical leave?"

Ozar frowned, processing my flurry of questions before answering. "He will play this next game. The healers here aren't familiar with orc medicine, so most of the team doesn't go to see human medics or go to human healing facilities."

Once more, I thought of the lack of medical and dental providers for nonhumans. Demons and angels wouldn't need such things, but other beings clearly did. It was horrible that Morag had suffered when there should have been trained individuals to ease his pain and ensure he suffered no lasting or permanent damage from the injury.

"Could an orc healer come here to train the human doctors on your medicines and treatments for illness or injury?" I asked, truly worried about one of them becoming seriously hurt and dying before we could figure out appropriate medical care.

Ozar shot me a puzzled glance. "Why? We are tough and heal quickly. Even at home, we seldom go to a healer."

"But you're not at home; you're here where the human healers don't know how to treat you," I countered. "At the very least, the team doctor should understand orc anatomy and medical treatments. Right now, there are only a few dozen orcs among us humans, give or take, but what happens when there are hundreds of orcs living here? Or thousands?"

His puzzled expression remained. "There will never be hundreds or thousands of orcs here. We come in groups and will probably return home before a new group arrives."

I felt a strange heaviness in my chest at his words. What did he mean "return home"? Were they tourists or on some sort of supernatural H1B visa, forced into jobs by the angels? Was this thing between Ozar and me the equivalent of a holiday fling? Did he plan to eventually thank me for a lovely time, and go home?

Or maybe I'd misunderstood, and the whole "return home" thing was a hundred years from now. I had no idea how long orcs lived, or what constituted a vacation for them.

It was ridiculous to be thinking of that when I hadn't known Ozar for even a week. Still, it stuck in my mind. I couldn't let myself fall for him, couldn't get serious when I wasn't sure if he intended on sticking around for at least my lifetime.

"I'd feel a lot better if you and the team wore the same level of safety gear that's provided to the humans," I told him, forcing my thoughts back to the team and the potential for injury during a game.

He grunted. "No. We do not wear helmets and pads."

I bent to finish tying my laces, hiding my eye roll. Stubborn, grumpy male.

Skates on, I stood and waited for Ozar to do the same. He was a little wobbly getting to his feet, and put a hand out on the wall as he stomped his way out of the locker room and down the tunnel to the ice. I followed, watching him and wondering what I could do to make him more balanced and confident on his skates. After our mock knife fight last night, I knew that the huge orc was incredibly light on his feet and could move with a nimble grace that belied his size. There was no reason for him to be so unsteady now, aside from perhaps a lack of experience.

Ozar hesitated at the end of the tunnel where the carpet met the ice, then launched himself forward. As I watched him, I noted that he had improved since the game last weekend. He still tended to stomp his blades into the ice and propel himself forward by digging the toe of one skate into the ice and using it to push off. Wincing, I felt sorry for whoever maintained the surface, wondering how much time the Zamboni needed to spend going over the ice to fix the divots the orcs dug out each day.

I glided onto the ice, slowly circling around to get a sense of my surroundings and skating backward a few feet before stopping. The stands were dark, but the ice was lit like it was game day. For a second, I felt the exhilaration of what it must be like to play professionally for a packed crowd. I imagined the roar of the crowd, the echoing din of the announcer, the adrenaline rush as teammates took the ice. I loved my career and wouldn't have made a different choice if I'd had the opportunity to do it all over again, but for a brief second, I wished I could have been good enough to play any sport in the big leagues.

Then I looked over at Ozar, who was watching me with his dark eyes.

"How do you make that look so easy? How are you so graceful on these knife-blades?"

"I've been skating since I was little. Growing up, we all skated. Winters were long and cold in Buffalo, and we bundled up to hit the ice after school almost every day. We'd play pickup games of hockey or make up fancy figure skating routines and pretend we were in the Winter Olympics. Even when I went to college, I would occasionally go to a rink. Skating is just something I've always done. Kind of like knife and sword fighting is for you."

He nodded. "I had practice weapons since I could walk. All the orcs in my tribe did. Females...uh, women and men, we all were trained to hunt and fight from an early age."

I held out my hand. "You showed me how to fight. Let me show you how to skate."

He scowled, then nodded and slid his way over to me with that stab-and-push motion. He did get a lot of distance and speed with each push, but the chunks flying off the ice were nearly giving me a heart attack.

When he was close enough, he took my hand.

"We're not going to skate fast," I told him. "This isn't a game. It's not a competition. Pretend that we're dancing, slow and smooth."

"Orcs do not dance slow and smooth," he informed me. "We leap and spin and fling ourselves into each other."

Lord. It sounded like the mosh pit at the metal concerts I'd been to.

"Then pretend like we're making love. Having sex, slow and smooth. Every movement will be coordinated between us. Just follow my lead."

His dark eyes were intense as they bored into mine.

"Orc males lead when they have sex, but for you, my human fe...woman, I will follow."

From a human, that would have sounded insufferably arrogant, but from Ozar, it came across as tender and vulnerable.

I turned so his front was to my back and positioned his hands on my waist. "Angle your left skate like this and gently push yourself forward on the right skate. Don't dig in with the toe like you were doing before, just angle, give some gentle pressure on the blade, then push."

Even though I couldn't see him behind me, I could feel that he mirrored my movement.

"Now with your right skate pointing straight ahead, return the left blade to the ice and shift your weight to that leg, angling and pushing off with your right foot."

We quickly fell into a rhythm, gliding slowly around the ice. The second lap we increased speed, and during the third lap, I pulled Ozar's hands from my waist, darting forward to put a little space between us before spinning around and taking his hands in mine. We circled that way, me skating backward and Ozar guiding our path as we increased speed once more.

I let go of his hands and cut to the right. He skated forward a few paces, then surprised me by turning around to skate backward. The turn involved a shower of ice chips, but he used the technique I just taught him to smoothly glide in reverse.

For an hour we skated, not like hockey players, but like a couple enjoying a romantic evening on the ice. By the time we headed back to the locker room, Ozar could coordinate his movements alongside mine, twirling me around in front of him to his other side, then turning to skate backward while holding my hands. It amazed me how quickly he'd caught on and how much innate talent he'd shown. Maybe my wishful thinking was right, and this hockey team might be able to hold their own against a human team by the end of the season.

After changing out of our skates, we headed into the night. The mild temperature of the day had vanished with the sun, and a cold breeze was sliding clouds across the stars and moon. I shivered, and Ozar pulled me against him, the warmth of his body and his arm slung across my shoulders, chasing away the chill. It probably wasn't an ideal night for ice cream, but since I'd enjoy a cup of mint chip even if I lived in Antarctica, we were going for ice cream.

The teen girl behind the counter looked up as we walked in, then did a double take. Her eyes widened as she took in the giant orc. Ozar had needed to duck his head coming through the doorway and turn slightly sideways so his shoulders could fit through the opening. His eyes widened as well, but it was because he'd seen the rows of ice cream in the long, counter-topped freezer.

"Is all this iced cream?"

His voice held so much awe that I laughed. "Most of it. Some are sherbet, which doesn't include milk. You can try a taste of any before you order."

Ozar walked over to the freezer cases and shook his head. "This is amazing. What is your favorite?"

"I've always been a mint chip fan, but I also love rocky road and dark chocolate with strawberries and almonds sprinkled on top."

I watched as he carefully perused the containers. Ozar was so refreshingly open about his emotions. His excitement over trying ice cream, his willingness to let me teach him to skate. And that picture of him playing with children at the park. This guy seemed too good to be true, but the optimist inside of me wanted to believe that this was real, so I did.

"I saw the article in the paper. The one where you were at Patterson Park with the kids this weekend," I told him.

His shoulders tightened. "Orc males teach their young to fight and survive. They don't usually indulge in play with them."

I put a hand on his arm. "That's a shame. I love it when a man finds joy in playing with children. I love it when a man talks to me about his hopes and dreams, about his fears. I love it when a man shares both the good memories of his past and the bad."

His shoulders relaxed. Then he said, "I like milk."

It sounded like a confession, and I got the idea that enjoying a glass of milk was another thing orc men weren't supposed to do.

"We're all about our dairy products here," I told him. "Cheese. Cream sauces. Lattes. We even have non-dairy options for humans who can't easily digest real milk. No matter your age, everyone deserves to enjoy milk products. Including ice cream."

He pointed a finger at one of the tubs of ice cream. "Can I try that one?"

"Sure can." The girl dug a tiny pink spoon into the mocha-fudge swirl and held it out to Ozar. The orc tasted it and made a low growling noise deep in his throat.

"I want that one," he announced.

I smiled. "Cone or cup?" He looked confused at the question, so I told the girl to put two scoops in a waffle cone and make me the same with mint chip.

And as we walked out of the ice cream shop with our cones, I grabbed Ozar's hand and led him toward the Inner Harbor.

Chapter 22

Ozar

We had nothing at home that tasted at all like this ice cream. It was cold and sweet and rich. The milky flavor melded with the taste of vanilla and the burst of chocolate in the thick ribbon swirl. I'd assumed the cone was some sort of biodegradable container, but when Jordan bit into hers, I did the same. The crunch was a perfect complement to the ice cream, and I quickly devoured the treat, vowing to stock my freezer at home with this delicious stuff.

From her occasional shiver, I could tell that Jordan's vest was not keeping her warm, so I was doing my best to snuggle her close to my heat. The last few days had been magical. *Tonight* was magical. Skating with Jordan had transformed a job-related training exercise into a...a dance. Not the orc sort of dance, but a gentle lovemaking waltz.

Orcs didn't waltz, but I'd watched the video Bwat had sent me a few days ago and while I'd at first scoffed at the two humans twirling about together, I changed my mind. There was a beauty in a soft touch, in the synergy of movement, in the coming together and the tease of edging apart.

I'd come here expecting to grab a breeding-age female and drag her home. I hadn't thought I would find my mate in a human woman. I hadn't planned to discover a whole side of myself I'd never known. And I hadn't expected to revel in human culture, to find myself thinking there were some customs and beliefs here that I liked better than the ones back home.

Jordan steered me down toward the waterside where the unbelievably wide Patapsco River was the backdrop for restaurants, bars, and an aquarium that Jordan promised to take me to. It was too dark to use one of the paddle boats to explore the water, so that was filed away for a future outing. Instead, we sat on a bench, holding hands and talking as we watched the distant lights of the ships heading to the city's freight harbor.

It was a romantic evening, Jordan curled against me with my arm around her shoulders. The crowd thinned as we left our bench and veered away from the waterfront into a commercial area. The buildings were clearly vacant this time of the night and the streetlights did little to lighten the shadows of the massive buildings.

"We should head back." Jordan glanced around nervously.

I let her pick the route, keeping her tucked under my arm as I admired the giant stone buildings reaching toward the heavens like the mountain peaks back home.

Two human males in dark clothing approached, and Jordan stiffened. I'd been told there were areas of the city where ruffians congregated to conduct illegal transactions, and while some places might be safe during the day, they weren't so at night. This was clearly one of the latter from Jordan's reaction. But she'd brought me here. She trusted that she'd be safe with me nearby. Of course she would be.

I'd protect her at all costs. That trust was a valuable gift, and one I wouldn't take lightly.

The male with a shaved head stopped, looking over at us. I squared my shoulders, standing up straight and fixing him with a hard stare. Two humans would be easy to subdue. I wouldn't even need to use my knife.

"Hey! You're that orc from the hockey team, aren't you?" the bald human asked as he approached, his companion a few steps behind.

"I am Ozar with the Baltimore Tusks," I confirmed.

"You guys suck," the other male with long braids informed me.

I nodded. "We do. But that doesn't mean I can't cave your skull in with one punch."

Jordan sucked in a breath, clutching my arm. "Don't," she whispered in a warning.

Braided male scowled and lifted his baggy shirt to reveal the handle of a pistol protruding from the waistband of his pants.

When I'd arrived here, I'd wrongfully assumed that humans still used knives and swords, and their only projectile weaponry was the bow and arrow. Bwat's research had enlightened us all on the advancements the humans had made. Their explosive devices and firearms rivaled the magical weaponry we'd faced when battling the fae. I knew this pistol was not something I should underestimate. It might only disable me, but it might kill Jordan before I could make a move to protect her.

Thankfully, it didn't come to that.

"Idiot." Bald male slapped the back of braided-hair male's head. "You think killing a cop causes problems? Killing a hockey player is gonna get you the chair, if the local boys don't blow your head off first. This is Baltimore.

We love our Old Bay Seasoning, our state flag, steamed crabs, and our sports teams."

Braided-hair male dipped his head. "Sorry, man."

"We have no problems between us," I reassured him.

"Can I get a picture?" Bald male asked me as he pulled a cell phone from his back pocket.

I gave Jordan's hand a reassuring squeeze and walked toward the man. Bald male handed his phone to braided-hair male and stood beside me, an arm slung over my shoulder. Human males were quite a bit shorter than orcs, so he had to press against my side and extend his arm to its full length to reach my shoulder. I hunched down a bit to lessen the height difference and adopted the pose of the tuskless, clearly exiled orc in a movie called *The Hulk*. Bald male scowled, extending the hand not clutching my shoulder and arranging his fingers in what I assumed was some sort of clan symbol.

Braided-hair male took several pictures, then handed the phone over and pulled his own from his pocket. "Me too. If that's okay."

I nodded, assuming a slightly different pose for the second human. Afterward, the two males examined their photographs and excitedly commented on them. I turned to check in with Jordan, who seemed less apprehensive and more bemused.

"Thanks, man." Bald male extended his hand and slapped it against mine, so I did the same. "You want some Molly? On the house this time."

I glanced around, not seeing any nearby human woman who might be named Molly.

"No, thank you," I told him, walking to stand beside Jordan. "This woman is my mate. I have no need of Molly."

The two males laughed, then made several comments

speculating on my prowess and appeal toward females, warning me against something called a "honey trap." Then they left and I wrapped my arm around Jordan's shoulder again, snugging her into my side.

"That..." She laughed. It was a weak sound of relief more than amusement. "The Inner Harbor is so much better than it used to be a decade ago, but occasionally I forget that Baltimore is a big city, and even safe areas can be dangerous in the dark."

I straightened my spine and let out a low growl, scanning our surroundings "You have nothing to fear when you are with me. It would be my honor to die defending you."

She laughed again, this time with real amusement. "I don't want you to die, whether you're defending me or not. And I really don't like the idea that you would be bringing a knife to a gun fight, no matter how large or well-crafted that knife might be."

"You shouldn't have to fear walking in your home city, at day or at night," I told her.

"True, but that's life in a big city." Jordan sighed. "Buffalo had some bad spots as well, but it's smaller than Baltimore and I grew up there. That probably didn't mean I was any safer, but it felt that way."

I nodded. "In my clan, we all know each other, but some of the larger clans have the same problems with violence. And when we visit another clan to sell, buy, or trade, we are always more aware and suspicious. Theft and attack are easier to justify when the victim is a stranger or an orc from an outside clan."

"There are so many humans that everyone seems to be an outsider," she said. "Small, rural towns might know the locals, but there are strangers even there. It's not like you can know all two thousand residents of the town and surrounding areas. And Baltimore? Heck, I barely know my own neighbors.”

I grunted, suddenly worried about Jordan living alone in her house. Would she move into my den if I asked? If only there was a way to let it be known that her and her residence were under my protection.

“Oh!” Jordan paused to grin up at me. “I’ve been meaning to tease you about the picture in the paper—the one with you and the children on the playground equipment at Patterson Park.”

I shrugged, feeling a bit embarrassed. “I love children.”

Jordan’s grin widened. “I can tell, both from the picture and the fact that you have a bunch of rubber weapons to take back home. And you want six of your own?”

“Only if my bride also wants six.” I tugged her along, relieved that she hadn’t thought the fact that I had played with strangers’ children in the park to be odd. “Our team owner also saw the picture, and he has informed me that part of my duties is to interact with all human children. I am to talk to those who attend our games, and those I encounter throughout my day. It is not work,” I confessed. “Finding opportunities to make children happy brings me joy.”

“That’s amazing.” She smiled up at me, and the admiration in her eyes made me catch my breath. “In comparison, my annual contribution toward Children’s Hospital seems lame.”

“Help to those who suffer is always valuable,” I assured her. “And I know you help many humans in your career.”

She shrugged. “I know I make a difference in my patient’s lives, but I also earn a respectable living from that, so it’s not selfless charity. I *do* volunteer quarterly at a free dental clinic, though, and I love that I’m helping children and our at-risk community there. And I'm expanding my practice to supernatural dentistry! It's so exciting, and you're to thank for that idea. There are so many nonhumans in our city and in the area, and they deserve the same services as humans."

It was my turn to look at her in admiration. "You remind me of my mother in how strong your heart is, in how you pursue your passion with all of your being."

Pink flooded her cheeks. "Thank you. That's a very flattering comparison. I do love my career. It's an important part of my life and of who I am. A lot of people think it's silly to be this enthusiastic about dentistry, especially reconstructive work, but it means everything to me."

"Tusks are very important to orcs," I told her. "We may not focus more than basic care on our other teeth, but our tusks are our heritage. Both males and females have them. They are different for each of us, and a symbol of who we are. The loss of a tusk, or of both of our tusks, is like the loss of self. We admire warriors who have been so disfigured in battle, but those warriors never accept that they are whole, and they always worry they are not truly an orc without both tusks."

She nodded. "We have soldiers that have lost limbs in battle, and they struggle as well. The more I talk with you, Ozar, the more I realize we aren't so different. There are culture things, of course, but deep down, I think both of our people want the same things from life."

I felt dizzy at this revelation from her. "It is true. We want a home. A rewarding career. Someone to share our lives with in partnership. Children to love and to carry on our legacy. Peace and a clan where our needs are met, where our friends and family surround us."

Her smile was warm. "Exactly. Except with humans, a

good life doesn't always involve a marriage or include children."

It was as if I'd slammed into a mountain. I sucked in a breath and looked down into her face, feeling terror deep inside my chest. "No marriage? No children?"

She shrugged, not seeming to register the horror that had seized my very soul. "I haven't had the best of luck in my past relationships, but I do hope marriage might still be in my future. As for children...I'm thirty. And I'm really focused on my career right now. I'm not opposed to having kids, but it's not at the top of my wish-list. Maybe just one. Or two. But if I don't have children, it's okay. My brother has two adorable daughters that I can spoil rotten, and although he hasn't said anything, I'm pretty sure he and Whitney have another on the way. So far, I've been happy being their favorite Aunt Jordan and not having any kids of my own."

I couldn't breathe. I just couldn't breathe. Every couple in our clan had given birth to orclets. There were solitary orcs who were without offspring, but those who had married always reproduced. The idea that there might be marriage without children was inconceivable.

"I have always wanted children," I said, terrified that this pronouncement would spell the end of my relationship with Jordan. "Many children. Although as an only child, I accept that sometimes the fates have other plans."

"Yes, six, as I remember." She squeezed my hand. "I'll admit being a little frightened at the idea of that many kids. I'd be happy with one or two, but more than that is kind of terrifying."

One. Or two. My dreams of half a dozen orclets crumbled to dust. Jordan was my mate. There would be no other but her. And if having her meant giving up my dreams of a large family then...

I wasn't sure I *could* give up those dreams.

"What about your career back home?" Jordan asked. "Do you travel a lot?"

It took a few seconds for me to push the panic over children aside. "I specialize in taking a troop into the outskirts of our territory to ensure the major roads and the forests are clear of rogues and dangerous predators. I also accompany our traders during the season when we journey to other clans to sell our wares and purchase items for the clan. I am often away from the clan most of the year."

She eyed me. "So, it's like our military. You're always deployed and on the move. Seldom home with your family. I'd think having a wife and six kids would interfere with that, especially since you told me you wanted to be an involved parent."

The reality of that sank into me. "In the past, I didn't have a family beyond my father to be home with. Things would change if I was married and had children."

"Would they?" she asked. "Because—I'll be honest here—things wouldn't change that much for me if I decided to have a child. A few months after giving birth, I'd return to work, and my baby would have a nanny or some sort of childcare. I'd still be there in the evenings and morning, and on the weekends, but I wouldn't ever want to give up my practice. Would you give up your role as Clan Guardian when you had children?"

I'd never really thought of that. I mean, yes, I'd expected to be sent out less frequently with a new bride and a young orclet at home, but as my children aged and my marriage solidified, I had always thought my wife would remain home while I renewed my pre-marriage Guardian duties.

But now that Jordan had put that all into words, it seemed terribly unfair—both to my children and my bride.

It wasn't what I wanted. As much as I loved being a Clan Guardian, spending time with my mate and my children was more important to me.

"I think a change would be needed if I were to marry and have children," I confessed. "I *want* to be a major influence in my orclets' lives, and I don't want to spend that much time away from my bride unless there is an immediate danger to the clan."

"I could thankfully schedule my work around any major events, like parent-teacher conferences or sick days," she mused. "And my practice isn't open on major holidays or weekends, so I would be able to attend Little League games or ballet recitals or whatever. I'd make it work, but there's no way I could ever give up the business I worked so hard to create."

It sounded reasonable but worry wound through me. We'd just met, and these discussions were a way for us to explore our values and priorities. But I hadn't expected us to want such different things.

"This must be such a huge change for you," she commented. "Coming to a strange land, living among the humans, and playing hockey for a professional team. That's a long way from being Guardian for your clan."

I breathed out, trying to push the worry aside and talk about less emotionally charged topics.

"It hasn't been easy," I confessed. "Things are very different here. I cannot deny that I am often homesick, but I do find the human world intriguing and enjoyable even with the differences. Plus, I am glad to have met you. Meeting you has made all the difficulties worthwhile."

She sucked in a breath, her eyes huge as she looked up at me. "Really?"

"With you, I'm the orc I want to be." I dropped my arm from her shoulder and entwined my fingers with hers. "I'm more than a Clan Guardian. All the expectations of what I need to be as an orc, as someone who fights for the clan's territory. None of that matters right now. With you, I can be..."

"Tender? Thoughtful? Caring? Silly and playful?"

I nodded.

"I love those things about you, Ozar. I like that you're more than a warrior, a scowling gruff leader. Don't get me wrong, the whole powerful protector thing is sexy, but it's not as sexy to me as the orc who bought play weapons for his clan's future children and proceeded to have a mock battle with me in his apartment. Or the orc who plays with human kids in the park. I'm...I'm not the most flexible person in the world. I have my routine, and I like to keep to that. But with you? I might feel safe and in control enough to explore the idea of something different than what I'd pictured as my future."

My heart soared, and I gazed into her eyes.

"Spend the night at my house?" She smiled and her hand squeezed mine. "Please? My home isn't far from here, and I can always Uber to get my car at the stadium tomorrow morning before work."

All I heard was the invitation to spend the night with her. Which I quickly accepted.

Chapter 23

Jordan

The Ozar and Judy meeting did not go as well as I'd hoped. During the short walk back to my house I'd made small talk while silently fretting that my weirdo cat would not react well to my orc boyfriend. Judy judged, and she sometimes judged harshly. It had taken Abby and Willa over a month to win her over and she still glared and occasionally hissed at them the first five minutes they entered my house. My cat had never been a fan of men, and I had a horrible premonition about how she'd react to a seven-foot-tall orc walking into my home.

My little black-and-white tuxedo cat had raced toward me the moment I'd opened the door, then screeched to a halt, arched her back, and hissed as soon as she'd seen Ozar.

"This is my cat, Judy. She'll follow you around, glaring and hissing at you because she rules this house and humans live to serve her."

Ozar tilted his head as he regarded the cat, clearly not understanding my humor.

"Most humans are very attached to their pets," I explained as I picked up the still-upset Judy. "People who love cats love them, eccentricities and all. They are independent animals. Some are aloof, others are varying degrees of affectionate creatures. Their amazing speed, agility, and hunting ability make them a fun companion that doesn't require the level of attention and care that other animals like dogs do."

"Judy is a hunter?" He sounded awed by that fact. "But she is so small."

I motioned for him to follow me as I carried Judy into the kitchen, petting the cat to reassure her that Ozar was no threat. "Cats mostly hunt birds, small rodents, and bugs. They were initially domesticated to kill vermin in human settlements, homes, and buildings. Mice and rats can carry diseases that spread to humans, so having cats not only protected our food from being eaten but reduced the risk of their owners catching those diseases."

"It is incredible that humans have developed a relationship with such an animal."

He reached out toward Judy, who flattened her ears and batted him with her paw. She hadn't unsheathed her claws, so I was hoping that was a sign she didn't hate Ozar as much as she hated the rest of my visitors.

I put the cat down and she backed away, her fur puffed out and her eyes fixed on the orc.

"Your best bet is to respect her space and just ignore her," I advised as I pulled a bottle of merlot from the wine rack. "In time, she'll learn to tolerate your presence."

We settled on the sofa with glasses of wine and talked about his campaigns in protecting his clan back home. I told him about my more challenging dentistry cases and my ideas about serving our supernatural community. The whole time Judy sat on the coffee table in front of us, her tail twitching, and her narrowed gaze fixed on the orc. It made our little make-out session a little weird, so when Ozar began to unhook my bra, I stopped him.

"Upstairs," I ordered in a breathless voice.

We climbed the steps, pausing on the way up to kiss and discard bits of clothing while Judy stalked behind us. The cat ducked between our legs as we crossed the threshold into my bedroom. I broke off mid-kiss with my bra hanging off one elbow and my pants sliding down my hips to grab Judy and evict her. The cat stared at me with huge, incredulous eyes as I closed the door in her face and went back to the orc.

I loved my cat, but there were some things she didn't need to be watching. And Ozar tossing me on the bed and yanking my underwear low enough to fit his face between my thighs was one of those things.

I awoke at five a.m. as was typical, but this morning I stretched lazily, enjoying every sore muscle and feeling incredibly satisfied. If I'd been a cat, I would have purred.

Cat.

I bolted upright, realizing that I'd never let Judy into the bedroom last night. Ozar and I had made love over and over until I'd collapsed in a boneless heap, falling into a deep slumber with my head nestled against his chest. Judy always slept on my bed, and I'd learned that any variation in her schedule resulted in all sorts of little gifts distributed like landmines around my house.

Judy wasn't the only thing missing from my bed. The spot where Ozar had been when I'd fallen into a sexually satisfied sleep was empty. I'd kinda hoped to wake up with him and maybe enjoy some sleepy, morning sex, but I tamped down my disappointment. This whole thing was new for us, and I didn't know what he might have on his schedule today. I hadn't slept the night at his house, so I could hardly fault him for leaving. And for all I knew, he might have kissed me goodbye and had a short conversation with me before he'd headed out. I slept like the dead, and it wouldn't be the first time I'd mumbled something incoherently in the middle of the night and not remembered it in the morning.

Rolling out of bed, I threw on an oversized T-shirt, took care of my morning biological functions, and brushed my teeth. Whatever Judy had pooped and vomited on my floor would still be there after I'd finished my routine.

Finally, I opened the door and, being careful to look where I stepped, headed downstairs. Before I hit the landing, I heard a riot of sounds coming from my kitchen. Scrabbling of claws on the flooring. Chirping and squawking, and the trill of Judy having the time of her life. I raced down the final stairs, sure that my cat was after some bird that had managed to find its way into my house.

Sliding to a stop at the entrance to my kitchen, my mouth fell open. Ozar sat on one of the bar stools that flanked the kitchen island. He held the small mirror from my downstairs bathroom and was redirecting sunlight from it into a beam on the kitchen floor. Judy was chasing that beam of light like her very life depended on catching and killing it.

My cat still might consider Ozar a dangerous character worthy of suspicion, but right now, any anxiety on her part had been washed away by the thrill of the hunt.

"She is a truly ferocious creature." Ozar smiled over at

me. "I wish we had cats back home. I would have loved to have a companion like Judy when I was an orclet."

My ovaries had exploded when I saw the picture of him with the kids at Patterson Park, but now it was my heart that exploded. He liked my judgy cat. He was playing with my judgy cat.

I sniffed.

And he'd made coffee.

"I have a laser pointer toy that she loves to play with," I told him. "It shines a red dot, and she chases it all over the room. And she loves the mice toys as well. They're made of wool and stuffed with catnip. They're all in a basket by the back door."

He set the mirror on the counter, much to Judy's dismay, and poured me a mug of coffee. "I believe she was upset at being shut out of your bedroom last night. I found some....*mukaw* outside the door when I awoke."

I hadn't seen the *mukaw* outside my door—which I assumed translated to either puke or poop—which meant Ozar must have cleaned it up. How embarrassing that he'd awoken to that. Although he didn't seem particularly bothered by my cat's anxious digestive issues.

"I understand what you mean about serving the cat." He handed me the coffee, then picked up his own, half-empty mug. "I have just met this creature, yet I already have cleaned up her *mukaw*, entertained her, and provided her with morning food."

I nearly choked on my coffee. "The cat kibble? Please tell me you gave her the cat kibble from the container."

He frowned and consulted his phone. "Uhh, there is specific food for cats? Because Judy told me she was to eat the container of shredded chicken from your refrigerator."

Chicken wasn't as bad as a bowl of milk or a dozen raw

eggs, although I had planned to use that container for the topping of my lunch salads.

"She'll be okay," I reassured Ozar. "Judy has a sensitive stomach, so you can't rely on her opinion of what's good for her. I do give her chicken as a treat, but only after she's had her kibble."

He nodded. "I will remember that for next time."

Next time. I loved that. My weirdo cat hadn't scared him away. *I* hadn't scared him away. Yet.

Walking forward, I put my mug of coffee on the counter and wedged myself between his legs. Wrapping my arms around his neck, I pulled him toward me.

"Do you have anything planned for this morning?" I asked, pressing myself against him.

"No," he murmured before lowering his lips to mine.

I was a woman who lived by her schedule, just like my cat. I got up at the same time each morning. I ate the same breakfast. I went to the gym, then went to work. But today? Today was when I was going to deviate from that reassuring schedule.

And I was going to relish every moment of my illicit morning with Ozar. Even if it made me late to work.

Chapter 24

Jordan

I wasn't late to work, but it was a close call.

And it was one hundred percent worth it. Ozar and I had made love in the kitchen, then he'd cooked breakfast while I'd showered and changed. We'd eaten something that reminded me of a hash skillet, chatting about what we had planned for the day. He had a home game Friday night and told me he'd arrange for my friends and I to attend, with special tickets waiting at the on-call booth of the arena.

The Uber dropped him off in front of his apartment building, then took me to the stadium to retrieve my car. I'd texted the girls and had just enough time to grab another coffee at a drive-through before heading to the office.

Yeah. Three coffees before eight. Don't judge me.

During my morning appointments, I couldn't help my mind from drifting back to last night with Ozar. Under that grumpy exterior was a kind, caring, sensitive orc. While performing scaling and root planing on Mrs. Jackson, I kept thinking of Ozar and his homeland. His voice had softened when he spoke of his family and friends, of his childhood, of his mother who he'd lost at such a young age. He clearly loved it there, and it must have been difficult for him to come here in search of a better life. I wasn't sure I could have been that brave if I'd been in his position.

Three patients later, I was taking a much-needed break when Mike walked up to my office.

"Jordan, there's someone up front for a consult, but it's not about her, it's about her partner." Mike sounded disapproving. He'd framed the word "partner" in air-quotes, so it might be that the potential client was in a same-sex relationship, or it could be that she was a supernatural. Probably the latter since I'd never known Mike to be snobby about any of our LGBTQ patients.

I'd never been able to tell shifters apart from humans by sight, and I valued confidentiality, so I'd added an optional question on my appointment form for clients to self-identify. Humans hadn't bothered to answer the question so far, but the three shifters who'd stopped by my office yesterday had.

They'd all been excited, curious, and openly thrilled that we were potentially going to be offering services for them, even if my staff had to inform them of a three-month wait for non-emergency appointments.

I had a few minutes between appointments, so I told Mike to have someone escort the woman to my office. The woman who walked in was tall with a lanky athletic build and short sandy-blond hair. Freckles dotted her skin, and I immediately envisioned her as a Ralph Lauren model.

"I'm Jaq." She held out her hand and gave me a shy smile before sitting in the chair across from me. "I'm a Nephilim with a werewolf pack in West Virginia, and I was told you were taking on supernatural clients?"

I nodded. "But if you're a Nephilim, then..."

This was awkward. Nephilim were half angel and half human, and from what I'd read and what Stephanie had told me, they were incredibly powerful. They could shift into multiple forms, although most had a favorite. Some had the ability to heal others, and they had defensive and offensive fighting capabilities similar to angels. They were immortal and were revered in whatever shifter pack they chose to make their home.

"Oh, I'm here for my mate, not for me." Her smile showed adorable dimples on her cheeks. "My mate is a vampire who had her fangs removed before she was old enough to be able to regenerate them."

I blinked, trying to process this. "She lost her *fangs?*"

Jaq nodded. "I realize that technology might not be advanced enough for her to have fully functional implants, but I'd really like to gift her with ones that would at least serve a cosmetic purpose."

That had to be one of the most romantic things I'd ever heard. But then again, my passion was teeth, so I was a little skewed in my ideas of what a romantic gift might be.

"It should be easy to mold new fangs, but I'm assuming she'd prefer for them to retract like her original fangs did?"

Jaq nodded. "Would that be possible?"

Hmm. The deep cavities where the vampire's original fangs retracted should still be there, or hopefully easily reconstructed if there was any damage. There were muscles involved in the retraction, though, and I wasn't sure if they'd been torn or badly injured in the removal of the original teeth.

"Do you know if her glands are intact?" Vampires had two sets of glands, the most important of which was one that rendered their "donor" numb and in a state of euphoria during feeding. The other set of glands was rarely used. It transmitted the virus that caused the vampiric mutation. Turning a human was not often done, but I assumed Jaq's mate would like to have the option if it was possible to restore either function.

Jaq blushed. "I know that the feeding glands are intact and still connected to the cavities. I don't know if the glands that carry the virus are though. I'm not sure if she was old enough for them to have formed."

I nodded, making some notes. The glands to transmit the virus tended to form between one hundred and two hundred years after the human was turned. It varied quite a bit depending on the siring vampire. The very few naturally born vampires had these glands upon birth, so from Jaq's comment, it was clear her partner was a turned rather than born vampire.

"So cosmetic fangs at a minimum. Retractable if the muscles are still functional. And glandular attachment if possible." I chewed on the end of the pen. "Would she want to use them to feed?"

From the diagrams I'd studied, fangs had a hollow cavity that drew blood up and across an oral/nasal space before allowing it to go down the vampire's throat. The majority of the blood consumed was still directly from mouth to throat, but this cavity allowed a vampire an enhanced sense of smell and taste during feeding that added to the experience.

Jaq's eyes widened. "Could...is that even possible?"

I smiled at her. "It's not *impossible*. All of this is going to depend on the damage done to her muscles, bone, and glandular systems, the technology available, and the surgical success. Ideally, I'd love for all of her functions to be returned, but we need to be realistic."

"I know she'd be happy just having those gaps in her

teeth filled," Jaq admitted. "Anything else is a darned miracle. I've saved money. I'll pay whatever you want to restore anything you can. And I'll be forever in your debt. None of the other dentists have been willing to do this. When I heard you might be, I drove straight down here."

"I'll need to research this a bit in terms of what's available," I warned her. "And I'll need to examine your partner to see if there are additional surgeries needed to prepare her for the implants. Would it spoil your surprise to bring her in for an appointment?"

Jaq beamed. "No. If you can't make them retract, can you make them slightly longer than the usual canine teeth? She wouldn't want them full length unless they can retract, but just a little longer would make her feel like more of a vampire, if you know what I mean."

I completely understood. "Have the front desk schedule her for an evaluation appointment and ask them to prioritize it since she might need several surgeries and the implant fangs might involve a six- or nine-month manufacturing schedule as they're customized. In the meantime, I'll research what's available. There have been surprising advances in supernatural dentistry, so I'm hopeful we may be able to restore some the original function."

Jaq stood and extended her hand, shaking mine in a firm grip. "Thank you, Doctor Schooner. I'm thrilled to know there's a reconstructive dentist serving the nonhuman population in the mid-Atlantic region."

I continued my afternoon schedule buzzing with an adrenaline rush. Although my other appointments were all human patients, I'd received a shipping notification on Ozar's specialized implants and was mentally strategizing different approaches for my new vampire client. At the end of the day, I was still high with excitement and energy.

Staying a little late, I did some research in the office, then locked up and headed north to meet my friends at Abbey Burger.

Willa made us both laugh with her stories of a recent, disastrous internet dating encounter. Abby bragged about her niece's latest field hockey win, and I told them about last night's epic date with Ozar.

"Jesus, that guy is too good to be true," Willa said.

Abby swatted her arm. "Don't be a pessimist. Your internet match, Paul, might have been a loser, but there are plenty of amazing guys out there. And some of them seem to have green skin and tusks."

Willa rolled her eyes. "Pollyanna. I've heard your dating and relationship stories over the last three years, and you can't sit here and tell me that these good guys aren't as rare as hens' teeth."

"I'd about given up," I confessed. "With my track record, I was ready to spend the rest of my life as a single cat lady."

"I think that would require more than one cat," Abby commented.

I laughed. "I'm not sure Judy would share her domain with another cat. She barely shares it with me. But Ozar seems to have won her over. He got up early and fed her a bunch of my grilled chicken, then played a makeshift game of laser pointer using a mirror from my bathroom. She's not snuggling up to him, but with this kind of progress, it's only a matter of time."

Abby raised her eyebrows and nodded. "The cat approves. That's a good sign, especially because I know firsthand how prickly Judy is with strangers."

"Wait...he spent the *night*?" Willa asked.

Abby and Willa both squealed at my nod.

"And in addition to his efforts to win Judy over, he made me breakfast," I told them.

Willa chuckled. "I'm guessing that's why you weren't at the gym this morning?"

"Obviously," Abby chimed in. "You know she got quite the morning workout with Ozar. Maybe two or three workouts?"

Thankfully, our food arrived, and I didn't have to answer that question, because the answer was yes. But as soon as the waitress left, my friends got right back to interrogating me for all the details. I thought about how to tell them enough without turning our dinner out into the recitation of an erotic novel.

"So, is the sex good?" Willa asked as she layered the lettuce and tomato on her burger. "He's taking care of your needs first? He knows where your clit actually is and how to treat it right? There's substantial foreplay before the zipper on his pants goes down?"

"Yes, yes, yes, and yes." I sighed, thinking of how the sex with Ozar seemed to get better and better each time. Everything with Ozar was better each time. "It's not just the physical, either. There's this weird emotional connection that's hard for me to describe. This all really *does* seem too good to be true."

"Jordan is in love," Abby teased in a sing-song voice.

I absolutely felt as if I were in love—more in love than I'd ever been before. And that scared me. We were moving too fast, but I couldn't seem to help myself. I wanted to see him, spend time with him, have sex with him. I kept envisioning a life with Ozar, a family with Ozar. Was this bordering on obsession? Should I back this whole bus up and try to put some distance between us just to ensure my feelings were real before I got in too deep?

"I don't believe in insta-love," I told my friends. "It's never love. It's just lust clouding both people's judgement. And in time, when that settles down, you realize it wasn't love at all. You realize he's a selfish asshole who was lying about nearly everything just so he could get in your pants. You realize that he's commitment phobic and has an eviction, a repossessed car, and a hundred grand in defaulted credit card debt—"

"Yikes," Abby muttered, sliding my drink closer to me.

"He always forgets his wallet, so you end up paying for dinner, and you're too nice to keep hounding him to Venmo you his share like he promised," I continued. "He tells you he's a Software Engineer for Google, then you realize he is unemployed."

"You've dated Paul too?" Willa asked. "Because that sounds a lot like Paul."

I laughed, snapping out of my bitter rant. "Ozar is none of those things, but I can't help but be paranoid."

"Just go with it," Abby said. "Ride the wave of awesome sex and perfect guy and just enjoy it."

"Yeah," Willa agreed. "Especially the sex. Ride that... what did you say he called his peen? A spear or something?"

I grinned. "His hand-axe."

Willa snorted. "Yeah, girl. Ride that hand-axe every chance you get. And if things go to shit, then drop him to the curb like garbage on Tuesday night."

"But things won't go south," Abby told me. "Be positive. This might be the *one*. Don't let all the crappy experiences color your judgement. Don't miss out on what could be the love of your life."

Abby *was* a Pollyanna, but I couldn't help but hope she was right, because Ozar just felt...like a puzzle piece that easily snapped into place—both in my life and my heart.

"Better take a pregnancy test every week though," she added. "Just to be on the safe side."

I shrugged, thinking that was a weird concern given how many discussions about various birth control methods we'd had over the years. "You know I'm on the pill. And I'm super careful about taking it on time, not missing a dose, and watching any drug interactions. No unplanned pregnancy for me. Nope. Not gonna happen."

Abby shot me a sideways look. "Are you sure? I've been reading a lot of orc romances in the last few days, and they supposedly have some sort of super sperm that overcomes birth control."

"*Orc romances?* That's a thing?" I asked.

"How the hell does the sperm force her to ovulate when she's on hormonal birth control?" Willa wondered. "That doesn't make sense. And does orc sperm burn through condoms? Diaphragms? Okay, *that* I can kinda imagine, but causing ovulation?"

I frowned, suddenly very worried. "There's no way that stuff is caustic enough to do any of that. I mean, it didn't burn my esophagus, so how could it burn condoms?"

"Hot damn. Jordan swallowed." Willa saluted me with her beer.

"I still think you should take a pregnancy test." Abby picked up a French fry and popped it into her mouth.

Taking a bite of my burger, I considered her suggestion. I'd be lying if I didn't admit that the suggestion freaked me out a bit. The whole thing sounded improbable, but in a world where demons, angels, werewolves, and now orcs openly lived, where magic was a thing—you could buy amulets and spells at a store—super-powered sperm wasn't really out of the realm of possibility.

"Is there anything else those orc romances mentioned?"

I asked Abby. "Unusual customs or physiological things I should know about? Is Ozar going to sprout a tail and a second cock? Do orcs have harems? Shed their skin? Need to take a six-year pilgrimage to a cave during their lifetime?"

Willa wrinkled her nose. "Eww. I mean eww on the shedding their skin. And the second cock. The tail I could probably live with."

"No, but they often have soulmates," Abby informed me. "Two orcs will meet, and it will be more than just a love-at-first-sight thing. It's like they're meant for each other. Fated to be together."

Uh oh.

"I do kind of feel connected to him," I confessed. "It's not just great sex, and it's not just compatibility and friendship. It's weird." Although maybe that was just an orc-orc thing, and not a human-orc thing.

"It's bullshit, is what it is." Willa rolled her eyes. "You two are such romantics. I'm gonna barf over here. Love? I'm all on board with wanting someone as a best friend and a lover. Soul-connection, fated mates? That's in the same fantasy realm as super-sperm as far as I'm concerned."

"You're just jealous," I teased. "Don't worry. I'll introduce you to one of Ozar's teammates, then you too can have a green-skinned, muscle-bound soulmate with super-sperm and a magical dick."

"Sold. Sign me up." Willa's laugh seemed oddly high-pitched.

"Me too," Abby added with a sigh of longing.

Chapter 25

Ozar

"**O**zar! Get your head out of your fucking ass and pay attention," Ugwyll shouted after a hockey puck nearly caved in my forehead.

"The stick is down here on the ice, not between my eyes," I yelled back.

None of us were proficient at pushing the puck around the ice with the curved sticks, Ugwyll included. He had a habit of launching it through the air each time he attempted to pass the turd-like object. But he was right, I *was* distracted.

Thinking of Jordan.

Last night had been amazing. This morning had been amazing. I liked her spacious home, and her decor, although I didn't understand the complete lack of furs. Her bed didn't have even *one* fur. It was quite comfortable otherwise, and I was more than happy to make love to her wherever I could, but I was absolutely going to get her some furs—the best furs I could buy, since skinning a kill and tanning its hide seemed a nearly impossible task in the modern human world.

But none of that would matter because we would soon be returning home, and I had a lovely house with plenty of furs prepared for her there. My mind wandered, envisioning me and Jordan in the home I'd built before I'd left to find a bride. There was a beautiful view of the Swael Mountain Range from the back porch, but it was close enough to my clan's town that she could easily visit others each day. Our orclets would lack for nothing. I was hoping that I could change Jordan's mind about the number of our offspring once we were wed. If not, then I would try to be satisfied with one or two. I hoped others from our clan came here to find human brides, so our children would never want for playmates. And of course we'd bring Judy with us. Jordan loved her cat, and I would make sure the little furry animal was safe in my homeland.

"Ozar!" Another puck almost cleaved my left ear off.

"You are very bad at this hockey," I growled at Ugwyll.

"We are *all* bad at this hockey," he snapped back. "At least I'm trying. Your mind and hand-axe are with your mate right now, rolling in her furs in your imagination."

He wasn't wrong. None of this seemed to matter anymore. I knew Jordan returned my feelings. She'd let me spend the night in her furless bed. She'd introduced me to her beloved Judy. Why should I bother to care about hockey or this team when we would soon be home, wed, and making orclets? Orclet. Surely, she would want more than *one* child?

But I couldn't let Ugwyll down. The others on the team might not care about hockey or winning, but he did, and I'd be leaving him behind. Who knew how long that idiot would need to wait until he found a human female willing to put up with him and agree to be his bride. It was my responsibility as the leader here to help him. Since I could hardly help him find a bride, then I might as well help him win at the hockey.

From what I'd learned of Ugwyll, winning our game was probably more important than finding a bride.

Another puck whizzed a few inches over my head and cracked the clear plastic that topped the wall around our ice arena. I didn't know much about this hockey game, but I didn't think concussing the other team with the puck would be considered winning.

"We should practice skating and disabling our opponents." Hopefully that would help us tomorrow night, because there was little chance we were going to get the puck into the net of our enemy.

Ugwyll thankfully agreed, and we spent the next three hours trying to skate as fast as we could without falling. We moved side by side and occasionally tried to knock the other down by elbowing and trying to trip each other with our sticks. Plowing into Ugwyll resulted in us both falling to the ice in a heap, so we both decided our strategy should only involve elbows and sticks.

We both showered and changed in the locker room, then I went home for lunch, feeling that my apartment was small and lonely compared to Jordan's home. At least I had plenty of furs, though.

Maybe I should get a cat of my own. It could keep Judy company when Jordan and I returned home. She'd said the cat didn't like change, and relocating to my homeland would be a huge change. A friend might assist Judy in making the transition with minimal stress.

I ate some meat and drank a large glass of cold milk, then headed out for my afternoon run. Checking my phone, I adjusted my route and let it guide me to the place where pets were waiting for homes.

My phone guided me to a location off Giles Road with huge paw prints painted on the side of the building and two stories of glass windows framing the entrance.

Two human women and a human man were working behind the front desk. The man was helping a human couple with some paperwork, presumably about the tiny dog hopping excitedly around their feet at the end of a colorful rope. One woman with bright red hair was talking on a phone. The other woman had wrinkled pale skin and short silvery hair that was curled in neat rows across the top of her head.

"Are you here to meet your friend?" The silver-haired woman beamed at me with a broad, toothy smile.

"Yes?" I assumed that was what the humans called their pets? Friends? Jordan certainly seemed to treat Judy as if she were an honored close relative, and I would like to have a friendly relationship with my own cat.

"He's through that door and down the second aisle to your left." The silver-haired woman pointed to a door, still smiling.

It seemed fitting that my cat would be male, so I didn't question the human woman's assumptions.

Going through the door, I was hit with a wall of sound. Shrill yaps, deep bays, loud barks, and through it all, the occasional plaintive meow. Following the human woman's directions, I went down the second aisle to my left but didn't see any cats. Instead, I saw Bwat.

I knew the other orc had been tasked with assisting homeless animals, but I hadn't realized he would be doing it here, or at this time. And I hadn't expected him to actually *do* it. Eng and Ugwyll had both ranted about their assignments, vowing to defy the demon who owned the team. I didn't mind since I actually enjoyed playing with the children at the parks and was excited at the prospect of visiting schools and spending time with the little humans who attended our games.

I should have realized Bwat would follow through. It wasn't that he was the kind to obey orders from a demon—no orcs were really the kind to obey orders unless they truly respected and felt a sense of loyalty toward their leader, and none of us respected or felt loyal to the idiot demon who owned our team. No, Bwat was an orc filled with endless curiosity. He would see this as an opportunity to learn about the various animals humans kept as pets. He'd dive into this assignment with gusto.

Except Bwat did not look particularly gusto-filled right now. He looked bored. Until he saw me, that is.

"Ozar!" His face brightened and he rushed toward me, still carrying the broom he'd been sweeping the floor with. "Is there something important I need to do for the team? Right now, that is?"

"No. I'm here to look at cats. I didn't expect to see you." That might have been a little blunt, but I was irked that Bwat wasn't practicing like Ugwyll and I were. Not that it would matter since Jordan and I would be returning home soon.

"The cats are in another area since the dogs' barking scare them," he told me. "I'll show you."

We walked past the long row of cages with the loud, excited canines who jumped and battered their front paws against the fencing. The enclosures were well made, and none of the dogs were in danger of escaping, but the noise and the excitement was excessive. Poor Judy would have been terrified.

The cats were separated from the dogs by two doors and

a hallway. I could still hear the barking, but it was suitably muted. Still, many of the cats seemed alarmed, huddling at the back of their cages with raised fur and big eyes.

"Have you learned much about these human pets?" I asked Bwat as I surveyed the available cats.

"No," he snapped. "I am only allowed to sweep floors and clean empty cages. I don't talk with the humans who come to adopt animals. I don't interact with the animals. I am taught nothing about their care or what makes humans love them so."

No wonder he was bored.

"Jordan has a cat," I told him. "Judy-the-cat is a fierce hunter and a judger of character. I believe I am winning her over."

"How?" Bwat looked at a large gray cat that stared back at him.

"Chicken. Feeding the cat makes them happy. And they enjoy games that simulate hunting. I reflected light from a mirror and Judy joyously chased it around in an attempt to kill it."

Bwat stuck a finger through the bars of the cage and rubbed the gray cat's cheek. It purred, and he yanked his hand away in alarm.

"That is a happy noise." I'd been similarly frightened when Judy had made that sound, thinking she had some sort of respiratory infection that might require emergency care. "If they no longer want you to stroke them, then they will either walk away or bite your finger."

"Bite?" Bwat sounded uncertain, but he stuck his finger into the cage again to pet the cat. "I can't believe a small animal like this would be considered a fierce hunter."

"Their teeth and claws are very sharp. They have the

ability to jump up to six times their height. And they can employ an impressive burst of speed. I do believe that Judy can easily take down an animal her own size, but Jordan says she prefers to hunt insects, birds, and mice."

Bwat seemed impressed by that. "Their fur is very soft. Maybe I'll come back and eventually be trusted with additional duties."

The door opened, and the older human woman with her short silver hair in rows of curls approached. "Bwat, you should be sweeping. I know you're a volunteer, but we're counting on you to keep the dog kennels clean."

Bwat sent me a pained look, then left with his broom as the gray cat meowed in protest.

"Are you interested in adopting a cat?" the woman asked me once Bwat was gone.

I nodded. "The human woman who will soon be my wife has a cat, and I thought it might be good to have one of my own. That way when we return to my home, her cat will not be lonely."

"Some cats are very particular about sharing their home with others," she informed me. "They are territorial animals, and it can take a long time for them to get used to another cat in the home. If you introduce them slowly and carefully, and keep your expectations low, they can learn to coexist."

I stared at her for a moment. "I...I don't understand any of that."

She patted my elbow. "We have booklets to guide you in introducing the cats, but basically you need to keep them separated for a while. The new cat can stay in a bathroom where it will feel safe and the current cat will become familiar with its scent. Like I said, it's a slow process. And some cats never really become friends with the newcomer.

Some bond and will play and enjoy each other's company, but some just tolerate the new cat and stay as far away as possible."

"That does not sound ideal," I mused. "I hoped to provide company and a playmate for Judy. I don't want her to be lonely living somewhere without cats."

"Most cats don't care about having another cat around. They're not herd animals like sheep or horses, and they do just fine living independently. As long as you provide Judy with human companionship and interesting toys to keep her mind sharp and her body fit, then she'll be happy. I would be concerned about predators wherever your home is, though. I'd recommend not letting Judy outside the house when you and your fiancée move."

"Judy is not allowed outside of the house now, and I would take her safety very seriously. Jordan loves her, and I am already fond of Judy."

The woman beamed. "You sound like you'd be a wonderful cat-dad. While Judy might not need a feline companion, you still might want to consider adopting one so that you and your fiancée each have your own cat. We have so many that are looking for a good home."

I looked at the stacked cages that held what seemed like dozens of cats. It was overwhelming. And while I *would* enjoy a cat of my own, I didn't want to alienate Judy or do anything that might annoy the cat.

"I sometimes travel for work," I told the woman. "Our hockey games are not always in Baltimore, and I wouldn't want a cat to suffer while I'm gone."

"Cats are the perfect animal for people who might be gone for a few days at a time," she countered. "You can set up an automatic feeder and watering fountain, and since they go in a litter box, you don't need to worry about coming home to a mess. And if you're going to be gone more than a day or two, you can pay a pet sitter to drop by each day to check on the cat and make sure everything is okay."

I did like the idea of having a furry little killer waiting for me at home. And while I was certain Jordan and I would return to my homeland, there were logistics that might delay our marriage and move. Even if I proposed this weekend, we had several months of games that I felt I'd made a binding commitment to. Honestly, I felt uncomfortable about leaving mid-season, even though the reason for my journey here was complete. The team needed me. Could I really abandon them?

Either way, I was not going to make a decision on a cat today.

"Is there one that you recommend?" I asked the woman. "I would want to talk to my mate before adopting one, but I would like to tell her about a specific cat in that conversation."

The woman nodded and led me down the row to a cage toward the end. Inside was an ebony cat with startling orange eyes.

"This is Coal, although you could always change his name. He's a relaxed and easygoing cat who would quickly adapt to a new home and would be good with other cats. He's not going to be pushy with Judy if she doesn't like him, but he'll be happy to play if she wants. His favorite things are sitting on your lap, perching on top of kitchen cabinets, and his little mouse toys filled with catnip."

She opened the cage and scooped Coal out, depositing him in my arms. The cat's ebony fur was short, shiny, and soft. He purred instantly, staring up at me with his orange eyes before rubbing his head on my chin. I instantly loved him, and with great reluctance, put him back in the cage.

"I'll need to discuss this with Jordan first," I told the woman.

"Of course," she said, closing the cage and putting steel wire between me and the cat I already felt had sunk his claws into my heart. "We always want to make sure every member of the family is on board with a new adoption."

Chapter 26

Ozar

That evening, I texted Jordan a picture of the cat from the shelter to get her opinion. She texted me back a series of hearts along with a picture of a burger on a plate. I was confused and somewhat alarmed about what a black homeless cat would have to do with food until she texted again that she was out to dinner with her two friends.

There went my tentative plans to ask her to meet me for a late meal.

Should I adopt this cat? I texted back, not wanting to interrupt her friend-time but feeling like I should make a decision on Coal.

Yes. Always adopt the cat, was the reply followed by another heart.

Would Judy approve? Does Judy like other cats?

There were several seconds of those pulsing dots alternating with their disappearance before I got a reply.

Judy would take some time to get used to another cat, but she's not unfriendly. I don't want that to keep you from adopting your own cat, though.

I frowned, not sure how to read what was behind that message. It was good news that Judy would eventually warm up to a cat-friend, but the last bit of the text confused me. Of course Judy's preferences mattered, as did Jordan's. If they did not want a second cat, then I would not adopt Coal.

I know you've got some away games coming up. It might not be the best time to bring a cat into your apartment, only to leave when they're adapting to a new home.

Oh.

She was right. As much as I wanted to adopt Coal, it wasn't fair for the cat to be abandoned right after he was brought into a new home. And having a stranger checking on him every day probably wouldn't help him settle in like my being there would.

Thank you for your advice. I will wait until I come home from the away games. Hopefully Coal will still be available at the homeless animal building because I like him.

His name is Coal??? Is he at BARCS? Maybe I'll go over to see him when you're away.

My heart twisted. *If he finds a good home, then I will love and adopt another cat. The shelter-woman informed me there are many nice ones there waiting for families.*

That's a good attitude to have. There are so many wonderful cats that need homes. I love that you're thinking of adopting.

The number of hearts following that text made me wonder how much Jordan had drunk while having dinner with her friends. With a smile, I told her to have a good evening, and that I would see her tomorrow morning.

My own dinner consisted of leftover *Swakega* stew and a cold glass of milk. I sat on my balcony for a while, looking out over the city, then changed clothes and walked back to the arena in search of companionship.

Sadly, the only one who was there was Eng. I really didn't like the arrogant jerk, and doubted he'd be good company, but figured he was better than no one.

I really did need a cat.

Eng held up a magazine with pictures of naked humans engaging in intercourse. "There are stories in nearly every issue of this magazine in which a male delivering pizza sinks his hand-axe into females on a regular basis."

"I am already having copious amounts of sex," I informed him smugly. "There is no need for me to deliver a pizza for that to happen."

Still, I filed the information away in the back of my mind, in case Jordan ever expressed the need for a pizza.

"I am considering quitting this hockey team and working at a place called Domino's where I can deliver pizza to women needing the services of my hand-axe." Eng frowned. "Except none of the human males in this magazine are wedding these females. Are the females just casually enjoying a roll in the male's furs? Are the males evaluating the females as potential brides by testing out their sexual prowess? Perhaps that's a method I should consider."

I snorted. "That would require you to actually convince a human woman to invite you to her furs. So far, you can't even get one to accept a beverage. Or a steak from the grocery store."

"That waitress must have already been married, because it was a very good steak," Eng complained. "Clearly I need to offer a pizza to the next female I consider making my bride."

"Excellent idea. What sort of activity should I plan for

my next date with Jordan? Should we workout together Saturday morning and then have breakfast? Should we run? Practice knife fighting? Skate on the ice?" I tried to steer us back to the topic of me and my future bride.

"Yeah. All of that." Eng leafed through the magazine, clearly not listening to my suggestions or caring one bit about my dilemma.

I picked up one of his discarded magazines, the one that showed a mostly naked woman with strategically placed coffee filters improbably attached to her nipples and shaved garden. I wanted to respect Jordan's need for friend time, but Eng's suggestion intrigued me. Waiting outside her home for her to return with a pizza in my hands seemed like it might suggest desperation rather than devotion, and besides, the pizza would be cold by the time she arrived home.

Plus, I'd learned that Jordan was a woman who liked her routine, just as her cat did. She'd made an exception for me today, and I knew how significant that was. I'd just texted with her. She'd be at the game tomorrow. Making plans for Saturday felt right, even though I wanted to see her before then.

The game. I'd promise to get Jordan and her friends passes.

"How do we get free tickets for friends and family members?" I asked Eng.

"Hmm," he replied before turning the magazine around to show me a picture that took up two pages. "Look at how flexible this female is. I don't know any orc that could possibly be able to perform this act. Are all human females this bendy?"

"If you're lucky, yes. I want special tickets for tomorrow to give to Jordan and her friends. Who do I get those from?"

Eng reversed the magazine to stare in awe at the picture. "I've got no idea. That guy in the booth up front, maybe? Or the human male guarding the entrance?"

I tossed the magazine I'd been holding aside and headed up front. There was a woman at the booth this evening and a surprising number of humans were lined up around the lobby.

A voice from the line shouted, "Hey, Ozar!" and the entire crowd turned to look at me. Half a second later, I was mobbed by humans wanting me to sign various pieces of paper and to ask me about our strategy for the upcoming game.

Strategy? Stay on our knife-blades and if we were lucky, get the puck into the enemy's net? I didn't want to relay our lack of planning, so I just grunted and scrawled my signature on the various papers and body parts they shoved my way.

It was the male security guard who finally came to my rescue, moving the humans away from me with the claim that I was needed on the ice. He cleared a path, and when we were securely behind the locked doors of the arena, I asked him about the tickets.

He grinned and slapped my shoulder. "Your girlfriend from last night? Absolutely, dude. She's smokin' hot, and I can tell she's not the usual puck bunny, either."

"She's a dentist." I had no idea what a puck bunny was and assumed that smokin' hot was a compliment I might not appreciate coming from this male, but he'd helped me escape a mob of humans, so I decided I should overlook the comment.

"Damn, dude!" He slapped my shoulder again. "Congrats! How many tickets do you need? I'll have them at the will-call box."

"Three tickets with the best seats," I told him.

"They'll be in the VIP box right behind the team," he assured me. "I hope she inspires you to a great game. I want to see lots of fights. And maybe we'll score a goal."

It was humiliating that he didn't think a win was possible, or even that more than a goal was a "maybe" for us. But fights? That I could try to deliver.

I thanked the male guard and headed back to the locker room. Even if I had to drag Eng out by his hair, I was getting him on the ice. Whether I could make him actually skate or do more than lean against a wall all night was uncertain, but at least I'd get him on the ice.

Ugwyll showed up, and between the two of us we managed to not only get Eng on the ice, but half a dozen of the others on the team as well. Eng refused to participate, but with Ugwyll and I bullying the other orcs, we spent two hours working on our skating and our passing skills with the puck. We were horrible, but I was sure we'd be less horrible than we were last week.

The Tusks probably wouldn't score a goal, but maybe we'd stay on our feet and manage to keep possession of the puck for more than a few seconds at a time. And fights? That might be the only thing we could deliver.

Fights, and several mortifying moments that the audience would laugh at.

Chapter 27

Ozar

The next morning, I was up early, going building to building to ensure that every orc on our team came to practice. We ran laps around the arena, then went back to the ice to work some more on our skating and puck handling. Or "turd handling," as the team called it. It was well after noon by the time I ended practice and assembled everyone in the locker room.

"Tonight, we are going to show these humans what a team of orcs can do," I told them.

"We're going to get the *akot* beat out of us, that's what," one muttered.

I glared at the orc until he lowered his eyes. "We might not be as skilled at this game as the humans, but there is something we *are* skilled at. We can fight. We can knock them down. We can slam them into the walls. We can find their weaknesses and exploit them."

Ugwyll nodded. "Scare the *akot* out of them, and they'll be timid. They'll make mistakes. And with those mistakes, we'll have a chance to score goals."

"We will defeat our enemy tonight," Bwat shouted and

raised his arm. The other team members did the same with varying degrees of enthusiasm.

"And as a reward, every teammate who gives it his all, who fights and defends, and attempts to score even if the turd misses the net...those orcs will receive a cannoli."

I'd faced bull-wraiths in the mists of the Wrenga Mountains. I'd battled fae in the Valley of Shadows. I'd led the forces that defeated *mwilla-mka* who'd come from the depths of the ground when the quakes split the earth. But none of those had me on edge like Friday night's hockey game.

With boxes holding three dozen cannoli in my arms, I entered the arena and made my way to the dusty coach's office where I hid the baked treasures in the corner fridge. In the distance, I could hear the hum of the Zamboni machine on the ice. None of the team had arrived, but the whole arena had a sense of anticipation about it. Anxious excitement. A battle about to begin.

Finding a remote corner in the depths of the arena's mechanical areas, I cleared my mind and focused on the game. It wasn't easy. I'd texted Jordan about the tickets and her reply had conveyed excitement, but I still worried. What if she didn't come? If her friends had other plans, would she choose them over a night of watching us probably lose against the humans? Or worse, if she watched us lose for the second week in a row, would she reconsider her feelings for me? I knew her heart was mine, but would her pragmatic side insist on a more capable mate? Would her heart be fickle after watching yet another disaster of a game?

She's not the usual puck bunny.

I'd looked that term up on my phone and winced at the description. Jordan was not a woman who sought a famous mate, *or* a mate who was famous for losing. She would support my goals but not turn from me if achievement took time. Or never happened. Besides, this hockey thing was temporary. Soon we'd be wed and home, and I could impress her with how respected I was a guardian of my clan.

Forcing those thoughts from my mind, I focused on the game as I would an upcoming battle. All other concerns needed to be locked away. Only winning mattered.

Winning. As if that were even a remote possibility.

I slammed the door shut on that. The inner battle was most likely worse than the one I'd face in a few hours, but I did my best, and when I emerged from the mechanical room, I felt at peace.

That sense of peace lasted through the chaos of the locker room, through the booming of the announcer's voice, through the initial skate onto the ice, through the anthem where we stood respectfully with our arms by our sides. It lasted until we skated to the benches, and I saw Jordan in the stands.

She and her two friends cheered and shouted, waving their arms at us. The look on her face...it was enough to stoke those hot coals deep inside myself to a bonfire. I wanted to make her proud. I wanted to see that look of joy and love on her face every day of my life.

"I've got a plan," Bwat said, handing us each a sheet of paper. "Ozar asked me to find an advantage, and I've got one. We need to say these things to our enemies every chance we get. It isn't enough to yell 'fuck' at them; we need to insult them in this particular way."

"They make fun of each others' mothers?" Ugwyll asked as he read the paper. "That can't be right."

"It's crossing a line," I agreed, wincing at some of the insults.

"This is what my research revealed," Bwat insisted.

"I'm sure this is wrong," Ugwyll told him.

"I don't feel comfortable with these either," I said. "Let's stick to insulting their manhood, their strength and skill, and their appearance."

My resolve vanished the moment I took the ice to face off against a human male for the puck. He looked me in the eye, head tilting upward as I was taller by a foot, and told me that he'd enjoyed my mother sucking his hand-axe last night.

Bwat was right. These humans *did* stoop so low as to degrade another's mother. For a split second, I was too shocked to react, then I said the first thing that came to my head.

"She has been dead for ages. You enjoy face-fucking corpses?"

The male's pale face turned the color of the ice. "You son of a bitch," he snarled.

"My mother is a dog-corpse and that is what you enjoy having suck your cock?" I wondered, not sure how any of this was insulting to either me or my long-dead mother.

"Fucker," he roared, tossing off his gloves and diving at me.

It was a mistake. I had seventy pounds of muscle on this human. I tossed my own gloves aside and pounded my fist into his shoulder, sending him flying backward across the ice. The arena erupted with shouts of approval and chants of "fight, fight." Other human players engaged the orc nearest to them and soon realized that we might not have padding or even shirts, but we were stronger than any hockey player they'd ever engaged in the past. By the time the demons in uniforms disengaged us, the ice was striped with red and green blood—mostly red—and several human males, including the one who had faced off against me, left the ice with a weaving, unsteady gait.

Since we'd yet to begin our first match, I found myself again facing off across from a different human male. This time, I took the initiative as far as insults went.

"You're so weak, a gentle spring breeze could blow you over." My taunt didn't seem to offend the human. In fact, he looked like he was amused.

"That's not what your mother said when I was balls-deep in her last night," he shot back.

Again with my mother. What was with these idiotic humans?

"My mother is dead. If you had sex with her last night, that makes you a neophiliac."

The human looked confused. "You mean *necrophiliac?*"

Yeah. That.

"You like to fuck corpses because they can't make fun of the tiny twig you've got between your legs," I continued.

The human dove at me, tossing off his gloves and flinging his stick across the ice before swinging a fist at my face. Gloves flew and again we pummeled the humans.

Clearly, someone with a more level mind had spoken to the human team, because the third time I was unable to taunt my enemy into a reaction beyond shooting the puck past me and to the expert stick of his teammate.

We scrambled after them, but even with practice, the humans could skate at double our speed. Immediately, I saw our error in having only Bwat and Eng positioned and ready near our goal. The humans reached our end of the ice without an orc in sight beside our goalie, who waved his arms ineffectually as our enemy shot the puck between his legs and into the net.

By the time we left the ice for our break, the enemy had scored four points to our zero. Back in the locker room, we collapsed on the benches and the floor.

"See? There's no sense in all that practice you're forcing us to do, Ozar," Eng growled. "These fucks were born with knife-blades on their feet. We can practice every day this year, and it won't make any difference."

Ugwyll snorted. "As if you ever actually practice. Unless by 'practice,' you mean leaning against the wall."

"They're faster. They're too good at evading us. We can't hurt them if we can't catch them, and there's not a chance in our lifetime of us getting control of that puck-turd," Bwat moaned.

"We need to spread out," I said. "All of us shouldn't go after the one with the puck. We should work on taking down the other humans by any means necessary where our best skater concentrates on trying to chase the puck-human."

"If one of us tries to chase the puck-human, then the others can move themselves into positions where it would be difficult for the human to change direction and get away," Ugwyll suggested.

I nodded. "It's an excellent idea. Like when we are driving a herd of *vokelna* through a canyon to better pasture. We will close in on this human, then steal the puck."

That was our plan. Unfortunately, it didn't work. The humans were smarter than *vokelna*. They saw us moving close and were able to quickly maneuver around us. At the end of the second period, the human team had scored another four points. By the end of the game, they'd won with ten points to our zero.

I didn't score a point in this game. No one had scored a point in this game. And for the first time ever, I didn't want to see Jordan tonight. I just wanted to go back to my den, drink my cold milk, and suffer the bruises to my pride alone.

Chapter 28

Jordan

"We've got this whole section to ourselves," I commented as Willa, Abby, and I scooted down the row to sit right behind the Tusks' bench. We'd arrived early to make sure there was enough time to get our tickets from will-call, grab beers, and find our seats before the teams were announced.

"It's for friends and family." Abby frowned as she took in the empty seats. "I get it that the players wouldn't have much in the way of family, but what about friends?"

"They're still pretty new in town," I told her. "It's not like they've had time to make friends."

Abby sniffed, clearly not believing that explanation. "Fine. But these unused seats should have been comped for PR. These should be filled with Make-A-Wish kids, or winners from a charity drive, or teachers, or first responders."

"I'm going to guess they don't have a public relations firm." Willa picked a seat at random and sprawled into it, propping her feet up on the wall. "The owner isn't even springing for shirts or pads, so he's obviously running this whole thing on the cheap."

"The shirt thing doesn't make sense either," Abby complained. "I love seeing a naked, muscled chest as much as the next girl, but if they don't have jerseys, then that cuts out significant revenue from product sales."

She wasn't wrong. Baltimore residents loved their sports teams and gobbled up merchandise at an astonishing rate. Sports jerseys and team logo-covered clothing items were second only to stuff with the Maryland flag or pictures of blue crabs on them in terms of sales. Or Old Bay Seasoning. Heck, the locals even "O!" in the "Oh say can you see" portion of the National Anthem in an enthusiastic nod to the Orioles baseball team—or the "O's," as they were affectionately called. The Tusks were missing out on some serious money here.

Abby and I sat next to Willa, sipped our beers and people watched. The arena wasn't even half full, and there was a noticeable lack of Tusks colors in the crowd, although a boy a few sections up did have one of those huge number one foam hands in lime green.

Wishful thinking, kid.

The Maple Leafs were on the ice practicing, but as the music changed, they headed down the tunnel to their locker rooms. The announcer made a few comments about parking and concessions, then brought the Toronto team back to skate around the edge of the rink while the overhead showed their headshots and introduced each one.

"Here they come!" Abby announced with a seat-bounce.

Willa sat up straight, and I leaned forward to see as the orcs took the ice. I noticed the improvement right away. The one guy remained along the wall as before, but the others were actually gliding into the center of the rink, even if they did have some issues stopping.

"No one's fallen yet," Abby said with crossed fingers.

Keyword: yet.

We screamed and yelled as the team was introduced, even though Abby had a few things to say about the head-shots on the screen.

"Tough day at work?" Willa asked her once the last team member, an orc whose name didn't appear to have any vowels in it, faded from the overhead.

Abby sighed. "I can't stand crappy PR work. This is our home team, and I want better for them."

Willa nodded. "Me too. It's not like it's packed here, but it could be. People come out even if the team is on a losing streak."

Abby snorted. "They *would* if they pimped this all out at even the most minimal level. Lots came out the first game for the novelty, but there is going to be decreasing atten-dance unless the owner gets his shit together."

"Get your sales staff over here," I told her. "There's an opportunity. Someone should be closing the deal."

Willa's expression turned thoughtful. "Yeah. Closing the deal," she murmured. "You know, it's a good idea."

"We don't usually go for demon-owned business." Abby held up a hand. "I know, I know. The owner is worried they will skip out on payment. I've tried to explain that demons are very respectful of contracts and with a properly worded one, there won't be any more problems than we have with human-owned businesses. Less, actually."

"Make a solid pitch," I advised her. "This isn't a corner vape shop, it's a major sports team, an NHL franchise. If the NHL felt the owner could abide by the rules of their contract, then your company's owner shouldn't be so worried."

Our discussion abruptly ended as the announcer instructed us all to stand for the National Anthem. Once the song had finished, we sat and watched as the players not starting took to their benches. Ozar was facing off against the Maple Leafs' center, flanked by Ugwyll and the orc with no vowels in his name. Eng remained against the wall, his location such that I think he was supposed to be playing defense. The only other player I recognized was Bwat, who was hovering near their goalie in a defensive spot.

I couldn't hear what Ozar and the Toronto center were saying, but it was clear they were riling each other up. The puck dropped, and all hell broke loose. Instead of gaining control, the two players lost it. Gloves came off, and the Toronto center dove at Ozar with a shout of anger. The crowd got to their feet in excitement, screaming encouragement as the players all began to brawl. It took the referees and the few level-headed Maple Leafs to settle everyone down. The next time the fight started even before the puck hit the ice.

"Damn. Best gladiatorial fight I've ever seen," Willa commented.

"All we need is some lions to come out of the tunnels," Abby added.

"And a couple of chariots," I agreed.

The refs sent both teams to their benches to think about what they'd done for a couple of minutes, and this time when the puck dropped, a hockey game actually ensued.

Well, sort of a hockey game. The Maple Leafs literally skated circles around the slow-moving, clumsy orcs, remaining far enough from them that they wouldn't be pummeled by the orcs' superior strength. At the end of the first period, the opposing team had casually scored four points.

I strongly believed the human team was taking it easy on the Tusks because that score should have been much higher.

During the second period, the Tusks tried a new approach. They appeared to be herding the human with the puck toward the wall where he had limited options, then closing in so one of the orcs could check their opponent. The move, which Willa had named "The Border Collie," worked the first few times until the Maple Leafs caught on and used their speed to evade the orcs. Even with several of their players injured, the Toronto team still scored an additional four points in the second period, then another two in the third to win ten to zero. The Tusks never got possession of the puck once during the whole game.

We sat in silence after the buzzer, mourning this loss.

"They *are* skating better." Abby's voice was soft. "It's only their second game. And the Maple Leafs are looking really great this year."

"They scored a goal last week. This shutout has to hurt," I said.

Willa blew out a frustrated breath. "You can't have a team full of Hulks in a game where speed and agility are critical. Who the hell is in charge of their training? They need to be doing weighted sprints and fartlek. Is anyone tracking their VO2 max and customizing a program for each player? They need speed work and a decent flexibility program in addition to skating lessons, or they'll never be able to win a game."

My eyebrows shot up, and I turned to Willa.

"Tough day at work?" Abby teased her.

"If it's not a tough day, then I'm not working hard enough," she shot back with a grin. "You hate crappy PR; I hate unfocused and inadequate sports training."

"And Jordan hates poor dental hygiene." Abby held out her empty beer cup and I tapped it with mine in agreement.

"Shall we drown our sorrows at a nearby pub?" Willa asked as we got to our feet and gathered up our coats and purses.

"I'm game," Abby chimed in.

"Me too." I'd spent the morning with Ozar, and while I did want to see him tonight, I knew he'd probably be here at the arena for at least another few hours. Maybe he could meet me at my house. Or I could go to his.

Or maybe I was going too darned fast with this whole thing.

Luckily, Willa steered us over to McHenry's where we'd met the orcs after their last game. Just in case this wasn't a team routine, I sent a text to Ozar, letting him know that we appreciated the tickets and how much we'd enjoyed the game. It ended up being a stupidly long post in which I rambled about how unmatched they were against the Maple Leafs, how proud I was of the team's performance and improvements since last week, and expressing confidence that they were on the right track to an eventual win.

Staring at the text before hitting send, I realized it read like I was cheering on a toddler who'd just lost a pee-wee soccer game. Yes, the loss sucked, but Ozar was a grown man. He'd fought minotaurs and other scary beings. He didn't need a participation trophy from me to make him feel better.

So, I deleted most of the text, sending my thanks, a brief

commiseration for their loss, and an invitation to dinner tomorrow night. Then I shoved my phone into my purse and focused on enjoying the rest of the evening with my friends.

Chapter 29

Ozar

I stared down at a tray full of water-insects. They were covered in some sort of spicy-smelling orange powder and had arrived at our table with small plastic cups of hot yellowish liquid. Jordan and I were dining outdoors at a river-side establishment. The temperature had dropped, and all the humans were wearing several layers of clothing even with the pillar-shaped heaters scattered throughout dining area. The chill wasn't dampening anyone's enthusiasm. Conversation and frequent laughter filled the air as a band tested their amplification system in the corner. The sun had almost vanished from the sky, but boats still came in to dock, disgorging their passengers to enjoy an evening of food and drink.

The drink was good. I wasn't so sure about the food, though.

Glancing around, I noticed that most of the humans had also ordered the water-insects which Jordan had said were pretty much the official food of the state.

"Let me show you how to eat these." Jordan grabbed one of the insects from the tray and held it up by the largest set of legs. "Start with the claws. You want to crack the joint here, then twist and gently pull apart."

She demonstrated and the claw separated from the insect's body, pulling a thick wad of white flesh with it. Picking up one of the creatures, I mimicked her movements and snapped the claw off without the white flesh.

"Is mine empty?" I scowled, thinking that the restaurant was ripping us off, selling us carapaces without meat.

"No, you just have to be gentler. Crack the shell, but don't break the claw all the way off. Then gently twist and pull. If the meat doesn't come out, then you'll just get it when you open up the body."

This had to be the strangest meal I'd ever had. Humans had many foods in common with us, and we weren't opposed to eating large insect-like creatures, but we would never go to this much trouble for such a small amount of food.

"Here."

Jordan dipped the white flesh in the yellow liquid and shoved it toward my mouth. I was in love, so I didn't hesitate to eat it.

She watched expectantly, hopefully, as I chewed and swallowed.

"Butter?" I'd only spread the stuff on bread and hadn't recognized it in the melted form.

"Some people don't bother with the butter," she explained. "And others like to butter, then add extra Old Bay Seasoning. Personally, I think that's too much Old Bay, that it overwhelms the flavor of the crab, but that's pretty close to a heretical sentiment here in Maryland. The Maryland natives believe you can never have too much Old Bay."

"It's very good," I reluctantly admitted. The flesh was mild and sweet and tender with a rich peppery spice and a faint brackish, salty tang. It tasted like nothing I'd ever eaten in my life. I wished I could bring these home to my clan to show them that the flavor was worth the effort.

Half an hour later, I wasn't sure that the flavor *was* truly worth the effort. The next time Jordan wanted us to go out for crabs, I would need to remember to eat a full dinner beforehand because I would starve if I needed to fulfill my evening caloric needs with these water-insects. Those tiny little legs were absolutely not worth bothering with. It was a struggle to release what amounted to a splinter-sized piece of meat. The body was a bit more satisfying in terms of sustenance. Jordan advised me not to eat the gray bits that she called lungs and let me know that many people enjoyed eating the mustards, which were basically the innards of the creature. Jordan carefully scraped them aside, but I'd always been taught not to waste any edible part of an animal—to do so would be a disrespect to the creature who'd lost its life so you might survive—so I ate the mustards. And I liked them almost as much as the flesh.

As we took the last two crabs from the tray, my stomach growled, and I wondered if we might stop off for something more filling after we left here. Before I could voice my request, our server was back with yet another tray of the water-insects.

Jordan quit a few crabs into our second tray, sipping her beer and nibbling on the balls of fried bread that the server had also brought us. "Hush puppies," she'd called them, explaining that the story behind the name was that you could throw them to a barking dog who would be silent as they ate the bread. I didn't know much about dogs, but from what Bwat said about the ones at the shelter, canines would be silent if given just about any item of food.

As we ate, we talked. She spoke more about her childhood home and her family, telling me that while she missed them, she enjoyed living in Baltimore. She loved the rivers, the Bay, being close to the ocean and the mountains. And she loved that the weather wasn't as harsh as back in Buffalo.

I told her about the mountain caves near our clan's home, about how we purchased and used fae magic lanterns and other spells and had indoor plumbing and heating systems similar to what the humans had here. After polishing off a third tray of crabs on my own, I sat back, my hunger finally satisfied.

Our dining area looked as if a brutal insect battle had occurred. The brown paper that covered the tabletop was damp and torn in spots and littered with clumps of the orange spice. Broken bits of shell, stray leg segments, and smears of mustard covered the surface. Wadded paper towels and buckets full of dissected crab parts flanked the empty bottles of beer.

Our server didn't seem at all disturbed by the scene. She efficiently scooped everything into a large, black plastic bag and cheerfully asked us if we'd saved room for dessert.

Jordan laughed, eyeing me. "Ice cream?" she asked.

I grinned, then turned to the server. "What do you suggest?"

"I'll be right back." She toted the plastic bag off and returned a few moments later carrying a tray with samples of all the dessert offerings.

"Ooh, Smith Island Cake." Jordan winced. "I'm not sure if I can eat more than a few bites, though."

I sniffed, then frowned. "None of these smell like food. They smell like plastic."

The server laughed. "Because they are. Trust me, the

ones you'll get to eat are real. We have these plastic replicas to show customers."

"If they used real desserts as displays, they'd melt or have flies dive-bombing them, or look really stale a few hours into service," Jordan explained. "Lots of restaurants do this."

I nodded, bemused by the idea of fake food. This would never work back home since the aroma was so unappealing, but humans didn't have our acute sense of smell, and they were very visual.

Visually, these selections were attractive. But none enticed me without being able to scent the combinations of sugar, flour, spice, milk, and fruit.

"I'll take a slice of the Smith Island Cake." Jordan glanced over at me. "And let's get the warm bread pudding with caramel as well. We can share."

"No ice cream?" I didn't intend for that to sound so whiney, but I was truly sad over not having what had become my favorite treat.

Jordan's smile brought adorable dimples to her cheeks. "I have ice cream at home in the freezer and will gladly serve you some. If you're coming home with me, that is."

I perked up at that. As much as I loved ice cream, the best part of that offer was that I would be taking Jordan to her lack-of-furs bed and spending the night bringing her pleasure and having her body against mine.

The server returned with Jordan's selections. I inhaled deeply and knew that my mate had made an excellent choice.

"Smith Island Cake is a bit of a local legend, although you can now purchase it all over the country," she explained as she pushed the plate to a spot between us and handed me a fork. "In the early eighteen hundreds, women on Maryland's Smith Island would bake this cake to celebrate the autumn oyster harvest." She gestured out to the river, dark with lighted boats bobbing at the pier. "If you haven't realized, Maryland has a love affair with the water and the bounty the Chesapeake Bay brings. The whole state is covered with creeks, streams, and rivers—all tributaries leading to the Bay and the ocean."

I nodded, thinking of how, back home, we were all about the mountains, the stone, the caves. While we did have streams, rivers, and lakes, my clan's territory did not have anywhere near the number of waterways that this state did.

"The cake has always been distinctive for its multiple thin layers. Usually there are anywhere from eight to ten, each with icing in between. No one is exactly sure how the unusual number of layers originated, but I like to think that the women baking the cakes had a friendly rivalry over who could create the thinnest and the most layers."

"I am not a skilled baker, but I cannot imagine creating layers this thin without them breaking," I confessed.

"Me either. But I'm sure it's a lot easier with our modern automation." She dug her fork in and scooped up a large piece. "The original was yellow cake with a chocolate buttercream, but nowadays there are lots of flavors, and the chocolate icing is usually fudge so it remains stable at a warmer temperature. It's the official state dessert. And since Maryland is my adopted home, it's my official favorite."

She extended the fork toward me, and I hesitated. Courtship involved male orcs feeding the female they wished to marry, not the female feeding the male. But humans had their own culture, and I'd noticed Jordan doing many things that would be a male orc's wooing actions. She occasionally purchased food for me. She planned some of our dates. I'd been thrilled that she was physically demonstrative, initiating many of our sexual activities.

Jordan leaned forward, touching the fork and the cake to my lips. I opened my mouth and let her feed me, my hand-axe growing hard at the gesture. The cake was good, an explosion of sugary crumb and sweet chocolate, but that all faded into the background of my sudden fantasies.

Jordan pushing *me* back onto her furless bed. Her restraining me with those small, fragile, white hands. Her issuing demands. Her taking control of my body. I would lie there, helpless as she used me however she wanted.

It wasn't the sort of fantasy that a Clan Guardian should have. It wasn't the sort of fantasy that a male orc should have. But the idea of this slight human having her way with me almost had me ejaculating in my pants.

"And now for the bread pudding." Jordan pushed aside the cake, putting down her fork and picking up a spoon. "This isn't a particularly Maryland dessert or even one originating in the U.S. It dates back to the Middle Ages in England and was a good way to make use of stale bread."

I stared at the gooey mess with horror. Stale? Stale bread?

"Oh, stop!" She laughed. "It's soaked in custard which is eggs, sugar, and milk. You're going to love it."

Again, she fed me a spoonful. In spite of the stale bread, this dessert was much better than the sugary cake, but not nearly as appealing as Jordan's delight in feeding me.

Unable to resist, I picked up a spoon of my own and fed her some of the bread pudding. Caramel clung to her lower lip from the bottom of the spoon. That, along with her noise of pleasure, so like the one she made when I tasted her body, nearly undid me.

I put down my spoon, swiped my thumb across her

lower lip, and licked the sweet caramel. The faint taste of her mouth made it all the better.

Her eyes darkened, and her lips parted as she focused on my mouth. "I think I've had enough dessert."

The breathless tone of her voice increased the sweet agony of my need. "Me, too."

I barely remember the tussle over who should pay for dinner. I barely remember the Uber ride back to her house. Everything was a blur until I took her in my arms and gave all of myself to her.

Jordan was my mate. My love. She held my very soul in her hands. And I would be nothing without her. Nothing. As I lay in her furless bed, her head on my shoulder and her chest rising and falling under my arm, I knew that now was the time.

In a week, I would be leaving with the team for a series of what the demon owner had called away games. It would be agonizing to be separated from Jordan for so long, but I'd made a commitment and felt as if I must see it through. But before I left, I needed to let Jordan know my intentions. I needed to tell her I wanted to make her my wife.

Chapter 30

Ozar

The following week went by in a blur. I spent every night with Jordan. Sometimes we joined her friends for dinner, and sometimes we ate only with each other. There were nights when she stayed at my apartment for the night, and nights when I slept at her house.

Unable to tolerate the lack of furs on her bed, I had asked Bwat for assistance and had a fifty-pound box of assorted pelts delivered to her house. These were much nicer than the odd-smelling ones I'd purchased at the Home Store for my own bed, and it had given me great satisfaction to place the red, gray, black, and white pelts of various textures throughout her house.

Judy had approved, making happy chirp noises and kneading her claws in the long hair of the ones draped across the back of Jordan's couches. Jordan had seemed somewhat shocked when she'd returned to see my gift, but had let them remain in place, admitting that the furs were soft and warm, if not really her style of decor.

While my wooing was hitting new heights, the Tusks

were on a descending trajectory straight to hell. Everyone was disheartened after Friday night's game, and I was lucky if three orcs showed up for morning practices. Ugwyll was the only one who consistently joined me on the ice, and I'd taken to running through the Baltimore streets alone. Normally the disintegration of the team would have infuriated me, but thankfully I knew I'd only need to endure it another month or so, then Jordan and I would return to my clan, where I wouldn't have to deal with such humiliating defeats or a team that wouldn't follow my lead.

"Good skating today." Ugwyll clapped a hand on my shoulder as we walked into the locker room. Eng had arrived but was dozing on a bench. Bwat was sorting through a box of books. Five other orcs were playing a dice game in a corner.

I grunted, glaring at the others. I might be leaving soon, but that didn't make their indifference sting any less.

"How is the wooing going?" Bwat smiled up at me from the box of books. "Are you to be wed soon?"

I plopped down on a bench. "I believe I am ready to ask Jordan to be my wife. But I don't want to approach this without thought and consideration. How do human women like a proposal of marriage to proceed? Should I set a tree on fire, prepare an offering of gold and incense, and hand-feed her pickled *Xlinea*?"

Eng nodded approvingly, but Bwat winced.

"What do you suggest?" I asked Bwat, because I valued his opinion far more than I did Eng's.

"I have read of many human proposals, and the most popular ones seem to involve asking the female while at a sporting event with the request to marry projected on the large screens so that all the attendees can witness the joyous event."

I shuddered at the thought of such a public spectacle. Besides, the only sporting event Jordan seemed to attend was our hockey games, and it wouldn't be easy to orchestrate a proposal while I was on the ice and she was in the stands.

"In addition, human proposals involve gifting the female a ring with a large high-value rock," Bwat added. "You're supposed to lie down on the ground when presenting the ring. That way, the female knows you are not a threat to them."

"Jordan knows I am not a threat to her," I told him.

Eng shrugged. "Sometimes these things become tradition and continue to be done even if the original reason is no longer an issue."

Bwat nodded. "Like the white dresses human females wear during the marriage ceremony. It is supposed to indicate virginity, but modern human females like to test the virility of their potential mates and ensure they can perform to their satisfaction before they bind themselves in marriage."

"It's a good practice," I said. "I was happy to show Jordan how I would devote myself to her pleasure." I assumed I should also show her I was sensitive to human culture and traditions. "A ring. A prostrate position while proposing. Is there anything else I should know about?"

"The element of surprise is important," Bwat continued. "Some males hide the ring in food items, then propose when the female uncovers it."

"She might chip a tooth," I argued, horrified at the idea. "Jordan takes the care of teeth very seriously, and I don't think she would appreciate that sort of proposal."

"What if she swallowed the ring?" Eng asked. "It would be difficult to propose with the ring in her stomach. You'd need to make her throw it up, or sort through her excrement for the next few days."

Ugwyll shuddered. "Neither of those options sound appealing."

No, they did *not* sound appealing. "I think I will just do the basics," I decided.

"Will you hold the exchange of vows here or back home?" Eng asked me.

I frowned in thought. "Jordan has many friends and family here, and I know she will want them to be present. Perhaps we can have two ceremonies—one here and one when we return home."

Bwat nodded. "And excellent idea. Expect her to want several of her closest friends to stand next to her in lavish dresses as she delivers her vows. And you will be expected to have an equal number of your friends next to you as well."

"I'm not wearing a dress, no matter how lavish it is," Ugwyll informed me.

"The males wear suits made of penguins," Bwat told him. "It's a bird, so I guess the suits will be feathered, although they all seem to be black and white."

Humans were so strange.

"I'll wear feathers," Ugwyll grudgingly agreed.

"After the ceremony, all the guests join together to feast and dance and drink to the point of excessive inebriation," Bwat continued.

"I'll absolutely wear feathers if there's a feast involved," Eng said.

"You and Jordan will receive many gifts of toasters and Instant Pots, which you can promptly return for cash."

"I think you should keep these gifts," Eng informed me. "An excess of toasters and Instant Pots must be the way humans show their wealth. You could display them in your home to show visitors how important you are."

"Traditionally, her family pays for the feast, but in the newer generations, the male and female often contribute significantly, if not entirely, for the festivities. The male's family usually pays for a dinner following a rehearsal of the vow ceremony, and the male pays for the honeymoon."

All the orcs, including me, were intrigued. "What is a honeymoon?" I asked. It sounded like one of those fancy cakes or cookies that Jordan was always buying for me to try.

Bwat's smile was smug. "A trip somewhere interesting for a week or two where the married couple have copious amounts of sexual intercourse."

Eng snorted. "Why do they have to go on a trip for that? They can have two weeks of sexual intercourse in the male's den."

"And why does it need to be an interesting locale?" Ugwyll asked. "If they intend on remaining in the furs for two weeks, how will they ever know if something outside of their room is interesting or not?"

Bwat shrugged. "I don't believe human males are as virile as orc males. Perhaps they need breaks and use sight-seeing and shopping as a way to keep their females from becoming bored while they recover."

All of us immediately made comments about how we would not require such diversions.

"We will return home immediately after our wedding, so perhaps a honeymoon would not be necessary," I mused.

"I would recommend a short honeymoon at least," Bwat said. "You will be living with your clan, so it does not count as a new and interesting place. Plus, you will both want to have lots of time in your furs before traveling."

True. The very thought had my hand-axe twitching.

"There are some places in Baltimore that would provide a suitable honeymoon spot," Bwat added. "They will bring you all the food and beverages you wish, so you do not even have to leave the furs. And the view out the window from the bed is very romantic if you book the correct room."

It was an excellent idea. First step was to get a suitable ring. The next step was to propose before I needed to leave for our away games. Then Jordan would plan our wedding while I found an appropriate local room and a dining area for our vow-rehearsal dinner.

And then we would go home to live with my clan and build our family. We might only have one or two orclets, but I'd be with Jordan for the rest of my life and whatever offspring we had would be loved beyond all measure.

It ended up being far more difficult to find a ring than I had thought.

The first store was insistent that I purchase a thin gold band with a large clear stone, stating that this was the classic engagement ring. It might have been traditional among humans, but even though the stone sparkled, the lack of color made it feel empty and devoid of emotion. The second store steered me toward a series of giant cluster rings so big that I wasn't sure Jordan would be able to use her finger while wearing it.

"I need to propose before we leave on Thursday, but I can't find a suitable ring," I complained to Sizzle, who was the only one in the locker room Wednesday afternoon.

The demon grunted, which I'd come to learn meant he wasn't listening.

"Those clear stones are soulless, no matter how much they sparkle," I added, thinking that such a bland stone would never convey the depth of my love for Jordan.

"Humans like them because they're the most expensive of the gems. And clear stones go with everything. Human women like to color coordinate, and colored gems in a ring they're supposed to wear for the rest of their life would limit their clothing choices."

Huh. I guess the demon was listening after all.

"Is there another choice that isn't so...bland?" I asked Sizzle.

He shrugged, his hands never pausing as he replaced the blades on our skates. "Emeralds. It's not easy to find a sizable stone without inclusions, or one that has a truly vivid color. Plus, they look best with not as many facets. The flatter cuts emphasize the color, but that means you've got a stone that sparkles less than what is currently in style."

I searched my phone and eyed the pictures of green stones. They were pretty but didn't feel right.

"Her eyes are like the waters during a storm. Are there stones like that?" I asked.

Sizzle nodded. "Yeah, but smokey topaz are cheap as shit, and you don't want to propose with some budget-ass stone. How about a ruby? Humans consider red the color of love and passion. And demons like them since they look like blood. Vampires too. And probably shifters. Can't go wrong with red."

I looked that gem up on my phone and recognized several of the ornate ring designs I'd seen at the second shop I'd visited.

"I like the color but hate the...fussy style." I'd had to consult my translation app to come up with the word "fussy."

Sizzle glanced up at the image I was showing him on my phone and winced. "Yeah. That is damned ugly. How about a solitaire?"

"I want something different. Something special. Something that not only shows how I feel but also says that I am an orc. This…" I pointed at the picture on my phone. "This looks like something a fae noble would give the woman his parents had contracted for him to marry."

That brought forth a snort from Sizzle. "Yeah. It's very fae, isn't it?"

"No one has gems set in iron or hammered metal," I complained. "No one has rings that don't look like a thousand identical ones were produced and shipped to stores across the human world."

"More like a million," Sizzle agreed. "Cookie-cutter fuckers. Your woman deserves better."

"Yes, she does," I agreed.

The demon tossed aside the pair of skates he was working on and stood, brushing his hands on his pants. "I know a place. I'll take you there, but you can't tell anyone I was the one who showed you this jewelry store. I've got a reputation to maintain, you know?"

I had no idea how a demon's reputation would be damaged by knowing of a jeweler but nodded in agreement. Before I knew it, I was stuffed into Sizzle's tiny electric car and enduring an uncomfortable ride out of the city. After a short stint on a congested highway, the demon took an exit heading toward a place called Reisterstown. He parked next to a battered sedan in a strip mall. The jewelry shop was wedged between a dining establishment called Hunan Gourmet, and a store that sold vape and tobacco products. It was a narrow store with thick metal bars on the entrance. The door squawked loudly as the demon opened it.

I blinked, my eyes adjusting to the dim light. There was a row of hip-high glass cabinetry that held a variety of jewelry, but the majority of the square footage was taken up by workbenches, magnifying apparatus, and tools.

"Sizzle!"

A small woman with frizzy red hair vaulted the counter and ran toward the demon. I eyed her, inhaling as the two embraced. She smelled a bit human, a bit demon, and a bit like the werewolf I'd met while at the deli last week.

Sizzle disengaged himself from the woman and turned to me. "Pru, this is Ozar. He's—"

"One of your hockey orcs." Pru reached out to grab my hand, shaking it with a firm grip. "It's nice to meet you. What are you looking for today? I've got a gorgeous chain-link collar with a leash ring that would look amazing on you."

Sizzle turned an interesting shade of red. "No, Pru. He's not...that's not...he's not..."

"I want to propose to my forever mate tomorrow night, and I want a suitable ring. I'm thinking of a ruby gem, but a setting that says 'orc' and not 'fussy fae.'"

Pru gasped, placing both hands on her upper chest. "Who is the lucky individual? Guy? Girl? Non-binary? Demon? Orc?"

"Jordan is a female...er, woman and a dentist. She has her own company and is a strong independent human who lives with a fierce hunter-cat. She might lack furs on her bed, but her home is warm and welcoming with comfort and space in the design. Her hair is the color of sunshine on tree bark, and her eyes are like storm-tossed waters. She is kind with a generous spirit and a curious mind."

Pru sighed, still clutching her chest. "God, that's the

most romantic thing I've ever heard. Sizzy, why can't you say stuff like that?"

"Your hair is like a burning shrub, and your eyes are the color of mud," Sizzle declared.

I eyed the two of them, expecting an argument. But Pru smiled, twirling a frizzy lock around one finger. "Burning shrub, huh?"

"Yeah." The demon's smile was downright sappy.

"Later." Pru waved a hand at him. "Right now, I've got an engagement to facilitate. Now, Ozar, let's take a look at some of my more artistic pieces. I like to work with moderately priced stones, but I can deliver a high-quality rock in spite of that. I like to give a whole lot of effort into the custom settings. I do a lot of work for some of our local... uh...communities, and I think you'll vibe with the aesthetics."

She led us to the back of the store and pulled a few drawers from under one of the glass displays, setting them on top of the counter. "I've done these in black gold, and several have a hammered finish, which I think you'll like. Rubies are a particular favorite of mine. The square and emerald cut ones are shaped to emphasize the depth of red, but these ones are cut with facets that bring extra light to the stone. You sacrifice some of the deep color, but I think the brightness makes up for that."

I was immediately drawn to a ring where the hammered black band split to sweep above and below a huge red ruby. The stone was lighter and brighter than the others, practically glowing in contrast to the ebony band.

"One of my favorites," Pru said as I picked up the ring. "That stone is a carat and a half. It's a much higher quality than I usually buy, but I just couldn't resist. The red color radiates from the gem, and I hand-polished the hammered black gold so every flat surface shines. It's light inside the darkness. Passion through pain. Love in blood. An ouroboros of life and death."

Her words faded. The store, the odd expression on Sizzle's face, the softness in Pru's eyes...it all blurred into the background and all I saw was the ring. And Jordan's hand wearing the ring.

"I'll take it," I said, not even caring how much it cost. I would give a year's salary for this gift. It was that perfect, that much of an expression of how I felt about my love, how I felt about Jordan.

"Special discount for a friend of Sizzle," Pru said with a smile. "If you need it sized larger or smaller, you let me know. And I wouldn't mind if you'd spread the word about the amazing artist who created it. Not that I especially need more business, but I do like the recognition."

"Absolutely," I told her as I pulled the piece of plastic from my pocket. "I will make sure everyone knows of your talents."

Sizzle made a strangled noise, and Pru grinned. "Well, maybe not *all* of my talents."

Chapter 31

Jordan

"**B**runch after the gym?" Stephanie asked.

The werewolf was on the equipment next to me, bench pressing the entire rack of weights without even a labored breath while I curled a scant ten pounds with shaking arms.

"Maybe a quick cup of coffee?" I countered. "Got some early patients this morning and was up late last night."

"Ooh, I know what that means." Stephanie shot me a knowing glance. "That hockey-orc still pounding you into the headboard?"

I smirked. "Sometimes it's *me* pounding *him* into the headboards."

Things with Ozar just seemed to be getting better and better. Judy adored him. He fit so well into my life and routine. And the adjustments I'd needed to make hadn't been a problem at all. Well, aside from the fur rugs and blankets he'd hauled over to my house. They didn't exactly go with my decor, and I wasn't sure how I felt about dead animal skins, but I'd given in. It meant a lot to Ozar to have them in my house and on my bed, and I had to admit they were very soft and warm. Plus, Judy loved to curl up on them, kneading her claws into the fur and purring happily as she snuggled up for a nap.

"Damn. You go, girl. Every morning, I expect to see him here with you at the gym," Stephanie said.

"We sometimes work out together, but usually at the arena or jogging around Baltimore." I wrinkled my nose, a little uncomfortable with the confession I was about to make. "I want to ask him to move in with me. And get him a membership at the gym. I love it when he spends the night, and I really would enjoy having him here for my morning workouts."

Stephanie eyed me. "Not you moving in with him? I mean, he's an NHL player. He's probably got a swank penthouse or McMansion."

I laughed. "He's got a tiny rental apartment a few blocks from the arena. It's cozy and utilitarian, and I do like staying over there. But my place is bigger, and I own it. Plus, Judy would have six months of explosive diarrhea and vomiting if I moved her to another place."

The werewolf halted her workout to turn toward me. "He doesn't have a problem moving into your house? Because I know a lot of guys don't want to feel like they're being kept."

I put the weights down as easily as my shaking arms could and faced her. "He seems okay with it. I mean, I haven't exactly asked him yet. He's leaving tonight for a series of away games, so I was going to wait until he returned to ask him to move in. But he's been talking about adopting a cat at the shelter and has been really concerned about how Judy might react to a cat-friend, so I think he's been considering us moving in together. And with all the furs he's been hauling over to my house, I assume he knows my place is the better spot to cohabitate than his rental apartment."

Stephanie turned back to her weights. "It sounds promising. Keep me updated. And I expect an invite to the cohabitation party."

I smiled, shaking out my overworked arms. "That's a definite."

My day was insanely busy. There were two tricky extractions, a bone graft, three consultations, and a denture fitting along with a bridge placement. We'd all stayed over, even though I'd insisted several times that my staff go home while I finished up the last-minute crown replacement for a long-term client. When my staff and I locked the door, I was exhausted and ready to collapse on my couch with a container of leftover shrimp fried rice and one of Ozar's fur blankets, but he and the team were leaving tonight for their series of away games, and I couldn't stand to have him go without seeing him once more. Picking up carry-out hibachi, I drove to the arena, pulling into the parking lot just as the busses were lining up.

There was no doubt in my mind that I loved Ozar. I was already picturing him living in my home, making my life with him. I imagined our children—one or two or *maybe* three. I'd get a partner to take some of the pressure off me at work, and Ozar would spend as much time with our kids as his job allowed. Me too. There would be two cats running through our home. We'd visit his clan on holiday when the kids were older. We'd grow old together, happy and content, and enjoy our lives in Baltimore.

I'd given up on love. I'd given up on marriage and children. I'd lost hope that I'd ever find the loving partnership that my parents and my brother had found. I'd thrown myself one hundred percent into my job and my social life with my friends, not expecting anything more. But that chance meeting in a parking lot after a hockey game had changed everything.

Change. It was a good thing. And here I was full of hope and dreams for the future instead of fretting over the loss of my routine.

Parking my car, I walked over to the line of buses, clutching my coat tight against the chill breeze from the river. They were just starting to bring the crates and bags of equipment out to the idling buses when I saw the first of the orcs exit the arena.

My eyes scanned the line of tall, green-skinned, muscle-bound guys until I saw Ozar. I felt my very soul light up, my lips curl into a smile. Jumping up and down, I waved and shouted, thrilled as he smiled and waved back before breaking from the line of hockey players to jog over to me.

"You came." He enfolded me in his huge arms, curling me against the warmth of his body. I hugged him back, already feeling the ache of being separated from him even though he hadn't yet left.

"Brought some hibachi for you to take with you." I pulled away and awkwardly handed him the bag. "Beef and veggie with Hunan sauce, extra cabbage."

He took the carry-out. "My favorite. And you don't need to suffer from the effects of my cabbage consumption, either."

I laughed, feeling sorry for the teammates who'd be on the bus with him when the extra cabbage worked its way through Ozar's digestive system. "Better them than me."

He gathered me in his arms again. "I will miss you terribly, Jordan Schooner. You are my breath, my heartbeat, my life. And every second away from you is agony."

I squeezed him tight, feeling the same way. The thought of not seeing him for weeks, of not having his warmth next to me in bed, his scent filling my lungs, his laughter booming through my house...it was painful to think of even a day away from him.

"I wish you didn't have to leave," I confessed. "But I understand. My career is important to me, and I know yours is to you as well. Just know that I'll be thinking of you every moment, waiting anxiously until you return to my arms again."

What sappy nonsense. But it was true. I'd never felt this way about anyone, and I really did ache to have him with me. Forever.

Ozar pulled away from me and suddenly flung himself on the ground, digging his hands into his pants pockets. I stared in shock, not sure if he was having a seizure or some other medical emergency, or if this was part of a cultural ritual that I was in ignorance of.

"Jordan. I want...I would like to...I...*xheba morat wenda ghilba.*"

I blinked, looking at him as he squirmed on the pavement, digging in his pockets before glancing over at the other orcs from his team who were eyeing him with concern.

Finally, he yanked a hand free from a pocket and flicked open a velvet box. This one didn't hold teeth. Instead, a gorgeous ruby caught the glow from the parking lot lights in a burst of red fire, radiating from a band of black metal.

It was the most beautiful ring I'd ever seen. It was Ozar captured in the artistry of jewelry, all rough edges, dark broodiness, passionate fire, gentle and feathery smokey touch.

I gasped, putting my hands to my mouth.

"Jordan Schooner, I want to marry you," he said, still lying on the ground at my feet. "You are my forever mate. I am nothing without you in my life. Together, we will build a family, light a fire of joy, live a life of love and partnership. I dedicate my life to you, to our family. No one, nothing, will ever be put above your needs and wants. Accept me as your mate and accept this ring as a symbol of the love I have for you."

My eyes blurred with tears. "Yes," I whispered.

He sucked in a breath, his eyes so dark. "We will have the wedding you desire with your friends and family. We will be gifted many toasters and Instant Pots and have a honeymoon with so much sex we will not have time to see any interesting sights outside our room. Then we will journey to my clan where I will gift you with the home I have built for my bride. Any modifications you desire will happen. You will become a beloved and revered member of our clan and each of our children that you bear will be blessed by the mountain gods who overlook our home."

Wait. What? It was like a record screeched to a halt in my mind.

"Your home? You expect us to live in your homeland? With your clan?" I felt the parking lot spin around me.

He froze, sprawled on the ground with the box and the gorgeous ring still extended toward me. "Yes. Of course. I am an orc, and my wife and my children should be with me and my clan in our homeland."

The pain radiated from my chest up through my neck to my forehead. "Ozar, I have family here. Friends. My business. I can't...there's no way I could give all that up to be a wife and mother in a clan where I know nothing about their culture, where I don't even know their language. I've built a life here. I thought that you came here to do the same. I thought...I thought we'd stay here and live here, that we had a future together *here*."

He hesitated a few seconds, then scrambled to his feet, still clutching the jewelry box. "You could easily learn our language. And there is a need for dentists in our land. You would not just be restricted to wife and motherhood. Many orc females have careers. It would not be unusual for you to do the same."

This wasn't at all what I'd envisioned when I'd dreamed about my future with Ozar. "I thought you came here in search of a different life. I'd thought you came here to stay, to live among us and become a citizen. I never expected that you intended to return home in the near future."

He blinked at me in surprise. "I came here to find a wife. I told you of the plague among our people, how female orcs made up the most of our fatalities. If we orcs want to continue our lineage, our clan culture, to bring up orclets as we have for multiple generations, then we need to bring home human wives as there are not enough orc females to continue our race."

That stung. Deep in my heart, I knew that Ozar loved me, that his feelings went far beyond the need to procreate or continue his culture. But in that instant, all I saw was that I would be a broodmare for him, a beloved but useful womb in the service of continuing the orc race.

"No." I took a few steps back from Ozar. "I love my career. I built my business from the ground up and am expanding into supernatural dentistry. I don't want to leave that all behind to go to live in a place I've never been before, where I don't speak the language and don't have any value beyond the children I can birth. That's not what I want for my life, Ozar. That's not me. I have friends here. And family. And a life. I want to get married *and* stay here. I'm so sorry, but if that's not what *you* want, then I can't marry you."

Chapter 32

Ozar

There had been no time for a lengthy discussion.

There probably had been no *need* for lengthy discussion. Love, a mate bond, a companionship like none I'd ever felt before...and it had all fallen apart before Jordan and I had ever had a chance at a life together.

I dumped my two bags with the others beside the transportation beast I'd been told was named "Bus" and climbed the stairs. The beast rumbled with caged energy, impatiently waiting while humans loaded our gear and bags underneath. Thankfully the beast was large because we orcs occupied many seats.

My teammates were mostly at the back, so I found a spot midway between them and the half-asleep driver. No one spoke. No one approached me. Which was a good thing, given my mood.

I'd told Jordan about my home, about my clan and my upbringing. She'd seemed interested, fascinated even. Why wouldn't she want to make a life there with me? Never had there been the slightest hint that she would not want to marry me and make a life with me. She'd said she loved me.

And I knew that humans married, had children, and grew old together just as orcs did.

We'd talked about marriage and children during our courtship. Jordan had clearly longed for that sort of partnership, although she'd accepted the possibility of a life without it and had resigned herself to replicating that connection through friends and family.

A sort of bitter anger rose from deep in my chest.

She won't be able to have that same connection with anyone but me. I'm her mate. No one will ever be able to please her as I have. No one will ever stir her heart like I have.

My stomach turned at the thought of Jordan laying with anyone but me. I shoved that thought away and tried in vain to push that anger back into the depths of my body. Humans were not like orcs, and it was possible that Jordan's declaration of love had meant something different in her culture than in mine.

Take her. She's yours. The orcs of old had the right idea. Grab the female you love and force her through the portal to our home. You'll both be gone before the angels know, and she'll come to love your clan and way of life in time, just as human females in the past have done.

No.

I could never do that to Jordan. If she didn't love me enough to be my life-mate, then I would not force her.

Escellates climbed onto the bus, and the door swished shut behind him. "Twelve hours until we hit Chicago. Get some sleep and be prepared to draw in the crowds tomorrow night."

The beast roared, and the driver steered our conveyance out of the parking lot and away from the arena.

Away from Jordan.

We'd joined the other vehicles on the speedway when my phone beeped. I glanced down at it, expecting to see some message acknowledging my pause in milk deliveries or from the humans who seemed insistent on discussing my non-existent car's extended warranty.

It was Jordan. My breath caught, and I debated whether I should read it or not. She was probably telling me this was over and that she never wanted to hear from me again. I didn't want to know that. I wanted to keep some sliver of hope that maybe she'd change her mind, that she'd miss me enough while I was gone to rethink her hasty rejection of my proposal. I'd suffered enough rejection tonight. To have her completely toss our love aside would destroy me, and I wasn't ready to face that level of hurt.

I was Ozar, the Guardian of Clan Heregut, son of Meig and Oala. I did not hesitate in battle. I was known for my bravery and fierce defense of our clan against our enemies. But there was a limit to bravery, and I'd reached it, so I silenced my phone and stuffed it into my pocket with the message unread.

After hours of staring at passing cars, the rhythm of lights and the purr of the transportation beast finally numbed my mind and lulled me to sleep. I dreamed of walking through Patterson Park with my son in my arms, only to have him vanish by the time I reached the swings. I dreamed of the building that housed my dwelling burned to the ground, and I needed to live in the arena locker room. I dreamed a human hockey-enemy hit me in the face with a stick made of steel, knocking both of my tusks from my mouth with a rush of blood. I'd fallen to the ice and looked up at the stands to see Jordan, dispassionately turning away as if repulsed by my disfigurement.

That dream had been the one that jolted me awake. The transportation beast still purred as the human guided it along a looping stretch of black road. Huge buildings appeared before me, with a large body of water to the right. I stared, awed at how strange it felt. Baltimore was giant compared to the largest of cities in my clan's territory, but this...this was beyond imagination. Lights stretched as far as I could see—to the left, in front, and toward the stars above. Once more, I was reminded of how the human world had changed since the time my ancestors had brought back their white- and brown-skinned brides.

Sorrow gripped me at the sudden thought of Jordan, but I loosened its claws and tried to focus on the lights and on the huge expanse of water to the left of us.

"That's Lake Michigan." Bwat had moved to the row of seats opposite me sometime during the night and he pointed out at the water, dark gray in the pre-dawn dimness.

"Much larger than our lakes back home," I commented.

He nodded. "It's actually considered a freshwater, inland sea. There are a joined group of these great lakes, marking part of the border between this country and the one to the north."

I nodded, trying to take any interest at all in these facts.

"Chicago is a city with a lively history," Bwat continued. "Blues music. Various ethnic groups of humans. Incredible varieties of food choices. They are fiercely loyal to their sports teams, even though they yell slanderous insults to them when they perform poorly. Their city is under the control of an angel and a demon. The demon serves as the mayor of the city, and the angel...well, I'm not sure what the angel does besides keep her demon spouse in line."

That got my attention. "An angel and a demon are *married?*"

Bwat shrugged. "Evidently it is not uncommon. Even the Ha-Satan is married to an angel—an archangel, to be precise."

I wasn't sure what most of that meant, but I wasn't about to reveal my ignorance to Bwat, who prided himself on knowing everything.

So instead, I just grunted and turned to look out the window at the passing buildings.

Bwat continued to prattle about mermaids and sirens in the lake, and some rich human, who was evidently a famous recluse living north of the city. He continued on about steak and some sort of root dumplings until Eng threw a red plastic cup at his head, yelling at him to shut-the-fuck-up. After that, we rode in silence until Bus pulled to a stop in front of a large building with brass-framed glass doors and a human standing at attention out front.

The door swooshed open, and Escellates hopped down the stairs. The team rose and walked along the narrow space between the row of seats as if we were sedated. Bwat and I were the last to leave Bus, grabbing our bags from the pile alongside the transportation beast. Inside the opulent building, we waited for Escellates to procure our key cards and inform us which rooms we'd have. I'd expected that we'd share rooms, but I was annoyed to find that my roomie for the next two nights would be Eng.

Eng didn't seem pleased either, but he probably wouldn't have been pleased to share a room with anyone since he considered himself above us all.

The pair of us took the lift-box up to the sixteenth floor

in silence. It took us a bit of walking around to find our room, then longer to figure out how the cards worked to open the door. Once inside, we dropped our bags and looked around, each of us scouting out how to divide up the minuscule territory.

There were two narrow beds separated by a tiny table with a plastic lamp, a clock, and a blocky plastic device with a glowing set of numbers. Two feet from the right-side bed was an open closet door and another door leading to a cramped room with a toilet, a sink, and a shower so small I wasn't sure either of us could comfortably fit in. The left-side bed was so close to the heating device that the thinnest human couldn't squeeze between them. Over the heating device was a thick swath of curtain. At the end of the left-side bed was a narrow desk with a chair barely wide enough to accommodate *one* of my butt-cheeks.

"This is the shit of Morfests," Eng snapped. "Do they know I am a prince of a kingdom? An orc of significance."

"You're nobody here," I informed him. "Just another oaf entertaining humans on the ice."

"Well, this entertaining oaf is claiming the bed on the right." He threw himself down on the mattress before I could protest.

Mine would be the bed on the left—the one inches from the heating device. I sighed and headed into the bathroom. Eng might have claimed the better bed, but I was going to shower first.

The hot water washed away the grime of travel but did nothing to soothe the ache I felt all through my body and heart. Thinking of Jordan, I brushed my teeth, taking special care to scrub my tusks to a shining white. When I went into the room with the beds, I noticed Eng was fast asleep, even though he'd slept the entire ride from Baltimore.

Naked, I sat on my bed, pulled aside the curtains, and gasped.

We were high above many of the buildings around us, and our tiny room with its minimal luxuries more than made up for any deficiencies by this view. In a straight line between two high-rises, I saw the giant lake before me—the inland sea of Michigan. Tiny waves rippled toward the shore. The lake was so vast that I could not see anything but an expanse of water before me. A boat bobbed in the dawn light, and as I watched, a woman breached the surface of the water, arching her back and flinging her red water-drenched hair over her shoulders. A pod of mermaids followed her path.

I smiled, awed by the wonder before me. Homesickness always retreated when I saw these sights. Children at a playground. Judy-the-cat playing with a reflected light. Jordan's expression when she looked up at me as we cuddled together.

Would it be so horrible to stay here? Could I? There were promises I'd made, a life I'd mapped out. What would happen if I remapped that life? What would happen if I tried to create a new future for myself?

With Jordan. Because without her, the old plans of my future seemed empty.

Chapter 33

Jordan

"He hasn't texted me back," I fretted to Willa and Abby.

It was an emergency friend meeting. With ice cream. And Judy sitting on the coffee table with her tail swishing back and forth as she sent a narrow-eyed glare my way. I'd told my friends the whole story from proposal to my panicked refusal. I'd hated that Ozar and I had left things that way, that Ozar had gotten on the bus with so much unresolved and unsaid between us.

"Do you think it's over?" I asked. "That him ghosting me after my text means we're done?"

"I'm sure he just needs time to process this whole thing." Abby patted my arm sympathetically.

"Yeah. Process the fact that you kicked him to the curb," Willa said, much less sympathetically.

"I didn't kick him to the curb," I argued. "He surprised me. With the proposal and the whole going back to his clan to live forever thing. I said no because I could hardly accept his proposal with those strings attached."

"Strings." Abby snorted. "More like chains."

"I'm sure Ozar didn't consider them chains," Willa countered. "Seriously, you guys never talked about this before? I mean, you really never imagined that he might intend on going back home after a short stint here, and that a relationship with him might involve moving on your part?"

"No," I snapped, annoyed at her taking the orc's side in this.

"Willa does have a point," Abby said. "You had to have known he'd want to go home at least to visit."

I stared at her, feeling betrayed.

"My friend Marisa married a guy who was here from Taiwan for his postdoc," Abby continued, seemingly unaware of my glare. "It's an insanely long and expensive flight, and they both obviously wanted to be near friends and family, and to bring their children up immersed in each parent's culture...it took a lot of negotiation for them to work it all out."

She wasn't wrong. Ozar's and my situation actually *was* similar to Marisa and her Taiwanese husband, except her husband and his family and friends were human, where Ozar's weren't. But did that really matter? Cultural and language differences along with geographic distance had destroyed many a human romance over the centuries, too.

"What happened with Marisa and the postdoc guy?" Willa asked.

"He found a company that would sponsor a H1B for him. Once he and Marisa were married, he applied for permanent residency. The big wedding was in Taiwan with a smaller ceremony and reception in the U.S. for her friends and family, although her parents and two brothers flew over for the Taiwan shindig. They both live and work here, but the plan is to spend a month in Taiwan the year their first child is born and to do that every other year. Plus, his mother wants to come each year for a month to stay with them and see the grandkids."

It sounded expensive, although if I was frugal, Ozar and I might have the funds to do that sort of schedule. The biggest issue would be leaving my practice for a month every couple of years.

"Do you think Ozar might compromise and agree to live here with regular visits to his homeland?" Willa asked.

I frowned. "It didn't sound that way from our conversation. I'm sure he'd agree on visits *here*, but he clearly wants to return home and for us to live there full-time."

"What did *you* envision?" Abby asked. "Because I know you were thinking about a long-term future with him."

I felt my face heat up. "I thought that he'd play hockey, and I'd continue with my practice. We'd live in my house in Federal Hill, and we'd have one or two kids. I'd imagined he'd be with them a lot during the off season, but we'd have a nanny when we were both swamped with our careers."

There was a long, awkward silence until Willa finally spoke up.

"You never thought about taking the kids on an extended stay to meet his clan? Or for you and him to spend any significant amount of time with his friends and his family?"

No. And that made me feel like an absolute asshole. I knew how much he loved his clan, his Guardian role back home. I knew how proud he was of being an orc and of his culture. He'd just assumed I'd give everything up to return with him as his bride, and I'd assumed he'd give everything up to stay here with me as my husband. I was just as much to blame for this whole mess as he was.

Abby patted my arm again. "You both haven't known

each other for long. This romance was fast and hot, and while I think that's really amazing, it doesn't leave either of you with much time to discuss your expectations, your hopes and dreams for the future, or how those can mesh together."

I sighed, feeling worse than I had before this emergency friend meeting. "He hasn't returned my text. He doesn't want to see me again. He's done. There won't be any chance to discuss any of this."

Willa rolled her eyes. "Oh, for fuck's sake, Jordan! He's been on a bus to Chicago. Maybe he's in a dead zone with no signal. Maybe he accidentally stowed his cell phone under the bus with his luggage and hasn't gotten it out yet. Maybe he turned the ringer off to catch some sleep while they're on the road and never turned it back on. Have some faith, girl. He loves you."

"Yeah, he loves me. I love him." It sounded like one of those affirmations you were supposed to repeat in hopes of willing the universe to deliver, and all three of us knew how I felt about those stupid affirmations. "How could he throw what we had away just because I refused to give up every-thing I have here to be a wife in a clan in his homeland? I don't speak his language. I don't know more than a handful of his customs. What the hell am I supposed to do there besides spit out kids and be a good wife?"

Okay, that sounded pretty damned bitchy.

Willa's lips twitched. "Yeah. They don't have cars there or cell phones. What the fuck?"

"Or Starbucks. How *will* you survive?" Abby grinned.

And how would Ozar survive without his organic, farm-fresh, milk deliveries? Or his coffee machine? Ice cream? Suddenly, all these happy memories flashed like a photo slideshow through my mind. The rubber sword fight. Ozar presenting me with his tooth in an engagement ring box. The steaks on my front porch that I had eventually realized were little gifts from him. His expression as he tasted ice cream for the first time. The look in his eyes when he'd glanced up into the stands mid-game and saw me cheering for him. The way he wrapped his arm around my shoulders and snuggled me close to his side as we walked. How he'd stood on the curb half-naked in the cold and watched until my Uber was no longer in his sight. He was a great guy. He was the most amazing man I'd ever been with, the most giving and passionate lover, the kindest and most gentle man I'd ever dated. He loved me. He loved my cat. He'd gone out of his way to show me how much I meant to him.

He wasn't the sort of man, or orc, to throw that all away after our first fight. Ozar was a warrior, a Guardian. He didn't give up at the first sign of adversity.

He wouldn't give up on me. And I wouldn't give up on him. Not without a fight. Not without giving everything I had for us to reach a compromise.

Chapter 34

Ozar

The enemy Blackhawk team slaughtered us. Try as we might, we weren't able to gain control of the puck even once. Our net-defender was useless, and the ending score was twelve to zero. Worse, we were unable to even lay a bruise on our enemies. They laughed at our attempts to enrage them, which enraged *us* and made our skating even worse.

I didn't care. All I could think of was Jordan.

Back home, I was an important orc, a Guardian of my clan. Back home, I was someone Jordan would be proud to marry, an orc she would be honored to spend her life with. Here, I was a fool for the entertainment of the humans.

If I stayed, I'd be the sort of man she'd grow to not respect. I would never be her equal. Any love she felt for me would be chipped away bit by bit with each lost game, with each failure. Even if I left hockey, what could I possibly do in this human world to prove myself as worthy of her?

The future I'd dreamed of had vanished in a sea of self-doubt and frustration.

If I went home to my clan, it would be without Jordan.

If I stayed here, she'd grow to despise me, and I'd end up without Jordan as well. Either choice resulted in my losing everything.

My mate bond was proving to be just as doomed as this hockey team.

With barely enough time to shower and change, we were back on the transportation beast again, heading south for a game in Tennessee. Then after losing that game, we went further south to lose in Texas, then twice in different parts of Florida, then somewhere on the east coast before heading north again. I was losing track of the locations as well as the names of the teams that humiliated us each night on the ice.

It had been a week since I'd seen Jordan, since she'd turned my offer of marriage down. I'd buried the ring deep in my duffle bag, unable to stand the constant reminder.

As if I needed the ring to remind me. The constant ache in my chest would never let me forget.

On the bus once more, I stared out at the other vehicles on the roadway, at the lights that flashed by. Then, as I always did, I pulled the phone from my pocket and stared at the empty black screen. I'd turned it off while in Chicago, unable to continue seeing the notification of Jordan's message, and I'd never had the courage to turn it back on. I should have stowed it in my duffle bag with the ring. It wasn't as if I really needed the device. Jordan was the only one who would text or call besides my teammates who were all on the bus with me. And I hardly needed to use the language application or the internet library with Bwat at hand to cheerfully answer any question.

What if she never wanted to see me again? I swallowed hard, trying not to let the agony of that thought overwhelm me. If that was her text message, I'd just go home to my clan.

She was my life-mate. There would be no other for me. Staying and trying to find another bride would be a logical next step, but that woman would never have my heart. It would be unfair to her, and I would feel I was betraying Jordan every time I took another to my furs.

No, if Jordan rejected me, I would return home. Like my father, I would not allow my loss to end my life. I would continue, helping my clan any way I could until I died a natural death. Or maybe a hero's death in battle.

Stop with that maudlin nonsense. You don't even know what her message says. You don't know if she's tried to call you or sent another message. What if it wasn't a break-up message, and here you've been sulking around with the text unread for a week.

I was Ozar. Guardian of Clan Heregut. Son of Meig and Oala. My future, my fate, was in this small magical box that humans used to transmit knowledge and to communicate across great distances. And Ozar was not an orc to shy away from his fate.

I turned the phone on and waited for the screen to light up. A few seconds later, I was staring at the notification. No missed calls. No additional texts. Just that one sent last week—the message that would seal my fate.

Inhale. Exhale.

I closed my eyes, waiting until my heart rate had returned to a normal pace before opening them to click the notification and read the text.

I'm so sorry. I love you, and your proposal both thrilled and terrified me. I can't abandon all I've worked for and who I am to just be your wife and the mother of your children in a place where I know no one and have no other value. I need to be more.

My heart twisted, and I struggled to breathe. The words

blurred, and it took a few seconds before I could continue to read.

This isn't something we can fully discuss a few minutes before you leave for weeks on the road. When you get back, I want to talk about this some more. I love you, and I hope there is a way we can both be happy together forever. Because I do want to marry you. I want to spend my life with you. I'm going to have faith that there's a way we can work this out.

I'll be watching and cheering for you. Always.

The whole way to Ohio I thought about the text. There were moments of elation—she hadn't given up on us. She loved me and seemed confident we could come to a solution. Then there were moments of understanding—she was struggling with the same dilemma I faced. Living in my homeworld meant she'd have to give up a huge part of her identity that brought her joy and fulfillment, that made her Jordan. And by staying, I was afraid I would be giving up the same. Being her husband, her mate, and the father of our orclets...would that be enough? Would I still be Ozar if I had to leave all of my dreams for the future behind?

But the most terrifying part of Jordan's text was the last bit. She was watching our games. Cheering? Her rooting for me and the Tusks was a small comfort. I was painfully aware that she'd spent a week watching the human teams decimate and humiliate us.

Uncertain what to say, worry that I'd waited too long to reply, and the embarrassment of our losses kept me from texting her back.

The sun was coming up as the transportation beast pulled up to our hotel. We staggered down the steps as humans unloaded our luggage and our demon owner yelled at us about when we needed to be ready to ride to the arena for our practice today and our game tonight.

It was six in the morning, and we were shuffling into the lobby like we'd just returned from a two-week march through the mountains. We were terrible skaters, terrible with the sticks and puck, and in terrible shape. I winced to think of what Jordan would see during tonight's game.

The same thing she'd seen for the last week, no doubt.

That was what motivated me to quickly change into workout clothes and begin banging on the doors of my teammates and barking at them to dress and be in the lobby by seven-thirty. Humans poked their heads outside their hotel-room doors, initially protesting the noise until they saw me. Then their eyes widened, and they quickly darted back inside, slamming their doors. The sound of chains and bolts quickly followed.

I didn't care.

Honestly, I did feel a bit guilty that I'd woken all the human guests so early in the morning, but I hadn't been able to figure out how the plastic hotel communication systems worked, and no one had answered their cell phones.

Those who arrived at the lobby at or before 7:30 were able to have coffee and the offered light breakfast. Those who didn't had both the front desk staff harassing them on the plastic phones as well as me returning to beat on their doors. Finally, the whole team was assembled, with a good number of human guests as well as staff watching us with curiosity.

"Attention!" I shouted in Orcish with enough volume to startle the humans and snap the orcs' heads my way. "We will not have a repeat of what happened during the last six games."

"Seven games," Bwat corrected. "Actually, all of our games if you're talking about losing and not just getting our asses handed to us."

I ignored him. "Our skating and hockey skills require more practice, but one thing we can work on as well is the level of our fitness. You have grown soft and lazy. You are an embarrassment to your clans, your ancestors, and your future descendants. Each morning, we will run and perform acts of strength. And before each game, we will strategize how to strike fear into the hearts of our enemies and keep them from shooting their puck into our net."

One orc snorted. "Puck. Net."

I rolled my eyes and switched to English. "Fucking your mother, Mohak. An extra twenty bench lifts for you because you are not serious."

"No. Ozar, no!" Mohak complained.

I cut him off with a glare. "I am leading the run. Ugwyll will be the tail and will punch anyone who tries to shortcut or cheat." Ugwyll made a fist and hit his palm at that. I nodded to him. "Let us go."

The team grumbled but complied. Each time I came across one of the glass shelters with benches, I made the team rotate through a series of handstands, push-ups, and presses-of-the-bench. I discovered that humans had a strange habit of bolting the benches to the concrete and securing them with chains, which made our strength endeavors all the more challenging. At each stop, humans watched, clapped, and encouraged us as we broke the benches from their chains and bolts, then pressed them upward, sometimes with humans still sitting on them.

I had never been to this city—or even this state before—but I figured that if I could navigate the dangerous, ever-changing fae forests back home, then a human city should be no problem. I was wrong. My planned three-mile run became an unplanned fifteen-mile run. Some of the team ended up puking their meager breakfasts into the streets, but that was their own fault for having allowed themselves to become so weak and feeble.

When we finally arrived back at the hotel, I was a little concerned. Yes, the team needed to be whipped into shape and to take our mission seriously if we were ever to become more than a group of fools for human amusement. And if we were ever to become a team I could be reasonably proud of.

We didn't have to win. We just needed to not be fools. And I needed to know that I'd guided the team in the same way that I'd guided our scouts and troops back home as a Clan Guardian. But I might have pushed these orcs too far this morning. I'd been running and lifting heavy objects since I'd arrived here among the humans, but I knew many of our team had not. They'd eaten and drunk and become lazy, confident that their size and initial strength were so superior to the humans that they didn't need to remain fit. I hoped this morning had shown them the error of their ways, because I would drag every one of them from their beds each morning and force them to exercise as long as it meant I did not need to be ashamed of Jordan watching our game.

That afternoon, we rode Bus to the arena for practice and I noticed groups of humans lining the sides of the walkway. I vaguely recognized some of them, realizing that many were either from the hotel or had been among the groups of humans who'd witnessed our early-morning exercises. They nodded, a few of them shouting encouragement. Given that we were intruders in their town, opposing their hockey team, I was surprised.

But there was no time to think about the humans. Once inside, I bullied everyone into their knife-blade shoes and forced them onto the ice. We skated around the edges, everyone following me and trying to keep up as I increased speed and began a series of circles and turns. The ice was littered with fallen orcs, but I shouted for them to get up and keep moving, just as I would my troops back home. Knowing I was depleting their energy, I considered cutting this practice short. But I didn't. Instead, I made them all shoot pucks toward each other, stopping the black turd-like object with their sticks before shifting it to their other side and shooting it back. At first, everyone was chasing pucks across the arena, and we'd lost several into the stands. Eventually the orcs learned some basic amount of control and were able to pass the puck back and forth, stopping it and controlling it with a minimal, basic skill.

It wouldn't be enough for us to win, but hopefully we would not appear as buffoons. And with some luck and determination, we might end this game with a point on our side of the scoreboard.

Chapter 35

Ozar

I knew that human sports teams were often named after ferocious animals or a job that reflected an employment option in the area. Our name, the Tusks, was obviously because of our tusks, given that we were all orcs. Some of these other team names perplexed me, though.

The team we were to play next was called the Blue Jackets. I knew there were horrible insects in the human world called yellow jackets, and I'd encountered those nasty beasts once while jogging in the park. After several hours of pain and then a day of intense itching, I'd realized that size did not necessarily equate with the level of suffering an animal could deliver in this world.

But *Blue* Jackets? I had no idea what the fuck Blue Jackets were supposed to be.

I was going to assume they were yellow jackets, but worse. So, I made my locker-room speech especially energizing.

"We will not be bested by a bunch of humans using an

insect as their totem animal," I shouted. "We are orcs, and orcs do not lose."

"*This* group of orcs loses," Eng sneered. "We lose over and over again."

"There's losing after a valiant fight, and there's losing twelve to zero because all you'll do is lean against the wall and watch the enemy score goals." I was arguing back, but I could tell a lot of the team felt the same as Eng.

"*I* didn't lean against the wall, and it hasn't made any difference at all," one orc shouted from the end of a row of benches. His comment spurred on a chorus of "me too."

Ugwyll stood and slammed his fist against a locker, denting the metal and silencing everyone. "One orc alone is a powerful force, but against a highly trained enemy? Such a disadvantage is hard to overcome. The more of us who fight, acting as a team, the more likely we are to win."

Eng snorted and Ugwyll pointed at him with a growl.

"If you lean against the wall tonight, I will pick you up and throw you over it into the crowd of humans."

Eng took a step forward. "I'd like to see you try."

I jumped between them, arms outstretched. "Save it for the ice. I want us all to put the fear of the mountain gods into our enemy. Charge them. Slam into them. Hit them with our sticks—"

"That's against the rules," Bwat protested.

"I don't care. If half the team ends up in the box, then so be it. I want them so scared of us that they abandon the puck and run away when they see us coming for them."

Ugwyll lifted his chin. "A good plan, Ozar. And if one of us gets the turd-puck, the others should skate along with him and guard him from the enemy. Protect the turd-puck holder until he can violate the enemy's net."

"Who is with us?" I raised my fist in the air, but the only

response was some half-hearted grumbles. "Who. Is. With. Us?" I shouted and glared at each orc until they all assented —well, all of them except Eng.

I taunted the enemy as usual during the puck-drop, adding several criticisms about the human's inability to perform in the furs and questioning his parentage. When the puck hit the ice, I surged forward with a growl. The enemy got the puck, but I managed to wedge my stick between his skates by accident, and he stumbled, cursing at me. Before he could throw his gloves off and fight, Ugwyll snaked his stick in and stole the puck from him.

The crowd roared. I'd expected that they would be supporting their home team but was surprised that many seemed to be shouting approval at us. One group even had a banner that said "Go Ozar" on it.

That feeling that I'd had back in Baltimore returned. I remembered the children wanting to talk to me, the Starbucks employee and random strangers on the street who'd greeted me by name and expressed confidence that we'd win next time. They hadn't thought we were jokes, and although we had yet to win a game, humans were still supporting us.

Jordan still supported us, supported me.

Digging the knife-blades into the ice, I pushed off and skated as fast as I could after Ugwyll. Our strategy was to guard whoever on our team had the puck, but Ugwyll's skating practice paid off and the rest of us orcs were quickly left behind. The enemy closed in on Ugwyll and he fought valiantly to keep them from taking control, using his elbows and wide shoulders to create distance. It was a losing battle. With their long sticks and greater skill on the ice, the enemy swarmed Ugwyll like their namesake, and I knew he would soon be overcome.

Suddenly Ugwyll dug in his knife-blades, sliding to a stop and spinning around. The enemy overshot him but quickly recovered. Ugwyll had a split second of freedom before he was mobbed, and he took that second to slap the puck my way.

I had to slow down to gain control, and that brief pause cost me. A human snaked his stick under mine and tapped the puck out of my reach. In retaliation, I skated into him, and we both went down in a heap.

What happened next was nothing short of miraculous. Another human ready to take the puck was flattened by one of my teammates, who managed to send the thing flying toward the wall—directly at Eng. Without hesitating, Eng twisted his stick and smacked the puck midair. It hit the ice with incredible speed and whizzed into the enemy's net. There was a moment of stunned silence, then the arena erupted with a mixture of cheers and groans.

We'd scored a point. We'd scored the first point of the game. And even more unbelievable, Eng had been the one to land the puck in the net.

Sadly, it was the only point we scored. Since the final score was eight to one, I was still counting this as significant improvement even though we were a long way from a win. It gave me enough confidence to actually return Jordan's text from my hotel room once Eng was asleep and I had a bit of privacy.

I love you and also want to talk more about our future when I return to Baltimore.

I stared at the phone after hitting send, afraid to even blink in case I missed her reply. Not that I was sure of a reply at all. It had been a week since she'd originally sent me the message. It was late. Jordan might be asleep or out with her friends. Or she might not want to acknowledge my text since I hadn't replied to her in a reasonable amount of time.

Finally forcing my eyes away, I rolled over and tried to sleep, still clutching the phone. It felt as if I'd tossed and turned for hours when the device vibrated against my palm, but when I turned the screen face-up, I saw it had only been ten minutes. And that Jordan had replied.

Call me.

I jumped out of bed, ran into the bathroom, closed the door, turned the water on, and climbed into the tub with the shower curtain pulled, hoping that all of this would give me a bit of privacy in case Eng woke up.

She picked up the phone in the middle of the first ring. "I miss you."

"I miss you too." For the first time, I wasn't sure what to say to her. Thankfully, she took the lead.

"You all did great tonight—especially you. Grabbing that pass, fighting off the Blue Jackets...and you scored a point!"

"Eng scored the point," I reluctantly reminded her.

"But you and Ugwyll and Morok set it up. You were part of the assist."

"Eng didn't mean to score the point. He refuses to help the team. He wouldn't have hit the puck if it wasn't coming straight at him. Our point was an accident."

Jordan let out a sigh. "Lots of life is a happy accident. Take the point and celebrate it either way."

She was right, but I couldn't keep from focusing on all the things the team was doing wrong. "We were terrible this whole week. Fools for the humans to laugh at. And the Blue Jackets still won tonight." I tugged at my chin and tried to change my attitude. "They did win by less than the other enemies, though. And we had sixteen tackles tonight."

Jordan laughed. "That's football, sweetie. Tackles don't count in hockey, although intimidating the other team with threats of violence and fights are definitely part of the appeal."

"We're good at intimidation, but the enemy is too fast for us. They get away before we can hit them." I was complaining again. I hated being that grumpy orc with Jordan, but she was the only one who ever seemed to understand my frustration.

"Your skating will improve with time," she assured me. "You are *so* talented when it comes to physical ability. It might not happen this season, but the Tusks *will* win a game."

I had my doubts about that. Half the team wasn't committed to the contest, and the other half of us lacked any skill. The human children who'd played on the ice during the first intermission were better at hockey than we were.

But I'd unburdened on Jordan enough for one evening.

"How is your dental business going?" I asked. "Do you have any new werewolf or vampire clients?"

"I *do*!" Jordan's voice raised in pitch. "No vampire clients besides the one woman who is coming in next month for an evaluation, but in the last two days I've had six appointments scheduled for werewolves— that's in addition to my friend Stephanie. And my new drill came in. Your implant should arrive by the time you're back in town, so we can get your new teeth installed whenever your schedule allows."

I grunted, less interested in my replacement teeth than seeing Jordan again. And I wasn't particularly excited about the mention of a drill. While Jordan's Instagram photos were interesting and filled me with admiration for her skill, passion, and intellect, they also made me a little nervous about this procedure.

"I will always make time for you," I promised. Even if that involved her drilling a hole through my jawbone.

"You'll be back when? Next week?"

I counted the games. "Yes, next Friday, but we have a home game the following day." Which sucked. I really wanted to spend the whole weekend with Jordan, especially after not having seen her for so long.

If hockey could somehow be a career for me, one that I could excel at and feel a sense of satisfaction performing, it would involve long weeks, or even months, away from Jordan. But what was the alternative? Even if she'd accepted the idea of returning home with me as my bride, I would face the same painful separation resuming my Guardian duties. Even more so since Guardians did not have off-season breaks like hockey players.

"I understand," she said softly. "I miss you, but I would never want you to give up something that adds meaning to your life. Just as I need my career, I know you need something outside of our relationship. If that's hockey, then I'll cheer you on, attend every game I can, and welcome you home with all my heart."

My own heart tightened at that.

"The girls and I are getting together to watch tomorrow," she added. "Tusks against the Penguins in Pittsburgh. Go Orcs!"

I grunted, hoping that we made her proud—that *I* made her proud.

"Can I ask you a favor?" Her voice hitched, uncertain and nervous.

"Anything." My own voice was husky and full of promise. Anything. And I meant it.

"Um...I told my parents about us...and they are planning to go to your game in Buffalo. I wondered if...if you could...I mean, if it's too much trouble..."

It took me that whole stumbling speech to realize what she was trying to ask.

"How many tickets would they like? Do they want to bring friends? Maybe your brother and his family?" I grimaced, realizing something. "The seats will be behind our bench, not the Saber-enemies' one."

She laughed. "That's perfect. Trust me, they have completely changed allegiance. The moment I told them we were dating, they became rabid Tusks fans. Expect some embarrassing displays of support."

I smiled, thrilled that her family was ready to cheer for me and my terrible team, that they had welcomed me into the family sight unseen, just because their daughter loved me. If only my father could meet them.

If only my mother could have met them.

"Just let me know how many tickets you need, and I will arrange for them." We were allocated a certain number of tickets each game for friends and family, but they always went unclaimed since none of us had friends or family here. Maybe we should arrange for those tickets to go to one of our special interest areas. Children. Elderly. Homeless. Animals from the shelter.

Although, I'd never seen animals at any of our games. Were they not allowed? Either way, it might be interesting to have a bunch of dogs and cats behind our bench as we played.

"Thank you, Ozar. They're so excited to see you play."

I winced, knowing Jordan's parents would be watching yet another game that we would lose. But I'd make sure we did our best. And I appreciated their support.

"Can I ask a favor in return?" I hadn't meant to bring this up on our first phone call, but something had clicked the moment she'd texted back, and we were fully connected again, as if the disagreement two days ago had never happened.

"Anything."

It was such a weird ask, but I powered on. "Can you send me a cannoli?"

She burst out laughing. "I've created a monster, a cannoli addict. Just one? How about a dozen? I want to make sure I'm feeding your cannoli cravings. And should I send some milk as well?"

Milk. How I missed the amazing milk deliveries. The stuff they had at the hotels just wasn't the same.

"I want to award our best player a cannoli at the end of each game." I hesitated. "But I would like one for myself as well."

"Two, because *you're* the best player," she purred.

That low, husky voice shot right through me, hardening my hand-axe.

"Two for me, and one for the second-best player," I replied.

"Text me the address of your hotels and I'll overnight freshly made cannoli the day before each game. A dozen, because it's important for my orc to have all of his needs met."

Yep. Hard as iron.

"My needs right now are going unmet." And it was downright painful.

Jordan's soft laugh added to my agony. "Where are you now? Somewhere private?"

"In the bathroom standing in the tub."

"I hear the water running."

Her voice was so low and sexy. It was taking my breath away. "Eng is sleeping in the next room," I told her, wondering where she was going with this. "I turned the tub water on so he wouldn't hear."

"So...you're naked in the shower?"

I frowned. "No. I am standing in the shower but not naked."

"What are you wearing?"

I glanced down at my tented-out shorts. "Basketball shorts."

"No underwear?"

By all the mountain gods, her voice was driving me to the edge of insanity.

"No. Just the shorts."

"You need to take them off," she purred.

I'd never removed an item of clothing so fast in my life.

"Close your eyes," she continued. "Reach down and gently grasp your hand-axe. Imagine it's my hand touching you, stroking you."

I did as she said, my breath hitching.

"I'm touching myself too, and imagining it's you. Your fingers brushing the inside of my thighs, dipping into the wetness between my legs, teasing my clit."

I groaned, my hand tightening on my hand-axe.

"But I'm in charge tonight, so I push your hand away and kneel down in front of you. My hand is sliding up your cock as I lean forward. My breath is warm on your skin. I hesitate just a moment, looking up at you as I kiss the tip of your cock. My tongue flicks along the slit, tasting the sweet pearlescent bead there, a treasure, just for me."

Agony. Downright agony. My hand-axe leaked, and I ran my fingers along the lower ridge, actually feeling her tongue and her mouth, as if she were right here with me.

"I'm licking, sucking at the skin of your hand-axe gently with my lips, working my way up and down your glorious length. And when I've made my way back to the head of your cock, I open wide and take all of you into my mouth."

"Mountain Gods! Jordan!" My breathing was rough and ragged. It was all I could do not to spill my seed right then, but I gripped my hand-axe tight and tried to hold back.

"I'm sucking as I slide you out of my mouth, only to sink you in again so deep you hit the back of my throat. My one hand grips your thigh and the other is on your ass, steading myself as I speed up my rhythm. You're so hard. I want to make you come. I want you to spill your hot seed down my throat. Then I'll lick you clean."

I could take no more. With a shout that I'm sure woke Eng as well as the hotel guests on either side of us, I surrendered to my release.

When my mind stopped spinning, I realized that my legs were wobbly, and I was bracing myself against a strong metal bar along the side wall of the shower. Mountain Gods, this was the sexiest masturbation I'd ever experienced. Maybe weeks and months away from Jordan wouldn't be so lonely if we could do this every few nights.

Except I'd need to live here, since we didn't have cell phones back home and communication spells weren't exactly ideal for long-distance sex. One more thing I liked very much about Jordan's world.

"You are amazing," I told her.

"I miss you." Jordan's voice held a note of smugness, as if she knew exactly how she'd ravished me tonight.

"*Grumem-esch-ach metanekan schlonakanap-tsknt,*" I told her, meaning every word.

Chapter 36

Jordan

My FedEx bill was going to be insane. I'd looked up the Tusks' game schedule, called the main office to beg the address to their hotels, explaining that I was Ozar's girlfriend and wanted to send him some care packages. Then I'd gone to town on the purchases, shipping the orc cannolis, cheesecakes, gourmet chocolates, and even a half-gallon of his favorite farm-fresh milk.

We talked every morning, just before my office opened for the day and after he and his team had finished their grueling run-and-lift routine. We talked every night after he'd returned to the hotel room from the game. There had been no more lucky scores for the Tusks, but they were at least narrowing the gap between their zero and the winning score. And the fights! No matter how the other team tried, eventually the orcs would needle them into action. As the team's skating improved, so did their ability to slam the opposing team against the glass or cut them off at the goal.

Ozar and I celebrated the improvements, mourned the

losses, then went on to have epic phone sex. It was our nightly routine, and I looked forward to it.

Each morning, I started the day on a high after our call. Even the most difficult procedure seemed easy. I was more focused, cheerful, happy. Ozar made me a better me. Just hearing his voice energized me and inspired me to work even harder for my patients.

But the games... Ozar seemed more optimistic than he'd been during that first call from Ohio, but I knew these losses and shut outs were taking a toll on him. The Tusks needed a coach, a trainer, marketing campaigns, and hype. They needed an owner who truly gave a shit about the team improving and winning instead of treating them like a circus sideshow.

And Ozar needed some sort of recognition for the work he was putting in trying to pull this team together.

I'd been keeping an eye on the animal shelter site, and by Tuesday I couldn't wait any longer. I went in and adopted Coal after setting up a spot for him in my master bathroom.

As expected, Judy had a shitfit. The moment I walked in with the little cardboard box holding the small black cat, Judy's eyes bugged out, her back arched, and the deepest yowly-growl I'd ever heard emanated from her chest.

Coal meowed plaintively from inside the box, but Judy was not about to be won over, so I took Ozar's cat up to my bathroom and introduced him to his temporary space. He explored the area with curiosity, taking immediate advantage of the litter box. After watching him play in the fountain water bowl, I gave him some kibble and left him to enjoy the space. It wasn't ideal, but it was a whole lot bigger and had more amenities than his cage at the shelter. Plus, I needed to give Judy time to get used to our new friend.

Judy was pacing outside the master bathroom door when I emerged. She'd already pooped in the middle of my bedroom floor.

"I know, I know." I picked her up and carried her downstairs. "Change is hard, but Ozar wants a cat of his own. I want to marry him, so you're going to need to get used to Coal living with us. He's a sweet cat. You don't have to love him, but you will have to tolerate him."

Judy made what I can only describe as a grumpy harrumph. Trying to make amends, I let her have some grilled chicken from the fridge while I cleaned up her mess. Then I sat down to watch the Tusks play against Pittsburgh.

Knowing it would be a few hours before Ozar finished up and made it back to the hotel for our nightly call, I went upstairs after the game to check on Coal. The cat had managed to pull down my towels and scatter them across the room. I found him curled up in one of the sinks instead of the comfy bed I'd bought for him. Blinking his bright eyes up at me, he stretched and yawned, then strolled across the counter with a confident meow.

I liked this cat. It would have been normal for Coal to be anxious his first night in a strange home, especially with a hostile feline roommate, but the little black cat had been nonplused by the whole situation. He bumped his head against my hand and purred as I scratched him behind the ears.

"It won't be long before you have the run of the house," I told him. "I'm pretty sure you'll be able to stay out of Judy's way and calmly ride out her tantrums. And when Ozar comes back, you'll be at his house most of the time. Until you both move in, that is. It'll give Judy some time to get used to you before you're here for good."

The cat kept purring. I loved on him as long as I could, then filled his food bowl and left, ready for Ozar to call.

On the way downstairs, I encountered another turd. And on the bottom step, a coughed-up hair ball. It was going to be a long transition, but Coal was worth it.

Ozar was worth it.

Chapter 37

Ozar

Our team's progress was incremental, but it was still progress.

The orcs had struggled during our morning workout along Pittsburgh's hilly streets, but no one grumbled, and everyone managed to keep their breakfasts inside their stomachs. Practice that afternoon had gone about the same. We worked on speed, turns, skating backward, then practiced with the puck. That was about all I knew. If we improved past those things, I would be at a loss. We needed a coach. We needed a trainer who could tailor our workouts. Without those things, I was pretty sure we'd soon hit our ceiling in terms of skill and ability. We also needed someone who actually knew the rules of the game, although Bwat was reading a book called *Hockey for Fools*. It was a surprisingly appropriate title for us.

We lost at Pittsburgh. We lost at Philadelphia. We lost at New Jersey. And we didn't score a goal since that accidental one in Ohio. But the sharp bite of humiliation had diminished each game. We were skating better. And the teams we faced often lost the puck when they saw us barreling down on them. They'd quickly regain it, but I liked knowing they were afraid of us and the hurt we could deliver if we slammed them up against the glass.

Tuesday, we arrived at Buffalo, where we had a day to rest and recover before our game against their team. I was both anxious and excited for our final game before we returned to Baltimore. Only a few more days until I saw Jordan again, but only a few more days before we had to discuss the looming obstacle that blocked the path to our happiness. And this game.... Buffalo was Jordan's hometown, and I was nervous to be playing here—especially with her family watching.

There were VIP tickets waiting for her parents, her brother and sister-in-law, two sets of aunts and uncles, and three cousins. Jordan's relatives would be occupying most of the seats behind our bench, and it made me sweat to think of how they might judge our team, and judge *me*.

Orcs made their own decisions about marriage, but everyone valued their parents' input. Parents knew us best, and these humans who would be watching tonight knew Jordan far more than I did. They loved her. And if they thought I might not be able to provide her the love and support she needed as my wife, their opinion would carry weight.

Summoning every bit of courage, I left a note with their tickets, asking them to meet the team after the game and giving them passes to the area outside the locker room, inside where even the press was allowed.

While we were supposed to rest Tuesday, my nervous energy wouldn't allow for that. Which meant that I didn't let the team rest, either. Getting off the bus, I barked at the orcs to meet me in the lobby of the hotel in an hour, dressed and ready for a workout. Hearing the chorus of groans, I threatened anyone who was late with an extra mile run. Yes, it wasn't all that easy sleeping on the transportation beast, and the team could use some extra shuteye, but the hours of sitting as we rode from New Jersey wouldn't be helped by falling onto the hotel's furless beds and lying there until tomorrow morning either. We'd complete the workout I'd put together. The guys could shower and sleep for a few hours, then I'd make them get up again to practice on the ice until dinner time.

For the first time, I didn't need to harass anyone or personally bang on their doors when it came time to meet for our workout. The humans followed us or cheered along our running route, as they had since Ohio. Their numbers had been steadily increasing, too. I'd attributed it to the larger population in certain cities, but today I realized that our routine had attracted an unexpected fan following. I overheard humans on their phones, telling others of our route. Humans took pictures, shouted our names, even turned around to do something that Bwat called "a selfie" with us in the background.

It was cold enough in Buffalo for us to be wearing shirts, but the humans in the city entreated us to undress, even though they were bundled up as if they were summiting Gronalek Mountain. I ignored them, but a few of the younger orcs obliged, tossing their shirts into the crowd and flexing for pictures.

I rolled my eyes, but knew I'd do the same if Jordan had asked with that appreciative glint in her eyes. We were all here to find brides to take home. Who was I to fault these orcs in their efforts to attract suitable marriage partners?

After our workout, I led the team back to the hotel, where once again I was in a room with Eng. I'd hoped to be assigned a different orc to share with, but it seemed no one else was willing to tolerate Eng. I didn't like him either, but since he seemed to mostly sleep or ignore me, I didn't complain.

By midafternoon we were on the ice, working on speed as we skated laps. After practice passing the puck, I made everyone skate backward, turning back around to forward, then again to backward when I shouted instructions. It was a total shitshow with orcs sprawled across the ice, so I decided we needed to only skate forward during our games and to make slow and wide turns as often as possible in order to stay on our feet. We'd lose time and distance in the process, but not as much we would lose having to scramble up from the ice each time we needed to head in a different direction.

The next day, we did our workout and practice again. When it came time for the game, my stomach was in knots, but at least I felt as if we'd done our best to prepare. The roar of the crowd when we took the ice was almost as loud as it had been when the home team skated on. Glancing over behind our bench, I saw a row of human faces with tiny white tusks, Tusks emblazoned shirts, and signs that said, "Go Ozar!" and "Ozar is our STAR!"

It took me a second to realize that Jordan's family had on plastic teeth that poorly simulated an orc's tusks. They waved enthusiastically when they saw me looking, and I returned the gesture, bemused.

At least my nervousness was gone.

"What the heck is that?" Ugwyll asked as he skated up to me and slid to a sideways stop with a degree of effortlessness that I envied.

"Jordan's family." I grunted, not wanting to examine how I might feel about the fake teeth.

"That's a huge show of approval. Congratulations,"

Bwat said as he slowly approached us. "It's typical for fans of human sports to dress and carry banners in support of their team and favorite player. But we're not the home team here. Jordan's family is clearly demonstrating their approval for your courtship as well as your chosen profession."

But this wasn't my chosen profession. My mind shot back to my Clan Guardian duties at home, the campaigns I'd been on with my troops, the battles we'd fought. That was important work. This? This was a game for human enjoyment. And I had mixed feelings about making this game my career.

First, we sucked. Jordan's optimism aside, I didn't see that we'd ever win a game against the agile and skilled humans, no matter how much we worked out and practiced. Secondly, while I was competitive, I didn't view this game with the same level of intensity as Ugwyll. Winning any contest, always being the best, had been Ugwyll's life. I was driven to protect and preserve, to guard our clan and our territories. While I was happy to indulge in feats of strength and stamina during a friendly competition, I didn't see that as a driving motivator of my life. Being a Guardian satisfied everything I desired. This? I wanted to keep my commitment to the team and to my demon employer. I wanted us to succeed and improve because developing others' potential and maximizing their abilities was important to me. But did the end goal of this sport really matter? I wasn't sure it did— at least not to me.

Thirdly, I'd always assumed this was a part-time, temporary gig until I found a bride to take home with me. But with the disastrous result of my proposal, I needed to rethink what I'd always envisioned about my future.

It hurt to think that I might never see my home and my clan again, but it hurt more to think that I could lose Jordan over this. There were things I loved about this world outside of Jordan. Would that be enough? Could this team be enough of a career for me? My breath caught at the thought, and uncertainty flooded my heart.

But Jordan. Together, could we forge a life that might make up for everything I'd be leaving behind?

I had to say that the team gave this game every ounce of effort. Well, except for Eng, that is. Eng still positioned himself along the edge, folding his arms across his chest and glaring at us all. I was relieved when he was cycled out for Mohak, who might be a terrible skater but who at least put in an effort.

In spite of it all, we had a great game. We might suck, but the Buffalo team messed up enough to allow us to score two points. They won the game, but I left the ice energized. According to Bwat, this was a reasonable score for the end of a hockey game. No more twelve to zero. We were in the big leagues—at least tonight.

I had managed to score a goal with some dedicated assistance from my teammates. Ugwyll was the star of the show, though. He'd put the puck into the enemy's net, showing off the speed that his dedication and obsessive practice had delivered.

The locker room atmosphere was jubilant, even though we'd lost. I awarded the post-game cannoli to Ugwyll for his point and incredible improvement in skating, then gave up my own cannoli to Ttonel, who'd slammed one of the enemies into the glass, which allowed Ugwyll to steal the puck and skate to a goal.

We showered and changed, fatigue slowly descending like a heavy fur blanket over us all. I hurried, throwing on my street clothes and heading out to where I knew Jordan's family were waiting.

It was bizarre to walk into a crowd of humans with matching bright-green shirts. At least they'd removed their fake tusks before coming to the pre-press room.

"Ozar!" An older man approached me and clapped my shoulders with his hands. He was bald with wisps of silver-gray hair at his temples. A similarly colored beard bristled from his jawline, chin, and above his mouth. His stormy-gray eyes were startling in contrast to his weathered, tanned skin. "I'm Todd, Jordan's dad."

He went on to introduce me to the crowd. I struggled to keep track of the names, only managing to retain that Jordan's parents were Todd and Eileen, that her brother was Jake and his wife was Ella, and that one of the uncles was named Oscar.

"That was an amazing game," Eileen said. "But I worry about you all on the ice without any shirts. Aren't you cold? I'd think that you would be cold. Do orcs not feel the cold like we humans do? I feel like I should knit you and the others on the team scarves at the very least."

"Eileen makes great scarves." Todd fingered a thick, red-and-white striped scarf dangling from his neck to his rounded stomach. It reminded me of the candy cane I'd bought at the food store in Pittsburgh. The strong mint bite had appealed, and I found myself wanting a candy cane colored scarf like Todd's.

One of the aunts pushed between Todd and Eileen to tell me how she was thrilled at Jordan having a boyfriend. According to her, the family had given up all hope at Jordan getting married and having kids.

Jordan's brother Jake came forward, sighing and glancing sideways at the aunt. "Dude. So glad to meet you. I'll admit that when Jordan said she was dating a hockey player, I had my doubts. But you seem like a stand-up kinda guy, and I was impressed at how well you all played tonight given that none of you orcs have much of a background in ice sports."

I nodded and shook his hand. "Thank you."

His grip tightened. I was sure that if I'd been human, it would have been painful, but for an orc the pressure felt mild. "Jordan is my sister," he muttered. "If you hurt her, if you break her heart, I'm coming for you. Understood?"

The human must have known how ridiculous the threat was, but I eyed him solemnly, knowing that this man would face terrible odds to protect his sister. Which was something I respected.

"I would never hurt Jordan. She is my breath and my life." I didn't add that I'd proposed, that I wanted to marry her and spend my life with her. That was between Jordan and me, and not something I should involve her family in at this point.

"Glad to hear." He pumped my arm again and scowled before releasing my hand and stepping back.

The other team members had begun to come into the room at this point, making their way to the press room. Seeing the crowd, they'd paused. Which gave Todd a chance to again name Jordan's family. I was impressed that he knew all the team members and could identify them, pointing each one out as he made the introductions.

That done, the family turned to me once more while the team continued to crowd into the room and watch.

"Ozar, I love the team's Insta account," Ella, Jordan's sister-in-law, gushed. "And the TikTok vids are amazing. I'm hoping to win the contest for the Buffalo game."

I frowned and remained puzzled even after I'd searched some of the words on my phone's translation app. Contest? Insta? TikTok?

"Social media," Jordan's dad told me. "Not just Instagram, either. You guys were nowhere, and suddenly last week, there were official Tusks accounts with pictures, videos, bios, and contests. It's a lot of fun. That's where we got the idea for the upside-down plastic vampire teeth. I'm hoping we make it on tonight's TV recap."

Nothing he'd said enlightened me any further, but Bwat had edged up beside me with his phone in hand.

"Instagram? This one?" He turned the phone toward Jordan's family, and there was a chorus of "yes."

Looking over Bwat's shoulder, I saw a mosaic of pictures and videos featuring us at workout, practice, games, even getting on and off the bus. Bwat touched a picture, and it filled the screen with an image of Trap lifting a woman in a wheelchair above his head with one hand while I scolded him in the background. That had been Miami, and while the woman seemed delighted by Trap's antics, I'd been terrified the orc would drop her. Trap wasn't the strongest on the team, but he'd been egged on by the crowd of humans and the woman's encouragement and had taken extra care even as his bicep shook with the effort.

The caption informed me that this picture was the Miami winner, and that HatTrick2001 would be contacted for an address to ship their prize package which included a beer koozie, a Tusks official poster, and a team Coolmax workout shirt. HatTrick2001 would also be entered to win VIP tickets to the next Tusks game in their area as well as a signed edition of our Hot-On-The-Ice calendar.

I shook my head slowly, looking up the translation for koozie and Coolmax to no avail. When had this begun? I couldn't imagine anyone on our team or Escellates Johnson organizing all of this, and I knew Jordan didn't have the time. It was a mystery—one that seemed to really intrigue Bwat even as I shrugged it off.

"I am so glad you came to the game," I told Jordan's family. "It means a lot to me and the team that you wanted to be here. And I am happy to meet you. You are all welcome to visit in Baltimore. Family of Jordan is family of mine."

I wasn't sure why I'd suggested they come to Baltimore. I didn't have room in my tiny apartment to host anyone, and I had no idea if Jordan was open to having her family stay with her without any notice on my invite. Luckily, no one jumped to take advantage of the offer. Instead, I was treated to a barrage of back and shoulder slaps, yanked down for cheek kisses, and given arm-pats.

Leaving Jordan's family with a wave, I led the team into the press room for the post-game interviews that I'd come to dread.

Microphones were shoved in my face, and a tall human male with spiky blonde hair asked me how I felt about the game.

This was all new to me, and I never knew how to answer these humans' questions, but I'd been informed that post-game interviews were part of our responsibilities.

"We are skating better and improving at keeping control of the puck," I announced, leaning into the microphone. "With added practice, we hope to keep the other team from scoring points."

The other reporters shouted questions, but I was exhausted and done. Leaving Bwat to take the spotlight, I headed for the solitude of the bus. There I'd relax, and when we got back to the hotel and I was sure Eng was asleep, I'd call Jordan for what had become our nightly ritual.

"Phone sex" she'd called it, although we spent a lot of time just talking before things got sexy between us. As much as I missed having her in my arms, I'd grown to enjoy this strange distance-intimacy with her. Separated by many miles, Jordan voiced all sorts of desires, detailing her physical reactions and telling me in detail what she would do if I were there in person with her. I loved these phone calls. And while I counted down the moments when we would be together again, this phone sex served to build our connection, to stretch the tension of our desire to the point of insanity. I loved it. I loved her. And as I sat on the bus waiting for the rest of my teammates to board, I knew that I'd rearrange my entire life to keep her. The future might be not exactly what I'd hoped for, but deep inside I knew that a life with Jordan would be worth that sacrifice.

Chapter 38

Jordan

Abby joined me at my house to watch Thursday night's game with a six pack of beer and a giant buffalo-chicken pizza. "Buffalo chicken. Game at Buffalo, New York. Get it?" she said as she handed the pizza box to me.

It was just the two of us tonight. Willa was out on what she'd called the long shot of all long shot dates. Stephanie was working to finish up her project in Hampton. I'd considered watching the game at a sports bar but decided it would be nice to curl up at home instead. Abby could shack up in my guest room if she was too tired or tipsy to drive, and this way I wouldn't have to scout out Judy's vomit after arriving home late at night.

Plus, I didn't need to rush home to be ready for Ozar's post-game call.

I put out corn chips and salsa. Abby and I settled on the sofa to watch the game, pizza box on the coffee table and beers in hand while Judy meowed for my crusts and wound around my legs.

The game was amazing. I swear that Abby and I hardly

said a word, our eyes riveted to the television. It was the best game I'd ever seen the Tusks play. Admittedly, Buffalo wasn't having the best season, but I saw a huge improvement in the orc team.

"They're doing daily workouts and practices," Abby said at the end of the first quarter. "It really seems to be paying off."

I turned to her in surprise. "Ozar told me. How did you know?"

Her lips curled up in a mischievous grin. "I did what you said and told my boss I wanted us to pitch the Tusks. The team owner went for it, and I've been running their public relations campaigns since last week. Gotta say, it's the most fun I've had in over a year."

"Abby, that's awesome!" I was rarely on social media except to post dental procedure pictures to my Instagram account and hadn't realized this. Making a mental note, I decided to look up the team's accounts and follow them.

"Ozar has been pushing the team hard with the workouts and practices," I said. "I keep telling him that it will pay off, and that they're improving at a remarkable rate, but I think he's getting impatient."

"Orcs seem to be physically gifted. I can imagine they'd struggle with patience in mastering a sport they'd never done before," Abby agreed.

I nodded, and we turned our attention back to the TV as the teams took the ice once more. It was a white-knuckle game which the Tusks ended up losing, but the score was close, and I was thrilled that they'd scored two points—one by Ozar.

And I'd seen several glimpses of my family behind the Tusks' bench, embarrassingly decked out in orc gear and signs. It was nice that they'd gone all out in support of my boyfriend, even though the fake plastic tusks were border-line cringe.

No, it was totally cringe.

Plus, my phone had completely blown up during the game with my family's texts, breaking my focus.

Wow, your hockey-guy is totally hot.

Is it safe for them to play without shirts? Aren't they cold? What if they get hurt?

Your man scored a point! Way to go!

Who is that other forward? Is he single? Does he like younger human females?

I rolled my eyes at Holly's text, assuming that she was talking about Ugwyll. I'd barely spoken two words to the orc, and there was no way I was introducing him to my barely legal cousin.

Setting my phone on vibrate, I shoved it under a pillow and concentrated on the game. It was the best the Tusks had played, and I was thrilled with the final score, even if they hadn't won.

I tossed the empty pizza box and got us the last of the two beers, returning to the couch to watch the post-game interviews.

"Soooo?" Abby eyed me, taking a quick swig of her beer. "Let's talk Ozar. How are things going between you two?"

My friends knew about the proposal, and the long silence before Ozar's reply to my text. They knew we'd been communicating every night since then, and that those calls had been glorious.

And they knew that there was a dark cloud hovering at the edge of our relationship.

"Right now, things are good," I told her. "But I feel like we're just holding back that storm on the horizon. He calls me each night, and it's amazing, but we both know that we're just putting off all the issues we need to face once he gets back to Baltimore."

Abby pulled a notepad out of her purse. "Okay. In preparation for what's looming on the horizon, let's do this like a relationship assessment. What are the traits you want in a husband?"

I thought about that for a few seconds. "He's got to be kind. Likes my friends. Family-focused. Has either a career or some charity or something he's passionate about. Loves cats."

She stopped scribbling on the notepad and looked up at me. "Extrovert? Introvert?"

I held up a hand and rocked it back and forth. "A little of each? I want someone who enjoys going to the occasional concert or game or party, but who also is okay relaxing at home at the end of a day. I do a lot of my research and writing in the evenings, so I need someone who is happy to do their own thing then as well."

"Mmmm." Abby kept writing.

"Not a super foodie, but willing to experiment and enjoy discovering new places to dine. I want someone who isn't an ass about keeping the house clean, who doesn't mind cooking occasionally."

Abby laughed. "Chili with hot dogs?"

I grimaced. "Ugh. If that's all he can cook, then I'm good with delivery."

"DoorDash for the win," Abby agreed. "Kids? No kids?"

It felt like my heart did a double-tap. "I've been thinking about that a lot lately. When I was young, I always envisioned myself married with two or three children, but then I never met the right guy. Or even close to the right guy. So, I changed my focus to my career and gave up on the whole husband and family thing."

Abby set down the notepad and pen, eyeing me with a somber expression. "Oh, Jordan. I totally understand."

"I'm thirty." And I was on a roll here. "It made sense to give up on all that and find satisfaction with my friends, my family, and my career, right?"

She nodded. "And it's not like you don't love your career. You've got a full life right now. Lots to be happy about. There's no need to be defensive about it. We women are more than wives and mothers."

"We are." I stared down at my glass of wine. "Ozar wants a ton of children. Like six or eight or a hundred."

Abby laughed. "Uhhh, how do you feel about that?"

This was beginning to remind me of a therapy appointment, but I answered her anyway.

"I'm uncertain. At thirty, I've got a limited child-bearing window, and I don't like the idea of spending the next ten years in back-to-back pregnancy."

She winced.

"But Ozar is so good with kids, and he wants to be an involved parent, so maybe?" My voice wavered a bit and Abby gave me a sharp look.

"Do you believe him? Sometimes guys have good intentions, but then all the housekeeping and child rearing falls to the woman," she pointed out.

"I know. But I think he really will be an involved parent. And..." I took a deep breath. "I'm absolutely on board for two. Maybe three. At first, I thought just one, but then I remembered growing up with my brother, and the Porter kids down the street that we used to play with, and I thought that two or three would be great. Maybe more, but I wouldn't want to commit to that until I saw how things went with the second. And the third."

Abby picked up her pen, biting back a smile. "So, six?"

"Oh, God!" I put my head in my hands for a few seconds before looking up at her. "What am I doing? Last month I was a dedicated single cat-lady focused on my career. And now I'm considering a husband and children. Again. After having given up on that and reconciling myself to a different but equally happy plan for my future."

"You are absolutely overthinking this whole thing." Abby scowled and jabbed her pen toward me. "Stop it. Life throws all sorts of surprises our way. We've got to be flexible, to be open to changing course."

"When have you ever known me to be flexible? I live by my routine, just like Judy does."

"You don't puke in the hallway if your routine is disrupted," Abby teased.

I sighed. "No, but it's tough for me to pivot. I'm not the pivoting kind of woman."

"You pivoted once," she gently reminded me. "Think about pivoting back. I'm not saying marry Ozar and have a hundred little green babies. I'm not saying dump your dental practice and become some sort of homestead trad-wife in his clan. Just ask your heart what it wants and take that into consideration when making your decision."

I was already listening to my heart. That's what worried me.

"Okay, let's rate Ozar one to ten on your list with ten being the highest score. Kindness."

"Ten." I didn't hesitate at all on that one. Ozar had to be the kindest man I'd ever met outside of my father and brother.

"Likes your friends?"

I wrinkled my nose. "Seven? I really don't know since he hasn't hung out a lot with you all. He always asks how you and Willa are doing though and never has an issue with *me* spending time with my friends."

"Family-focused?"

"Ten," I shot back. "Eleven. Maybe twelve."

Abby snorted. "Career or charity or something he's passionate about?"

That one took some thinking. "I...I don't know. He's passionate about being a Guardian for his clan, but that involves us living with his people and I don't want to give up my career. He wants to make this hockey team a success, but he swings back and forth with it. I don't blame him since it's not like he can control what the other orcs on the team can do. I think he has the capacity to be passionate about a career or a charity, but I'm not sure he's found that yet here in my world."

"Seven? Four?" Abby held her pen poised above the notepad.

I held up my hands. "Eight. Put down eight because I'm sure he'll find something."

There was a poignant silence before Abby spoke. "Sure? Or hopeful?"

I scowled. "Okay. Six."

"Loves cats?" Abby powered on.

"Ten. He's made a lot of effort to bond with Judy and she's responding. He really seems to love her."

"I'm pretty sure that's the most important question," Abby teased.

"It's up there," I told her. "Gotta say it's a dealbreaker of a question, but not the only dealbreaker."

"That's fair. Extrovert or introvert?" she asked.

"More introvert than extrovert, but he seems to enjoy hanging with the team and going out, so I'm going to say an eight on the compatibility scale."

"Foodie?" Abby continued.

I smiled fondly. "He's always willing to trying anything I put in front of him. He'll go anywhere, do anything. I really love that about him. He's not snobby about food or activities at all. He's open for any adventure. A ten."

Abby nodded. "We've already discussed kids."

"We're a five on that right now, but I'm hoping we can come to an agreement."

Abby put her notepad down. "He's scoring high, but the big roadblock seems to be that he wants to go home to live, and you don't. And the kid issue."

I glanced at the television. They'd cut to an image of the orcs entering the press area of the arena in Buffalo. Immediately, my eyes went to Ozar, wearing a T-shirt that stretched tight across his chest and a knit cap with his black hair spilling out beneath the edge. The orc fidgeted, looking like he would love nothing more than to bolt past the press and take refuge on the bus, which is what he did after answering a few brief questions.

Abby sighed. "Ozar and Ugwyll are the fan favorites. I really need to coach them on interviews."

"Bwat does a good job," I pointed out. "He's relaxed and seems to enjoy answering their questions."

"Yeah, but he's not seen as a dynamic player. He's…just kind of there on the ice. It's not all his fault. Defense just doesn't get as much attention." Abby frowned. "When they're back in town, I'll put together better profiles on the other players. We can't just focus on Ozar and Ugwyll all the time."

"You're really into this." I smiled, loving that Abby was doing this. Yes, she was getting paid, but any hype she and her company could generate for the team would help Ozar to be more satisfied in his job—and hopefully he'll be satisfied enough to want to remain here.

I didn't want him to leave. But I didn't want to go with him and live the rest of my life with his clan. And we'd need to address this issue soon. Tonight's game with Buffalo was their last on the road. The team would be returning home tomorrow in preparation for a game against the Avalanche. And *then*, we would have to talk about our future—one that we hopefully could spend together.

Chapter 39

Ozar

I was the first orc off the transportation beast, yawning and rubbing the shaggy beard I hadn't bothered to properly trim while on the road. The human assistants who'd hopped off before the bus had barely come to a stop were already yanking luggage and equipment from the storage areas under Sizzle's watchful eye. Feeling guilty, I turned to give them a hand. We were free to stagger back to our apartments, although we'd need to be up early for practice. The humans would be here late, though, ensuring everything was put into the appropriate storage compartment. Dirty laundry would be promptly sent off for cleaning. Equipment inspected. Skates sharpened. Sizzle might be a demon, but he took his duties seriously and demanded the same from the humans on his staff.

Strange. Back home I'd never thought I'd admire a demon for his work ethic. Or be working in the human world. Or come to the realization that as much as I loved and missed my home, this human world had charms of its own—charms beyond my beloved mate.

"Ozar!"

I spun around at the sound of Jordan's voice, abandoning my plans to assist the humans unloading the bus. She was bundled up in a puffy blue coat with white mittens. A thick lock of her brown hair had escaped the white knit hat to curl around her jaw. She ran toward me, and I opened my arms, catching her as she jumped.

Her legs wrapped around my waist. I held her against my chest, burying my face in the warm skin of her neck.

I would have been glad to stay that way forever, but Jordan pulled her head back to plant a quick kiss on my lips, then slid down my body to stand still pressed against me, her arms now around my waist.

"Get your bag and come home with me," she commanded.

I wasn't about to say no to that. As much as I'd grown to enjoy my little apartment, I wasn't ashamed to admit that Jordan's house was nicer—especially now that I'd bought her some much-needed furs. Plus, I knew that Judy didn't like being left home alone all night. There was nothing I desperately needed to do or to check on at my place, so I found my duffle bag in the pile next to the bus, wrapped my arm around Jordan's shoulder, and followed her to her car.

It feels so good to be home.

I started as the thought flitted through my mind. These streets were so familiar to me. I jogged them every day, waving at the residents on their front stoops, stopping to buy a bottle of water at a corner grocery, nodding as I passed humans walking their dogs, humans pushing baby strollers, humans with plastic grocery bags in each hand, or their phone pressed to their ear. There was the gas station where an old human with the tight silver curls of his beard framing a wrinkled brown face worked on his vintage Fairlane between helping customers. There was the tiny deli where a pair of male humans traded quips and made the best corned beef sandwiches. The barber shop where a twenty-minute haircut seemed to become a three-hour social visit. The nail salon. The row of houses with a sidewalk that had been decorated with a mural of local historical figures in chalk.

A warmth spread through my chest. It wasn't just ice cream and milk I loved about Baltimore. It wasn't just Jordan. Somehow this place had become home. And it had taken a two-week absence to realize it.

I still missed my clan, my friends, my father, my troops. I still missed the way the shadow of the mountain crept across the meadow in the late afternoon. I missed our traditional foods, the house I'd built by hand for my future family. It hurt to think of giving that up, of never seeing that again.

But it hurt just as much to think that I might never see *this* again, either.

As I folded my body into the small confines of Jordan's car, I began to think. Would it be so bad to make my home here? The hockey team was improving and our losses, while still humiliating, weren't quite as bad as they had been when we'd started. And we had fans that cheered us on even when we weren't playing in Baltimore. Maybe I could make something of this team—something that would satisfy my need to be a valued and skilled contributor, a leader of a team. It might not be a team of Guardians like I'd had back home, but a hockey team still seemed to provide something of value to the humans who enjoyed the sport.

Would that be enough?

As the other orcs found wives, they'd leave to go home. Our team would look completely different from year to year, and I'd find myself constantly having to train new orcs on the game and how to skate, as well as figuring out how to adjust our game strategy for each new player. I'd be the only orc in this world long-term. Jordan's and my children would be the only ones in this world who looked like them, who carried orc blood. How could I make sure they were accepted? How could I ensure they knew their heritage, learned my language, carried the stories of our ancestors in their hearts? How could they be orcs in a human world?

And while I'd encountered so much support, I knew there were humans who hated our presence here. I'd seen the scowls, the glares. I'd heard the occasional shout to go home, the angry words telling me I didn't belong here. I'd agreed with them, ready to return as soon as I'd found a bride, but now I was contemplating living among humans—some of whom would never accept me, or my children, or Jordan for having chosen me as her mate. Would her practice suffer? Would some humans refuse to go to a dentist that married and had children with an orc?

"Penny for your thoughts." My beloved's soft, concerned voice broke me from my spiral of anxiety.

"The team has improved, but we are still not winning." I was a complete coward for not being honest, but we'd knitted a fragile repair of our relationship after the disastrous proposal of marriage, and I didn't want to risk further damage.

"Oh, honey!" She reached out to take my hand, entwining her fingers in mine. "Don't discount those very significant improvements. Rome wasn't built in a day. And the games are energizing and so much more fun. People aren't watching because they want to see silly orcs-on-ice, they're watching to see you all score, defend the net, and fight back against the other team. You're real hockey players, even if it's another season or two before you win a game."

I knew she meant that speech to be inspiring, but her belief that it might be a year or two before we won even *one* game was disheartening.

"Thank you." I squeezed her hand gently. "And I'm tired. For some reason, sitting on Bus for hours at a time is more exhausting than the actual game."

"Oh, I know that." She smiled. "I used to take the bus home for Christmas break when I was in college, and I always felt like I'd run a marathon and been beaten with a leather strap by the time we arrived in Buffalo. My parents would pick me up at the station, and I'd fall asleep in bed the moment I got home."

I eyed her. "I think I have enough energy for sex if you limit your expectations."

The laugh that burst out of her did more to energize me than a dozen cups of coffee.

"As much as I want to feel your touch and have you inside me, I'll be perfectly happy to cuddle up with you in bed, feeling your body against mine as we sleep. And in the morning, I'll wake you with my mouth on your cock, just so you know how much I missed you these last two weeks."

My hand-axe began to harden at the thought, but I knew that I would be happy having her against me in our furs as we slept. And I was already envisioning all the things I would do to her in the morning.

Morning. Because I truly *was* exhausted.

Jordan found a parking space only a block away from her house. I carried my duffle bag, which seemed to have gained a hundred pounds since I'd gotten off Bus, and held her hand as we walked up the street. Even this felt warmly familiar, like home. She let go of my hand to unlock her door, and I was surprised by a chorus of meows as we walked in.

"Surprise!" Jordan's smile wobbled with uncertainty as she turned and extended an arm toward the two cats racing across the living room.

I instinctively shut the door, knowing that Jordan wouldn't want Judy to escape. Or the other cat...

Small. Black. Friendly, but displaying obvious deference to the tuxedo cat that ruled this house.

"Coal?" I could hardly believe it. Cats often looked similar, but this little feline was identical to the one I'd fallen for at the animal shelter.

Jordan twisted her hands together in front of her waist. "I couldn't risk him being adopted before you came home, so I got him. For you. And after a few days, he and Judy seem to be getting along great. It helps that he lets her get her way in everything and is so chill with her temperamental outbursts of hissing and growling."

"For me." Like an idiot, I was repeating her words, barely able to absorb all she was saying. I wanted to claim it was due to exhaustion, but I think surprise was more to blame.

"For you." She put a tentative hand on my bicep. "If I acted in haste and you weren't ready to adopt, it's okay. I've gotten really fond of him, and like I said, Judy gets along with him as well. What I'm saying is that I'm happy to keep him if you're not ready to be a cat-dad yet."

"I am very ready to be a father," I blurted out. "I mean, a cat-father."

I meant both. Hopefully the other kind of father would happen eventually, but for now I was beyond excited to know that I would be Coal's orc-father.

"Good." She let out a long breath. "Honestly, I was a

little worried that I'd acted in haste and was putting you in a situation where you'd have to make a decision you might not be ready to make."

"I wanted him before I left but felt it wouldn't be fair. Thank you so much for adopting him for me and letting him stay here until I came back." I gathered her in my arms and kissed her. "This is the best of all surprises."

She snuggled against me. "I'm happy to have him stay here when the Tusks need to travel in the future. That way, he won't be lonely in your apartment when you're gone."

"Thank you." Again, there was the reminder that she had no intention of leaving this human world, no matter how much she might love me. Something ached in my chest, and I ignored it. This wasn't the time for that discussion, not when I was so tired and had just gotten back to Baltimore after two weeks on the road.

"Bed?" Jordan asked with a soft smile.

"Bed," I agreed. Then I put my arm around her shoulder and walked with her up the stairs, two cats bounding up behind to join us in the bedroom.

I did awaken to her mouth on my cock, and I returned the gesture which allowed me enough time for my hand-axe to recover and extend our lovemaking until the sunlight sent its morning rays through the bedroom windows. I wanted nothing more than to spend the day in bed with Jordan, but I knew she had to go to work, just as I needed to prepare for tonight's game.

And the cats were growing impatient for their breakfast. There was only so much ignoring cats would tolerate before they climbed onto the bed and meowed plaintively in your face while you were attempting to sexually satisfy your mate. It was similar to having icy water poured on my hand-axe, so I gave up on another round of sex, told Jordan to take her time in the bathroom, and accompanied the cats downstairs to ensure they did not starve to death.

After swearing Judy and Coal to silence, I added a generous helping of chicken to their kibble. Putting the coffee pot on to brew, I began to pull food from the refrigerator for Jordan's and my breakfast.

My two weeks on the road had taught me a lot about what humans enjoy as their first meal of the day. All of our hotels had buffets, and I'd learned from the staff how to make omelets, French toast, pancakes, biscuits and gravy, and how to cook a variety of what humans called "breakfast meats."

They were pretty much just cured meats that had been seared. I had no idea why humans limited these delicious things for only their morning meal but had taken note. So, with confidence, I put eggs, vegetables, milk, and bacon on the counter and got to work.

By the time Jordan came down the stairs, her hair clean, dry, and styled and her work clothing on, I was just sliding a huge omelet out of the pan.

"That smells amazing!"

I smirked, cutting the omelet in half and dividing it between two plates. I added some sliced fruit and buttered toast, then set both plates on the table next to silverware and napkins before I turned to pour coffee into our mugs. I was so glad we'd gone to her house last night instead of my apartment, not just because of the cats, but because she had food and whatever scant items were still in my refrigerator had probably spoiled.

"A girl could get used to this." She smiled at me as she

took her seat and reached out for the mug of coffee I extended toward her.

"A girl should get used to this. I love to take care of you." Provide for you. Bring you not just sexual pleasure, but emotional and intellectual pleasure as well.

I kept the last bit to myself, worried that it might be too much for the fragile state of what we shared.

Her gaze was soft as her eyes met mine. "I love taking care of you, too."

My heart swelled. Choking on the emotion, I turned around to regain composure and to get my own mug of coffee. By the time I sat down, I was able to breathe once more.

We ate and talked about tonight's game, her new dental clients, the fact that she was doing her werewolf friend's dental implant today and was very excited to use the new equipment she'd received. She also informed me that she was ready to replace my two missing teeth and would like to do this procedure early Monday morning, since we had no game next week and she wanted my mouth to have the extra time to heal before I could potentially suffer another hockey puck to the face.

The pair of us cleaned up the dishes together, then Jordan dropped Coal and me off at my apartment with a box she'd filled with cat supplies. With a deep kiss, she told me she'd see me at the game tonight and hoped to meet up afterward, then drove to work, leaving me and my cat alone in my apartment.

I hadn't been here in two weeks, and in spite of my improvements, it felt sterile and empty compared to Jordan's home. Then Coal meowed and rubbed against my ankles, reminding me that I wasn't alone, and that I had a lot to do after being away for so long.

Cat supplies. Groceries. Resuming my milk delivery. And team workouts in preparation for tonight's game.

It had been a perfect welcome-home. And I was grateful we hadn't immediately jumped into The Talk about our different visions of the future. Honestly, I was dreading that discussion. Things were going so well between us. Maybe we could delay The Talk for a few weeks.

Or a few months. Or a year.

I really wanted to avoid that discussion, but I knew the delay would be worse. Our feelings would continue to grow without the resolution of these significant differences. And I'd be in limbo, uncertain where I was going and whether our relationship would survive.

But for the first time in my life, I was a coward. I'd avoid the conflict until I couldn't. Then I'd face the prospect of a broken heart.

Chapter 40

Jordan

I was such a coward.

There were many good reasons for me to avoid discussing the future with Ozar. He'd just gotten back from a hectic two weeks on the road, and diving right into a possibly relationship-ending discussion wasn't the best way to welcome him home. He was exhausted and needed to sleep. He had a game tonight. I had to work this morning. All of them were good, sensible reasons to procrastinate.

But the main reason was fear.

Love sometimes wasn't enough when there were fundamental differences in what each person wanted in their lives. It scared me that we wouldn't come to a compromise, or that the compromise we agreed on would result in resentment and regret down the road.

Maybe we'd talk Saturday, when we both had time to truly explore the options. Or maybe next Saturday, or at the end of the hockey season.

It had to be *this* Saturday. Tomorrow. Because I wanted to move forward with our relationship. I wanted to talk about him moving in, and it would be insanity to take that step without knowing if we could have a long-term future together or not.

I pulled into my parking space and had time to grab a cup of coffee before my first appointment, thanks to having skipped the gym this morning. Normally deviations from my routine threw my day off, but I took today's changes in stride. It was so good to have Ozar back, to have him in my bed all night, to wake him up and start our day with some glorious sex and breakfast together. Life seemed easy with him by my side.

And the expression on his face when he'd seen Coal and realized the cat was his...it had nearly made me cry. The joy, the gratitude, the love—not just for the little black cat, but for me.

My first appointment of the day was Stephanie. Her implant was free of charge, as the tooth from DarRafi was not yet available outside clinical trials and this would be the first time I used the new equipment specially designed for shifter dentistry. It took extra numbing injections and the time to drill was extended, but Stephanie left with the screw for her implant installed and a promise to let me know how everything held up when she shifted into her wolf form for this weekend's pack hunt. If all went well, I'd put her crown on next week, and we'd have a few more weeks of regular checkups to make sure the tooth remained undamaged after a few shifts.

My first restoration for a supernatural client. I took a much-needed break to celebrate with an iced coffee before Mr. Gerwin's denture fitting appointment. Stephanie's implant today. Ozar's two implants on Monday, and next Wednesday I'd be doing X-rays and evaluating my vampire client to see what I could propose for her restoration work. I felt giddy with excitement about the expansion of my business, and all the new clients I could help.

The rest of the day went smoothly, and I raced home to take care of Judy and change my clothes for tonight's game. Once more, Ozar had provided the girls and me VIP tickets, including an extra one for Stephanie, who had taken the evening off her remodeling project to come see "these orcs of mine" in person.

Abby presented us all with team jerseys, even though the orcs were still playing shirtless. Of course I got one with Ozar's name on the back. The other three girls couldn't agree on who was going to wear which orc's name, so they left it up to chance. Willa ended up with Ugwyll, Abby with Bwat, and Stephanie with Morag.

The Tusks lost, but they put up a good defense against the Ducks and I felt like the ending score of one to three was worth celebrating, along with the fact that I had downed three beers and shouted myself hoarse cheering for the orcs.

I wasn't the only one cheering. The stands were packed. Abby kept calling someone to get the attendee numbers and by the time the teams took the ice, she'd finally begun to relax. Judging from the amount of Tusks jerseys, signs, and team merchandise in the stadium, I assumed she had a lot to celebrate besides the much-improved team performance.

More than the usual four orcs joined us at McHenry's Tavern for a post-game revelry. This time, the human customers didn't line the edges as far away as possible from the giant green-skinned hockey players. Ozar and his teammates were treated to jovial slaps on the shoulders, pint after pint of beer, and requests to sign shirts, menus, and even body parts. I loved how enthusiastic everyone was, even though it meant Ozar and I didn't have the chance for any private conversation.

Leaving him signing autographs for an older couple, I went up to the bar and squeezed in beside Bwat, hoping to get a refill on my beer.

"Yellow or brown?"

It took me a second to realize he was asking me what kind of beer I was drinking.

"IPA," I replied, then thanked him as he waved down the bartender and ordered me a "PIA."

The guy gave Bwat a thumbs-up, which made me realize he'd gotten used to the orcs and their language mistakes. A minute later, Bwat was handing me a pint, informing me that he'd put it on Ozar's tab because it wasn't polite to purchase food and beverage for someone's mate unless they were starving to death. Even then, he would have needed to have Ozar pay him back for the purchase.

I laughed, adding the tidbit of knowledge to what I had learned so far about orc culture.

"Can I ask you something?" At Bwat's nod, I continued. "What does *Grumem-esch-ach metanekan schlonakanap-tsknt* mean?"

Bwat frowned. "Can you say that again?"

"*Grumem-esch-ach metanekan schlonakanap-tsknt.*" My tongue tangled over the strange words, and I spoke slowly, trying to remember Ozar's exact pronunciation.

The orc laughed and shook his head. "Your accent is horrible. It sounds like you're saying, 'my best friend won't stop pissing in my window.'"

"I don't think Ozar is repeatedly telling me that his best friend is peeing in his window." Especially because he tended to say this during romantic and intimate moments.

"It's possible," Bwat pointed out. "I can see Eng doing something like that, and not as a joke, either."

"Ozar lives on the fifth floor of an apartment building. Eng does not seem like the kind of orc to climb up balcony railings when there are a million other, less physically taxing ways he could annoy Ozar. Besides..." I squirmed, my cheeks feeling hot. "Ozar says it when we're...we're...."

"In the furs together?" Bwat shot me a knowing look. "I think he's probably saying, '*Grumem-esch-ach metanekan schlonakanap-tsknt.*'"

"That's what I said," I huffed in exasperation.

One of the orc's eyebrows rose.

"Well, that's what I was *trying* to say."

He nodded. "That means, 'my beloved crushes my heart in her hands.'"

My eyes widened. "I'm not crushing his heart! How could he think that? I love him!"

"You're his mate," Bwat replied. "His heart belongs to you."

"Yes, but not to crush," I argued.

Bwat shrugged. "There is a cultural meaning that the word translation doesn't carry. You aren't *actually* crushing his heart, you are...cradling it? You have the power to crush it or to keep safe."

"Is that...is it something romantic to say to someone?" Because it didn't seem romantic to me, but I was trying to be sensitive to orc culture.

"Oh, *very* romantic." Bwat grinned at me. "But you must have known that. You're Ozar's mate. That means you're an important part of him, like a leg or an arm."

Or a heart.

"*Grumem-esch-ach metanekan schlonakanap-tsknt,*" I said again carefully. "Is that right?"

He winced. "Close. I'm sure he'll get the idea."

I headed back to the table where Ozar was finally done signing autographs. Abby had her nose in her phone, no doubt checking numbers from tonight's game and monitoring social media posts. Willa was arguing with Eng about something in a corner of the bar. Stephanie was holding court with six orcs, telling them about this weekend's pack hunt. I plopped down beside Ozar, scooting the chair over so my leg was pressed against his.

"Spending the night at my place tonight?"

He slowly shook his head. "I want to, but it's Coal's first night in my apartment. I'd feel neglectful if I didn't return tonight. Can you spend the night at my den instead?"

I grimaced. "I have an early morning breakfast meeting with a colleague, and I didn't bring a change of clothing. I'd need to be out of your place by six."

Which would completely throw off my schedule. I'd significantly deviated from it today, and the thought of missing my morning routine and gym-time was almost giving me hives. Still, I loved the idea of spending the night in his arms again after so long apart, and it was only fair that I slept over at his place occasionally, especially since he was trying to settle Coal in.

"When is your breakfast meeting? If we both get up at five, will we have time to go to your place, then to your gym before?" He smiled sheepishly. "I can take care of Judy while you get clothes together, and I want to join your gym."

"When you have a perfectly good gym at the arena?" It seemed like a waste of money to me.

He shrugged. "I don't need to go to your gym every day. I would like the option, though. Unless your gym is private time? For you to be alone or with your friends?"

I laughed. "Alone with fifty other sweaty humans? I'd love for you to join and go sometimes; I just don't want you to feel like you have to spend the money."

"I don't spend money on much else," he pointed out. "I have no car. The team pays for my apartment-den. I pay for my milk delivery, food, and furs. I can afford to join your gym."

"Okay." I took a drink of my beer and eyed him over the rim, trying to figure out how to approach this next topic. "About the car thing...I think you should learn how to drive. I mean, I'd like to teach you, if that's okay. If not, there are driving schools you can enroll in."

"I would love for you to teach me to drive."

Ozar practically bounced in his seat.

"We'll start out in empty parking lots," I warned him. "And you'll need to get a learner's permit. I'm not sure what the requirements are for adult orcs getting their license for the first time, so we'll need to check into that."

"I'll get a car of my own." His eyes gleamed, and I wasn't sure he'd even heard what I'd said. "Or a truck. It will be blue."

I laughed. "Okay. Blue truck it is. But license first, okay?"

He grinned. "Okay."

There was so much more I wanted to say, so much more that we needed to talk about, but this was all I could manage tonight. And maybe it was enough for now. There was still the subject of our future looming over us, but for now, these little discussions about how we could merge small parts of our lives together were progress.

"*Grumem-esch-ach metanekan schlonakanap-tsknt,*" I told him.

Ozar blinked at me. "Is this some human custom? Which of your friends is pissing in your window?"

I sighed and tried again.

"Ah." He wrapped his arm around my shoulder and pulled me close. "*Grumem-esch-ach metanekan schlonakanap-tsknt*, my beloved Jordan. *Grumem-esch-ach metanekan schlonakanap-tsknt.*"

Chapter 41

Ozar

We were up at five in the morning, stopping to get Jordan's car at the stadium parking lot before heading to her house. She quickly added a change of clothes into her workout bag while I fed Judy and searched the house to clean up any of the cat's "little gifts," as Jordan called them.

It was easy to join the gym, even if I struggled to answer some of their application questions about my fitness goals. The manager was thrilled to have a hockey player as a member, and I had to pose for several photographs with employees. Jordan was mostly done with her workout by the time I was done, so she showed me how to use some of the equipment, then ran off to shower and change for her meeting, asking me to come over to her house tonight for dinner.

I was intrigued by the traditional food from her hometown that she was going to make for me, something called beef on weck, which she described as a roast-beef sandwich on a hard roll with salt and horseradish. Everything had been so easy and relaxed between us since I returned, but I still carried the engagement ring in the small box with me, hoping that we'd be able to resolve our differences and that I could put it back on her finger. She hadn't once mentioned that horrible night in the stadium parking lot. I didn't want to mention it either, but that ring would never have a chance of returning to her finger unless we were aligned on what our future held.

She had a career here. She had friends and family here. I had all of those things back home, but none of that would mean anything without her.

One of us would need to compromise. *I* would need to compromise if I wanted to spend my life with Jordan. So, after a brief workout at the gym, I jogged home to check on Coal, showered and changed, and went to the stadium.

Ugwyll was just finishing up his skating practice. I outlined my plan to him and together we went in search of Escellates Johnson, finally finding the team's demon owner in a large office going over sheets of numbers and cackling gleefully.

"What?" the demon barked as we opened his door.

Holding our reply, Ugwyll and I entered, closing the door behind us and sitting in the two chairs in front of Escellates' desk.

"The team has been improving," Ugwyll began. "We no longer look like fools on the ice."

"Which I'm not happy about," the demon grumbled. "But the numbers last night look decent, so I'm willing to let that go."

"We are losing by less points," I continued. "And we are able to regularly score a goal or two each game."

The team owner shrugged. "So what? Are you two asking for more money? Because you're not getting any more money. I'm still angry at what the angels told me I have to pay you as it is. Fair wage. Fair to who? Certainly not me and my wallet."

"We don't want more money. We want a coach," Ugwyll told him.

"And a team trainer," I added.

For a second, I thought Escellates' eyes would bulge right out of his skull. Then he laughed. "Why in all of Aaru would you need a coach and a team trainer?"

I cleared my throat, remembering the speech I'd rehearsed on the way over. "So the team can improve. We need someone who knows hockey, understands the strategy of the game, and can help us work together in ways that will counter our opponents. And we need a team trainer to help us use the equipment in the gym and practice on the ice. If we have these two things, we can win games."

"Winning games isn't important." Escellates waved a hand as if he were wiping the concept off of one of his many white boards in the office. "I don't care about whether you win games or not, I care about making money."

"Teams that score and win bring more humans to see the games," Ugwyll pointed out. "And they sell more of the T-shirts, coffee mugs, and other things that are now available."

The demon thought about that for a moment. "Maybe, but I doubt you all would improve fast enough to cover the cost of a coach and a trainer."

"We might," I said, even though the owner was probably right.

"Come back next year and I'll think about it." Escellates looked back down at his paperwork.

I took a deep breath. "We won't be here next year. If you do not hire a coach and a trainer, then Ugwyll and I will quit the team."

The demon looked back up at us, his eyes narrowing. "You're bluffing."

Both Ugwyll and I had to look that word up on our phones.

"We are not bluffing," Ugwyll said. "We will quit."

"We're your best players," I added. "The humans know our names. I've been in the local paper already. Ugwyll and I both are approached by large groups of humans both after games and on the streets wanting to talk to us. Humans are wearing shirts with our names on them, even holding up signs with our names on them at games. Losing us will lose you money."

"If we leave the team, the team will not survive," Ugwyll said. "A few humans might come to watch the others, but the stands will be mostly empty. You need us."

"And the pair of you needs me, needs this team," the demon snapped. "Without this job, you'll need to go back to your homes and your primitive clans. If you quit, the angels will send you back."

I shrugged, trying not to panic, trying to...bluff. "Perhaps we have another job offer. The angels don't care which hockey team we work for or even if we play hockey. They only said that we needed to 'maintain gainful full-time employment.'"

Escellates sputtered, his face red. "Which team is trying to poach you two? Is it the Lightning? It's that Vinik with the Lightning, isn't it? I hate that guy."

Ugwyll and I sat back, saying nothing and letting the demon rant about various other team owners, all of whom he seemed to hate. Finally, he glared at us, picking up a pen and throwing it across the room.

"If I hire a coach and a team trainer, you both are going to sign twenty-year contracts."

"One year," I countered.

"Five."

"Two."

"Three."

I glanced at Ugwyll, who gave me a slight nod. "We will sign three-year contracts, but the trainer and the coach need to start within the next thirty days, and if we are ever without an experienced hockey coach or a trainer, our contract is void."

Escellates threw another pen and let out a string of curses. Then he stood. "Fine. Deal. Now get out so I can add up how much money I made last night."

"I'll do it." I strode inside and made the announcement the moment Jordan opened her door. "I'll stay here. I'll keep playing hockey and will live here in the human world."

"But what about your family? What about your job back home?" she argued.

I cut her off with a wave of my hand. "Now my career is hockey. I have signed a three-year contract with the Tusks and I'm staying. Yes, I will miss my family and my home, but the human world is beautiful and amazing. I will be happy here, especially with you."

"Ozar...are you sure?"

"I have never been surer." I took a deep breath, knowing that I needed to give her more. "Ugwyll and I talked with Escellates Johnson this morning. We told him that if he didn't bring on a coach, and a trainer, that we would leave the team."

Jordan's eyes widened. "Did he call your bluff?"

"It was no bluff. We intended to leave and find another job if he refused, but he didn't." I couldn't help my smug smile. "Escellates Johnson agreed to our terms. Our new trainer starts in two weeks, and we will have a coach within a month."

"But will hockey give you a satisfying career?" she asked with a frown.

"It will. I like the challenge of hockey. What I don't like is not having the support the team needs to improve. I don't want us to be fools. And if the other players"—like Eng—"refuse to be serious about our team, then we will recruit new ones for next year."

"So, you'll be happy?"

"Yes." I hesitated a second, then dug the ring box out of my pocket. It might be a mistake not to lay on the ground first, but I wanted to propose standing up this time. "I want you to be my bride, Jordan. I want you to be my life partner. You are my mate, the only woman for me. If you are not ready to make this decision, then I will wait. If you do not want to be my bride, then I will still stay here in the human world and play hockey. But I hope you will say yes."

"Oh, Ozar." She gave a watery laugh and swiped a hand across her eyes. "I love you, but I can't let you sacrifice your home and your family for me."

"There is no sacrifice," I insisted. "I love you. The time I spent traveling with the team made me realize that I was being stubborn and clinging to old ideas. Maybe when we are older, we can visit my homeland, but I am ready and excited to call this place my home now."

Her smile widened. "I love you. I want to be your mate, your wife, your life partner, the mother of your children. I'm happy that you've got a great solution for a career in hockey. But I don't want you to never see your friends and family, your home and your clan ever again. I don't want our children to grow up not knowing what it is to be an orc. I want them to meet your father, to eat the food you grew up eating, listening to the music and the festivals and being immersed in their orc culture. I don't want us to raise our children to be just humans, but as humans *and* orcs."

"I choose you over all those things." I did, but I couldn't deny how much my heart ached at the thought that my orclets might never see the home I loved.

"Ozar, that's not fair to you or our children, and to be honest, I want to know your home as well. That's why I've decided to bring on a partner to my practice. My breakfast meeting this morning was with a colleague of mine who I've known for years. He's getting ready to welcome his first child into the world and wants more flexibility in his business practice, just as I do. We're going to combine our businesses, bring on an additional dentist, and make the time for ourselves and our families outside of our careers. Once we're established, I'm going to start shifting my workload so I can take time off each year. When the hockey season ends, we can go to your home and visit, maybe even stay there until you need to be back in the late summer. At first, we might only be able to take a few weeks off, but I eventually want us to live among your clan for two or three months each year, especially after we have kids."

"You are speaking the truth?" My English faltered, and I could barely contain my joy at her words.

"Truth." She extended her left hand. "Now put that ring on my finger and take me upstairs to our bed where we can roll naked in all those furs and celebrate our engagement."

Chapter 42

Jordan

A small black ball of fur streaked across the living room, jumping onto the back of the couch and diving behind a cushion. All that showed was a twitching black tail.

If a cat could have rolled her eyes, that's what Judy was doing. We'd brought Coal over whenever Ozar spent the night, and she still little more than tolerated him in her house, but that was okay. Secretly, I think she liked the little cat but was too proud to admit such a weakness. I wasn't so proud. I'd grown to love Coal and was happy he and Ozar were moving in.

Actually, I was more than happy that Ozar was moving in. It had taken a couple of months and lots of long discussions about important things like separate hampers for our laundry, how often towels should be changed, how much additional milk needed to be delivered weekly, and which direction the toilet paper should roll. Once we'd compromised on the major issue of where we would make our home and how often we would visit Ozar's clan, everything fell into place.

Except the furs. There were too many furs. But that was something I compromised on, since according to Ozar, there was no such thing as too many furs when it came to home decor.

Our wedding date was over a year away. Neither of us was thrilled about the delay, but it wouldn't have been possible to arrange the wedding and honeymoon we wanted during the break between this hockey season and the next, and I needed time to merge my business and arrange for coverage since our honeymoon would be for three weeks in his homeland.

I couldn't wait. In preparation, I was learning Orcish so that I could at least have minimal, stilted conversation with his friends and family. Ozar seemed under the impression that we were going to spend three weeks, seven days a week, twenty-four hours a day having sex. I informed him that unless he was trying to kill me, I would need some time out of the furs and away from the bedroom.

"Where should I put these?"

I turned at Ozar's voice, dismayed to see that he had a dozen more fur pelts stacked up in his arms.

"Um...the guest bedrooms?" The things were already all over the couches and even the dining room chairs. Some were serving as throw rugs. There were enough furs on our bed to withstand a sub-zero arctic blast.

He nodded. "Yes. Our guests will need furs on their beds as well."

They most certainly didn't, but if it made him happy, then I'd hang them on the walls and from the curtain rods.

"Come here first. I have a present for you."

His eyes lit up at that. Tossing the furs onto the sofa, he came over to where I had a wrapped box on the dining room table.

"What is it?"

I motioned toward the gift. "Open it up and see."

He made quick work of the wrapping paper, then carefully read the words on the box. "An ice cream maker?"

"I thought it would be fun. There's a book with all sorts of recipes, and we can look on the internet for more." I eyed him, letting out a breath at his excited grin.

"We can make ice cream with the special farm-delivered milk!"

I wrapped my arm around his waist. "I even bought ingredients so we can make some tonight, to celebrate our moving in together."

"A perfect way to celebrate." He pulled me into his arms and leaned down to kiss me. When he was done, I was thinking about other ways to celebrate as well.

And from the gleam in his eyes, Ozar was thinking the same.

"I have two more armfuls of furs to bring in, then we can make the ice cream," he announced.

More furs? I eyed my curtain rods but smiled and agreed. He could have all the furs he wanted, all the milk and ice cream he wanted. Because I had him. Forever.

My mate. And soon to be my husband.

COMING SOON

Want more Jordan and Ozar? Join my newsletter list HERE and get the bonus epilogue Grumpy Pucking Wedding plus all the info on sales and release dates!

Also by Debra Dunbar

<u>IMP WORLD NOVELS</u>

<u>The Imp Series</u>

A Demon Bound

Satan's Sword

Elven Blood

Devil's Paw

Imp Forsaken

Angel of Chaos

Kingdom of Lies

Exodus

Queen of the Damned

The Morning Star

With This Ring

A Crown of Imp and Bone

<u>California Demon Series</u>

California Demon

Sinners on Sunset

Ventura Hellway

The Devil Went Down to Glendale

Route 666

Half-breed Series

Demons of Desire

Sins of the Flesh

Cornucopia

Unholy Pleasures

City of Lust

Imp World Novels

No Man's Land

Stolen Souls

Three Wishes

Northern Lights

Far From Center

Penance

Northern Wolves

Juneau to Kenai

Rogue

Winter Fae

Bad Seed

The Templar Series

Dead Rising

Last Breath

Bare Bones

Famine's Feast

Royal Blood

Dark Crossroads

Accidental Witches Series

Brimstone and Broomsticks

Warmongers and Wands

Death and Divination

Hell and Hexes

Minions and Magic

Fiends and Familiars

Devils and the Dead

The Bremen Shifter Band (short story)

White Lightning Series

Wooden Nickels

Bum's Rush

Clip Joint

Jake Walk

Trouble Boys

Packing Heat (TBD)

Acknowledgments

A huge thanks to my copyeditor Kimberly Cannon whose eagle eyes catch all my typos and keep my comma problem in line, and to Sylvia and her team at The Book Brander for the awesome cover design.

Most of all, thanks to my children, who have suffered many nights of microwaved chicken nuggets and take-out pizza so that Mommy can follow her dream.

About the Author

Debra lives in a little house in the woods of Maryland with her sons and two slobbery bloodhounds. On a good day, she jogs and horseback rides, hopefully managing to keep the horse between herself and the ground. Her only known super power is 'Identify Roadkill'.

For More Information:
www.debradunbar.com